ADVANCE RAVES FOR
UNDER THE OVERTREE
AND JAMES A. MOORE!

"A creepy novel recalling vintage Stephen King."
—*Publishers Weekly*

"Fans of *The Shining* and *Phantoms* will welcome James A. Moore into the ranks of horror master. *Under the Overtree* is fresh, complex, and totally enthralling."
—*Midwest Book Review*

"Here is a talent. Here is someone to watch."
—Bentley Little, author of *The Summoning*

"An ambitious novel with echoes of Bradbury and King and McCammon. James A. Moore has arrived!"
—F. Paul Wilson, author of *The Keep*

"*Under the Overtree* is a wonderfully creepy, well-written book. The best book of the dark fantastic that I've read in ages."
—Joe R. Lansdale, author of *Mucho Mojo*

"*Under the Overtree* firmly establishes Moore as a major force in the world of dark fantasy."
—Matt Costello, author of *Unidentified*

MORE PRAISE FOR JAMES A. MOORE!

"Great things are to be expected of James A. Moore. Get your tickets early."
— Christopher Golden, author of *Strangewood*

"James A. Moore is a rising star in our galaxy."
— William D. Gagliani, *Cemetery Dance*

"This is horror fiction at its dazzling best. Wonderfully human and touching and frightening, *Under the Overtree* is everything a good novel should be."
— Rick Hautala, author of *The Mountain King*

"*Under the Overtree* is a spine tingler. I devoured the book and then slept with the lights on. James A. Moore is a true master of horror fiction."
— Owl Goingback, author of *Darker Than Night*

"One of the ten best horror/dark fantasy novels of the year. Moore is no longer just a writer to watch, but has graduated to 'must read' status."
— Garrett Peck, FeoAmante.com

THEY BITE

Something hard hit Pete in the ass and he bashed his head against the side of the car in his rush to look. Rubbing his head, he looked for some asshole throwing rocks in the distance.

Nothing. The only change he saw was the light in Old Man Terrell's little dumpy house going on.

He was thinking about the best way to bribe the old goat-faced boot-licker when he felt the searing pain in his right little toe. With a yelp of surprise, he stood up and felt the world tilt wildly, as the blood rushed eagerly from his head. When he could see again, without dark swirling explosions of color in his way, there was nothing to look at.

Except for the gaping hole and bleeding stump, where shoe and little toe had been before. Upon viewing the damage, he really started to feel the pain. It flared across his foot and ran up his leg in a blazing streak of agony. He let loose with a string of foul words as he hobbled over to the hood of his car for a better look. He was numbed enough by the alcohol in his system that he could actually bother with looking at the wound and not with passing out immediately. The meat had been torn clear off his toe and white broken bone glared up at him, mostly concealed by the free-flowing blood that insisted on pouring from the open wound.

While he was busy looking, something attacked the back of his left calf. Pete screamed as he felt the flesh tear from his body. . . .

UNDER THE OVERTREE

JAMES A. MOORE

LEISURE BOOKS NEW YORK CITY

A LEISURE BOOK®

October 2002

Published by

Dorchester Publishing Co., Inc.
276 Fifth Avenue
New York, NY 10001

ISBN: 0-8439-5110-9

Visit us on the web at www.dorchesterpub.com.

For Inge Moore, my mother.
For Bonnie Moore, my beloved wife.
For my siblings Andrea, Nela, Kurt, Steve and Rowanne.
For Rick Hautala, thanks for the scares.
For my friends, you know who you are,
thanks for everything.

Special thanks to Stephe, Kevin, and Teddi
for making this novel painless and
better than it was when it started.

UNDER THE OVERTREE

(Excerpt from the unpublished autobiography of
Phillip James Sanderson)

It was a long time ago that I first learned the meaning
of life; perhaps it would be better to say that I learned
one of the meanings of life, the meaning of life's end.
Death. I was a great deal younger then, and thirty-five
years more innocent. I would gladly have sacrificed
the youth, but the innocence I would snatch back to
me greedily, if only I could. I'd like to think that the
world was a simpler place to live in back then, but it
wasn't really and I try not to lie, not even to myself.

If I must tell the truth, and in my eyes to do otherwise is possibly the worst of all sins, the town of
Summitville was almost the same back then as it is
now. Only the faces have changed, and not all of those
are so different today. I feel it safe to say that the biggest apparent changes came from within, from somewhere in my heart and soul. Back then, I had friends.

Not many mind you, less than a handful of people I
could call anything but buddies. If you haven't learned
the difference between friends and buddies by now,
there is nothing that I can do to help you. Even the
music that lived on the radio in those days was somehow friendlier than most I have heard in the last decade. The music spoke of love, friendship, and just
how cool it was to be true to your school. Today, the
music seems to be about pain, the lack of jobs on the
market, and the best sex a person has experienced to
date. I know it's just the ramblings of a man past his
prime to most of you, but to me that says it isn't just
me that has lost the magic of innocence; to me that
says the whole world has grown too old for its own good.

I was fifteen when I met the boy who would change
my world for the worse and, like so many of my con-
temporaries, I had just started to notice that girls had
a way of looking at you that could stop a truck trying

to beat the sun on a thousand mile race. I like to think of myself as a knight in shining armor, someone that was always for the right way of life, just like my parents had taught me. But in truth, I was one of the people who had it all made.

I was well on my way to being "Mister Popularity" back then, I had an easy smile, and I had a way with words. Naturally enough, there were more than a few who resented those meager gifts. One of them was Charlie Hanson. Charlie was from the area of Summitville we all referred to as the Slums, not because the area was in horrible shape, but because the people there were not quite as well off as in the rest of the town. The Slums was an area with nice enough houses that weren't quite as nice as those peppering the rest of town, the part of town where roofs in need of repair were normally patched with plywood instead of with shingles. Somehow, by the time I had reached the age of fourteen, that fact seemed important. It made me better than someone like Charlie by the simple virtue of how much money my father made.

Charlie and I had been the best of friends only a few years earlier, playing football and baseball together, and even fighting side by side when some of the older kids would decide it was time to smear the queers and then elect us to be the queers. I wish I knew when that changed. I wish I could have stopped it from happening. Charlie was bigger than me—by almost half a foot, but it was just one of those things you do your best to ignore—back then.

I guess what finally drove that last nail into our separation as friends was the arrival in town of Alex Harris. Alex came to Summitville from San Diego, California; but in Summitville he was received as if he had come from another world. Then like now, Summitville was a fairly secular town, less receptive of strangers than any other place I have lived. He moved into town with his family in the last days of summer, in 1958.

I keep trying to imagine what that must have been like, moving from your life-long home to another part

of the country, from the flat shoreline near the Pacific
Ocean, to an isolated town surrounded by mountains
on all sides. I haven't a clue as to what he and his family must have felt; my imagination simply isn't that
powerful. Whatever it was, resentment, awe, or even
fear, Alex Harris hid it well.

Alex came to school for the first time on the same
day that the rest of Summitville's youth attended their
first day, the day after Labor Day. Most of our town
simply ignored him; having never met the boy before,
and having no love of strangers, we simply went on
about our business as if he didn't exist. Charlie Hanson
wasn't most people; he took the appearance of the new
kid as a personal insult, an affront on his good small
town sensibilities. On the first day of school, he did his
very best to start a fight with Alex. Alex ignored him.
Charlie took that even more personally than he did
the boy's appearance, but he did nothing about it at
that time.

Alex managed to fade from existence for most of
us, just another shadow on the wall when we walked
down the long hallways to our next class in the eternal
school day. That seemed to suit Alex just fine, he
seemed no more interested in becoming our friend
than we were in becoming his. Summitville's just like
that, even today. I would have probably never even
come to know Alex, if it hadn't been for Charlie
Hanson's hatred of him.

I should explain a little more about the both of
them, I suppose, just to help you understand the hatred that I can now look back on and see so clearly.
Charlie was a big kid, like I've already told you. But he
was a fairly good one for the most part. Charlie would
have stopped on the side of the road to help you in a
heartbeat, even if it would mean being late for work
and possibly getting fired because he had already
stopped to help others on the road that week. He was
just that kind of guy. But Charlie would have only
stopped to do so if you were a local. Summitville is the
only town I know of in Colorado that hates the very

idea of tourists. When other places with similar slopes
on the nearby mountains were preparing to open ski
lodges and were starting to make money from the winter tourists, Summitville was still doing its best to forget that the rest of the world even existed. Summitville
had gotten on for most of its hundred and twenty years
without need of strangers, and it intended to keep on
doing the same thing for the rest of its life. Charlie was
like that, only more so. Charlie never liked strangers;
it brought out the worst in him to see one lost and asking for directions. At the age of twelve, he happened
upon a woman whose car had broken down near the
farm that he and his folks ran. When she called out to
him, he ignored her salutations for about ten minutes,
until she speculated out loud that he must be retarded.
After that, he screamed a blue streak of profanities at
her, and actually tossed a couple of cow patties from
the field at her. The woman called him a young hooli-
gan or the likes and Charlie flattened her tires with a
pitchfork for her troubles. Charlie's mom came from
the house then, and swatted him across his head with
one of her ham hock hands for his behavior, and then
called her husband Emmett over to help the poor
woman with her car. I'd have never heard about that
at all, even in a town as small as Summitville, but
Charlie told me about it later, explaining that his father had told him he'd had his heart in the right place,
but the best way to get rid of a stranger was to help
them along their way out of town. Had almost anyone
else in town done what he had done that day, they
would have lost a few layers of skin from their butts.
Not Charlie; his father gave him a beer for his troubles.

Charlie was always big for his age, and with his
brown hair and brown eyes on top of a tan from working the fields after school, he looked rather like an Indian in one of the old Technicolor westerns that came
a few years later. Even back then, more as a term of
endearment than as an insult, people called him Chief.

Alex looked almost nothing like Charlie, except that
he was male, and even that would have been debated

by a few of the people in town. Where Charlie was broad across the shoulders and chest, Alex was lean, almost scrawny by comparison, but still athletic in build. Where Charlie had a lantern jaw that would have easily fitted a bull, Alex's face was long and narrow. Where Charlie's face was strong and wide, Alex's was almost heart-shaped, bordering on being girlish. Alex was one of the most beautiful men I ever saw. Not handsome, beautiful.

Alex was also darker in hair and lighter in skin than Charlie. His hair was the color of the darkest night, and his eyes the same shade of blue as a winter sky when the sun is out and the clouds are just a memory. His eyes seemed like the promises of childhood, deeper than the threat of death or pain and as shallow as the concept of Santa Claus when you've turned sixteen. I could have gotten lost in his eyes, had I but noticed them in those early days.

In those days, I was head over heels in lust with my sister Antoinette's best friend, Susan Hailey. Susan was a pretty girl, the kind you think of as the girl next door, but only if the girl next door is extremely chesty and likes to tease the older brother of her best friend. Anita knew how I felt about Susan, and that meant that Susan knew as well. Both of them took full advantage of this knowledge for endless hours of fun at my expense. What I would have given to kiss her only once in those days...

It was on a day when Susan was over that I heard about the troubles between Alex and Charlie, and it was Susan's anger at Charlie that drove me to interfere. Susan was talking with Anita about the horrible way Charlie kept trying to pick a fight with the new kid, and I was in the same room as my sister and my heart's desire, pretending to do my homework, while I listened to an angel's voice. A wiser young man might have picked up the underlying desire in Susan's voice to be closer to Alex, in the same way that I wanted to be closer to Susan, but I was far from wise in those days, and in truth I still can't tell you what a woman is

thinking from moment to moment. All I knew for certain was that the sandy-haired beauty that I so loved
was in need of a knight in shining armor, and in my
own eyes, I fit that bill. Too many comic books when I
was a kid, I guess. I made a silent promise to Susan, to
watch over the new kid from that moment on. It was
made without a word being spoken, but I still wanted
desperately to believe that she had heard me all the
same. Now and then I still like to think that she did,
because after all of her talking about poor Alex, she
looked over my way for just a brief second, and smiled.
It was on the strength of that perfect, summer day
smile, that I became an enemy of Charlie Hanson.

A few days passed, with me pricking my ears every
time that I heard Charlie's voice, before I had my
chance to be the hero. I finally raced for the glory on a
Friday afternoon, just as the school bell was ringing
the final release from prison for another weekend.
With a quick smile at Mrs. Carpenter, the most beautiful ninth grade teacher any school ever had, I grabbed
my books and rushed into the hallway that smelled
sweeter for being a hallway in a school on a Friday afternoon. As I spun the combination on my battleship
gray locker, I heard the sounds of Charlie's voice, raised
in outrage.

To my left, not a hundred feet from where I was
standing, stood Alex Harris and Charlie Hanson, looking ready to take on the world and each other over the
books that Charlie had just knocked from Alex's hands.
Loose papers fluttered to the ground, sifting aimlessly
and spilling like the sad insides of some jackrabbit just
a little too slow when it came to crossing the street out
near the road out of town. The look on Alex's face said
all that needed saying, without a word being spoken:
Charlie had just pushed him too far, once too often.

Charlie looked a little nervous about the whole situation, and that struck me as funny in an odd sort of
way. Funny and a little sad as well; you come to expect
a certain attitude from the people you know, and seeing him looking worried about taking this kid down

after wanting to for so long...well, that was almost like finding out that Jesus was just human, it didn't fit with the way the world was supposed to be.

I was just as eager as the next person to see how this would turn out. Like every fourteen year old I have ever met, the promise of a good fight was enough to make me forget about my silent vow to Susan, especially if I could watch all of the action and not have to feel any of the pain. I would have been perfectly content to just watch, even then, if I hadn't been able to see Susan, standing with Antoinette and another of her friends, looking at me, silently begging me to stop all of this before it went too far. I think I hated Susan in that one moment: she was stealing from me the right to simply enjoy the show and be a face in the crowd, a right that I had always enjoyed to the fullest extent. I was never much of a fighter, I had other things to do, like pine away over Susan, and read about other people's fights. I never had a chance. Even as I was starting to hate Susan, I was achingly in love with her; her wish was my command. I knew it and I suspect that she knew it as well.

I stepped up to the two opponents, and stared my once-close friend Charlie in the eyes. "Charlie, leave him alone. He hasn't done anything to you, c'mon." I wanted to sound authoritative, like a man who had a plan, but I sounded like what I was, a fourteen year old kid with a serious case of the "I'm gonna get my head stomped in" blues. I guess I was lucky anyway, Charlie took my words pretty seriously as he looked down into my eyes.

"It ain't nothin' to do with you, Philly. Get on away from here. This is between me an' him." The words were serious: I had done my part, I had tried to stop him, and I was relieved of my duty as peacemaker.

Except. Except that I could feel Susan's eyes boring into the back of my head, I could feel her wanting me to stop this before Alex got hurt. I think that was the first time I knew she liked him, and wanted to be with him. I think that was when I knew I would never have a chance with her. But hope springs eternal as they say, and I had already gone this far for her...I couldn't simply stop myself and walk away. I had to do this as much for my own pride as for sweet Susan's new love. "Charlie, leave it be, the teachers are gonna be here in a second. They'll make you stay after. Leave it be." Charlie shook his head once, twice, a third time. As he reached out towards me, I felt something break inside, and I saw it break in his eyes too. He shoved me hard out of his way, and in the process, he broke the last strands of what had been our childhood friendship. It hurt me more to realize that what we had once had was finally over, than it hurt me to bounce off the lockers when I landed. I cried out in that brief instant. Part of it was fear of having Charlie hurt me, but most of it, I think, came from the knowledge that he already had hurt me. I think I realized that the money our folks made had driven a wedge between us in some senseless way, and I knew that I had somehow hammered that wedge home, by standing up for a stranger. It hurt my heart a lot to realize my loss. I would never again be able to go fishing at Lake Overtree with my old chum, I would never again tell frightening old ghosts stories with Charlie as we camped in the pasture out in back of his family's farm. What had been a trial separation had become a complete divorce of our feelings for each other, and those feelings could never be the same again. I didn't think of it in those words, but I felt it in those ways. Our friendship was gone forever in that one stupid moment, and I cried out at the loss.

I cried out, and Alex Harris hit Charlie with a right hook that staggered him backwards. I had never paid attention to the quiet new kid, but even in my sudden loss, I knew what it was to be in the presence of a god. I had never seen anyone move so fast, and I never thought I would. He only hit Charlie once, but it was enough to take the wind out of Charlie's sails. I like to think it was the feelings of loss in Charlie that stopped the fighting, I don't like to think that Alex was simply too tough for him, but it didn't seem that way. Charlie staggered around like a drunk on the fifth day of a four-day binge after he got hit, he held his stomach with both hands, and moved away from the crowd as if the floor was tilting madly under him. Everybody had wanted to see a fight; nobody had wanted to see anyone hurt, least of all Charlie. He was too good a person for that.

I watched him walk away for what seemed like hours, and only then did I notice the hand that was being held out for me. It was the new kid, Alex Harris. Until that second I hadn't even realized I was sitting on the ground. As I accepted the offered hand, Coach Braddock reached the both of us, grabbing a handful of each of our arms, and escorted us to the Principal's office.

In all of my time in school, I had never been to the Principal's office. I had never done anything to deserve it. I felt like a man on death row, ready to hang for his crimes against his fellow man. Principal Hagen had that effect on everyone. We were given two weeks detention; it would have been less but old man Hagen knew we were lying when we said I had fallen down and Alex was just helping me up. That's the way it was back then, you never narked on a friend, even one who isn't a friend any longer, or in Alex's case even a friend who never was. We accepted the punishment, and I was grounded for two weeks as a result of being given detention. My dad was never the type to be satisfied with the penalties placed by someone else, he always had to be in on the sentence himself. Dad had fought in Korea and in WWII; he wasn't going to let me off easy just because I was young. He was going to work my butt into the ground because I wasn't old. I suppose there was logic to those words when he spoke them, but they never have made sense to me since then.

During our two-hour daily detentions, Alex and I started to form a friendship. It was almost inevitable. You really can't spend twenty hours with someone in

complete silence, not when you're fourteen, not in the
world I grew up in. It just wasn't possible. We talked
about what it had been like for him when he had to
move here, and we talked about why he had been given
such a hard time by Charlie. We talked about everything, even Susan, and I had never told anyone how I
felt about Susan; she was two years younger than me
and it just didn't seem like the right thing to do. Not in
Summitville. I guess things had been different in San
Diego, because to Alex, it seemed perfectly natural.
Alex was like that; he seemed to understand where I
was coming from, even when I didn't. We became
friends very quickly.

As time passed, we spent more and more time together and we learned to be friends in a way that few
people ever are. Alex Harris was my first best friend.
By the end of September, he meant more to me than
my family did. That's just the way those things go, I
guess; there's no real way to explain well enough to
make them clear.

In the first week of October, when the sun was setting so much earlier than it had only a month before, I
met his family. His father was a lean and likable man
who I came to know and appreciate in a very short
time. Mr. Harris liked to read, and fostered in me a
love of something more powerful than a comic book
or detective magazine. He brought to me a love of novels. Whenever I went over, which then was very frequently, he had another book in his hands, and he
would nod politely as he puffed away on his briar pipe
and he would hand me another book to read. Most of
them were thrillers, stories that seemed like longer
versions of the stories I was already reading in True
Detective and in other trashy magazines in the same
vein. The man almost never said more than "Hello
Philly, got another one, let me know what you think."
But in those words he showed an interest in what I
thought. Me. As if my opinions were worth listening
to. He always gave me the books to read before he read
them, and it was like he wanted to know if he should

even bother with the stories, except that he would read them whether I liked them or not. I will always remember him fondly for that; it made me feel important. It was more than my own father had time to do. My father never was very good at being friendly; he was just good at being stern. Some dads never seem to understand the difference I guess; my dad didn't.

On one occasion, my father told me that I should clean out the attic of our big old house. He even offered me two dollars to do it, but I would have done it even without the money, I was very curious as to what was up there. There was a lot of junk, stuff that had sat around in that house since it had been built, and that was a good deal of time before my Grandfather moved into this town. (It's funny thinking back on that, because once upon a time my father was the new kid in town, and it took him almost fifteen years to be accepted in Summitville. I guess that's why he liked Alex from the first time he met him. I was lucky, and I was born in town, but until Alex moved here, I was still called "That young un' of Howard Sanderson, the new kid from a few years back," by the long timers in Summitville. Even after twenty-five or more years, my dad was the new kid in town to some of those old farmers and mill workers.)

Alex was good enough to help me, and he brought along his little brother, possibly the clumsiest three-year-old I had ever seen. His little brother's name was Todd, but I always called him Toddler, because it just seemed to fit with him. He didn't walk, he toddled along and as often as not he fell on the ground, skinning one part of his body or another. Todd normally had a dozen of those little baby Band-Aids on his hands, elbows and knees at any given time, and I often wondered how he managed to survive the day with the way he fell down. He was a cute little kid, though, and he loved his brother with the pure unsullied love that only a three-year-old can have. Alex had to take Todd with him that day, because Alex's dad worked in Denver for some big law firm, and he

was almost never home before seven o'clock at night.
Todd only stayed at Mrs. Phillip's house until Alex
got out of school, because Alex was big enough to
watch him, and Mr. Harris felt it better to have his
son influenced by a family member like Alex than by
a stranger like Mrs. Phillips. I never understood that
kind of thinking until I was a good deal older and
learned about life away from a small town like
Summitville. Summitville had almost no crime back
then and in comparison to some towns, it still doesn't
except for the occasional fight at Dino's Bar & Grill. I
guess I lived a very sheltered life growing up, especially next to someone like Alex or his father.

It was while we were getting to the last of the junk
in that old attic, that Todd found an old book, bound
in red leather, and closed with a tarnished brass clasp.
The book had no name, but it held a fascination for
Alex and me, it held the promise of secrets to learn.
Alex set it aside immediately, and when we finally finished in the attic, asked if he could take it home. He
was my best friend, and I trusted him even with so
great a find. I said yes. Whenever I think back on that
day, I wish I had told him no. I wonder if things would
have been different if I had. I like to think not, but I
suspect it's still so.

I forgot about the book for the next couple of weeks,
but Alex didn't. He spent hours going over the thing
nightly, while I spent those same hours reading the
latest book on loan from his father. Mr. Harris had a
large library, and I guess he must have had the books
that Alex needed, because he managed to figure out all
the things that were written in that book, and most of
what was there was written in three different languages. One of them I later realized was Celtic, one old
English, the other I still have no clues about. Whatever books his father had in the library must have been
very diverse, because I have looked long and hard, and
even sent copies to some of the universities I have visited in my time, and I have yet to get an answer that
told me what that last language was.

It was at the end of October, on Halloween day, that he told me the book was the journal of a man named Stoney Miles. Once upon a time, that name would have terrified me, but by then I was fourteen and I knew better than to be afraid of old ghosts. Maybe I'll tell you about Stoney later, but he's really not important now. Suffice to say that he had a very dark reputation in my hometown. Alex wanted to have a kind of seance, out in the woods where Stoney had written in his journal about a special place, one that was closer to the nature of other places than this world. I didn't like the idea, but Alex was so excited about it, that I simply couldn't say no to him. I especially couldn't say no when he told me that Susan and Anita would be going as well. He said it would be great fun, and maybe we could give them a scare while we were at it. Hey, I was only fourteen, and if you try to tell me that the idea of scaring a couple of pretty girls didn't appeal to you at fourteen, then you either don't remember your childhood well, or you are a liar. It was a Saturday, and the girls were agreeable; we left less than an hour later. Antoinette and Todd were along for the show, and we had a good time. Todd delighted Anita and Susan, along with Antoinette, and that left Alex and me all the time we needed to study the little notebook in which he had written the "Magic Spell" that we would be trying. We had everything that we needed, except for the blood of a lamb. In substitution we took the blood from one of the chickens that was in my refrigerator, waiting for mom to chop into pieces and fry. It would have to do; besides, it was just for show.

Everything went beautifully, Alex made dramatic gestures and intonations as he cast the various tidbits like toads' eggs and such about the area he claimed was Stoney's special place. And we all got terribly frightened by the dramatics. Even Todd. Todd got very frightened, and screamed and stumbled and fell and cut his hand. And that was the end of the show. We all laughed about it later, but Todd had managed to give himself a good scraping when he fell against one of the big rocks that decorated the woods. The winds promised snow in the near future, and in Colorado you take that kind of promise as a threat. It was a long walk back home, and then we all went our separate ways so we could get ready for the Halloween Party at the school.

Alex never made the party that night. We had planned on hanging around together, and generally having a blast, but Alex never made it. I waited for about three and a half hours, having as good a time as I could without my best friend, and even dancing with Susan once (it was a faster song, and much as I wanted to, I couldn't hold her in my arms) before I finally called it a night.

The next day, I went over to Alex's place, and I saw his haggard tear stained face. I almost missed the moving van. All I could see was the agony that enveloped my friend. Beside him was a woman I had never seen, carrying Todd as if he were the most fragile of crystal vases. She too looked incredibly sad. I found out that day that a man I had come to love in the way any boy can love a substitute father had died on his way home from Denver the night before. He'd hit a patch of black ice on the road, never even saw it would be my guess, and his car had spun into one of the Tarkenton Lumber trucks from over near Boulder. My friend, the father of my best friend, was dead. Buried under several tons of red oak on interstate seventy. The strange woman I saw with Alex and Todd was their mother. She had divorced Mr. Harris just four months ago, and I guess maybe she realized that she still loved him. Maybe she always had. I can never say for certain; she was the one thing that Alex never talked about.

That was the last time I saw Alex Harris for more than a few moments at a time. I wrote a few times, but I never had anywhere to send the letters. He never gave me a forwarding address. I never asked for one. I guess I never thought it possible for my best friend to leave me, especially so soon after I had found him; I always felt I'd see him again, even when he climbed into the station wagon with his mother, the station wagon with the California license plates.

I only knew Alex and his family for a short time, but I remember them very fondly. Years have blown past like leaves in a strong wind, and I guess you could say that I am now in the autumn of my life. I would be willing to bet money that Alex is long dead; I feel he would have come back here if he were alive, if only to say goodbye properly. All I have left to remember him is a book he once found in my attic and the unreadable script that he translated. I never knew what words he said that day so long ago, but they chilled me when he spoke them.

Now and then, when I'm feeling particularly morbid, I wonder if that "Magic Spell" he cast caused his father's death, and his being torn from my life. I hope not. I don't like to think that such things are really possible, and I like the idea that it was in part my fault even less. I guess I had to write this down. I guess this is my way of finally saying goodbye to Alex and his Father, and even little Todd.

Hold your friends dearly, you never know how long you'll have with them; like the seasons that change so abruptly when their time is due, life changes, and all too often it changes without warning.

Good Bye Alex.

P. J. Sanderson
October 31, 1991

Chapter One

1

Mark Howell stared absently out the window of the moving car, only vaguely aware of the mountains that now blocked his view of the horizon. *Not just any mountains, the Rockies*, he thought to himself. *A long way from where I was last week.* It was only June, but the air here was already considerably cooler than it was back home.

The thought of the temperature change and the thought of considering Georgia *home* brought a sad smile to his face. *Is there such a thing as a home, or just different places to live?* The words were silent so as to hide from his mom and her husband, Joe, just how much the thought hurt. He needn't have bothered. Neither of them ever paid him the least bit of attention anyway. Atlanta, Georgia had never been home to Mark. Neither had any of the dozen or so other cities and states in which he had lived, but at least in Georgia he had started to make friends. That in itself constituted a minor miracle in his eyes. The thought of moving to another new town in another new state was enough to bring tremors of fear to Mark's insides. New towns meant no friends, no one at all with whom he could talk. New towns also promised a great deal of suffering. Suffering normally caused by the local bullyboys with nothing better to do than make the new kid's life a living hell.

Mark stared at his reflection in the window, faint and insubstantial, but still showing the soft features that went with being a good fifty pounds overweight. His hair was short and very dark, framing a face cursed with delicate features and the general shape of a basketball. His eyes were a pale blue and the closest thing he had to a good feature on his heavy jowled face, at least in his own opinion. Mark believed that he was possibly the least interesting person on the planet. Unless there was someone out there who enjoyed chatting merrily with the Blob.

The road up ahead forked suddenly, as it wrapped around the mountain's edge. Joe took the left fork and smiled brightly. "We're almost there, Marko! You're gonna love this place, kid. It's a lot smaller than Atlanta, but at least you don't have to worry about the crime rate or any of that stuff. Wait'll you see the houses, they're unbelievable! No more apartments for us, guy, just nice comfy houses." Mark smiled towards Joe's reflected eyes in the rear view mirror, as the curving road descended sharply between the mountains. The smile never went past his mouth. Joe had been talking about how much Mark was going to love Colorado from the first day he had accepted his new job with the publishing firm in Denver. He'd never bothered to ask Mark how he felt about another move. The thought probably never entered his head. Joe didn't think that way; it was Joe's way or no way. Mark had never been overly fond of his mother's choice for a new husband and he knew that the feeling was mutual. Mark thought Joe seriously needed to consider a few hundred good books on how to not to treat a stepchild. Joe probably felt Mark was a sissy, owing to the fact that Mark almost always came home from whichever new school he was attending with at least one black eye in the first week alone.

Mark looked to the side of the road, where Lake Overtree made its presence known. He could understand the name well enough upon seeing it. The lake was literally over the trees. Whether there had been a catastrophic incident, perhaps a now-dead volcano blowing its top, or something else, he couldn't possibly have guessed, but the lake looked to be carved from a smaller mountain, and sloped gently down to the woods. He'd seen dams that were built over towns, but in the case of Lake Overtree, nature had done the job. The cool waters glistened in a natural bowl that rose over the forest and made for a stunning site. Mark looked at the lake, allowing himself a brief moment to appreciate the natural oddity, before his mind moved back towards depression.

Sometimes Mark really wished he were still living with his grandparents. He'd been happier back then, before Joe had shown his stupid face in the picture. Sometimes he wished he'd never been born at all. At least then he wouldn't be such a burden on his mom.

He looked over at his mother and came to the same conclusion as always; she was beautiful. Not just because she was his mom, but because she had a dynamite figure, corn-silk hair and a face that looked almost ten years younger than it should. Considering that she would be thirty-one this year, that said a lot. His mind still reeled when he realized that she had been his age when she'd gotten pregnant with him. She'd given birth to her first and only child at the age of sixteen. Fifteen years later she still looked incredible and still managed to smile most of the time. He chalked that up as another minor miracle; no matter what his feelings for Joe, his love for his mother was complete. He forgave Joe's numerous trespasses because Joe made his mother happy. It would have to be enough.

As the car erupted into Summitville, Mark stared around in something like awe. He guessed the town might have a population of six thousand, but that was being overly generous. The road they were on became, of course, Main Street and was surrounded on both sides by cute little shops and cute little restaurants and even a cute little hardware store. He doubted that he would be able to keep up with his comic book collection in this town. He seriously doubted that they had ever seen a comic book in the tiny little Norman Rockwell town of Summitville. At least Joe had told him that they had cable. In the far distance, off into the woods behind what town there was, he could see the faint glimmer of the lake. Maybe he would be able to go swimming there, later on, when the air warmed a bit more. The thought brought a smile to his face that was tentative but real. The smile positively glowed when they cruised past a solitary store on Third Avenue, a good mile and a half past the town proper, that bore the legend WE SELL COMIC BOOKS! in big bold letters. The tiny town of Summitville was looking up already. Then Mark saw the house they were about to move into. In that moment he knew everything would be okay here. The place was even bigger than Joe said and had a lawn that was more than just a postage stamp in size.

As they were getting out of the car and stretching muscles that protested having been in the same position for too long, Mark spotted a girl who was approximately his own age jogging past. He smiled, thinking about how pretty she was and, amazingly, she smiled back and waved. Mark blushed furiously, knowing in his jaded heart that the smile she flashed had to be a way of teasing him, lulling him into a false sense of security…and praying mightily that it might be real just the same.

Maybe, just maybe, Summitville Colorado wouldn't be such a horrible place after all. With a small secret smile and a spring in his step, he grabbed his suitcases and started toward the house.

2

Tony Scarrabelli watched from outside the main building of the Charles S. Westphalen High School as the new kid stepped out from the back entrance, facing the woods. A thick, slow grin spread across his face. The fat boy looked in every direction and finally started walking. He'd missed Tony and the whole crew by some twist of fate. The new kid, Mark Howell, knew that his life was over if Tony caught up with him.

Next to him on his left, Andy Phillips tapped him lightly on the arm and pointed towards Mark Howell. "Hey. Tony, there he is," Andy whispered urgently. "We gonna take him or what?" Tony closed his eyes and counted to ten, trying to remember that Andy was a little slow and that he should have patience with him. The fact that Andy was also five inches taller and over forty pounds heavier than he was made the job much easier.

Tony glared at his best friend and whispered back urgently. "No shit, Andy. Now shut the fuck up, before he hears you." Snickers from the rest of the merry little band filled the air behind him. Most of them were assholes, but a town the size of Summitville didn't permit you to be too picky when it came to your friends. Jerry Sanders and Rob Blake, like Pete, Tony and Andy, were riding high on whatever the hell it was Patrick Wilson, Summitville's only connection to the world of chemical fun and games, had sold them this time. Pete Larson was the worst of the lot: he was giggling quietly and it looked like he was in pain. Any second now, he was going to start laughing out loud unless Tony did something.

Tony looked over at the new kid. He'd almost made it to the woods. "You shouldn't have gotten me in trouble, fucknuts, now I'm going to hurt you." By hurt, Tony meant he was going to blacken both eyes and maybe bruise a few ribs, nothing permanent. Tony was a bastard, even by his own standards, but he wasn't really a vicious bastard. Pete was a vicious bastard, maybe even Jerry, but not Tony. The others were starting to do just what Tony had feared; they were starting to laugh instead of giggle. Tony rolled his eyes towards the Heavens and prayed for patience. Then the chemical stupor hit him as well and he started snickering too.

In the distance, maybe a hundred yards away now, the new kid looked over towards the laughter and his eyes grew wide in his fat face. Just looking at the kid made Tony angry, he had a pretty-boy face and Tony wanted to smash it into the ground. In the back of his mind, he heard his own voice warning him not to cause the kid any real harm, a throwback to his days in the private Catholic School his dad had forced him to attend in the elementary school years. The voice simply made him angrier than ever, everything was making him angrier right now and he couldn't help wondering if the drugs were responsible. He hoped so, because then he'd have an excuse he could live with. Suddenly he wanted to do a great deal more than just hurt the fat kid; he wanted to kill him. He wanted to cream the fat fuck into the ground and make him bleed and scream. He wanted to destroy the little prick. The rage filling Tony was apparently contagious, because he could hear the others starting to growl deep in their throats as the butterball made it into the woods.

"Get him!" The words were barely audible, hidden in a throaty snarl that jolted Tony and his friends into action. In the distance, Mark Howell ran even faster, faster than Tony would have thought possible. And that too made Tony angrier. The pack took off like all the demons of Hell were right on their asses, with Tony leading the way. A feral grin spread across his face, showing bared teeth and red gums as he covered the grassy hillocks in leaps and bounds.

He could hear the sound of the fat boy's wheezing, gasping breaths within a matter of seconds. He could hear the tub o' lard's whining little noises as he closed in. Behind him, one of the others started to howl like a wolf on the hunt; Tony liked the sound so much he joined in.

With a whoop of savage joy, Pete passed him on the right, heading for the jiggling backside of the new kid. As Pete prepared to land on the squealing little piglet, Tony heard a new sound among all the others. It was a sound that he would have never expected from the woods: the sound of laughter and applause as if someone, or a group of someones, was watching a truly fabulous show and it was just getting to the good part. For just a second, he almost stopped what he was doing. Then Pete took fatso down hard, hard enough to draw blood. The sight of the crimson stain on the rock took all self-control from Tony. The beating began in earnest. Somewhere, deep in the back of his head, the rational and caring part of Tony Scarrabelli closed its eyes and covered its ears. Some things are best not remembered. By tomorrow, he wouldn't even remember the incident at all. Later, he would wish that it had been the drugs. Later, he'd have reason to.

3

The day was bright, the air was cold and crisp and, in the autumn woods, Mark Howell was running for dear life. Tony Scarrabelli and Pete Larson ran after Mark Howell with blood in their eyes. Again. For some reason that was just the fate of the perpetual new kid in Summitville.

He looked over his shoulder and saw that Tony and Pete were gaining on him; not rapidly, but they were gaining just the same. Tony and Pete; where were the others? The thought made him run all the faster, what if the others were waiting somewhere, ready to pounce? Two to one was bad enough, but if Jerry Sanders, Rob Blake and Andy Phillips joined in, he would be a dead man for certain. That was the thought running through his mind when Pete crashed into him. For the second time that day, he fell to the ground, his hands, neck and face catching the brunt of the fall. The mulchy autumn leaves covering the forest's floor slid freely away, revealing the rocks and burrs waiting eagerly to sink into Mark's flesh. Certainly, not all of the rocks connected, but it sure as hell felt that way. Sharp pain ripped into his right cheek and then into his neck and chest, as he slid to a stop with Pete riding his back as if he were a sled in the wintertime.

Mark was too stunned to look up or try to fight as the fists started to fall. Around him the aspen trees were silent, stark skeletons reaching for the sky and ignoring his pain. He simply lay still, feeling agony upon agony and counting the number of feet around him. Seven...Eight...Nine...Ten. Well, whaddaya know...the rest of the Asshole Patrol had shown up after all. The beating seemed to last forever, blast after blast of numbing pain tore through his entire body, before the shoes disappeared, one pair at a time. He was fairly certain that he heard names and words and he was guessed they were directed at him, but none of them made sense.

For a minute or more, the world faded away, bringing memories of how the fight started:

The fight started as Mark's fights always started these days, with Tyler opening his mouth and Mark stepping in against his better judgment. He just couldn't help it, Tony practically begged to be verbally cut apart. Mark had learned only one solid lesson since his family had moved to Summitville: Stay away from Tony Scarrabelli. He had been in Summitville and at Charles S. Westphalen High School for just over one month and on every day he attended, Tony, Pete and the rest of their little gang, started in on the fat jokes. Most of the time, he ignored them.

Today, Tyler's mouth opened wide and the battle of wits started in earnest. This time, it went a little too far. This time, Tony meant to hurt him. Not just a little, Tony meant to make him bleed.

It was right after lunch, and Mark was talking excitedly with Tyler Wilson, possibly the only kid in the school with a worse reputation. Tyler was thin, not really skinny, with coke bottle glasses that made him look downright owlish. But that wasn't what made Tyler's life miserable— even with the thick glasses he could almost be called handsome in an impish way. No, Tyler suffered from a near terminal case of Foot-in-Mouth disease. His tongue was simply too sharp and his mental reflexes too quick, for him to have a great life expectancy. So, naturally, when Tony and four of his friends stepped in front of Mark, Tyler immediately prepared for battle.

And just as naturally, Tony was less than prepared. Tony stepped directly into Mark's path, crossing arms just slightly thinner than Arnold Schwartzenegger's and grinning good-naturedly. "Hey, fag-boy, I mean fat-boy, what's new?" he asked with enthusiasm.

Mark shifted on his feet, prepared to walk around the bully, but Tony was having none of it. Neither was Tyler. With the eagerness of a prizefighter, Tyler started with the verbal assault. "Gee, Tony, it's so good to see you again. Is it true you finally learned to breathe with your mouth closed?"

Tony responded with silence, and a puzzled expression. "I mean, seeing you always makes me realize that Darwin was right on the ball." Seeing Tony's perplexed look, Tyler moved in for the killing stroke. "Y'know, Darwin. No? Well, he's the guy who figured men evolved from apes like you."

Mark could have almost laughed at the amount of time it took Tony to realize he'd been insulted. Almost. When understanding sank through his, no doubt, chemically induced stupor, Tony lashed out with truly phenomenal speed and lifted Tyler off of the ground by his hair. Even realizing that Tyler barely passed the one-hundred-and-fifteen-pound mark on weight, it was an impressive sight. Tyler immediately started out with a high pitched keening sound as he was lifted off his feet. His perpetual grin was gone, replaced by a pained baring of his even white teeth. Tony was grinning, though. Tyler had just given him another excuse to impress all of his friends with a show of his physical prowess. Oh my, how Tony was grinning and so were all of his buddies.

Mark looked at the smaller, paler, version of The Incredible Hulk standing before him, holding the only person he could call a friend in the entire damned school by his hair and laughing, and something inside snapped. Were Mark a stronger or more violent person, he would have used his fists, something Tony could have understood. But Mark, like Tyler, was more experienced with his brain than his brawn. Before he could stop himself, he opened his mouth. "Posing for your fag boyfriends, Tony?" he asked, horrified by what he had just said and simultaneously exhilarated by the thought of another good staring match.

But, when Tony turned his tanned, dark-haired head towards him, the excitement was replaced by cold, hard, terror. It seemed to take forever for Tony's columnar neck to finish turning. And, after that slow neck-crank finished, time stopped. Dark, fearsome eyes narrowed and Tony smiled again, viciously. "What," Tony started with a frighteningly-sweet voice, "the fuck did you just say?" Tony dropped Tyler to the ground, turning the rest of his powerful frame to face Mark. The hideous grin grew larger and more imposing. His grin promised whole new worlds of pain just for Mark. "Did you just call me a fag?"

Inwardly mortified, Mark smiled too, in an effort to match the feral expression on Tony's face. He knew that he couldn't hope to make amends; he knew that one more word would seal his fate, but his mouth didn't seem to care. Even Tyler— the mouth that roared—was shaking his head at Mark, silently begging him to stop before it was too late. Mark already understood that there was no stopping now. "No, I called your friends fags. Calling you a fag would assume that you're human and male. I figure they keep you around to scare off any women who might want to get near them."

His mind reeled in abject horror as Mark realized that he had brought in the whole herd of Tony's friends. He knew he couldn't take Tony, but at least if it was only one guy, he could HURT that guy, before he went down. Looking around at the five Neanderthals before him, his mind went into automatic over-drive. With no connection to his body's actions, he watched his left fist swing hard and connect with deadly precision, against Tony's granite jaw.

Tony's head snapped around and the impact ran all the way up to Mark's elbow. His mind howled victoriously, even as Tony was turning towards him, with honest shock in his eyes. Then his traitorous mouth spewed out words, even as the shock in Tony's eyes was replaced by a seething rage. He sneered at Tony and spat out, "Why don't you try that shit with someone your own size, Scarrabelli? Only pussies take on kids fifty pounds lighter."

Somebody yelled, "Fight!" at the top of their lungs and Mark turned, realizing they had drawn a crowd. Along with this realization, came the knowledge that he had just turned his back on the biggest, meanest sub-human he had ever had the displeasure of meeting. Tony took full advantage of the fact and drove his fist directly into the back of Mark's head.

Mark's whole world exploded with light as he staggered forward. If Mark had been anywhere but in the hallway known school-wide as the skating rink, he might have managed to stay on his feet. These were the floors that Otis the janitor waxed to a glassy sheen every day and even after three periods the floors were as smooth and slippery as ice. He flailed his arms frantically as he fell to the floor. The linoleum tasted like a thousand tennis shoes. He barely had time to notice the flavor before Tony landed on his back. The air erupted from his lungs and he felt his body flare with a desperate hunger for oxygen as Tony struck him in the head again. He supposed he would have been beaten to death then and there if it hadn't been for Coach Malloy. Andrew Malloy stood just over five foot eight and seemed to be just as wide, but from Mark's point of view, he was a towering god. Even as he turned his head and torso, fully prepared for another sledge-hammer to smash into his skull, he saw Tony's hand stopped on its descent by the blocking hand of his savior. Tony looked up, perplexed by the interference, as Malloy hauled him off his victim.

Tony hit the wall with enough force to stun him and Malloy grabbed a fistful of Mark's jacket, in a hand slightly too large for the rest of his body. The next few minutes were a blur. He didn't really remember being hauled down to the principal's office and he didn't really remember the acid stares of his adversary, but his mind made up reasonable facsimiles. He remembered the principal's look of astonishment, as he told his side of the story and he remembered Tony's smile of satisfaction, when the overweight man informed them that they both had two weeks of detention. Detention meant walking home every day. Alone. With only Tony to keep him company. The thought sent tiny tremors through his body, similar to the ones just before the real beating began, but much smaller. After all, then it was only a possibility. Now, it was a past event.

It was almost an hour later, with his clothes torn and dirtied, his skin scraped and bloodied, that he finally stood up. He staggered home, reaching that special destination some twenty minutes later. He noticed the stunned stupid look on his mother's face as he walked in, remembering to wipe his feet off—a big point of pride, that. And then he kissed linoleum, in the kitchen this time. It tasted like Pledge and dust balls.

4

It went better than he had expected. Although she was obviously horrified by his condition, his mother explained that she understood about him defending his friend and even though she didn't say it, he got the impression that she was even a little proud of him. His stepfather, Joe, (never Dad) even treated him decently, a rarity indeed—he normally looked at his stepson with barely hidden contempt. Or at least, it seemed that way. No parent ever seemed to understand their child's thoughts and the opposite was certainly true. He suspected it was worse when the kid was fat, plain, and not your own. Joe was a good friend of Principal Samuel Watkins—that friendship being one of the reasons for moving to Summitville—and a brief phone call ended the detention. Hell, the man even apologized to Mark, an act that had never before occurred in the history of Westphalen High.

Right after that, a trip to the Summitville Emergency Clinic was necessary. After a thirty-minute wait, through which Joe grumbled continuously, seventeen stitches were placed in his face. Mark still didn't understand the logic of calling old man Watkins before the trip to the clinic, but he wasn't about to make waves. He may be stupid upon occasion, but why ask for another argument?

He slept the rest of the day and most of the night. When he woke up it was six-thirty. It just wasn't worth the effort to try to get back to sleep. Instead, he tried to prepare himself for the hellish day at school, fully prepared for more humiliation. He winced at the thought and immediately regretted it—the damn stitches *hurt*. With a sigh, he settled in and painstakingly placed his contact lenses into his eyes. He told himself the tears were only there because his eyes were sensitive. He almost believed it, too.

He'd been outside for forty-five minutes when the school bus arrived. He couldn't hold back a rueful grin when Tyler looked at his face. "Shit, Howie, what the hell happened to you?" Tyler looked positively sick. "Cut yourself shaving with a pickax?"

Sitting down beside him, Mark looked over and shook his head. "No, that prick Scarrabelli and his good buddies decided to thank me for yesterday. I'm bound to impress the girls now, huh?" He spoke in a whisper; Tony Scarrabelli had too many friends for him to speak loudly. Not that he really had to worry. They were just leaving the third stop on the bus's trip to school and the two other passengers, both being females, had little that they would talk to Scarrabelli about. They weren't the types of girl he'd bother with; they weren't good looking enough for the bastard to even consider.

As Mark closed his eyes for a moment, Tyler looked at him with a great deal of regret and more than a small amount of admiration. The last thing he'd wanted was for Mark to pay the price when he opened his damned mouth again. In reflection, he realized that Mark was simply too damn nice for his own good.

If Mark wasn't so damned shy, he'd likely have a girlfriend by now. Mark wasn't like Tyler, Mark looked human. Oh sure, he was a little pudgy, but only a little. Anyone with half a brain would realize that nature had been more than generous to Mark when it came to natural muscle-tone. That easily explained why Tony and his butt-buddies chose to tackle him en masse. None of them was quite brave enough to try it on their own.

Tyler looked over at Mark's pale face and studied the line of stitches that ran glaringly across its surface. Ouch. That had to have hurt. That was another thing about Mark, he very seldom complained about anything, but he was always more than willing to listen to Tyler's bitching about life in general. Tyler had him pretty well pegged. He was willing to give it five years, before Mark climbed into a bell tower and started shooting. He snorted to himself, appalled by his own cynicism.

He watched quietly as the kids from all over the neighborhood got on the bus, stop after stop. Most of them knew about what had happened in the halls yesterday, most of them knew what brought the wounds that covered Mark's face, but he was the New Kid, a stranger to Summitville, and so they ignored him completely, expressed no sympathy. Summitville was a great place to live, in Tyler's opinion, provided that you had always lived there. Strangers were tolerated at best.

Tyler saw Cassie before Mark did, he nudged Mark when Cassie climbed the three stairs up into the bus. Mark was immediately awake and stared at the girl with cow-eyes. Cassie was only fifteen and already stood over five foot eight. A fact that probably tore her up inside. Cassie used to live right next door and Tyler knew she'd had dreams of being a world-class gymnast until her last growth spurt had hit. In her words, being that tall was as good as a death sentence when it came to gymnastics. Tyler didn't know a damn thing about that, but he knew she was still hurting where it counted. She hid the grief well and to prove that it didn't bother her, she took up jogging. Watching her jog was one of Tyler's favorite pastimes; she bounced well. She had dark red-blond coppery hair and eyes the color of a pre-dawn sky. And, although she seldom showed it, a smile that could light every house in Summitville—she seemed to show her smile a lot more when Mark was around, but that was probably just his imagination. There wasn't a feature on her face that wasn't damn near perfect. There wasn't a feature on her face that she liked. Frankly, if her body kept developing the way it was now, he might decide it was time to re-develop his crush on her.

This time, he'd definitely have competition. Mark Howell was in love. Or at least in lust. He'd never even said hello to her after the first day, Tyler doubted that he ever would, if he didn't get some help. "Yo, Cassandra!" he bellowed at the top of his lungs, "get a load of Frankenstein, over here!" Cassie looked over with a frown and her eyes flew wide at the sight of Mark. Mark was far too busy trying to kill Tyler with a look to notice. Tyler just smiled innocently and pushed his sandy-blond bangs away from his glasses. *Ah, Tyler, you sly devil you.*

Cassie touched Mark lightly on the arm and Mark felt electricity course through his body. Tyler who? He turned to face Cassie and saw the look of worry on her face. "What happened?"

Before Mark could answer, Tyler butted in and told of how Mark had saved him from certain death at the hands of the evil and stupid Tony Scarrabelli. He continued on, to tell of the later beating in the woods. "Does it hurt?" she asked, wincing in sympathy.

Mark smiled, "Only when I look in the mirror." Cassie smiled back and his whole world seemed better. He'd have to remember to thank Tyler, sometime after he'd beaten the little weasel into the concrete.

By the time that the bus finally stopped at the high school, Mark was convinced that he was in love. Her voice was musical, her face was magical, her body was phenomenal and, as an added bonus, she had a brain. Cassie was a great deal nicer than he would have suspected; if past experience had held true, she should have been a true bitch. Mark had seldom been happier to be wrong. As they went their separate ways, Cassie smiled and Mark felt a comforting warmth spread through his entire body. The warmth disintegrated in mere seconds, as Tony passed by.

Tony was looking particularly gruesome today, a fact that Tyler immediately pointed out. Loudly. Mark flinched inwardly, as Tony turned their way. Without thought, Mark punched Tyler in the arm, not hard, but hard enough to make his point clear. That was a particularly stupid thing to do, especially after yesterday. Much to his relief, Tony simply glared and went on his way.

Tyler looked over at Mark and grinned sheepishly. "Sorry, my mouth still has this nasty little problem with staying shut when it should."

Mark arched an eyebrow and frowned slightly. "Ty, are you trying to get me killed? What did I do to you," he mused aloud, "that makes you want to see me bleed? Weren't the stitches enough?"

Tyler looked wounded, until he saw Mark break a grin; it was twisted by the stitches and by the pain they caused as they pulled, but it was a grin just the same. He lightly thumped Tyler on the back of the head and gestured towards the school's entrance. "C'mon, we're gonna be late."

Smiling to himself, Tyler thought about what Mark's reaction to the same situation would have been the day before. He was very pleased with himself —he had just given Mark the only gift he could afford, a good mood, however briefly it lasted.

5

Joseph Howell was angry, primarily with himself, for not having paid better attention the few times that Mark had mentioned troubles at the school. It was hard to think that there were any serious problems, the kid always seemed to be in a good mood; as long as he had a book to read or a decent horror movie to watch, nothing seemed to bother him. Somehow, Joe doubted that another round of Nightmare On Elm Street would make the scar seem like less of an affliction. He was just grateful that the scar would be minimal, that the stone had cut him cleanly rather than tearing the flesh from his face.

He wished he understood his stepson a little better and he had no one to blame but himself. From the first time he'd met Mark, he'd felt a mild repulsion for him. The kid seemed, well, wimpy. Joe had spent two years working as a paramedic in the worst part of New York City and had always kept up a strenuous regimen of exercise even after days when he felt like passing out from exhaustion. After all of the blood-shed he'd seen, after all of the cruel deformities he'd had to patch up on people who had been in perfect health ten minutes earlier, he just couldn't stand the sight of anyone who was less than physically fit. Oh, he realized deep inside that it was a prejudice, he just couldn't seem to do anything about it. To be honest, he hadn't really tried to, either.

Well, it was time to try now. He hadn't realized how strong his feelings for Mark were until he'd seen the crusted, bleeding gash running across the boy's face. He shuddered at the thought, paranoid little scenarios of what could have happened running rampantly through his mind. Try as he might, the hideous images of his son—*Yes dammit, his son! He'd been with the boy for ten years, longer by far than the bastard who'd fathered him. That made him his son!*—lying dead on the forest floor, his skull cracked open by the rock, wouldn't go away.

Pulling into a spot at the fitness center a block from the agency, Joe grabbed his workout bag and headed towards the entrance. His mind was made up. When he got home, he and the boy would talk.

It was time for his son to learn a little bit about self-defense. If he'd been a man about it, he'd have taught the boy years ago.

6

The sun had yet to burn away the morning's dew when the first of Them came into the opening between the trees. They gathered quickly, knowing that the sun would soon rise high enough to kiss the glen with its fiery light.

Eagerly, They caressed the Stone and felt the flaky red crust on its edge. Their bodies sang with the promise that the blood offered. As they whispered urgently, the animals grew silent. No bird dared call for its mate, no insect dared move, for fear of the noise its chitinous shell might make. The glen was silent save for the whispered calls, save for the promise made by the Folk. They danced excitedly about the Stone, carefully setting the leaves and mulch back in place. No sign must show, no hint must give away Their presence. Only the One could know. That was the way. As it had always been. The One had been chosen, the One had been marked. Now, They must wait. Despite Their excitement, despite the closeness of the One, They would wait patiently. They had waited so long, years and years, They could wait a small while longer. They had all the time in the world.

The light of day topped the trees, touching the ground that was sacred to Them. Silently, disturbing not even a single leaf, They found Their special places and hid away.

"Soon, Soon..." the wind promised, "The time is almost here."

The Stone sat impassively. It pulsed with the power that the Chosen One would soon provide. It was a slow change, nothing that a person would actually see, but in the glen where it had always waited, the Stone began to grow.

Hidden away, the Folk crowed with joy. The Stone was growing and soon They would be free to roam as They pleased, wherever and whenever the notion touched Them. They had but to wait and to protect the Chosen One in his time of Change.

7

Tony sat in his third period study hall, trying to figure out just what the hell had happened. He knew that he had had a hand in the damage done to Howell, but he couldn't remember it and he sure as shit hadn't meant for the puke's face to get slashed that way. News of the kid's beating had spread through most of the classes like wildfire. There hadn't been anything even close to an event worth gossiping about since Tanya

Billingsley had disappeared earlier in the year, and even in Summitville, that was old news. So Tony brooded, knowing that at least half of the class around him was looking at him with a new sort of fear. Very few people doubted that he was responsible for what had happened to Mark Howell's face. He'd just wanted to put a good solid scare into the fat slob. Hell, the kid wasn't even that fat, it was just, well, the kid pissed him off. He couldn't even say why. *Yes you could.* He didn't know just what it was, *oh, don't you?* about Mark Howell that always made him angry. He shook the thoughts out of his head and looked over at Cassie Monroe. She was facing away from him, hunched over a thick book on Biology. Lord, but how he'd love to teach her some biology. She had a damn fine body. Every time he walked down the hall, he looked for her. Seeing her muscular body glide down the hallway always made him ache. Made him hard.

He looked down at his notebook, just for something else to stare at and started drawing more than slightly vulgar illustrations. He wasn't a talented artist by any stretch of the imagination and his anatomy was horribly off, so he didn't worry much about a teacher understanding what he had drawn. No problem.

He looked up again, just in time to hear the bell ring. He stayed where he was and watched as Cassie stood and stretched her shoulders. Damn, she was a knockout. She looked his way and he smiled. She was coming over to talk to him. He forced his heart to stay out of his throat and nodded to her. "Hey, Cassie, what's up?"

Cassie frowned slightly, looking at him where he so casually draped himself over the chair. He very quickly closed his notebook, before she could see his doodles. "Hi, Tony," she started, "I heard you and Mark Howell got into a fight yesterday." She looked honestly perplexed. "Why?"

Tony felt suddenly uncomfortable and forced his eyes away from hers. "I don't really know, I guess, maybe I teased a little too hard." He looked back up at her and shrugged his shoulders. "Hey, I didn't even throw the first punch, he hit me."

Cassie looked at him intently and he started to feel like a bug under a microscope. The temptation to squirm was very difficult to resist. "Well, I hope you guys work it out. He's not a bad guy. You should get to know him."

"So, maybe I'll give it a try. If you say he's okay, maybe he is."

Cassie smiled briefly and he felt like a real worm. No way, was he going to make nice with that fat prick. He hated to lie about it, but it was easier than arguing with Cassie. Anything was easier than that. "Great. Well, I'll see ya later, Tony. Time for the old work out."

"Yeah. Later, Cassie." He watched her leave, mesmerized by her walk. How could anyone move like that and not know the effect she was having? *Standards*, he grinned to himself, what was Pete going to have to say about the gash on Howell's face? He couldn't wait to find out. Cafeteria, here we come.

8

Pete had it all planned; when the lard-ass came around the corner, Pete was gonna nail him in the balls. Not hard enough to make him go down, but hard enough to make him ache. His math book at the ready, he smiled to himself and listened for Tyler Wilson's nasal voice to come creeping up.

He'd watched for two weeks and every day of those two weeks Tyler walked about three feet from the wall of the hallway, leaving just enough room between himself and the wall for pork-belly to squeeze through. Mark always walked about two steps behind Wilson, too. So when he heard Wilson he'd set himself and as soon as he saw the skinny little shit, he'd swing the book. He could barely stifle the snickers that threatened to erupt from him.

It went like clockwork. Pete heard him, he saw him, he swung. *Whap! Home run!* The pig fell to his knees and dropped his books. Just as he was preparing to offer a sickeningly sweet apology, he saw the stitches on Howell's face.

His voice caught, looking on in shock, as Mark Howell stood up. The look in the guy's eyes spoke volumes. He knew instinctively that if he said another word, the kid would jump on him. Pete would never admit that he was afraid of anyone, even Tony, but his better judgment made him bend and pick up the books that Howell had dropped. He muttered a small apology that was acknowledged by a curt nod and beat a hasty, if dignified, retreat.

He'd seen that look a few times, it was the same look that Tony'd had on his face yesterday, after detention. When they'd gone after...who?

He remembered chasing someone. He couldn't see a face, or remember what had happened, but he definitely remembered chasing someone. He thought about it for a few seconds and then toyed with maybe stopping on the amphetamines. They were a good high and cheap, but maybe they were playing with his mind. Pete was fairly proud of his mind, he'd yet to fail a course at school. Why risk it?

A few minutes later he saw Tony heading his way. Should he ask him who they'd chased? Naw, last thing he needed was to get ragged by Tony. He thumped Tony on the back as he passed and started up a conversation they'd had to stop at the end of second period. In five more minutes he'd forgotten all about Mark Howell. What a pity that Mark had not forgotten about him.

9

Mark smiled and kept up the conversation with Tyler, but inside he seethed. A dull ache crawled through his stomach and groin, reminding him that he was alive and in pain. His face didn't even seem to hurt anymore and, truth be told, he barely even felt the ache in his lower body.

He had been humiliated again. By the same son of a bitch that had torn his face open yesterday. Try as he might, he couldn't stop thinking along those lines. A part of his mind cowered, thinking of nothing but the fact that he had been pounded into the ground the day before. But it was a small part, it was nothing compared to the rage that filled him. He had divine images in his mind of what he would do to Pete, if he ever got him alone. *It's a good thing,* he thought to himself, *that I'm a pacifist.*

"Yoo Hooo…Earth to Mark, come in Mark."

Mark pulled himself from his inner thoughts and looked over towards Tyler. Tyler was waving his hands in Mark's face, a slight frown on his forehead. "Hmmm? Oh, sorry. I was thinking about other things."

"Shit, I didn't know I was *that* boring to talk to." The words lacked sting, mostly because of the exaggerated look of woe on Ty's face. Mark smiled and this time, it was a little more real. "So, what're ya thinkin', Howie?"

Mark looked over, with a pained look on his face. "I'm thinking how much I'll miss you, when you're gone."

Tyler frowned, obviously confused. "Gone? I'm not going anywhere."

"Sure you are. To the hospital. The next time you call me 'Howie.'"

Tyler grinned, exposing his teeth in all their glory. It was a very open smile, it challenged and apologized simultaneously. Mark doubted he would ever understand his friend, but he certainly enjoyed his company. "Shit, Howie, you wouldn't hurt me. If you did, who'd remind you to get your thumb out of your ass? Who'd point out all of your faults, or tell you when you were drooling?" Tyler's grin changed to one of pure sadistic glee, as he continued. "Who'd tie your shoes when your mom had to go to work early? And who'd give you all the information you so desperately wanted?"

"Information? About what?"

Tyler grinned victoriously and Mark marveled at the mobility of his horse-like features. *Horse-like? No, more like a slightly tamed vulture…* "Not what. Who. A certain flame haired vixen, the apple of your eye, the bulge against your thigh, none other than…" Mark glared, but Tyler was on a roll and nothing could stop him now, short of violent death. "One Mizz Cassie Monroe." Mark's cheeks flared with warmth and, with his usual tact, Tyler leapt at the new opening. "My God! You're blushing! Oh, this is too perfect, wait'll I tell Cassie! She'll die!" Mark felt his face grow warmer still, as Tyler Wilson slapped the table, laughing uproariously. Mark could *feel* the eyes of the cafeteria against his back, he imagined the stares of every student in the school on him. A panic started in his chest, rapidly spreading throughout his body, as his mind pictured every last one of them telling Cassie how he felt. If he'd had a rock to crawl under, he would have. Desperately, he looked around the large room and realized, with relief, that no one was paying any attention. What could the losers of the school have to say that could be of the least bit of interest?

Tyler wiped his eyes, still chuckling at Mark's expense, "Oh. Ah ha. Had ya goin' there," he crowed triumphantly. "Didn't I?"

"Why don't you just fucking broadcast it over the goddamn P.A. system, asshole?" he hissed back.

With deadpan innocence, Tyler responded. "Do you think I should? I work in the office y'know."

"If you even think about it, I'll—" Mark sputtered, he felt like his heart was going to erupt from his chest, as if someone had pulled his pants down around his ankles in church and he wasn't wearing any underwear. Tyler's face cracked into a sincere smile and he thumped Mark on the arm.

"Relax, Mark. I'd never really do that to you. You should know that by now." Mark felt his body start to relax, as Tyler continued. "Hell, you're just about the only person I can hassle around here, who doesn't feel the immediate need to tear me a new asshole. I wouldn't do anything to hurt you." Again Tyler's expressive face became solemn, "Where the hell would I find another punching bag so willing to be abused?" Mark grinned at that one and realized that Tyler had, once again, manipulated him into a good mood. He would have thanked him, but

Ty would probably take offense from someone knowing how he operated. Ty thrived on his subtlety; he considered it his one true gift.

The bell blared its dismissal and before Mark could move, Tyler had thumped him on the top of his head, grabbed up his books and bolted away. Mark shook his head, wondering just how he'd managed to find a friend like Ty. He was goofy, obnoxious to a fault, and too loud for his own good, but he was also a helluva good guy. Mark made it all the way to the end of the day with a smile on his battered face.

Mark stepped into the house and realized that he was alone. Joe was probably still at work and God alone knew where his mom was off to. She never left a note. He dropped his books on the counter and went to sit in the den. The den was almost his private area, with endless piles of science fiction and horror books piled on almost every available piece of furniture. The room was huge, easily three times the size of his bedroom and decorated entirely to Mark's taste. Freddy Krueger leered down from one of the walls, promising a thousand painful games with his eyes. From the opposite wall, dozens of magazine cutouts stared into the room. Prominent figures included The Phantom of the Opera, The Creature, Michelle Pfeifer, Pinhead, Drew Barrymore, and the Lost Boys. It was against that wall, that Mark had placed his drawing board.

The board was a gift from his mother. She'd given it to him when he moved here, knowing that Mark loved to draw when he was depressed. Mark was always depressed after a move, so she'd opted to give him an inexpensive form of therapy. It wasn't the best drawing board around, but it suited his needs.

Mark sat at his drawing stool and stared at the poster of Julia Roberts intently, seeing nothing. He pulled a sheet of paper close and stared at the white blank expanse in front of him. Here, he could see thousand of different things. Here, the potential was limited only by his imagination and his ability. His imagination was fine—his ability, on the other hand...

As he started moving a number two pencil across the paper, with smooth easy strokes, he let his mind move to other things. This was the best way he knew of to think. As happened so often, he thought about the past, about all of the friends he had said good-bye to and about how much some of them had meant to him. Without his mind getting in the way, the picture started to develop.

Depression is a seductive trap. It can lead you into a warm familiarity, wrap you in its protective blankets of numbness and lull you into a false sense of self that has nothing to do with the way that you really are. It drains away your other emotions and bleeds away the colors that you would normally perceive. It can be addictive. Mark Walter Howell was most definitely hooked. The compelling traps of the past had him almost looking forward to his near daily trips into the realms of melancholia. Mark's hand made motions on the Bristol paper before him, while he spun through time, contemplating the many failures in his young life.

He'd never known his father; he had been too young when the man left his mother, never to return. His mother still had photographs, candid shots of the man that so resembled his son. The same night black hair, the same slightly effeminate features, the same sky blue eyes. But, he was leaner and harder; his eyes seemed to look at the world with certain disdain, his tight smile spoke of a sneering contempt for the people around him. Mark had trouble seeing himself in the man, despite the remarkably similar features. He looked far too confident and fit to have spawned the quivering slug that Mark perceived himself to be. Never having even met the man to his knowledge, he idolized him and missed him.

Moving on in his memories to the years where he was finally old enough to go to school, finally old enough to have more than brief snapshot memories, Mark contemplated his mother. Jennifer Gallagher Howell was far too young to have a fifteen-year-old son. In three months, she would finally break into the early thirties age bracket. She'd given birth to Mark when she was sixteen years of age. Mark knew that she loved him, but he knew that she also harbored a great deal of bitterness for the loss of her childhood at such a young age. Her parents had been furious when they found out that she was pregnant. They had forced her to have the child and had intended that he be given up for adoption. She took one look at her newborn son and decided to raise him. Her parents, his grandparents, never seemed to regret her decision. Obviously, his father did. He knew, from the stories that his mother would tell and how she would tell them, that his father had been only a few years older than Jennifer herself. Before she had turned seventeen, he had left town.

He also knew that if it hadn't been for the support of his maternal grandparents, she would have had to go on welfare. His grandparents practically raised him after his father had flown the coop, while his mother went to college and learned a trade. Grandfather Gallagher had insisted. Nobody argued with the man when he had made his mind up. His mother had opted to study commercial art and, to her credit, was talented enough to make a good living at it. It was while free-lancing for a fantasy and science fiction magazine that she met Joseph Howell, a man almost a decade and a half older than she was, who fell in love with her almost at first sight.

One year later, they were joined in holy matrimony. At the ripe old age of three and a half, Mark had his new father. On the day she turned twenty, his mother gained a new husband. It made her life much easier, having someone other than her parents or son to share her triumphs and pitfalls, and for that Mark was always going to be happy. But, it made his life a great deal more difficult. Joe was a good man, he treated his mother right and provided a home for Mark, but he had never shown any real affection to the boy. He was too busy working or being macho or hanging with his friends to give time to Mark. And they moved too much. Joe was always looking for a better job or being relocated, when a company that he worked for expanded. Mark had trouble comprehending that a job in the magazine industry could be the cause of so much trauma. He had counted them a thousand times: fourteen schools and he was just now in the tenth grade of his education.

By number eight, he'd built solid walls around himself to avoid getting too close to anyone. He felt like a plant that had been uprooted and relocated too many times. He actually flinched at the thought of another move; his soul had been battered too many times for him to control the spasm.

Joe had promised that this would be the last time; Mark just couldn't believe it. He wanted to, desperately, because he could sense the first touch of caring leaking through his armor, could feel himself wanting to make friends, and that could easily lead to the collapse of his already torn soul if he allowed it. If they moved again. He'd made so many friends, and lost them all to the need for more money and better benefits for his family. He didn't think he could stand to make any more just to lose them a few months later. Just the thought was enough to push him deeper into his growing depression.

With a sigh, he pushed the pencil out of his hand and stood, ignoring the grisly, bloodied form of Pete lying broken on the paper. He was eager to get out, walk in the sunlight and forget. Oh, how he wished that he could forget. It was the season—autumn always brought the blues with it, eager to befriend and embrace him. He hated autumn passionately.

Grabbing his coat, Mark walked outside, into the chill air and started to walk a circuit of the subdivision he lived in. The Red Oaks subdivision was a fairly new addition to Summitville, barely older than Mark himself. In the early sixties, Tyler Wilson's grandfather, Alexander Prescott Wilson, had decided that the town needed new blood. Old Alexander didn't believe in hesitation: he started construction on the subdivision, building where Summit Town had once thrived over a century ago.

Summit Town had been even smaller than Summitville, a fact that Mark had trouble swallowing, if the old stories could be believed. It had been settled early in the eighteen hundreds, by Dutchmen. The town had only been around for some thirty years, when Albert "Stoney" Miles had come there to live. In less than four years, he had murdered the town.

Stoney had come from the east, with his small family and a small fortune in merchandise to sell. Hungry for news about the world outside of their little community, the people of Summit Town had accepted the family eagerly. They helped Stoney in the building of his house and in the building of his mercantile, they helped make him a part of the town. They helped destroy themselves.

He didn't mean to murder the town, it just sort of happened. Stoney liked to drink, as the legend went, and Stoney liked to smoke his pipe. It was in the latter part of August, with a nasty drought turning the town and its wood mills into dry kindling, that Stoney struck the killing blow.

While on a fearsome drunk he picked a fight with Abraham Smythe, a younger man who seemed to dote a bit too much on Stoney's wife for Stoney's peace of mind. After a particularly scandalous bit of gossip, saying that they had been together near the lake above town, reached his drunken ears, Stoney severely beat his lovely wife in front of their three year old son, Joshua.

Grabbing his hatchet, he set out to find Abraham Smythe. And find him he did, in the woods, heading towards the Miles' residence with a cluster of wild flowers in his hand.

Stoney went berserk. The first seven blows were concentrated on Abraham's handsome face, the remaining fifty or so on his crotch. He was found almost a week after the town was murdered, by one of the town's last surviving founders. The man stopped counting ax blows after seventy-three.

Considering himself to have found all the proof he needed, Stoney stalked down his wife, raped her savagely and killed her.

After only a moment's contemplation, he tossed his son down the well. He apparently couldn't bring himself to hack the child to pieces, but he also couldn't trust that the boy was his. It has been hypothesized, by various rumor mongers and story tellers, that the boy's drowning would have been acceptable to his father.

The town's constable found the boy, half-drowned, hanging onto the rope and perched on the bucket that Stoney used to pull water. (Visions of Daffy Duck being reeled in from the bottom of such a well with a glare of disgust came to mind immediately. Mark's mind worked that way.) Joshua had spent over twenty-four hours treading water and clinging to the rope. His vocal cords were never quite the same after that. Not a single member of the small town expected the child to live —he was, after all, only three years old. But the boy was strong enough to survive the resultant pneumonia and, due to the uncertainty of the boy's heritage, the remaining members of the Smythe family later took him in. Those that survived the day, that is.

Stoney went on a drunken rampage that ended at a still one of the local boys had built in the woods. When he arrived there, he found several bottles of the rotgut halfheartedly hidden in the shrubs nearby. Murdering your family was mighty thirsty work apparently and Stoney took full advantage of the supplies available. He drank his newfound bounty and smoked his trusty old pipe, until the sunset. He may very well have been content to leave it at that, if it hadn't been for Jon Stewart making an appearance. Jon owned the still and was less than pleased to find that Stoney had helped himself to over half of the bottles available.

Jon screamed at Stoney, demanding payment in full for the whiskey that he had consumed. Stoney refused. It seems fair to say that had Jon known of Stoney's earlier activities, he would have let him go with all the whiskey he wanted, free of charge. As it was, the slightly larger and younger man threatened to call the town's law on Stoney, after he threatened to beat the frail-looking man severely.

Well, anybody who has ever had a serious hangover, the kind that amplifies sound and makes the faintest light a solar flare, should be able to sympathize with Stoney's dilemma.

He took his trusty hatchet in hand again and went after Jon, screaming like a banshee the entire time. He didn't kill Jon, but he managed to knock the man senseless with the flat edge of the blade on his third attempt to behead his opponent.

He probably would have killed him, if he hadn't over-extended his last wild swing and thrown himself down on the still. It should be pointed out that Jon had freshly stoked the small flame under his poorly built contraption, before he realized that Stoney was even in the vicinity. Jon was always cautious and he had cleared away all of the dry scrub brush in the area, but he hadn't expected the fool thing to explode. He hadn't counted on Stoney leaping out of the flaming debris, still clutching his hatchet, and streaking off into the dried-out woods nearby.

And he hadn't even considered the possibility of a burning man running most of the way to the town, a quarter of a mile away. The rest, as the say, is history. With the town sleeping away snug in their beds and the winds blowing from the lake to the town, they never really had a chance.

The larger part of the populace of Summit Town managed to escape the flames; they only lost all of their worldly possessions and twenty-eight people to the blaze. Stoney's house was one of the few left unscathed. They took the problem in stride—they'd had more than their share of troubles and hardships since they and theirs left the homelands, and they were used to it.

Within three months, they were well on their way to rebuilding; a few trails away from their original site, granted, but they worked hard and fast and soon Summitville rose from the ashes, birthed from the smoldering corpse of Summit Town.

After hearing the stories of all the witnesses able to speak, the town's elders pieced together what had happened and condemned Albert "Stoney" Miles to an eternity in Hell. They even put the curse on his headstone, in a grave set away from the church proper. There was no body in the grave, only a scorched and charred hatchet.

Of Stoney, no sign was ever found. For years on end, he became the town's bogeyman, an evil creature that chopped little children to pieces if they were naughty. Mark found it amusing that every little town he'd lived in had at least one such character woven into its history. But he liked the story of Stoney Miles best. It seemed to have some small basis in fact. He'd even seen the tombstone, Tyler had pointed it out to him. The inscription was faint, worn by the years, but readable. ALBERT "STONEY" MILES—MAY YOU BURN IN HELL—FOR ALL TIME.

He thought it was priceless. He found particularly hilarious the fact that some people even crossed themselves, hoping no one would notice, when they heard the man's name. At least twice a year, according to Tyler, some child claimed to have seen the burned man running through the woods, demanding to know where he had left his hatchet.

Mark lost himself in the story for a few minutes, then settled down, remembering the rest of what Tyler had told him about the town's history. From the moment that the town heard of the plan for the subdivision, some of the people started protesting. They claimed the land should be preserved, as a sign of respect for the town's founders, or that the town was large enough, thank-you-just-the-same. Wilson didn't care. It was his dream and he could afford it with the money he had made after the great depression. (He never told of how he'd made the money, but most people suspected that it was by keeping up the old town tradition of bootlegging.) To make them all shut up he built the school. It was a beautiful school, even Mark had to admit that, and it was named after the man who had founded the town. Charles S. Westphalen. Mark often pondered such a British name being the name of a man who founded a Dutch settlement, but no one seemed to have an answer to that one. Before the project was finished, old Alexander kicked the bucket. He had a massive coronary, one that left his only son to finish the project, or let it die. Out of respect, he finished the development and then proposed strict rules about building any new structure to the town council. He had been one of his father's strongest opponents when it came to the project, but he wouldn't deny his father this last dream. Tyler and his parents were the first to move in, giving up the mansion that was the family's ancestral home, in order to establish a town library and historical society. Like his father before him, he had learned that to get what you wanted, you had to give something as well. His proposal about building restrictions passed through the town council and was accepted in near record time. By the time all was said and done, easily half of the town had become historical monuments, most often kept up by the older, wealthier families as a tax write-off...

Mark's reflections were broken when he ran straight into Cassie Monroe.

10

Cassie slammed into the tree, hard. She stepped back and lost her balance, landing on her ass in the Nelson's unmown lawn. *S'funny*, she thought, *I don't remember any trees on this part of the sidewalk*. Mark Howell was towering above her, looking absolutely terrified. It took her about half a second to realize that he was the moving tree that she had run into.

"Oh God," he stammered, "did I hurt you? I'm sorry, really, I should have been looking where I was going." He held out his hand and when she accepted it, he lifted her easily into a standing position. He was practically glowing with embarrassment. "Are you all right? Did I hurt you? Jesus, I really am sorry, I don't know what I was thinking. I didn't mean to hurt you. Do you need a doctor? Should I get your parents? Oh, shit, I..." The words flew at around a hundred miles an hour.

Cassie smiled and thought about the fact that he was kinda cute, in a teddy bear sort of way. "I'm fine, don't worry about it." He looked like he was about to pass out and she realized that he had a crush on her. He couldn't even look her in the eye, without turning a darker shade of red. "Are you okay?"

Then he did look her in the eyes and she started to feel slightly uncomfortable. His eyes were so intense! She looked towards the side of his face, where the angry red welts of the stitches could be seen, and felt for him. "Uh, yeah, I'm fine," he managed to stammer out. She brushed herself off, watching his face as she did so. He seemed paralyzed by the thought of being so close to her. She reached her hand out and touched him lightly on the arm and he practically jumped out of his skin. "Relax, I'm fine. And I don't bite, y'know?" He blushed even more furiously and she wondered how a person could turn that red and not rupture blood vessels. "Hey, look at me." He looked and she thought it must be causing him actual, physical pain. How was she supposed to handle this? Cassandra Monroe's mother had always told her to be direct in her statements. That she should always tell a person what she felt and hope for the best because at least she would know that the person's reaction to her would be an honest response to the real her, not just what the person perceived to be real.

If she could have followed her mother's advice, Cassie's words for him would have probably been "Geez, this is awkward. Look, if it helps, I think you're cute, too. But don't get nervous around me, okay? And don't put me on a pedestal." Nope. Couldn't do it. Not a chance in hell. He already looked like he was ready to die—just lie down and let his life flow away. She felt like an idiot, not knowing what to say, so she smiled and risked more than she was comfortable with, in proposing a plan for getting to know each other. "Make ya a deal? Get to know me, don't expect anything and we'll see what happens. Okay?" She finished her argument by giving him a small kiss on the uncut side of his face.

She could see that he was flustered and more than a little stunned by the peck on the cheek. If his mouth opened any wider, she'd be able to see his heart thudding in his chest. She smiled and he smiled back, tentatively. "Uh," he started and she waited patiently while he tried to kick his brain into gear. "I—um, okay. Shit, I didn't think it was that obvious." He looked like he was relaxing, as if he'd just shared a guilty secret, one that it had been a torture to hide inside.

She had mercy on him and answered the question he seemed so desperate to ask. "Listen, I take a jog around the Red Oaks everyday. If you want, you can join me. We'll talk, get to know each other. 'Sides, you look like you could use a little bit of exercise." The smile she gave him took the sting out of the last words and he laughed with her. He had a nice laugh, it came from deep in his chest and was obviously heartfelt. She squeezed his hand and started jogging in place. "I gotta get back home, s' almost dinner-time." She waved enthusiastically as she started into motion again. "Bye."

Cassie listened to his mumbled response and accelerated into a full scale run. In less than a minute he was out of sight around the curve of Red Oaks Circle. She smiled to herself as she ran. Definitely cute, but she decided to hold any kind of judgment until she saw whether or not he showed for the run tomorrow.

Cassie was sitting at home at the dinner table by the time Mark Howell walked into the woods with a smile stuck to his face. He didn't even feel the stitches pulling, he was too busy with the warm burning spot on his face, where her lips had touched him.

11

He had shown himself again. He was here. They thrilled at how close He was, but dared not move. "Not yet," They whispered to one another. "Soon, but not just yet." He settled down next to the Stone, a smile on his face and They shuddered with joy.

They sang to Him and he slowly responded to Their silent words. He closed his eyes and lay back. In a matter of minutes He was asleep.

Still, They waited. They fidgeted, They shook from the tensions. They waited. Twenty minutes later, They approached.

12

The dream was glorious, He was in the woods and the sun was setting and She was there. Her straight red hair fell to her shoulders and past. She smiled at him and took off her clothes and stood before him, the hunger clear on her face.

She knelt before him, planting tiny kisses on his face, where the wound stung. She caressed his body with her hands and, after an eternity of teasing, opened the fly on his pants. He gasped as her slim fingers stroked his length. *Oh, dear Lord, don't ever stop.*

He ran his hands over every inch of exposed flesh that he could find, probing and squeezing and wanting more. She pulled the pants away from his hips and kissed him, there. His body shook with barely suppressed needs and she climbed atop him. He thrust slowly, eagerly. She matched his pace. They came together in a screaming, writhing, bucking explosion of energy that left them both drained and fulfilled. She lay atop him, winded, content. He kissed her delicate features softly, repeatedly.

He wanted to cry as she stood, pulling the warmth from him. Cassie bent and redressed him and, with a thousand tiny kisses, she promised that she would return soon.

In his dream, she walked away and the darkness enveloped him. It was a safe warmth; he knew that his friends were with him. In his dream, he had so many friends and they comforted him. They loved him and would protect him.

Mark woke up as the sun finished setting. He felt content and happy. He wished and hoped that his dream would soon come true. He knew it had been a wonderful dream, about Cassie, but he couldn't remember the details. From all around him the sounds of nature crept slowly away. The leaves no longer sighed when the wind moved, the thousands of sounds so mundane that most everyone ignored them, faded one by one until there was only a silence that was almost overwhelming. The very universe seemed to be holding its breath. Then he heard little noises around him and knew immediately that they were not the normal sounds of the woods. He looked around, alarmed momentarily by the sounds. And stared in shock as he saw the Little Ones.

They were beautiful and evasive. They danced around the edges of his sight and darted close enough to touch him, whenever he was looking somewhere else. The sounds They made were musical, whispered hints, and promises of delight.

Slowly, They came to where he could see them. He knew. They were friends, he could trust Them. He sat with the tiny little creatures and They talked to him and he to Them. Secrets were shared, promises were exchanged and then They were gone.

He felt wonderful. With a casual ease, he found his way home in the dark. He had friends, real friends, not just imaginary little dreams to talk to. He had talked to Cassie; in time, possibly they would be more than friends. In time.

He was home and eating his solitary dinner, when his parents came home. Joe looked over the stitches and remarked on how well he was healing. Mark just smiled and then he told them of Cassie, his new jogging partner. He didn't tell of his time in the woods. A secret shared is no longer a secret.

13

Jennifer Gallagher Howell looked over at her sleeping husband and smiled. She was tempted to wake him ask what he thought about Mark having a little girlfriend, but she already knew the answer. He was nearly ecstatic about the idea. For the first time she could remember, he and Mark had talked to each other, not just around each other. It made her feel wonderful.

Mark had tried so hard to win Joe's affection and had failed, she was sure, because Joe was afraid the boy was too effeminate. Possibly even homosexual. That would have been a shattering blow to Joe's manhood.

Joe was masculine, well muscled and macho, at least in public. He didn't like to show that he had feelings, not to anyone but her, and she loved him for it. She knew that he had looked at other women from time to time, but he had never done anything but look. Other women didn't know him, how fragile he was in his own way, how he sometimes clung to her, as if she were a life raft, and shook, the fears of his childhood trying to tear him apart. It was that weakness that made him all hers and her all his. He was afraid of having that secret revealed and knew that he never had to fear her telling.

She remembered the first time they made love, and his guilty confession that he was a virgin. She had already known, but she feigned surprise and they made love again, with Joe being more confident than he had before, more commanding. He knew that all of his secrets were safe with Jenny, and that made him a better man.

Pushing the nonsensical thoughts away, she looked at his rugged face and ran her fingers through the mane of chestnut hair on his head. He shivered and awoke with a smile that said more than his words ever would or could. She hoped with all of her heart that her son would find a love as powerful, when his first love came to bloom. She hoped he would never run across a woman that could be as cruel as his father had been, when the mood switched to anything less than perfect.

Mark's father had been an incredible lover, possessed of skills far beyond those of most men twice his age. Every move that he had made, every caress, had kept her on the edge of ecstasy. For what seemed like hours, he would tease her and then he would satisfy her. Just when it seemed like nothing more could possibly happen, he would start on her once more. Joe didn't even begin to compare, but he made up for that lack in a thousand ways every day.

They moved together in the same motions that they had used for years, motions that seemed the only ones known to her husband, and in a very short while, Joe had finished. He fell asleep with a smile on his face. As she heard his gentle snores start, Jennifer smiled. She was very thankful for Joe. When he had reached a constant, rhythmic rumble, she thought of her first love, not her true love, and satisfied herself. She managed not to cry out his name, but only with an effort.

14

They rejoiced, the woods fairly quaked with the sounds of Their celebration. He was Theirs, They had waited so long but, at last, He was Theirs. Promises had been made, gifts exchanged, and the patience They had shown had been rewarded. His hopes had been satisfied and would be again, as was necessary. Such small hopes, so easily fulfilled. Ah, but hopes can change so quickly, one day a friend, the next, a foe. They would listen and watch from a distance and when the time was right, They would move to satisfy. Nothing must hurt the Chosen, until the time came that He was no longer important.

They calmed, They rested. The watch had to be extended, They had to be near at all times and They had to be prepared at all times. Several left the others, moving at blinding speeds, and ran to watch, to guard. It was Their sacred duty. They would have it no other way. As the sun rose, They positioned Themselves. As They waited, quietly, patiently, They shivered with ecstatic joy. The time was here again. It was so good to be needed.

Chapter Two

1

The last two days of the week went by in a blur. Mark barely acknowledged school, it was only a time to think about Cassie. The jogging wasn't easy, but he managed to keep up with her for the most part. She had to slow her pace for him and even stop now and then as he paused, panting and red faced, to catch his breath. To spend time with Cassie, he would gladly run three times the distance, barefoot. *On salt covered glass shards*, he mused. *In the Sahara desert. At noon.*

By Saturday he was certain that he was in love. He was also certain that he was about to be late for work. P. J. would not be happy, he'd been late too many times before.

With a groan, he rolled out of bed and started getting dressed. The same jeans he had worn Tuesday and his Pinhead t-shirt. Within ten minutes he was out the door and on his bike. The Basilisk's Books and Hobbies store was over a mile away and he'd have to really push himself if he wanted to make it in before the end of P. J.'s five minute grace period.

P. J. Sanderson was one of those rare people that Mark had liked at first sight. The feeling was obviously mutual. He knew that he'd be in no real trouble if he was late again, but a single frown of disapproval was enough to make Mark feel like a slug. P. J. could make a nun feel guilty of every sin in the book and probably had a dozen times. Not only did P. J. own the Basilisk, he ran the store as well. And that was something he did more as a hobby than as a way to make a living. P. J. was, Mark felt certain, more than wealthy enough without the store. His many novels, seven of which had been on the New York Times best seller list, had netted him enough to close the store permanently, if he so desired.

The first time Mark had gone into the only comic book store in town, he'd almost dropped dead of shock. Standing before him was the author of such works as *Screams At Midnight, The Night of the Howler,* and *Stirrings.* He'd read all of the books a dozen times and knew the author's face on sight. He was tall and, like Mark himself, more than a little plump. His face was open and friendly, but held the potential for his trademark smile, a smile that could chill your blood and darken your soul with fear. He was older than in the photo on the back cover of his books. It was definitely the same face, but easily a decade older. If anyone doubted, they had but to look at the backs of all of his books where they rested on a shelf behind the counter, not quite hidden but not prominently shown.

When Mark had opened his mouth to speak and found himself without the ability, P. J. had made the comment for him. "Oh My Gawd! You're that writer! Oh, wow, I read one of your books!" He made the exclamation with such a look of profound shock, that Mark couldn't help laughing with him. P. J. had a grin that was infectious and a personality to match. By the time Mark had finished his window shopping and his thousand and one jabbered questions, he and the older man had become friends.

P. J. was easily the oldest big kid he had ever met. They would talk for hours on end, about the latest novels by King, Koontz, McCammon, Grant, and of course, Clive Barker. Both read all of the authors and Phillip James Sanderson knew most of them on a first name basis. His love of reading horror stories was only exceeded by his love of writing them.

By the time the third Saturday in a row had passed, with the two of them talking and comparing notes, P. J. had proposed that Mark start working for him part time. "Mark," he started, "you're here all day any way, you may as well get paid for all the help you give me." He would listen to none of Mark's protests and before Mark knew what had hit him, he was the Assistant Manager at Basilisk. The fact that he was the only other person working there took nothing at all away from the title. Neither did the fact that both the job and title were simply P. J.'s way of making sure he had companionship on the weekends.

He missed the five-minute grace period mark by two minutes and thirty-seven seconds, a fact that P. J. pointed out as soon as he walked through the door. "Mark, my boy, you're late again." The accompanying frown was exaggerated and made rather comical by the granny glasses perched on the end of P. J.'s hawkish nose. With mock seriousness, the older man continued. "I'll have to dock you the last three month's salary and I fear an hour in the Iron Maiden may be necessary, to remind you of the severity of this crime," he mused, as he pulled at his salt and pepper beard.

Mark was glad to see he was in a good mood. It was when he said nothing at all, that Mark knew he was in trouble. Mark clasped his hands together tightly and threw himself to his knees before the man. "Puh-lease, Mawthter, forgive poor Igor!" he pleaded. "The monster made me shine his shoes! Hasn't your poor servant suffered enough?"

P. J. grinned and helped Mark to his feet. With a swat at the back of his head, P. J. told him to get his butt in gear. "The latest shipments are merely waiting for your eager young hands to assist them to the proper locations."

Mark got right to it, knowing that the reason P. J. hadn't set the magazines and books in place was more so that Mark would have something to do, than because of the back pains he claimed to suffer from. Mark had seen the author in action a dozen times and knew the man was more than healthy enough to move the dozen or so boxes by himself. But he hated to ask the boy to sort the older comics; he took so long looking at each one and wanting to read it. Mark had found in P. J. the substitute father he had needed for so long. It wasn't quite the same as a real one, but he could talk to the store's owner, as he could with no other adult. He could tell the man his problems, no matter how trivial, and he was always ready with a comforting word, or solid advice. Even the silences, when Mark was ringing customers or settling stock and P. J. was writing, were comfortable. Mark often thought that it would be wonderful if his mother had met and married P. J. instead of Joe.

After he had placed all of the stock where it belonged, Mark sat across from the writer, placing a fresh cup of coffee before each of them. They both liked it sickeningly sweet, with huge quantities of cream. "How goes the book?" Mark asked.

Without pausing in his typing, the writer took a one handed sip of his coffee and replied. "Very well, thank you. I'm reaching the climax and it's going to be a good one. If you'd like, I'll make a copy for you and you can give me an advance critique before I fight it out with that joke I call an editor."

Mark was stunned by the offer. He knew from experience what the original manuscript could potentially net on the market. He forced himself to be calm, to keep the squeak of excitement out of his voice, as he replied. "Yeah, I'd love to see it. You're so secretive, that I don't even know what the blasted thing's about."

"That's the way I've always worked, drives Hathaway crazy." Mark grinned at that: the arguments between P. J. and Alberta Hathaway were practically legendary. He was fairly certain that if they ever saw each other in person, one or the other would leave in an ambulance. The author looked away from his manuscript and stared meaningfully at Mark before he spoke again. "Now, why don't you tell me what happened to your face? I suspect that there is quite a story in that as well."

Mark told him, leaving nothing to the author's imagination save the names of his assailants. P. J. was upset by the incident and asked why Mark hadn't pressed charges. "I just didn't think it was necessary, I mean I can't even confirm who most of them were," he explained, faltering when he saw the look on his friend's face. P. J. was furious.

Standing slowly, the writer punched a few buttons on his word processor and turned towards Mark. "You let them get away with that? What next? Mugging you for your paycheck here? Breaking your arm or leg? Mark, you have to stand up for yourself. In the long run, no one else will."

Mark frowned at that and shook his head. "I brought it on myself, I'm the one that started it."

"Bullshit!" Mark jumped slightly, shocked by the venom in his friend's voice. "They've been hassling you since you first came to the school. Don't tell me they haven't. I know the kind. They throw all the hassles they can at a few kids, to try to make themselves look bigger in the eyes of anyone they consider to be worth the effort. Don't you dare tell me you brought that on yourself! I've half a mind to call that father of yours and tear him apart for not pressing charges against those little bastards!"

Mark found himself suddenly uncomfortable as he looked up at P. J. and explained. "I wouldn't tell him the names, I told him I could take care of it myself. And I will, in my own way. I'm too old to go running to my folks every time somebody pushes me."

The older man's face softened then and he looked over towards Mark with a calm understanding. He obviously didn't approve, but he accepted. "So. Just make sure that you do handle it. Every young bird has to spread its wings, but don't try to fly too fast or too far. Get a little more experience under your belt first, okay?"

Mark smiled and nodded his head. P. J. put the closed sign out and went into the back of the store where his small kitchen was. When he came back, he had several sandwiches and two colas on a tray. "Let's eat and then we can look over the latest convention schedules. Screamicon is just around the corner in Boulder. Perhaps we can convince your mother to allow you to come along. After all, you are my assistant manager." Mark stuttered excitedly at the thought and the rest of the afternoon fairly flew past.

2

Andy Phillips watched as Mark rode past, heading towards his home. Andy kind of liked Mark. He never had anything bad to say except for that one time and he didn't seem to mind that Andy and the guys picked on him, it was almost like he expected to get picked on. Andy even considered waving, but thought better of it. What if one of the guys saw? What would they say?

Andy wasn't the brightest kid in school and he knew it, but he didn't mind. Not as long as he still had the guys to hang around with. They seemed to like him okay and they never made fun of him. At least not when he was around. People had made fun of Andy all his life, because he was kind of slow; not retarded or anything bad like that, just slow. He managed to pass all of his classes and he was due to graduate at the end of the school year, but he had to work harder at it than anyone else did. He wished he was smarter, but knew his wishes were wasted breath when it came to the brains department.

Andy remembered very little about the day that he and the gang had trounced Mark Howell. He remembered the fight between Mark and Tony, but he didn't really remember why they had fought, or going after school to find Mark in the woods. He didn't remember kicking Mark in the ribs nine times, he didn't remember laughing when he saw the split flesh on Mark's face. All he remembered was going into the woods with his friends and having a good time. No whys or wherefores lodged in his skull.

If he'd thought very hard about the situation, he might have regretted that he remembered so little about most of his life, but he never really thought about it. Andy's life had very little by way of serious distractions. Most events, most people even, were merely brief interruptions from the track of his thoughts. Those he saw often he recalled easily, but those who passed through only occasionally were sometimes a struggle for him to remember.

The one thing he never had any trouble remembering, were the girls that he saw. Andy liked to look at girls, realizing that they were different and fascinating, in the same way that children looked at bugs and made the same discovery. Except now and then he got uncomfortable. When that happened, Andy liked to—*No! Mustn't think about that!*—do things.

Things like he had done to Tanya Billingsly late in the summer. Tanya had screamed and hit him and had tried to run away. Andy had caught her. After that he really didn't remember too much except rubbing up against her and not seeing her when school started up again. He felt bad about that; he liked to look at her.

He remembered seeing her in the paper a while back and cutting her picture out so he could look at her whenever he wanted, but he couldn't remember where he had put the picture. He had that problem sometimes.

Andy was still standing in the same spot almost an hour later, when Cassie and Mark came jogging by. He waved, but they didn't see him. They were too busy looking at each other. He didn't mind. He was used to being overlooked. His parents did it all the time.

As they ran past, Andy stared hard at Cassie's rear end and at her coppery hair. She was pretty, almost as pretty as Tanya and he felt himself start to get uncomfortable. He'd have to remember to come here again, maybe tomorrow. Maybe he'd get to see Cassie run by again and maybe she'd notice when he waved next time.

3

Cassie liked to read horror stories too and she was excited about meeting P. J. Sanderson. She hadn't even known that the man lived in town and she certainly hadn't known that he owned the Basilisk. If she had, she'd have purchased her books there instead of at the Mall in town. Mark told her all about the writer and even said that she could read the original manuscript he was getting tomorrow, if she swore not to tell P. J. She promised it would be their little secret.

She had to admit it, Mark was doing better than she had expected when it came to the jogging. They'd already gone over half the distance to the Basilisk and he was barely winded. She looked at him and saw where his eyes were glued and smiled. *Men. They all looked at the same spots.* At least he had the decency to look her in the eyes when she was talking. That was more than she could say for most of the guys she knew. Even Tyler was talking to her chest these days and Tyler was practically her brother.

He noticed her looking at him and quickly turned his face away so she couldn't see him blush. He was like a puppy dog whenever he was around her; full of energy and almost bursting at the seams with the need to get and keep her attention. At least he'd gotten over being so nervous all of the time. He could talk to her and not blush; except when she caught him staring at her feminine parts.

She couldn't say that she was in love with him, not yet at least, but she certainly liked him an awful lot. Cassie was glad that she'd invited him to join her on her afternoon jogs. The only other guy she was even half-interested in was Tony Scarrabelli. She really wished the two of them didn't seem to hate each other so much. It made life damn difficult. Truth be told, she didn't know which of them she liked better.

She saw Andy Phillips on the side of the road and quickly turned away. Andy was a little on the scary side with the way he had of looking at her. He'd run his eyes over her whole body and lick his wormy lips and then, if he remembered to, he'd look at her face and wave. Cassie had suspicions that he wouldn't be a safe person to spend time with alone.

Without even thinking, she took Mark's hand in hers and squeezed, relaxing when she felt him squeeze back. Their hands seemed to fit together. For something to take her mind off Andy, she started telling him about Halloween in Summitville. Though she had no experience with other towns, if what Hollywood showed in the movies was accurate, Summitville took things a little differently. His face lit up and they began making plans.

After another fifteen minutes they slowed down and approached the Basilisk. Mark was panting and more than a little sweaty, but he didn't look like he was going to drop dead. He looked over at her, smiling brightly and gestured grandly. "Milady, the palace of hellish delights," he announced, "complete with yours truly as a tour guide." That was another thing she liked about Mark: he didn't hesitate to show his intelligence in the way he spoke and he didn't use it as a way of trying to be superior, either.

With a smile of her own and a final squeeze of his hand, she released her grip on his fingers and they walked towards the glass door.

P. J. was a delight—he smiled fondly, squeezed her hand affectionately and insisted they stay for a few hours. When she tried to protest the special treatment, his response was; "Cassie, any fan of mine is a friend of mine. Especially if they happen to be friends with my assistant manager." He then excused himself and ran to fix them a snack and tea.

She could tell that Mark had a special spot in his heart for the writer and it was easy to see why. P. J. was almost as eager to see her as Mark was. She couldn't help wondering if Mark had told the older man about her and maybe stretched the truth in the process.

As P. J. reentered the room, loaded down with cheese and crackers plus chilled fruit, Mark excused himself and went off to the bathroom down the hall. P. J. immediately took full advantage of the golden opportunity and started with the barrage of questions. "So, how long have you two been dating, or are you just friends?"

Cassie was a little taken aback, but she saw that the man was honestly interested and eager to listen. She also saw that he was aware of Mark's feelings and suspected that Mark hadn't had to tell the man anything, he'd just seen it on his young friend's face. "Well, I wouldn't say that we're dating, or anything like that. We really just met earlier this week, right after he got hurt."

P. J. frowned for half a second at the thought of Mark's injuries and then brightened when he responded. "But it's not an impossibility? Please say it's not; he needs a good woman to keep his feet on the ground. The boy's just too flighty, reminds me of me when I was his age."

She smiled and chuckled and admitted that the thought seeing him steadily had crossed her mind. And laughed whole-heartedly when the man rolled his eyes towards Heaven and proclaimed, "Thank you, Jesus. I've never even heard Mark talk about you, but I could tell he was in love with someone right after school started." He frowned when he heard the toilet flush from down the hallway. "Curses, here he comes. So much for the juicy gossip hour. So, tell me about how much you loved all of my novels." The man fanned him self with an imaginary fan and spoke in a false Southern accent. "We writer types have such delicate egos; we need all the morale boosts we can get."

They spent the next hour and a half, chatting away like old friends, with P. J. leading the conversations and directing the questions they each had about different writers and the many books each had read. Just before they left he raced back into his apartment in the back half of the old house and came out with two copies of the manuscript. "One for each of you, so we can discuss what changes you both feel are necessary when you both come over next Saturday."

And that was it. Feeling vaguely like she had passed a test of some sort, Cassie said good-bye to the man and was surprised by the kiss on the cheek that he gave her. He shooed the two of them off and Cassie knew she had made a new friend.

She and Mark walked slowly the entire way back home. They held hands, talked and enjoyed each other's company. For Cassie, it was a wonderful change of pace and it let her realize just how much she liked Mark. They paused once for a fledgling kiss. She enjoyed it almost as much as he did. They didn't see Tony as he cruised past in his car, but he saw them. It was one more reason to hate the new kid. Not that he needed any more.

They didn't see Andy, either. They didn't see the glazed look in his eyes, or the way he licked his lips. They didn't notice when he started following them from a small distance, his eyes locked on Cassie.

4

He was uncomfortable, but he knew how to take care of that. He might have to wait awhile, but he could be patient. They were heading for the woods and he knew the woods very well. It was in the woods that he'd finally caught up with Tanya. He liked the woods; the woods were his safe place, where he never had to worry about being hurt. They held his secret place, a place so secret that he seldom remembered it if he wasn't there.

Cassie heard him first, just after the sun had set. Mark was too busy thinking about their first kiss to have heard an elephant stampede.

It was a little sound, the snapping of a large twig, the rustle of a few autumn leaves, but it didn't belong. When she turned around, she saw Andy just as he dodged behind a tree. She didn't like the look on his face. He looked like he was angry and sad and expectant, all at once.

"Mark," she whispered, as she tugged at his sleeve. "I think we're being followed."

He turned to her and frowned, "By who?" He looked concerned, and remembering his recent experience in the woods, she understood his reasons.

"Andy Phillips, I saw him hide behind a tree," she whispered urgently. "Let's get out of here. I don't like the way he looks at me."

Mark frowned. Andy was, by far, the biggest member of Tony's little herd of friends. He could still feel the tenderness that Andy's foot had caused in his rib cage. But he wouldn't let Andy hurt Cassie, he couldn't. He held his few friends as far too precious to leave unprotected.

He felt the hidden angers inside of him start to stir and that, as much as the thought of Andy Phillips, stirred him into motion. He didn't know which to be more afraid of, himself or Andy. "C'mon, I know the shortest way home."

Cassie followed, holding tightly to his hand as he led the way through the rapidly darkening trees. He definitely knew the woods and she was stunned by how well. He hadn't even been in town for two months, but he pointed out pitfalls she would never have seen. He stepped around logs that were rotted and deadly without even a thought, save to warn her.

Andy was not as lucky. She heard his grunts as he fell several times, heard the sound of his body crashing to the ground and the sound of him struggling back to his feet. He never said a word, which was what frightened her the most.

The lights of the subdivision could be seen through the thinning woods when he caught up with them. Both she and Mark were taken completely by surprise as he stepped out from behind a tree directly in front of them. Luck had been his guide—while they had stepped around the forest's little snares, he had simply forced his way through all but the most tenacious ones. They had the path to consider; Andy had instinct and brute strength. The only serious challenge he faced was getting past the trees, and there was room enough to maneuver between them. He looked the worse for his shortcut.

Andy Phillips stood over six foot three and weighed in at easily two hundred and fifty pounds. Most of those pounds were now covered in dirt and leaves from his repeated falls on the forest's floor. He had several small scrapes on his hands and arms and a tear in his heavy metal tee shirt. She couldn't tell which band he was promoting on his chest today, but concert shirts were practically the only things he wore. Even if he'd had a big smile plastered on his wide face, he would have intimidated her. The pasty, blank look he wore did nothing to help her disposition. His eyes glittered darkly and his wide pinkish lips twitched, as if trying to remember how to smile. He was breathing hard, but didn't even seem to notice. "Hi, Mark. Hi, Cassie. How ya doin'?" The question was aimed directly towards her chest and both of them noticed.

Mark slid in between the two of them, his body tensed and trembling, like an over-wound spring. "Uh, hi, Andy, we're just going home, we're both late for dinner," he explained slowly, as if to a small child.

Andy almost managed a grin for him. Almost. "Yeah, I'm gonna be late, too. Why don't you go on, I have to tell something to Cassie."

"Well, I'll just wait here, I promised her I'd walk her home."

"I'll do it, I don't mind." He actually bothered to look away from Cassie and pin Mark with a black stare. To his credit, Mark barely flinched. Andy was a good six inches taller than he.

Mark tried one more time, "Well, I'd hate to break a promise, Andy. I'm a man of my word." He smiled tightly as he spoke, fully aware that Andy was having none of it. He felt his adrenaline glands going into overdrive, preparing him for his dismemberment. He had every intention of going down swinging, giving Cassie enough time to get away. He gave her a quick warning look and a gentle push that urged her to run. She stayed where she was. He could have throttled her; what was he purpose of getting himself maimed again, if she stayed around for Andy to grab when he was done with the maiming?

Andy appeared to swell, seemed ready to grow out of his skin as he looked at Mark. His voice, which had been a soft whisper, deepened, taking on a very threatening note. "Mark, leave. I have to talk to Cassie in private."

Cassie felt ready to scream, She could feel the tension in the air as Mark looked his opponent in the eyes and, gulping down a wad of spittle, replied. "No."

Andy hit Mark in the stomach and all of the air in his body took a vacation. He felt his lungs rebel, felt the bruised ribs scream in protest. Somehow, he managed to swing back.

Andy couldn't understand: Mark shouldn't have argued with him and he certainly shouldn't have been standing after he'd been hit. But mostly, he shouldn't have hit him in the balls. He felt his blood rise to his face and roared out in anger. Some little part of his brain knew that he had about five seconds before the pain hit him. He reached for Mark's face.

Mark screamed when Andy's blunt fingers grabbed at his cheek and he positively shrieked when he felt the stitches start to tear open in a blaze of hot agony. His hands flew in a frenzy, punching and clawing at the pain in front of him. He felt warmth running down his cheek and heard the sound of Cassie screaming in the distance. None of it mattered. When the pain in front of him let go, he followed it with a growl. He would stop the pain once and for all.

Cassie thought there was a bear in the woods after she heard the growl. Then she realized that the sound had come from Mark. She looked at the two figures in the dark and saw the arms of the smaller one lash out again and again. She watched, her eyes failing to believe what they saw, as Andy tried to run away and Mark went after him. She couldn't make out the words in Mark's war cry, but she knew he meant to kill. Andy moved with a speed that belied his size and darted around trees and shrubs that Mark never even saw. The third time he fell down, Mark stopped chasing after the larger boy.

It took fully a minute for Cassie's mind to accept what had just happened. When she did, she ran to where Mark lay on his hands and knees. At first she thought he was crying, the hitching sounds he made were very fast and faint. When she got closer, she realized he was in the grips of a full-scale giggle fit. "Mark?" She looked down at him and winced when she saw that three of the stitches had been torn out of his face. The flesh under them was raw and red, and the flow of blood soaked Mark's face. He didn't even seem to notice.

After a few moments, he sobered and felt along the line of stitches. They rushed back to his house and Joe immediately ran into the bathroom for his first aid kit when he saw the bleeding, torn cheek.

Joe cleaned the wound carefully, and found, to his relief, that the damage wasn't as traumatic as he'd initially feared. "Facial wounds," he commented. "They always bleed like there's no tomorrow." While Joe fixed the small tear using only a piece of gauze, he explained to Cassie that the stitches were due out on Monday anyway. He called the local clinic, got the answering service, and fretted over whether or not the repairs could wait until the next morning. A few minutes later, Doctor Lewis called back and said he'd be by within the next twenty minutes. Joe listened raptly as Cassie explained what had happened, over Mark's protests. Mark seemed horribly embarrassed now that the fight was over with. Joe, on the other hand, seemed damn pleased with his stepson's performance.

Mrs. Howell, though, was still worried about her son, and about Cassie. "Call me Jenny, dear," she said. "Should I call your parents? Won't they be awfully worried about you?"

Cassie smiled and explained that her parents were out for the evening, they'd gone into the city for a showing of one of her father's favorite operas. Jenny insisted she stay over until her parents got home. Cassie didn't mind. She didn't want to be alone just then.

Joe reacted differently to this than he had to his stepson's beating: the boy responsible had obviously been up to causing serious harm, and over Mark's protests, he called the police. The wait was short, but the questions went on forever, compounded by Doctor Lewis's careful ministrations. Lewis was rather surprised, really, that the boy's stepfather had been so worried. The wound was almost completely closed by the time he got there. A few pressure bandages were all that he needed to fix the damage. He removed the remaining stitches while he was there. The skin beneath them was healing beautifully.

Sheriff Chuck Hanson waited patiently, asking his questions through the doctor's minor surgery. Hanson believed in being very thorough, making sure that every detail was covered.

5

Andy moaned to himself and held his broken fingers to his chest. Mark had gotten lucky with one of his wild swings and forced his middle and index fingers all the way back to his wrist. It happened so quickly that Andy hadn't even had a moment to react. The fingers breaking were like a jolt through his body and suddenly all lust had left him. He simply wanted to get away. He was scared for dear life when he heard Mark growling at him. It hadn't sounded human.

He walked blindly through the woods, trying to remember which way his house was and praying that Cassie and Mark hadn't told anyone. His dad would be pissed if he found out. His dad would get nasty.

William Phillips was a giant by any standards. He worked in the mills about twenty miles out of town and had since the age of sixteen, when he dropped out of school. Andy's dad didn't drink, smoke, or curse. But he was hell with a leather strap. Willie believed in the old adage about sparing the rod and spoiling the child and he had never hesitated to prove it. Andy had more than his fair share of scars.

Years of heavy lifting and using chain saws to cut down the giant trees in the milling area had developed muscles the likes of which Andy had never seen outside of a muscular fitness magazine. His father used those muscles at home, too— whenever Andy back-talked him or forgot to do his chores. Try as he might, Andy never could seem to remember his chores. But this, this would get him a beating like none he had ever experienced. Andy was scared. If they had told on him his life wouldn't be worth spit.

6

They watched him as he stumbled around through the woods. The rage They felt was divine. They had seldom felt its like. He had hurt the One and that could not be permitted. He had to die.

They had always been in the woods, for as long as the woods had been there. They saw everything that happened, even when there was nothing to see. They hadn't defended the Chosen, preferring to see how well he fared on His own, first. They were pleased; his ferocity when confronted meant that the changes They had already made to him were as effective as They'd hoped. Still, They would get Their revenge and it would be sweet.

With nary another whisper, They ran to where the one who had hurt Their friend had hurt the other, before tonight. They knew just what to do. They knew what he would fear. There, under those shrubs...

7

Andy finally sat down, whimpering like a wounded puppy. Maybe he deserved to get in trouble, one part of his mind whispered. Hadn't Tanya asked him not to? Hadn't she begged him to stop?

She'd beat at his shoulders, she'd screamed at the top of her lungs and he'd done it anyway. Was that why she'd never come back to school?

No. Even as he asked himself that question, another part of his mind was answering him, a part that demanded nothing less than the truth. She hadn't come back, because she couldn't come back. He had pushed the truth far away and tried his best to bury it—just like he'd buried Tanya. He could not. No more than Tanya could come walking back into his life and forgive him.

He had murdered her. He'd slapped his hand over her nose and mouth and kept it there, while he forced himself on her. She could no more come back and forgive him, than he could go to her and beg forgiveness. The only answer he would get would be the silence of the grave. Her grave, unmarked and untended. Just a dozen yards to his left, in his special place. Involuntarily, he looked over towards the spot.

And there she was, staring at him.

He screamed, long and hard. The birds nestled in their trees took flight at the sound, startled out of their rest. He heard them flapping madly, but it was a small sound in comparison to the beating of his own heart.

She stood before him without a shred of clothing, smiling serenely. He cowered before her, certain that she had come back to kill him. "I'm sorry! I'm so sorry, Tanya, I couldn't stop myself, I knew it was wrong, but I just couldn't stop myself!" She looked down upon him, a smiling goddess of vengeance, and he cringed, scraped the ground at her feet, writhed in the forced recognition of what he had done that night, four months ago. A thousand years ago.

She reached down, gently touching his head with her long delicate fingers. He trembled at the lover's touch. She raised his head with gentle pushes on his chin, until he looked her in the face. She had lost none of her beauty, her silky raven hair still flowed across her shoulders and her angel's face was unblemished in the pale light of the rising moon. Her full lips gleamed wetly as she helped him to his feet and, in her hazel eyes, the light shone back with a hint of amusement. He looked at her, awestricken by the sight of her perfection. This was the woman he had dreamed of so many times, the woman he had wanted to marry in those dreams. The woman that he had murdered. Tanya Billingsley looked as lovely in death as she had in life.

Mesmerized by her beauty, he allowed her to move him like a puppet on its strings. She stood him up, dusted him off and took his hand in hers. All he could do was follow her mindlessly. When she wrapped her arms around his neck he knew that all had been forgiven. When she planted the tiny kisses there, he knew that she loved him as well. And then she kissed him on his lips fully, passionately. He fairly swooned to be so close to her again, living out a fantasy that he had held so tightly for so long. He closed his eyes and felt himself starting to stir. He drew her close, into his arms and felt the rounded curves of her body, as she pushed eagerly against him. She stroked his hardness and he groaned with the need for relief. He opened his eyes to look upon her angelic face—and saw the torn and ragged remains of what had once been a young girl named Tanya Billingsley.

The elements had not been kind to her earthly remains. She had putrefied and withered in the last four months. He pulled back from the lips against his mouth and the tongue that had danced against his own. He saw the living creatures that crawled across her face and felt the wriggling bodies of maggots writhe across his tongue and teeth. He saw the sunken pits where her eyes had been and felt the wormy flesh and jutting bone of her pelvis grind across his own in a mockery of lust. As he tried to step away, mind numb with horror, she pulled him close one last time and suggestively pushed her tongue into his ear.

In the place where Summit Town had stood almost two centuries ago, history repeated itself. Tobias Andrew Phillips, descended from the legendary Stoney Miles on his mother's side of the family, ran shrieking mindlessly though the woods, all the way to town. Stoney had been burned across his body; Andy simply felt his brain catch fire. He hardly felt the twigs and stones that lashed his body. He barely even noticed when he ran face first into an ancient red oak and he never even heard the screeching of tires on several of the late night streets, as he ran all the way to the sheriff's office.

Deputy Alan Fisk had never before seen a man so terrified, or so repentant of his sins. He looked on in amazement at the small giant before him, with eyes as wide as saucers and hair whiter than the first snow of winter and hardly recognized him as Andy Phillips. The stench of rotted meat wafted from him, the scent of the corpse that'd held him in its rotted arms and kissed him passionately. Alan almost gagged on the odor. Just the same, when he heard the boy's confession, he read him the Miranda and locked him in a cell, but not before taking a sample of the rotten flesh from the boy's clothing and ordering the almost hysterical teen to shower himself in the single shower reserved for overnight guests of the town's holding facilities.

He had to put the sheriff on hold when one of the other deputies turned out the lights in the cellblock. He'd never before heard a man scream as shrilly, either. Andy seemed to have developed a fear of the darkness in record time.

Early the next day, Sheriff Hanson found Tanya Billingsley's moldering corpse, exactly where Andy said he would. Andy would later refuse his right to counsel and plead guilty to murder in the first degree. He never told anyone what he'd seen that night, after trying for his second rape. Hanson had to admit he'd never seen anyone so eager to go to prison. He wished with all of his heart that he did know what had happened to the boy; if he could bottle it, he could sell it to the City's police and retire on the profits.

8

They had laughed merrily at the jest, and had found the boy's reaction of such rare humor that They'd let him live. He wouldn't hurt the One again; it was likely he would never hurt anyone again. Also, the Folk were not without mercy— he had been repentant. There were those among Them, that believed he would punish himself for as long as he lived. Oh, how They loved a good joke. They'd have laughed all the harder, had They known that Andy killed himself two weeks after he was sentenced to fifteen years in the state Facility (the minimum that the state would permit in a case of admitted murder).

Reportedly, after fourteen nights of screaming nightmares, he shrieked a name loudly and threw himself off of the railing on the fourth floor of the Waltsburg Maximum Security State Penitentiary's cellblock E. No one was quite certain what the name he called had been, but Tanya seemed like a good guess. He landed headfirst. Emmanuel Jorge De Carlo, a Lifer in prison for the shotgun murder of seven parishioners at the Holy Mother Catholic Church in the city, was later heard to say he'd never seen a more flawless swan dive.

With Their habitual enthusiasm, the Folk prepared for another span of watching, guarding the One. Oh how They laughed that next day, thinking of Their wonderful jest. They never considered that some might blame Mark, however irrationally, for the death that They had caused.

9

Mark had never met Tanya Billingsley, had only heard her mentioned once or twice, but he attended her funeral just the same. Tyler needed the comfort of a friend. He had been close to the girl.

Tyler was one of those rare people who never seemed to care what others thought of him. When he had heard of Andy's crushing defeat at the hands of Mark, he'd told everyone in the school, laughing merrily and adding to the story with each telling. When he'd heard that poor Tanya had finally been found, he had cried without embarrassment, right in the middle of the auditorium. Mark often envied him that freedom of feeling. He suspected that such a freedom must be very liberating.

Tyler cried again as they lowered Tanya's remains into their final resting place. Mark held him and hugged him fiercely when he needed the embrace. For once, no one made any comments about his sexual preference, or about his weight. Not even Tony, who stood close by.

Tony stood numbly, unaware of those around him, as he attended the funeral. Andy and he had talked just last week, during the visiting hour at the County Jail. Andy had told him exactly what he had told the police, almost word for word.

Frankly, if he'd been asked what the weather was, he, like as not, would have given the same response again. His poor feeble mind had been shattered. Tony had trouble believing that Andy, of all people, was capable of rape and murder. He had serious difficulty accepting the facts, even when it was Andy who told him. He felt very little for Andy: possibly the same affection a hunter feels for his favorite bird dog, but certainly no more than that; he felt even less when Andy went on to tell of his fight with Mark in the woods.

He couldn't care less that Mark had won. He knew the fucker had it in him; he'd known it since he first saw him, waddling into the school with his neck tucked between his shoulders like a turtle. It didn't matter at all. Except…except, that Andy and Tony'd had a few falling outs in their time and Andy'd always won. And if Mark Howell could take out Andy, who had in his time taken out Tony, didn't that mean that Mark could, possibly…? *No. Not a chance.*

Much as he hated the thought, there seemed to be something between Howell and Cassie. Maybe the fact that he had saved her from what would have likely been the same fate that Tanya had suffered had brought them closer together. Maybe, Hell.

It wasn't like he considered Cassie his property, or anything, but the thought of her with that fat turd did nothing for his self-esteem. *Fat turd? Doesn't Mark seem a great deal more fit, lately? Isn't he standing a little taller and looking more fleshed out across his shoulders and chest, than around his gut and butt these days?* Dammit all, he really liked Cassie. He wanted to ask her out, maybe to the Halloween dance down at the town square.

He looked over to where the minister was finishing his little sermon about ashes and dust and spied Cassie looking at him. He nodded to her and was rewarded with a small smile. She looked more uncomfortable than Howell did, and Howell was the one who was comforting that little shit, Tyler. *Another two points,* he thought — he respected Mark for being willing to risk the shit that would fly at school, when the word of *that* got around. He heard the hollow thumps, as the Billingsley family placed handfuls of dirt atop the coffin where their only child would spend the rest of eternity, and walked over to where Cassie stood. Her smile grew weaker, but friendlier, as he approached.

"Hi," she started, "haven't seen you in a while."

"Yeah, I've been kinda busy, talkin' with Andy's family an all that. His dad's really torn up, he blames himself for Tanya's dying."

Her pretty little eyebrows pulled together at that one. "Why? He couldn't know what A-Andy had been doing."

He noticed the nervous little stutter in her voice when she mentioned Andy and knew then that the story of him trying to get at her was true. Tony couldn't help wondering if he'd have stood up to Andy in the same situation as Mark. "I guess he figures he should have done that 'birds and the bees' talk with him. He said they never even talked about it. Mister Phillips is kind of heavy into religion, didn't think it would be appropriate." People were starting to leave and Pete was motioning to him. He smiled and waved a small good-bye to Cassie. She replied with the appropriate terms and they parted. He wished he could talk to her, about how he felt about her, *about everything,* but he knew this wasn't the right time. Looking up towards the heavy, sodden clouds above, he walked a little faster. The sooner he was home in the warmth of his house and out of the chilly October air, the better he'd feel.

10

Cassie moved closer to Tyler and Mark. Tyler smiled wanly and gave her a fierce hug. She hugged back with equal emotion. She'd never really liked Tanya, she felt the girl was a vicious little prick-tease—*shouldn't think that way about the dead, girl*—but she knew that Tyler had been close to falling for Tanya, hard. She loved Tyler with all of her heart, and to see him hurting, for any reason, was to be hurting herself. He cried against her shoulder and she held him, whispering nonsensical words of comfort to him and stroking his hair. He had always been her confidant and she had always been his, now she could only offer comfort and she did so without hesitation.

Looking past Tyler's head, she saw Mark, who understood instinctively the relationship that she and Tyler shared. If he was jealous of their friendship, he hid it well. She thanked him silently for that and he nodded, smiled, just before he turned away to leave them in peace.

His smile said it all: he'd see her later if she felt the need to talk. For now Tyler's needs were the most important.

11

The woods were his new thinking grounds; he could sit back and talk to his elusive little imaginary friends and they would comfort him. He rambled on for quite a while, before he finally grew tired and slipped into a comfortable, deep sleep.

In his dreams, she came to him again, as she now did when he was weary of life or just frustrated. She pleased him in a thousand ways, she teased him in a hundred thousand, before he felt himself release his seed into her. As always, she smiled and left only moments after they were finished. He knew they were only dreams but they always felt so real. He leaned against his favorite stone in his sleep, never aware that, in the real world, that stone had slashed his face with a will of its own. The Stone looked different than before, larger, more anchored in the real world. He'd have left the woods and never set foot in them again if he'd known the history of that thin blade of rock.

While he slept They touched him, caressed him, changed him. He felt only the pleasure of his dreams, not the hands that reached through his skin as if it was water and caused the small transformations in his very flesh and bone. Had he thought about it, he might have realized that his recent weight loss had all occurred in strange spurts and only after he slept in his special place. If he'd thought about it. Most of his thoughts, sleeping and waking, were only for Cassie.

Chapter Three

1

Tyler was fast on the rebound and Mark was increasingly convinced that nothing short of his own death would ever keep his friend down for long. He was in fine spirits indeed by the time Halloween showed up that year. It was unseasonably warm for October in Colorado, and everyone seemed to be enjoying the last chance for a little fun in the world beyond their houses, without the added weight of a heavy coat.

When Mark opened the door he stared Death in the face, and Death was smiling toothily. "Yes, I'm here to ask if you'd like to sell you immortal soul in exchange for eternal life," Tyler said as he swished past Mark into the living room. "Hi, Joe! Hi, Jenny!" he called as he swept over to where Mark's mom was sitting. He looked over at Joe, dressed in his traditional Dracula costume, and started speaking. "Now, Joe, don't let this seem like a *reflection* on your character," Joe and Mark both winced at the pun. Tyler turned to look at Jenny, dressed in a red bodysuit and wearing high-heeled red boots that ran up to mid-thigh. She finished the costume with a pair of horns and a pointed tail. Next to her on the couch, was a cheap plastic pitchfork.

Tyler winked, behind an obviously home-made skull-face that took into consideration his goggle-like glasses, and said "But the lady is simply too hot, to *count* you in." Jenny blushed and hearing the silence, Tyler looked over at the two. "Get it? Vampire? Reflection? Count? Devil? Hot?"

Joe grinned past his Glow-in-The-Dark fangs and said "Oh, we got it, but it wasn't a tenth as funny as your face."

Tyler opened his mouth, obviously ready to start the verbal boxing, when he finally noticed Mark. He shut his mouth and raised his eyebrows. Mark wore clothes that were ridiculously large, torn and patched everywhere. He'd shredded a plastic broom to get the bristles free and shoved them into the sleeves, waist, collar, and pants cuffs of his clothes, making them look like straw leaking out. In addition, he had cut an old canvas out of its frame and, with careful cutting, made a passable mask, that covered his hair and ears, but left his face exposed. He colored his face to match the canvas and added dark shadows around his eyes and colored the scar on his face so that it looked like black thread closing a tear in the fabric. An old straw hat completed his scarecrow outfit. The overall effect was a demonic straw man, something more fitting to *The Twilight Zone* than *The Wizard of Oz*. He was very proud of his costume; it had taken him several hours to get it just the way he wanted.

Tyler looked him over, nodded, mumbled to himself and frowned slightly. "Not the best Frankenstein Monster I ever saw, but not the worst either," he finally proclaimed. Then he looked at Mark's hangdog face and burst out in laughter, along with Joe and Jenny. Mark had finally joined in on the laughter when Cassie peeked through the still open door.

She had put together a costume, composed primarily of black fur and a set of pointed ears, adding on the whiskers and tail that made it obvious that she was a black cat. Mark felt like purring, himself. She was gorgeous. He grinned and howled, soon to be joined by Tyler, and Cassie blushed. After a few moments of conferring on meeting places and when to use them, the whole group slithered and stomped out to Joe's van. The night was rich with promise.

2

The Summitville town square was garishly decorated in shades of black and orange, but was nowhere near as colorful as the denizens of the town, dressed in costumes that ranged from cheap homemade specials, to rentals and purchases that must have cost thousands. Everyone there was planning on a good time.

No one there looked better than P. J. Sanderson. P. J. had dedicated every book he'd written to a slew of people, and at least one make-up artist was mentioned in each case. He had received a dozen letters, thanking him for the consideration and, in one case, he received a tailor-made costume. It was the stony countenance of Sligis, the Gargoyle from *Night Thunder*, his first novel ever to sell. Alan "The Blood-letter" Tolliver had outdone himself in the creation and when P.J.'d seen the costume, he'd practically shed tears of joy. He'd never received a finer compliment, a finer reply, to one of his stories. He turned his head and looked over at the podium, from which he, as the Guest of Honor, would make his speech.

Mayor Hollis had decided he was perfect for the part, seeing as he was also a fan of P. J.'s stories—and the man didn't charge anything for the speech. As P. J. scanned the crowd his eyes ran across various famous monsters and ghosts of every description and he cringed ever so slightly at the clowns, cowboys, and politicians that he saw among the crowd. It was his firm belief that if you were going out on Halloween, you should go out as a monster, not as a politician. Not, now that he thought about it, there was much of a difference in the long run.

Finally, when he'd almost given up, he spotted Mark and his friends. He waved his taloned arms above his head and called out loudly, until they noticed him. As they came closer, he manipulated the wires that folded and unfolded the leathery wings on his back. Several people nearby stepped away and there was even a patter of applause for the spectacle. He took a small bow.

"Mark, introduce me to your friends, my boy," he started and then spotting Mark's mother, made another small bow. "And certainly you must introduce me to this bedeviling beauty before my slitted eyes."

Mark made introductions all around and the group spent some time wandering around making comments about the various costumes around them. Mark also pointed out just how many people were looking forward to the story to be told by the guest of honor, "some crazy writer that was coming into town just for the occasion". The comment was humorous—but it wouldn't have been, if P. J. counted on his store to eke out a living. Looking at his watch, he begged off the conversation and stated honestly how much of a pleasure it was to meet them all.

With a mad flapping of his wings, he strutted towards the podium. It was eight o'clock, time to tell a story, time to liven up the party. The halogen streetlights flickered several times and a spotlight was directed towards the evil form of Sligis. "Good evening, one and all! I'd like to tell you a story, if I may. A story about a night not so long ago, when the demons of Hell found their way to a small town, rather like the very town we find ourselves in. On this blustery night…" It took only moments for the street to drop into deathly silence and P. J. smiled to himself behind the scowling countenance he wore upon his brow.

3

Pete Larson, whose idea of fun was still beating on the new kid or kicking the occasional puppy, listened to the story, as mesmerized as everyone else in the crowd. The writer spoke with a deep voice, rich in timbre and thick with diabolical charm, masterfully weaving his tale of destruction and horror. No one there that night was unaffected. Pete felt Sandy shiver and pull closer to him, as the writer finished the story, telling of how most of the creatures had been destroyed, but a few had escaped and waited for the right time.

When the story was told and the applause had faded, Pete stood and looked at his watch, peeling back the clawed glove on his wrist. "Geezus, he told all of that, in only forty minutes? C'mon, Red, let's get our picture taken."

Sandy reached for his hand and smiled a promise at him as she asked, "I don't know…can I trust you, Mister Big Bad

Wolf?" He looked over the body under her Little Red Riding Hood outfit and thought about it for a second.

"Not a chance in hell. So let's go get the picture taken and then we can find Grandma's house." She laughed, swatting at him playfully, as they got into the sprawling line, leading to where photos could be taken with P. J. Sanderson.

As they waited, they talked about the haunted house that the fair offered and wondered how it would compare to last year's. It was as they were considering whether or not to save the cost and buy a six-pack, that Pete noticed Howell and the little bitch that had had Andy put in jail.

Once again, the uncanny mouth of Tyler Wilson was about to cause irreparable damage. Tyler had spread the story of Andy's defeat far and wide with his usual enthusiasm. Unfortunately, his usual enthusiasm normally translated into gross exaggerations of the facts. By the time the story had reached Pete's ears, Mark had practically dragged Andy all the way to the Sheriff with his own two hands.

The first side effect to make itself known was that Mark became something of an underground hero to many of the underclassmen. The second side effect was that he became more of a target than ever before to the likes of Pete and his side-kicks. The only one who had never seemed to slander him in front of the entire school was Tony: that actually worried Pete to a certain extent, leading him to think that maybe Tony'd gone soft.

Also, Pete had honestly liked Andy, a great deal more than any of the other kids in the school. He'd grown up not far from where Andy lived and they had been friends since kindergarten. Andy was a little slow on the uptake, sure, but he was always there when Pete had needed a friend.

He looked over towards where the scarecrow stood laughing with his friends and gritted his teeth. Thanks to dick-head over there, Andy had been arrested and Andy wouldn't even talk to him. He'd gone to the penitentiary in Denver twice to see Andy, and both times it was the same: Andy'd just sit there and shake, like he had a fever. He'd really been sick, looking at Andy: his brown hair had gone white and he'd had cuts and bruises all over his fucking face. He'd also had a double splint on his right hand and tape on his nose, where Howell had apparently broken it.

He felt his fists clenching and almost let out a growl in public. He whirled suddenly, as a hand slapped him on the back.

Patrick Wilson stood before him, a grin splitting his angular face. "Say, wha's happenin', Pete?" Patrick was obviously sampling his own wares again, Pete thought to himself. "How you holdin' up?" It took a second for Pete to realize he was asking about his supply of "party favors"—when he did, Pete just shrugged.

"I'm okay fer now, but check with me later in the week, okay?"

Patrick smiled like the Cheshire Cat and nodded his head very slowly, three times. "Sure, listen, you seen my little bro'? I'm s'posed to see how he's doin', check up on him, y'know, for the old man." Pete pointed to where Tyler and Mark stood, getting their photograph taken with the rest of their little group, and Patrick nodded his head again, three times, slowly, before staggering off in that direction.

Pete had started thinking about Mark again, when Sandy interrupted him. "Why do you hang around with that loser? He's almost as bad as Andy." She shivered dramatically, as she mentioned the latter and Pete frowned under his mask. "God, when I think what he did to Tanya…"

Pete grabbed her by the arm, fed up with hearing all the bullshit about how horrible Andy was. "Why don't you get off of Andy's back?! I'm sick of everybody always ragging on him." He glared at the girl in front of him, enjoying the way the skin of her lean arm shivered beneath his grip. He almost said what was on his mind: *Andy didn't do shit to Tanya that she didn't deserve. She was a teasing little slut.* Instead, he amended the thought and blurted out, "Besides, I think Howell over there is the one that killed her."

Sandy looked at him, as if he'd lost his mind. "That's crazy! Andy confessed to killing her. Anyway, she disappeared before Mark came to town. He wasn't even around when Tanya was killed."

"Garbage. I say Howell killed her and that bitch Cassie helped him come up with an alibi. Shit, she probably paid him to kill Tanya. They were always competing for damn near everything."

Sandy pulled her arm out of Pete's grasp and stepped away from him, disgusted with his attitude. He had definitely been playing in Patrick's Pharmacy too much. He'd gone off the deep end, as far as she was concerned. Plus, she and Cassie were good friends and she knew that Cassie had never been jealous of Tanya. The other way around was more like it. "You're crazy, Pete. I'm going home. If you feel like talking later give me a call."

Before Pete could protest, she had merged with the crowd of people around them, disappearing from his sight. The world seemed determined to shit on him tonight. Well, he was damned if he was going to take it.

He spotted Howell and his group of butt-buddies, as they walked away from the photo booth. His eyes kept snapping from Mark to Cassie and he couldn't decide who he should hurt first. In the long run, he decided he'd hurt them both.

4

Joe looked over at Tyler and had trouble accepting that the muscular young man next to him was Tyler's older brother. They looked nothing at all alike and their personalities were so radically different that he felt it had to be some kind of joke.

Patrick stood almost six feet tall and had the body of a professional athlete, where Tyler was lucky to have broken five and looked more like a scarecrow in his civvies, than Mark did in his costume. Patrick had clear skin and wore contact lenses, where Tyler was a text book example of acne run rampant, and hid his owlish eyes behind inch thick lumps of plastic. And Tyler had a brain, while his brother seemed determined to burn his out with every illegal substance on the planet. He silently thanked God that Mark had never gotten involved with drugs. He couldn't help but think that maybe Patrick sold more than he used. His body wasn't wasted into a skeletal parody of a normal person—at least not yet, he added as Patrick nearly fell over himself while standing still.

Jenny had noticed too and sadly shook her head. He grasped her hand and gave her a peck on the cheek, as he pulled her closer. Cassie and Mark were next to them and at the same time, they called out "awww, that's cu-ute." Joe actually felt himself blush slightly, as he mock glared at the young couple. "Joe, if you and your date," Mark said, "could unclench for a moment, we could all go to the Haunted House. We're supposed to meet with P. J. in about ten minutes."

He and his date could, and the group went on their way—without Patrick, for which Joe was grateful. A moment before they got to their destination, Cassie called out to a friend and they were joined by a sixth person, a girl named Sandy, who was dressed in a Little Red Riding Hood outfit. The girl seemed upset, but soon agreed to join them. Moments after she'd met with them, Tyler had her laughing. Suddenly Tyler no longer seemed like a fifth wheel and Joe was very pleased about that.

The Haunted House was full of the normal badly constructed horrors, good more for laughs than anything else. The only redeeming quality about the monsters were the tiny ones scattered all around the place that moved slightly and had burning red eyes. He wished they had been larger, so that he could have seen them in closer detail. Not the best of attractions at the fair, but they managed to enjoy themselves.

By the time they left, Joe understood why the scrawniest kid in the school never seemed worried about being on the outside of the established cliques. He and Sandy were holding hands and talking about everything under the moon. P. J. seemed to notice as well and he chuckled throatily, as the writer mumbled something about there being tigers, where young Tyler was headed.

He couldn't have been more right, Joe realized, as he saw a young man heading their way. He was built like a linebacker and wore a Lon Chaney Jr. Wolfman mask. By the clenched fists at his side and the tight, angry stride, he had to guess that this was Red Riding Hood's beau. He looked ready to kill Tyler, and Joe had no doubt that this particular werewolf could. He was thinking about stepping in, when he heard Cassie call out, "Uh, Sandy? Guess who's here." She sounded nervous, and that worried Joe; she was too confident for the most part, too outspoken, for her to be easily worried.

Sandy turned her head and paled slightly. Joe decided that something would have to be done and soon. Sandy had started to speak, when the Wolfman interrupted her. "You bitch! I thought you said you were going home! You planning on having Howell frame me too? Is that what this is all about?"

Understandably, everyone was confused by the outcry—a sad side effect being that it gave Pete Larson a chance to plow into Tyler, who had turned decidedly green beneath his homemade skull mask upon viewing the boy advancing on them. Tyler went into the air, leaving his mask and glasses hanging comically for a moment before they fell to the ground. Even as Joe was starting forward, Pete rained blows down on Tyler as the boy tried feebly to defend himself. He had almost reached them when Mark landed squarely on Pete's back, knocking the wind out of him.

Mark stepped away and looked warily at Pete, as he cursed through his mask and stood up.

"Let's just all calm down," P. J. started, as Pete advanced on Mark. "Peter Larson, isn't it? Yes, you're a friend of my nephew's. I'm sure this can all be worked out, I'm sure it's just a simple misunderstanding." P. J.'s voice took on that mesmeric quality, as he stepped towards Pete. "Why don't we all just talk, nice and friendly, before someone gets hurt." Pete looked around himself at the small crowd that had formed, and thought carefully. Mark was looking straight at him, not paying attention to what anyone was saying. Mark continued to stand stock still, with a warning glare in his eyes, as Cassie helped Tyler to his feet. Jenny handed him his mask and magically produced a handkerchief from somewhere to clean the blood from his split lip. Joe stepped up to where P. J. was and stood beside him, giving Pete his silent alternatives: talk, or get smeared into the ground.

Pete nodded his understanding of the situation and then turned to glare at Mark and Tyler. His eyes promised retribution at a later date. Without a backward glance, Pete took off, moving like a stalking tiger.

Mark relaxed and the adrenaline in his system started producing quakes throughout his body. Joe was still taken aback by the sudden and savage assault he had thrown at Pete when he'd seen Tyler go down. A month ago, Mark had been beaten severely. Joe was beginning to wonder just what effects that had had on him.

Part of him was pleased by the change in his stepson, part of him deeply worried. The boy had looked ready to kill. Then again, maybe "boy" wasn't the right term anymore. Since they'd arrived in Summitville, Mark had grown over two inches in height and lost a good fifteen pounds. Maybe he'd have to start thinking of him as a young man.

Tyler was the one who broke the sour mood, with several sharp comments about his clumsiness and vain attempts to kiss Mark on the face, all the while screeching "My Hero!" in a high falsetto voice. Most people trying a line that corny would have gotten a snicker or two at best. Tyler managed to pull it off with ease. He managed to break the tension in the group, and used his natural flamboyance to bring everyone back into a good mood.

They had a good time for the rest of the night and had nearly forgotten the incident by the time they all headed home.

The Folk had not forgotten, nor did They forgive. There would be a reckoning. The threat in the voice of the One's opponent had been clear, as had the threat in his parting glance. It was a threat that would never be carried out. They would make certain of that.

5

Patrick Wilson was busy making a deal with Dave Brundvandt around the same time his brother was getting jumped by the Big Bad Wolf. Dave was the only one of his customers who purchased painkillers and amphetamines almost daily.

Dave was also the only person in town who probably re-sold what he purchased. Pharmacies didn't always supply the comforts that a lot of the kids in town wanted and Patrick rather enjoyed the safety that came from dealing with the bul-lies in the school and cutting them deals. No one wanted to crack Patrick Wilson's head open; everyone knew that Tony and the whole merry gang would stand up for him in a heart-beat. They had proven that several times.

Dave was the one person Patrick didn't like to sell to. Dave was the type that would sell it to twelve-year-olds. One of these days, he just might have to cut him off cold turkey.

Patrick saw Pete go storming off, Wolfman mask shoved in his back pocket, and almost made a comment about making sure he didn't get himself bitten in the ass. One look at the nasty expression on Pete's face changed his mind. Dave saw the look too and smiled about it. No love had ever been lost between Dave and Pete—opposite sides of town separated them as surely as the difference in what their parents made ever could. Even in Summitville, money meant too much to too many people. Patrick didn't think it should matter at all, but then Patrick came from *serious* money.

6

Pete was furious; now the lard-ass had others standing up for him. Well, two could play that game and the adults wouldn't be invited when the time came to rectify the situation. He couldn't believe that he had actually seen Sandy holding hands with that twerpy little shit, Tyler, either. He gripped the steering wheel of his Jetta in a death clutch as he turned off Main Street onto Second Avenue. His mind was awhirl with savage thoughts as he shot past his subdivision, heading out to the cemetery. He needed to think and he needed the clear air to aid him in his attempts.

He stopped about a hundred yards from the cemetery's main entrance. His family owned the cemetery, so he didn't worry about old man Terrell getting on his ass. The stupid fuck knew better.

Pete climbed out of the car and pulled out the bottle of Stoli he had been saving for later. Later, when he and Sandy got it on. *Yeah, right.* Thinking about Sandy started his mind going over the entire thing again and he felt himself getting angrier and angrier.

He thought about Andy and wondered just what the hell Mark had done to him. The fart wasn't that ugly, he couldn't have scared him badly enough to turn his hair white, fer Chrissakes.

So if he didn't, what the hell did?

Not a good thought for almost midnight, on Halloween, in front of a graveyard. He looked around the area, suddenly uncomfortable about where he was, and saw nothing but the same old hang-out he'd been using since he got his car. Well-kept lawns, a few trees and evenly spaced, tasteful headstones, for as far as the eye could see. He snorted at his own nervousness, taking a pull off of the Stoli for warmth—certainly not because it gave him courage, not a chance. He was plenty brave all on his own, thank you very fucking much.

He was just starting to relax when he heard something moving in the cemetery. He sat straight up, heart beating hard, and looked around the area again. Nothing out of the ordinary.

He almost screamed when he heard the four gun-like reports of his tires exploding. "Sweet Jesus, what the hell was that?" No one answered him. When he felt the car sinking, he suddenly had a flash of his Jetta sinking into quicksand and fairly flew off of the hood to land on solid ground. Pete saw the four rapidly deflating tires. He was ready to explode; it was over a mile to his goddamn house, what the hell was he supposed to do, walk?

How did the tires get flattened? he thought. *Does that sort of shit just happen?* "Oh, shit." he whispered, feeling his vocal cords tighten. "Shit, shit, shit, shit, and *shit.*" The movie *Night of the Living Dead* started playing in the back of his mind and he felt the first serious flutters start in his stomach. Images of zombies clawing their way from their final resting places beneath the ground whirled through his mind and made his nerves dance a mad tango. He slugged back some more liquor, coughing as it seared the inside of his throat.

When he had finished with his coughing fit and was silent again, he dropped to his knees and looked under the car. *No zombies, okay? No zombies and I'll give up the drugs. Deal?*

Something hard hit him in the ass and he bashed his head against the side of the car in his rush to look. "Sonuvabitch! Who the fuck is out there?!?!" Rubbing his head, he looked for some asshole throwing rocks in the distance.

Nothing. The only change he saw was the light in Old Man Terrell's little dumpy house going on. "Don't even think about calling my old man. Don't you even fucking think about it."

He was thinking about the best way to bribe the old goat faced boot-licker when he felt the searing pain in his right little toe. With a yelp of surprise, he stood up and felt the world tilt wildly, as the blood rushed eagerly from his head. When he could see again, without dark swirling explosions of color in his way, there was nothing to look at.

Except for the gaping hole and bleeding stump, where shoe and little toe had been before. Upon viewing the damage, he really started to feel the pain. It flared across his foot and ran up his leg in a blazing streak of agony. He let loose with a string of foul words as he hobbled over to the hood of his car for a better look. He was numbed enough by the alcohol in his system that he could actually bother with looking at the wound and not with passing out immediately. The meat had been torn clear off his toe and white broken bone glared up at him, mostly concealed by the free-flowing blood that insisted on pouring from the open wound.

While he was busy looking, something attacked the back of his left calf. Pete screamed as he felt the flesh tear from his body. He looked down quickly and saw Them for the first time. They stood no more than six or seven inches tall, but there must have been a hundred of Them. Tiny little demons, just like the ones that writer had talked about in his story. The one closest to his leg eagerly munched on something raw and bloody as It leered up at him. Numbly, he noticed that the mouth on this creature seemed huge in proportion to the rest of Its tiny little body. *My, what big teeth you have, Grandma.* It was dark, he couldn't see enough to make Them out clearly in the shadows on the ground. But what he could see sent shudders of blind panic through his brain. They had smooth, grayish skin that gave the impression of scales too small to be seen, and ridiculously powerful little torsos. Their eyes burned a feverish red, and wicked spikes of bone bristled across Their spines, leading to tails that lashed frantically. Their little triangular heads looked like they belonged on something from another era, a carnivorous dinosaur, perhaps. They had very nasty looking teeth and tiny little claws, that looked very, very sharp—like needles.

They studied him with a like intensity. Unlike him, They didn't seem to find the subject of Their studies very scary. But, judging by the bloody smile on the one chewing on his leg meat, They sure thought he was tasty—and maybe even a little funny. The tittering, giggling, little noises They made annoyed his senses like a constant, monotonous beep, the kind a phone left off the hook makes. Just as he was wishing that They would shut up, the silence of midnight fell around him.

The sudden quiet told him that he had been judged, and he wondered idly what the verdict would be.

They moved as one and he was amazed by the speed and savagery They displayed. With unnatural strength for such tiny little creatures They pulled him to the ground. The alcohol in his system didn't do a thing to stop the pain as They started to feed. Tiny little pieces of his body kept being shoved into Their tiny little mouths and he couldn't help but wonder where They were putting it all.

Pete thought about the Living Dead movies for a brief second and wondered if maybe the dead did come to life after all. *If they do, If I do, will it feel this bad all the time?* Pete screamed for as long as it took the tiny demons to reach his throat.

Old Clarence Terrell had heard the noise of exploding tires and it was enough to wake him from his fitful slumbers. He thought about getting up and then remembered it was Halloween. With a muttered curse, he rolled back over and went to sleep. Lord knew he'd have a fit when he had to clean up after that snot-nosed little Larson kid this time.

Almost took all the fun away from the times he had watched the punk and his latest little girlfriend doing their thing in the cemetery—but only almost. Larson had some fine looking little girlfriends.

The screams stopped. The thrashing motions that Peter Larson made lasted a bit longer. His last conscious thought was that he'd never get Sandy down here now.

The sound of bones being broken, chewed and swallowed lasted nearly until dawn. They liked the bones; many among Them even argued that the bones were the best part.

7

Doctor Richard Lewis hated having to do the Coroner's reports, but he hated not having the money that they brought in even more. Summitville was a small town and didn't have many violent crimes—with the exception of any given Saturday night at Dino's Bar and Grill—so he didn't really have that many bodies to examine. But, he still didn't like it.

He certainly didn't like having to examine the body of Tanya Melissa Billingsley. Working meticulously on the examination had shown him a taste of what the folks in the big cities must go through. Someone had torn her apart, and they had done it after she'd been dead for quite a long time. They had forced entry into her body from every available orifice and done serious harm to each of the body cavities in the process.

Rigor mortis had long since set in and faded; the stiffness that death grants for a few hours was gone. Most of her muscles and flesh were rotted away, and even her tendons were thin and brittle. But whoever had worked her over had forced the corpse into motion, and not just once either. And there was a fluid trapped in her decayed body that he couldn't comprehend. It was largely like an organic oil but like none he'd ever seen before.

Shivering to himself, he stepped away from his small desk in the Larson Mortuary and poured himself another cup of coffee. He just couldn't let this one lie. He had to understand what had been done to her.

His mind ran back to the actual examination and he ran over the details in his mind again. The mouth had been shredded, by whatever had been forced past the withered and tightly drawn lips, and tiny little cuts had been involved in the process; it made the good doctor think of what a baseball bat would do, if it had been wrapped tightly in barbed wire and then coated liberally with fish-hooks. A good deal of her teeth had been knocked out in the process. The same baseball bat must have been used in her pelvic region as well.

But, that still didn't explain the liquid. It didn't explain how the liquid could have gotten into her body, even as far in as the torso and the cranium.

He was still contemplating the fluids, when Chuck Hanson called him. "Shit, what the hell is it now?" he mumbled, as he reached for the phone. "Hello?"

Charles Emery Hanson had a voice like distant thunder: it rumbled menacingly out of the phone. But Rick knew the menace wasn't for him, just for any fool dumb enough to break the law in Hanson's district. "Rick? This is Chuck. Listen, I know you're busy, but I've got a real puzzle on my hands, out at the Cemet'ry. I need you out here, now if at all possible. Looks like we might have rain soon and I want you to see this in person, not just on film."

"I'm as good as on my way," he said. "Just give me ten minutes."

Hanson was silent for a rather long moment and Rick was starting to think he'd hung up, when the Sheriff finally replied. "Sounds good. Rick? Be prepared, it's not a pretty sight. Whatever the hell it is."

With that, the line went dead. Rick Lewis hated the job of coroner for the small town and felt a cold and certain dread that told him he'd hate it a great deal more before the day was done.

8

Lewis arrived at the scene and was eagerly greeted by Hanson. Chuck was a true bear of a man, with thick auburn hair, shot with gray, that fell in cascading waves down to his shoulders. Rick was certain that in most towns he would have been relieved from his position for the gross violation of what he was equally certain had to be a universal police policy on hair length; not here. Hanson was too well respected as a peace-keeper. Hanson nodded grimly and Rick knew that his troubles were about to begin in earnest.

Hanson talked easily and walked with amazing grace for a man that carried as much extra weight as he did. As always, he was out of uniform, wearing his badge on the blue jean jacket that he wore, regardless of the temperature, year 'round in his duties as sheriff. He was also wearing his cowboy hat, pulled down low, almost hiding his gray eyes. On any other man, Rick thought the outfit would look ridiculous. Hanson carried it off with ease. "Clarence called me out here, 'bout an hour ago. He found the mess I'm about to show you and thought maybe it was a prank at first. But, he remembered hearing screams early this morning and thought he ought not touch anything, just in case. Smart move."

Rick nodded to old Clarence, where he sat against the low stone wall in front of the cemetery. Clarence tried a smile that looked more like a wince and waved sheepishly. "How're ya today, Doc?"

Rick smiled back and stated conversationally that he'd know in about two minutes. But it took about thirty seconds to decide that he'd been much better. The pool of congealed blood looked almost black in the early morning light. In and of itself it wouldn't have bothered him in the least, but in light of the scattering of teeth and bone fragments mixed in liberally, he was glad that he'd skipped breakfast. He had to bend in close and use a small knife to move the fragments, before he was convinced that the remains were human. Four of the teeth had fillings.

"Photos already been taken?"

"Yeah, Dave's got em down at the lab now, getting 'em developed." Hanson lit a cigarette, snorting smoke out of his nostrils, before he continued. "What's the verdict, Rick? Human, or other?"

"Human, Chuck. No two ways about it." He got off of his knees and walked slowly back to his station wagon, which doubled as the Coroner's wagon. "Let me get all of my stuff and we can talk while I gather what I'll need. Whose car is that anyway?"

Hanson hesitated before answering, obviously less than pleased about the answer. "Belongs to Pete Larson. So does the wallet lying just under the car, least that'd be my guess. I haven't touched it, be careful. I still need to dust for prints."

Rick groaned, audibly, as he realized the situation that Chuck and Clarence were in. Theodore Larson was a mean old bastard and wouldn't be at all happy if these were his son's remains and the killer wasn't already behind bars. Not that he could blame the man—nobody liked to have a dead relative, let alone a son, go unavenged if there was a reason to believe that foul play had been involved. He was pretty damned certain it was in this case. His instincts told him this hadn't been an animal attack, it was simply too thorough.

Whatever had killed the person in front of him had torn every single bone into tiny little shreds, effectively peeling all of the marrow from the skeletal frame.

Most animals that he knew of would have either left the body intact for the most part, or they would have hidden the corpse where they could find it later. Not that he knew the habits of all animals, but he'd certainly seen enough documentaries that he'd remember having heard of one that did this kind of carnage. Also, he thought that most animals of a size to do this kind of damage would have left sizable tracks, and he couldn't see any, not even in the pool of blood which, he noted, the animals had left undisturbed.

"Maybe rats?" Rick almost jumped out of his skin: he'd forgotten all about Clarence Terrell. "Sorry, Doc, didn't mean ta startle ya. Figured you'd jest about hear the old bones creakin' yer way at a hunnert yards." The man placed an arthritic claw on his shoulder and Rick had to force himself not to scramble away from the old man's withered paw.

He looked at the older man and smiled tightly, seeing the need to be helpful in the old man's eyes. "I hadn't thought of that, Clarence, I'll have to look into it, though I don't honestly know if a rat-swarm could do a person in that thoroughly or not." He saw the sheer happiness at having been of use in the old man's eyes and smiled wider, filled with the simple joy of making some one else happy. "Good thinking on your part, I'll definitely make a note of it."

"Yup, well, I guess I better get back to the office," The man stood taller than he had before and Rick wondered just how nasty a boss that old bastard Larson was. "I 'magine the sheriff's gonna need ta use the phone, ta call Larson on this one." With that the caretaker turned smartly and strode with pride and purpose, towards the small shed that was his office and home.

"Better go on up there, Chuck, you'll break his heart, if you don't at least call the old man from his office."

Hanson smiled ruefully and nodded. "Yeah, Lord knows Clarence is gonna get shit enough for this. Let him have his moment in the sun." Hanson turned back, after only a few paces and smiled brightly. He didn't say a word, but his look spoke for him. After silently thanking Rick for giving the old caretaker a little dignity, he walked on.

With a sigh, Rick got back to work. It looked like he'd be here awhile, pulling bone chips and hair out of the bloody mess in front of him.

9

It takes little time for news to spread throughout a community as small as Summitville, and bad news spreads even faster. By noon, most of the town had heard about the death of Peter Larson. Most of them expressed grief or shock, but a good handful was glad to see him go. Although it was Tony Scarrabelli that led Pete's little pack at school, most would have eagerly admitted (though not to his face) that Pete was the most vicious when it came to punishing the different.

Mark didn't know what to feel. Part of him was deeply saddened by Pete's death, part of him was quietly pleased, and a shadowy part that truly horrified him was disappointed. That part had wanted the pleasure of removing Pete from the face of the Earth personally.

He didn't mention any of this to P. J. The man had enough problems of his own. At the present time, he was in the process of screaming into his over-abused phone, explaining once again to his editor that the story had been written in the present tense, because he liked the present tense, not because he was ignorant of the fact that it wasn't considered appropriate by his publisher. For the thirty-seventh time, he was explaining that he wouldn't hesitate to break his contract.

Mark had read the entire manuscript in just over three hours, and it had kept him enthralled the entire time. It was a sequel to *Night Thunder* and it brought Sligis back for a second appearance in the sleepy little town of Whisper Lake, where most of P.J.'s novels took place.

He and Cassie had talked excitedly about the novel the next weekend when they had come in to see the author, already at work on another story. P. J. had been very pleased by the reception that his two favorite critics had given the book and he had signed and dated both copies, after binding them in black leather that he stitched around each. P. J. had spent several months working with an old gentleman who restored older books, in the process of researching one of his grislier novels, *Stirrings*, where the dark figure of Gabriel Dante had bound all his tomes of knowledge in the skin of virgins. It was a great gift to receive and they'd been equally floored when he added a dedication page, to his two greatest critics and named them both, with a wish for happiness in the future.

P. J. called Mark over to the phone and demanded that he "Talk some sense to the crusty old bitch on the line." Hesitantly, he placed the phone to his ear and started off with a simple hello.

He found Alberta Hathaway to be a charming woman. After almost forty-five minutes of conversation with her, he said a simple good bye and promised to call again soon. Mark looked over to where P. J. was glaring at him and knew what was coming next.

"Traitor," the writer accused, lip shot out in an uncharacteristic pout.

"Am not," Mark countered immediately.

"Are too."

"Am not."

"Are too."

"Am not." Mark continued, adding the dreaded counter argument, " and I can prove it."

P. J. looked at him skeptically and Mark smirked, waiting to lay down the trump card of his hand. "Oh yeah," challenged P. J. "Prove it, I dare you."

"Ali said she's going to print it as-is."

P. J. sat gape jawed, staring at Mark as if he'd suddenly developed seven extra heads. "No. No way will you get me to believe that you convinced the old witch to go ahead with the novel unchanged."

"Ah," Mark lifted a cautionary finger. "There's a catch."

"I knew it! What does the old bat want, my first born child? My eternal soul?" P. J. looked as if he'd scored major points against Mark's argument. "What did you agree to on my behalf, boy? Speak! Your Lord and Master commands you!"

Mark buffed his nails against his shirt and looked nonchalantly over at the nervous writer. "Oh, nothing so extreme."

He was about to continue, when the author piped in again. "Gods, man, tell me you didn't agree to more books for the hell-cow!"

Mark smiled. "No, just one little thing." P. J. looked warily at Mark, knowing that this was the killing stroke, the one piece of knowledge that would devastate him, no matter how mildly the boy put it to him.

"What already?!" He demanded, as his mediator started pouring them both a mug of cream with coffee flavoring. "What have you done to me? I can't stand this! If you don't let me know, I'll strangle you with your own intestines!" That was Mark's favorite thing about P. J.: the man's penchant for dramatics was almost as bad in real life as it was in his novels.

Mark smiled triumphantly and said "Now you know what it's like, to be on the receiving end of a good piece of suspense."

P. J. stood, blood in his face. "What-did-you-give—that-*evil*-creature?" He punctuated each word with a small step forward. Mark backed up an even distance and smiled cruelly.

"I told her," he started slowly, "that you would have lunch with her when she comes to town this Friday. Tomorrow, to be precise."

Mark watched his friend turn deathly white, as the terror of what he'd just said struck home.

Mark's laughter was quickly blanketed by the raw shriek of horror that broke from the writer's lips.

He laughed all the way home, as P. J. tried without success to get through to Alberta Hathaway, desperate to let her know that he'd reconsidered and would write it her way. The real coup de grace had come when he told P. J. that she was already on her way.

Hathaway, it seemed, wanted to negotiate for more novels.

Chapter Four

1

Tyler's house was a massive, sprawling, three-story monster that had absolutely no reason to be in a neighborhood of smaller two-story homes. Except, of course, that that was where Tyler's dad had wanted it. Tyler's dad, Samuel Edgar Wilson, could afford to have things go his way, at damn near any cost. Fortunately for Mark and Cassie, Mr. Wilson had also wanted to have an indoor heated swimming pool; otherwise, they wouldn't be enjoying a good water fight with Tyler until Summer showed itself again.

Folding his body into a near fetal position, Tyler hit the pool like a small boulder, half drowning his two friends with the resultant wave. He then flew energetically out of the water to land on Mark, who was still trying to get his breath back.

Wrestling frantically, the two went under the turbulent waters. Cassie screamed excitedly, as they came out of the water and threw themselves at her wading form. After another twenty minutes of such frantic activities, the three gasped and crawled weakly over to the pool's ledge and flopped themselves down with a gusto.

Tyler looked over at the two heavily breathing forms next to him and grinned ear to ear. "You should see yourselves, you look like you both just had raunchy sex." The two lifted themselves up and looked at each other, then quickly away. That confirmed that they had not yet done the deed and Tyler relaxed a little. At the ripe old age of sixteen, he had seen too many couples complicate their relationships with physical satisfaction before they were ready. He wanted their relationship to last. They looked good together and they had a fighting chance, as long as neither one forced the issue too soon. They still had a lot to learn about each other.

Mark looked over at Tyler and casually tossed an insult into the air. "Why, were you wishing I'd look that way for you, you big stud?" Tyler gave him the bird. He wished that Sandy would've come over, but she had obviously been torn apart by the confirmation of Pete's death. He really liked her, but knew it couldn't work out. She was in love with a dead man. Or if not love, then at least infatuation. Tyler strongly believed that lust was the downfall of most romances. He'd seen it send his father through several live-in girlfriends before his mother had finally come back to stay. Off and on his parents had separated and reunited several times before the old man finally decided to stay with the woman he'd married in the first place.

"Okay, so you're not going to give me any juicy gossip on your love lives," he started. "How about the latest gossip on the 'I hate Tyler patrol'— any more gruesome deaths to talk about?"

Cassie grinned, familiar with Tyler's sick sense of humor; Mark looked appalled. "That's disgusting, Ty, you should wash your mouth out." Mark looked as if he meant it. Tyler just grinned.

"You can't honestly tell me you miss those guys, Howie, I know you better than that."

Mark frowned. "No, but that still doesn't seem like a decent thing to say about the dead. I mean, I hope I'm remembered a little more fondly, when my time comes."

Tyler looked at him and pushed his glasses up the joke he called a nose. "Good point, Howie. I hereby withdraw my previous statement." Mark seemed mollified and Tyler went in for the kill. "So anymore assholes get offed, or what?"

Mark and Cassie laughed along with him and Mark slapped him with a towel. "No, I think only two of your sworn enemies are out of the picture, so far." Cassie replied, "But, I'm sure that your efforts will be rewarded. What's next, arsenic in the cafeteria, or dynamite in the gym?"

Tyler leapt at the question with a special joy, saved only for friends who had left themselves open. "Hey, they see dynamite after gym, every time I take off my shorts for the shower." He leered at Cassie and winked. "Lose ol' Howie and I'll show you sometime," he stated, in a bad imitation of W.C. Fields.

"In your dreams," she stated, wiggling her little pinky in his direction. "You'd have to have something worth showing first."

With mock injury on his face, he threw a dramatic arm across his brow and wept. "You slut! I knew you'd given me up for Howie, but to tell him about my castration is simply going too far!" He watched as Mark reached for a Diet Pepsi and as his friend started sipping, threw in: "And all because I made you swallow the second time."

Cassie let out a loud "EEEUUUUWWW!" of disgust and wrinkled her face up, as Mark snorted cola out of his nose. *Ah, Tyler, you've still got it.*

"No reason to hide the truth, my love, I've told Mark all about our relationship, just as I told you of his, with me." Mark half choked on that one too. "Ah, I see that you remember our love affair with the same fondness that I do."

They caught him on the third circuit of the pool and worked in unison to heave him as far as they could into the deep end. After they helped him back out, they started the gossip in earnest.

"You should have seen the look P. J. gave me when I told him that Ali was coming over to his place for lunch. I imagine it was almost as good as when she showed up for dinner." Mark chuckled at the memory and continued eagerly. "If she's half as good looking as she is smart, he won't have a chance."

Cassie looked slightly wounded and he immediately added, "Just like I never had a chance." That earned him a smile. *Too close, Mark, too damn close.*

They talked a good deal more, as the day became night. Then Mark and Cassie said their good-byes and Mark led his girlfriend off into the darkness.

2

Mark was rapidly becoming someone special to Cassie. She didn't quite know how she felt about it, but there it was. They held hands as they meandered slowly towards her house, on the next street. They didn't talk much, but they communicated.

When they finally reached their destination, he pulled her close into a light hug and kissed her softly on the forehead. "You better get inside," he said, smiling gently. "Your dad's probably ready to be tied, waiting for you." She smiled back and gave his hand a final squeeze. He watched her the entire trip to the door and she knew he'd probably stand there for another five minutes after she had gone in. She'd timed him once. It was silly, but it made her feel special.

Dinner had been held for her and she and her parents discussed the day in the usual round of questions. "So, how's Tyler?" Her mom would ask and she would respond with a fifteen or twenty minute lecture on his latest antics, normally curbing the more sadistic comments because her mother was ever so slightly prudish.

"How was school?" her father would ask and she would tell him a fairly detailed run of how her day at school had gone and what she was studying in each of her classes. They never asked about Mark, not after that time last week. That was when her father made his little comments and pointed out that the troubles around town, as regarded that "young Tanya girl" and even poor Andy Phillips—"Did you hear, he was apparently thrown off of a balcony and crushed his head in, poor boy"—had started about the same time that that Mark Howell came to town. Her parents worked in the city, her father to pay the bills and her mother because she wanted a little extra spending cash, but they lived here, in Summitville, as their parents before them had. They had security here and could even leave the doors unlocked at night. They knew everyone in town, if not by name, at least as a casual acquaintance.

If anyone from Denver had asked them if they could recommend a place to live, away from the city, they would have hemmed and hawed for a minute or so and said that they couldn't think of any place. They had a P.O. box in the city, so that they didn't have to give their home address to anyone. They never invited anyone from the city to stay in town with them, or to come to dinner at their home. Dear Heavens, what if they wanted to stay after having seen the little town? Oh, that would never do! No, absolutely not!

Her parents, like most of the town, suffered from an extreme case of xenophobia. The very thought of strangers coming into the town was enough to send most of the families scrambling madly to lock the shutters and bar the doors, as if any newcomer must obviously be out to rape every female, no matter what age. Newcomers must want to murder all of the young children and kill the men in the process. Probably rape the children in the process.

Cassie smiled to herself bitterly, remembering how long it had taken Doctor Lewis to be accepted—and he had had the recommendation of Sheriff Hanson to back him up. She wondered if P. J. Sanderson would have been readily accepted into the town, if he hadn't been a native son returning from college. *Probably not,* she decided.

Still, it irked her that her parents had automatically assumed Mark carried a switch-blade in his pocket and had something to do with Tanya's death. She had let them know her feelings too, when they had suggested, ever so casually at the dinner table, that perhaps she should stick with her own, stop seeing that new boy. She'd let them know all right, at the top of her lungs. Cassie wondered how much of Tony's attitude towards Mark was based on his parents, if they had the same fear of anything different. His mother, maybe, but not his father. His father was from Chicago and couldn't possibly feel that way. He'd suffered a good deal of the town's stand-off-ishness himself.

It had taken most of the week just to get back on speaking terms with her parents. The unofficial decision not to speak of Mark had been made without a word being said. Perhaps that was for the best. She really didn't want anymore grief with her folks. She had enough problems of her own without having to hold theirs as well.

After she finished dinner, she went to her room to study. It didn't go well. Her mind was on Mark and none of the schoolbooks made any sense. Eventually she went to sleep and that was when They made Their move.

3

Mark walked aimlessly, thinking to himself that his life had turned around, since moving to the little town of Summitville. Suddenly he had a few friends at school; he'd finally started to lose the excess pounds he'd carried for years—something that his mother had assured him would happen, she'd lost her baby fat late in life as well—he wasn't getting bashed daily by the assholes at the school and, of course, he had met Cassie.

Yep, life had definitely taken a turn for the better. He liked Summitville and was fairly certain that at least some of Summitville returned the sentiment.

As he often did, he wandered through the subdivision and the surrounding woods, thinking to himself, as he headed on his way home. Somehow, he managed to find his favorite spot. If someone had asked him why he liked this spot, he couldn't have told them. Unless he'd been here for awhile. They never showed up, right away, They always waited for a small time before They showed Themselves, and he never remembered Them until They showed Themselves again.

He saw Them all at once and felt the tide of warm emotions wash over him as They scampered closer and danced around him on the forest's floor. They climbed across him as if he were a log, running up to his face and caressing his skin with Their delicate little fingers. He laughed with Them and shared in Their joy, never thinking that They shouldn't even exist. They were beautiful. Their pale skin glowed in the moonlight and Their liquid eyes shone with joy, as They whispered excitedly to him, telling him of the wonders that existed only in Their world.

When They told of a snake shedding its skin, it was a story of wonder and a story of celebration, for the snake had lived long enough to shed its old skin and grow a small amount larger. When They sang to him of the birds in the trees, he felt the feathered creatures' simple joy at being alive, no matter that the day had brought challenges the bird had had to struggle desperately with. They always had the finest things to tell of all his friends, P. J., Tyler, Cassie, even his parents. They always had the most amazing stories of his friends' lives. It was as if They had been with his friends, watching them all along, protecting them. He was very grateful that the Folk were his friends.

Soon, he grew sleepy and he closed his eyes, knowing that he was safe and would have such wonderful dreams. Dreams of Cassie, dreams of great passion, love, and warmth. And safety in a world without pain. Sometimes, he wished he could stay forever.

4

What seemed like hours took only some twenty minutes in reality. Mark was home in time for dinner with a smile on his face. Had his mother or Joe asked him, he would have simply said that he'd had fun at Tyler's. They didn't ask, they had other things on their minds.

He didn't know what the problem was, but he could sense the tension between them. It was a tension that rarely existed. After twenty minutes of eating in deadly silence, Mark could take it no longer. "What's wrong? You're both awfully quiet tonight."

Jenny looked over at her son and he knew what the problem was before she even opened her mouth. "Joe's been offered a job, in New York. It pays almost twice what Joe's making now. He wants to take it."

Mark felt his blood pressure shoot up to dangerous levels and controlled himself with a Herculean effort. "I want to stay here."

Joe looked over at Mark and clamped his jaw tightly shut. He'd been afraid of this. "Look, Mark, it's a job that only comes around once in a lifetime. The managing editor is retiring, I need to accept the position, if I ever want to move into the upper management level." He hesitated when he saw the look of raw pain on Mark's face and realized, possibly for the first time, just what all of the moves had done to his son. He added words that rang untrue, even to his own ears. "If it means that much to you, I'll talk to Rob at work and see if I can work out a raise. Maybe we won't have to move. Okay?"

Mark tossed a feeble smile his way and stood away from the table. His voice was hardly even a whisper, as he walked towards the front door. "Yeah, I understand. I'm goin' for a walk. I'll talk to you later."

He walked calmly out the front door, trying his best not to let the rage and fear inside of him show itself. He truly hated losing control of his personal demons, but the thought of going back into the house and ripping Joe's throat out with his own teeth was running through him, and he liked the visual image it conjured.

It was his own fault, for daring to tempt the Powers That Be and allowing himself to think the dreaded words that had destroyed him before: "Life's been good lately." Mark had once again cursed himself, by making the fates look down, snap their fingers and exclaim, "THAT'S WHO WE FORGOT!!!"

He didn't know if he should scream, laugh, or just break into tears; his body trembled violently with the indecision.

When Mark reached his special place, They showed Themselves immediately, chattering with concern, trying to understand why he was so distraught. He explained, as best he could, that he loved the town and Them and his friends in town.

And Cassie. He explained that he would have to leave soon and They bristled with rage, Their silky hair thrashing about Their delicate bodies, demanding to know the cause of his forced move.

He explained in detail. When They promised to find a way to help him, he sensed the threat to Joe and made Them swear that no harm would come to the man. Reluctantly, the Folk gave Their word, which he knew was as good as gold.

They comforted him in silence, stroking his flesh and kissing his eyes with feathery lips. In time, he slept.

Cassie came to him again, holding him closely, that he could weep his sorrows upon her breast. She comforted him as well and promised that they would always be together. They made love a thousand times, furiously, passionately, sadly, each fearing that it might be the last time.

When he awoke, the sun was hiding just beyond the horizon. He ran all the way to the house he so desperately wanted to think of as home and dressed with a wild urgency. He made the bus with minutes to spare, never knowing that his special friends had already made arrangements to keep him in town, near the woods with Them. Forever.

5

Robert Carter lived in Denver and had all of his life. Had you asked him directions to Summitville, the best he could have told you was that it was at least an hour's drive to the town. He had no idea where the town was located. It didn't show on many maps and even when it did, it was hidden by its tiny size.

Rob couldn't have cared less about Summitville. He had more important things to worry about on this particular night. Joe Howell was giving serious consideration to leaving the agency, moving to New York in the hopes of building a better life. He suspected that Joe could have a million dollars in his bank account and continue looking for that legendary treasure sought after by people the world over: The Better Life.

He didn't want to lose Joe. The man was a hell of a good worker. Unfortunately, Sonny Martin did not look at things in the same light.

Sonny was one of those men who couldn't find the forest for the trees in his way. He couldn't look at anything but the Big Picture. Details were not important to him as long as the work got done. He was, in short, a prick of monumental proportions. Rob fervently wished that he would just drop of a stroke and let the real world get on with its life.

He said so, aloud. When his wife, Amy, asked him to repeat himself, he did so with a relish. Amy knew the situation and had met both Sonny and Joe, she couldn't have agreed with him more. While sipping Budweiser number seven, they toasted the thought of the old fart passing away and, unknowingly, saved their lives.

The Folk could move like lightning when the need arose. They could leave the area where They lived for short times, if They needed to. They had run all the way to Denver intent on ripping the one called 'Rob' apart. He had given Them an idea that would end with the same result and prove much more amusing. It had been a very long time since They had actually scared a human to death. Oh, this would be a fine night. They needed the distraction; protecting the Chosen was hard work.

6

Sonny Martin hated women. He felt they had exactly one use in the world and that he could just as easily use his hand to take care of that little problem.

The only things he hated more than women, were men who didn't agree with his philosophy on the aforementioned. Not surprisingly, most men felt him just a tad too vocal to agree with him. On anything, with women right near the top of that list.

That was okay with Sonny. He didn't really care what any of them thought or felt as long as they didn't cross his path.

The only thing Sonny ever really cared about was power. Power to do as he felt, say as he felt and get away with both, was the most important thing in Sonny's life.

He'd left the orphanage in Tulsa when he was sixteen and never once looked back. He'd started working only a week later, when he reached Denver, and he had managed, as the years went past, to win his way to the top. If a few people got crushed underneath his feet in the process, all the better. It made those left standing realize that he was not a person to be taken lightly.

No one ever took Sonny lightly. At least no one who was still around. Oh, he'd never killed anyone, or caused them any actual physical harm; he'd just arranged for them to have incredible difficulty finding employment anywhere north of Florida. For all of his very obvious faults, Sonny had managed to make enough friends in the business to assure that. Sonny had a great deal of power.

Had Sonny heard of Joseph Howell's desire to leave the company, he would simply have laughed; a quick phone call would have destroyed the job opportunity and assured that Joe knew his place in the industry forever more. Not because Sonny really cared one way or the other, but because Sonny liked to flaunt his power as often as he could.

To look at the man, you wouldn't know any of these things. He was of average height, a little heavy and as plain as the day was long. His hair was a dirty blond color and fading from the crown of his head like a tide that refused to raise itself back up to the high mark. He even dressed in average clothes, all the better to fool people into a false sense that Sonny was an Okay Kind of Guy. That way, when the stomp of his foot came down, the sense of being crushed was all the greater.

The proudest moment in Sonny's life had been when he took the title of Executive Editor away from old man Carmody. He'd cackled happily for weeks, remembering how the bastard had squirmed under the knowledge that a man who didn't even have a high school diploma had pulled the red carpet out from under his Harvard Graduate, loafer enclosed feet.

Not surprisingly, Sonny didn't have any friends away from the industry. Nor did the friends he had ever bother to associate with him when he was away from the business. But Sonny honestly didn't care. He had Power and The Respect of His Peers. Well, at least he had power.

Take away Sonny's power and you had nothing. That was something that Sonny learned the hard way, some twenty minutes later. That was how long it took Them to find his house in the hills. Even by Their standards, it was a beautiful building; very modern, with its huge bay windows of tinted glass and its lovely manicured lawn. It rested majestically in the cleft of two small hills, situated so that the sun rose to its front and set to its back, thus giving Sonny the ability to have the light of day on him for as long as possible (he could then convince himself that the sun did indeed rise and fall to his beck and call. It enhanced his sense of power). The house was crowned by four stone chimneys, in which a fire burned constantly throughout the latter part of autumn and all the way through the cold Colorado winters. They were powered by gas, thus allowing Sonny to believe that he had power over that most powerful of the four elements, fire.

They planned to change all that. They could read Sonny as if he were a book. Take away his illusions of control...

7

Sonny sat, as he always did, in his recliner watching the television. At the present time, he was staring at Vanna. Lord, but wouldn't he like to spin her wheels. He listened to her honey coated voice and actually thought that a woman who looked like that might make him change his mind about the weaker sex. Then again, he thought, maybe he could make her his personal little love-toy and use her as often as he liked. If she gave him any lip, he'd just slap her around and go about his business with the next good lookin' bimbo he ran across.

He was watching her spin the letters on a puzzle that he knew he could have gotten, when the power went out in the house. Vanna was gone and so was his ability to see. He didn't like to be in the dark, about anything. Grumbling to himself, he stood and fumbled his way towards the cellar door.

The wind outside his house made him remember why he didn't much like the dark. It sounded too much like his mother's wheezing breaths in the last weeks of her life. He'd hated those sounds, they made him realize that he was losing control of the situation; his mother couldn't very well take him to the store for ice cream if she couldn't even get out of bed. She didn't have any money for him to go by himself, it had all gone into the various drugs she had to take just to stay alive. For all the good they had done her.

He found the doorknob on his seventh try and walked carefully down the stairs. The wooden steps creaked as he walked and he could feel the skin on his body pull into bumps of chilled flesh. Suddenly he wasn't so sure about going down to the fuse box; what if there was something waiting for him at the bottom?

His mind flashed back to the punishment center in the orphanage. It too was in the cellar, far toward the back. The punishment for any crime against the orphanage had been silence and darkness, theoretically to teach you the error of your ways by giving you time to reflect on the horrid crime of wetting your bed or talking too loudly or just catching the attention of Sister Maria, the prune-faced hag who liked to carry a ruler at all times, the kind made of metal for that extra sting when it slapped across your butt or hands.

The memory sent terror through his heart and he tried not to think of

Jose Rodriguez

the janitor, the only living soul, other than those being punished, who ever went down to the cellar. Jose always took the guilty down there to be punished and Jose had his own special punishments that he eagerly added to those handed down by the nuns.

Take down them pants, Sonny Boy, I want to make you shiiiine.

He quickly shrugged the thoughts away and forced himself to continue on. He was In Control! He didn't have to think of that fat old slob

You tell anyone, boy and I'll think of something reeeall special, just for you

anymore. The man was long dead: he'd killed himself when the nuns had caught him with Billy Parker, an eight-year-old habitual bed wetter. He couldn't bother Sonny anymore. He couldn't bother anyone anymore.

Sonny found himself unable to step away from the memories, try as he might. Some things exist, that make a person powerless, no choice, no way around it. Some things just were.

That was when he first heard the whispers: *"Sonny…Sonnnnny…Where arrre youuuu boyyyyy…It's darrrk in here."*

Sonny Martin thought his heart would stop, actually felt his eyes grow larger in his head. *That sounded just like…But no, he was dead. Dead and hopefully rotting in his own private hell.*

"Don't you worrrry, IIII'llll find you. You know I couldn't forget youuuuu, you're my Ffffaaaavooooorrrrite…I like the way you mooaaan, when I put it to you."

Sonny Martin felt his bowels go watery, heard himself whimper like a six-year-old boy. The whispers sounded closer and Sonny wasn't surprised to find that he'd wet himself, warmth running down his leg like a lightning stroke.

Jose always had that effect on him when he was coming closer in the darkened room. He half expected to smell the tobacco-scented stench of the old man's breath.

Something caressed his inner thigh, in the darkened cellar. *"Feels like yer already goood and wet, boyyyy…Guessssss yer as ready as yer gonnna get."* The whisper was right next to his ear and it was carried on a Red Man-scented breeze.

Sonny couldn't move. His body refused to obey his frantic, whimpering thoughts. The only sound he could make was a high pitched wheeze, that feebly tried to become a scream, lodged deep in his throat. *"That ain't all you'll get lodged in yer throat, boy, iff'n you don't get them pants down, right now."* Cold sweat stung at his eyes and he flinched, breaking the paralysis that locked him in place.

With a shriek of fear that tore his throat like glass, he started flailing his arms, trying desperately to knock Jose away from him.

His hands encountered nothing, no resistance. He staggered towards where his memory told him the fuse-box was and whined like a whipped dog.

There! Victory! Now he could put the power back on, force the world to obey his commands again. He desperately flipped every switch back to the "On" position and felt relief wash through him, as sweet, warm light flashed through the room.

He was back In Control and the cellar he owned revealed itself to him, just exactly as he remembered it. Shaken, but In Control, he made his way back towards the stairs. Filled with the wild shaky energy of a full-scale adrenaline rush, he took the stairs three at a time and pulled the door open, the door to freedom, Power, Control.

The *Wheel's* credits were rolling, by the time he'd changed his pants and gone back to his seat. He didn't care. He was In Control. That was all that mattered. He reached for the TV Guide, wondering what he would watch. Don't Be Afraid of The Dark was playing on TBS, that actually got a nervous chuckle out of him.

The lights went out.

Sonny threw himself out of the chair, furious. God damn, but the power company would pay for this! He did not want to go back down there, nossiree Bob. But, if he wanted to watch the TV and be In Control, he had to move now.

He was most of the way to the cellar stairs, pulse blasting his temples and bladder threatening another mutiny, when the

voice came from behind him, accented by the firm, thick fin-
gered hand that grabbed his crotch and stroked lightly. *"Therrre
you are, I been lookin' forward ta this, Sonny Boy. Lookin' forward ta
this fer a long time."*

Terror took over and Sonny's mind went blank as he sailed
towards the cellar door. Possibly he should have wondered
why the door that he had closed firmly was now wide open. It
never crossed his mind. The last thing that Sonny Martin ever
felt was sweet relief as his neck snapped on the last stair, his
feet never having touched the first one. His last coherent
thought:

*Never get me again, you sonuvabitch. Never again, 'cause I am In
Control of this situation.*

8

Two days later at eight o'clock in the morning, Joe Howell was
promoted to Managing Editor by Rob, who had just been promoted to Executive Editor and really didn't want to lose Joe.
The raise, while not quite what he could have managed in
New York, was substantial.

At seven o'clock the same night, Joe Howell came home
with the news that he had been promoted. He never explained
why he had been promoted and neither of the people he loved
ever asked. He was grateful for that—he felt like enough of a
ghoul as it was.

As he went to sleep that night, Mark Howell said "Thank
you," aloud, in the quiet privacy of his room. He was well
asleep before the answering "You're welcome," was whispered
in his ear.

Chapter Five

1

The following night, the first storm of the season hit without so much as a flurry of snow to herald its coming. It slammed into the town, carried by the force of the first Siberian Express to kiss the Rockies since the winter before. For most of the town this was easy enough to accept, they had all seen them a dozen or more times before and the blinding winter's rage was nothing of great import, save for the possible need to leave for work at an earlier hour.

For some, it meant pulling out the snow-chains and prepping their vehicles for the long trek to Denver. For a few, it meant setting their snow plows into motion, in the endless and sedate fashion that they used every year, when the powdery white and seemingly innocent threat to motor safety fell from the heavens.

For Mark Howell, it was a wondrous dream come true. A part of him always longed to see the snow's fall, that part of him that lamented the need to move from the northern regions, inevitably, before the first real snow of the year. To hell with Dallas, Texas and New Orleans, Louisiana and Atlanta, Georgia. The best you could hope for in those places was a light frosting on the ground and the panicky screech of tires. There were too many drivers who had absolutely no concept of how dangerous even that gentle touch of winter could be, who tried to force their cars into high speed races to the office, instead of avoiding the inevitable game of bumper cars that most inexperienced drivers seemed intent on playing. He reveled in the knowledge that he was once again where real snow fell and the people knew, by God, how to drive through it safely. It had been years since he'd had the simple joy of making a snowball, instead of a slush ball.

He watched the flakes of ice drift lazily to the ground with the eyes of a five-year-old child and thrilled to think of how clean the world would look when the sun rose tomorrow.

It sometimes seemed like the fat boy, who had run so fast and hard to escape Tony and Pete, blundered into the woods and had his face cleaved open by gravity, had existed only in the far distant past. He turned away from the window and looked at himself in the mirror on the back of his bedroom door. For the first time, he really noticed all of the changes in his body: he was taller, and thinner than he could ever remember being. He had muscle definition for the first time in his life. He could actually count his ribs without using his finger to probe under the flabby sides of his chest.

He was looking pretty damn good and feeling even better than he looked. He noticed, almost as a passing thought, that he smiled more than he used to. So much, in fact, that his face had actually hurt for a small time, as muscles he almost never used had to go into play. The fat boy inside of him quailed, fearing that the dream would end and he'd wake up as heavy and homely as ever. He did his best to ignore the voice of the fat boy, but it wasn't always easy.

Fortunately, he could use the fat boy's defenses against their creator. He simply thought of pleasant things, like Cassie's sweet kiss and the fact that he would not be moving away from the same, and the whispered fat boy terrors faded to an acceptable level of mental background noise.

He smiled, thinking about the tricks he'd learned to drive away what his mother called 'the Blue Funks' and went back to looking out the bedroom window, watching the clear white spectacle of ice fall to the ground. He felt at peace and opted to enjoy the sensation, rather than try to force it away. It felt so good, just to be happy for a change, just to feel accepted and loved.

And in the quiet recesses of his mind, the fat boy howled his fears and raced wildly in his cage, trying to remind his captor of the first rule of emotional survival: *Never Be Happy!*

Never Let Your Guard Down, Because That's When They Can Hurt You The Most. His cries fell on deaf ears.

2

Tony had been considering his predicament for a few weeks: Pete and Andy were dead. That hurt, a lot. They weren't exactly close friends, but they were all he really had, aside from his uncle, and he was too ashamed of what he'd become to risk staring into the man's eyes for more than a few seconds at a time. Contrary to popular belief, Tony wasn't really happy with the decisions he'd made in his own life, nor was he one of the inner clique of beautiful people. Despite being reasonably attractive, he bore the same curse that Mark Howell suffered from: he wasn't really accepted in Summitville. His mother was born in town, sure enough, but Tony, like all of his siblings, was born in Chicago. He was fine to hang with, but few people considered him worth getting to know. He was an outsider.

The girl he most wanted to be with was now associating with the boy he could most likely call his worst enemy. Certainly he was the only one who had ever stood up to Tony in the hallway, let alone thrown the first punch. All in all, it could be said in complete sincerity that Tony Scarrabelli was a very unhappy person.

He couldn't help but wonder about the occurrences that led to his predicament. If he were to be completely honest, he had to admit that he'd brought it on himself to a large degree. He'd never given Howell a chance to prove himself, either as a friend or as a foe. He had simply taken a dislike to the quiet, overweight new kid and started in on him as he had with any person that didn't make him comfortable. Part of it was simply that he was the new kid and that made it Tony's right to mess with him. Part of it was that the guy asked for it. He walked as quietly as possible and tried to hide in the shadows with his head tucked between his shoulders; he may as well put a sign on his head in bright pink letters that said, "I'm shy and don't wish to be bothered by you, please go away." As open an invitation to abuse as Tony had ever seen. Okay, so maybe he'd been a little rough the day Howell got the balls up to hit him, but he'd also been flying high on the Patrick Wilson Speed-ball Express; maybe if he had been straight that day, things wouldn't have turned out as badly as they did.

If he'd been completely honest with himself, he would have admitted that he'd been a prick. Alas, Tony was almost never that honest with himself. Very few people ever really are. So he blamed Mark for a great deal of woe in his life. But, he couldn't just trash the little shit; he had to be subtle.

Tony wasn't stupid, at least not when he was his own boss and not the slave of whatever Patrick's drug of the week was; in truth, he was really quite crafty in his own way, rather like a stalking panther. Mister Scarrabelli's only son was very much a predator when he felt the need to be one. Right now, the need was strong indeed.

So, it was time to make a few changes, fix the rules to his advantage. He'd have to cancel the chemical fun, immediately if not sooner; Cassie hated dope users. Secondly, he had to be nice, to Tyler and even to Howell. He could do that, he was nice to his three sisters, even when he felt like smashing them in the head with his fist for being such snotty little bitches half of the time. (That was okay in his father's eyes, his father seemed to believe that it was almost the sacred duty of rich WASP girls to be snotty little bitches, and claimed that Tony's mom was a perfect example of the fact. Tony had little doubt that that was why she had a stud boyfriend in the City. She and his father argued about her lovers often enough, and his dad had a very loud voice.)

Then, when the time was right, he'd make his move with Cassie and all would be well in the kingdom of Tony. First thing tomorrow, he'd put his plan into action. He smiled at the thought and then grimaced at the loss of the pharmacy he was about to flush: out of sight, out of mind.

3

Mark's built-in sonar warned him trouble was coming his way and he whipped his head around, just in time to see Tony coming up on his left. The school day only barely started, and already trouble was brewing. Tyler and Cassie saw him too; all three of them tensed, fully expecting the shit to hit the fan.

"Listen, uh, Mark, I need to talk to you." Tony was right in his face and smiling shyly. Mark trusted him and his pearly whites about as far as he'd trust a shark; just because he no longer allowed himself to be prey, didn't mean his instincts for danger had faded. Tony Scarrabelli was most definitely dangerous. With a skeptical look on his face, he shrugged his shoulders and forced his fists not to ball up. "Speak away."

Tony did a passable job of being apologetic. "I'm here to apologize to you. I've been a real asshole and I'm sorry."

Mark and his companions stopped dead, stunned by the words that had come out of Tony's mouth.

Tyler was the first to recover. "Tell me," he squeaked, "somebody please tell me, that I misunderstood. It sounded like Tony Scarrabelli apologized to Mark. Tony Scarrabelli doesn't even apologize to teachers fer Chrissakes."

Tony looked over at Tyler and Tyler prepared to die for his acid tongue. "I guess I owe you an apology too, Tyler. I haven't exactly been nice to you either, since about the third grade."

Tyler looked him dead in the face and spoke with great sincerity in his nasal voice. "Doctor only give you a week to live, Tony? Or did the pod people from Planet X replace you with an almost but not quite perfect duplicate?"

Tony noticed absently, that Cassie was looking offended at what Tyler had just said and was glad that *something* was going right in this conversation; Jesus, what the hell had he done to these guys, to cause such hesitancy on their part? *Oh, nothing much,* his mind responded, *you've just been beating the shit out of Tyler since you were both eight.* He accepted that voice well enough, but did his best to block out its next comment, almost succeeding and hating himself a little for the cowardice that voice revealed. *And who do you think left that huge fucking scar down the side of Howell's face the last time you and your good buddies tried to pound him through the ground?* He tried to grin and actually got embarrassed as he thought about the scar and the half-memories of what they'd done that day. He continued his apology. "Look, I know you don't have any reason to trust me on this, but I mean it. I'm really sorry for all the shit that came down. I know it was mostly my fault."

"Mostly?" came the immediate reply from Tyler, who arched his eyebrows and peered over his glasses, like a teacher in the process of driving home a disciplinary lesson. "Mostly?" he asked again, to insure that he had made his point.

Tony looked over at him and for the first time in his life, made Tyler uncomfortable with words. "You have a mouth that could get the Pope after you with a baseball bat, Tyler. As often as not you started in on me."

Flustered, Tyler conceded the point with a smile and his usual verbal assault, this time softened by the truth of Tony's words. "It was strictly self defense. I was just cleaning it, officer, and it went off, *boom* and he was lying on the ground in front of me."

Tony held out his hand and waited solemnly for Tyler to accept it. "Can we just forget it, try to work around it? Hell, maybe we could even be friends, I hear you're an okay guy, when you're in bed and your hands aren't under the covers."

Tyler laughed at that one and before his hand was even joined with Tony's, Tony knew he'd won the easy victory. Now came the tough one. After he finished shaking hands with Tyler, he turned to face Mark again. This was where it would get rough. He didn't have any pat answers for any accusation that Mark might make, they were all accurate. As his Uncle Phil was fond of saying; "Here there be Tygers."

He held his hand out again, this time to Mark, and waited. His eyes locked with Howell's and he realized that Mark was almost as tall as he was; whatever the boy was thinking, he hid it behind cold blue eyes. Tony started reassessing his nemesis, unaware he was even doing it.

They both stood that way for what seemed to Tony like hours and finally he felt Mark's hand clasp very firmly around his own. They shook hands solemnly, warring factions ending a long feud. Cassie's smile made them feel like they had both done the right thing. As always, her smile made just about anything seem okay.

4

The sight that greeted Mark as he walked into the Basilisk, would have had him losing his mind only a week earlier; Tony Scarrabelli and P. J. Sanderson were engaged in a warm, friendly, conversation. Beside him, Cassie was just as floored. "Son of a bitch," she whispered incredulously. "How do they know each other?"

"Beats the hell out of me," was Mark's earnest reply. He pushed the door open and continued with "Let's find out."

The two of them walked hand in hand, into the sprawling chaos that was the inside of the Basilisk, fully prepared for almost anything. P. J. looked over at them with pure delight in his expressive eyes and Tony looked over with a face that mirrored their thoughts. "Mark, Cassie, how delightful to see the both of you. Mark, have I ever introduced you to my nephew, Tony Scarrabelli? Tony, this is the lad I told you about, the only man I know who can match me and possibly beat me, when it comes to bad monster movie trivia, Mark Howell." He looked at all three of them, with great enthusiasm and walked over to give Cassie her usual peck on the cheek. "I imagine you already know Cassie, you both go to school together, if I'm not mistaken.

"Tony has graciously volunteered to drive us into Boulder for the convention." A week ago, the news would have destroyed Mark. The man he cared for so dearly was related to

Tony. He found himself oddly glad he'd never revealed who pulped his face at the beginning of the school year. He didn't think P. J. would have been thrilled by the revelation of his assailants' identities, not when he was related to one of them.

Tony was doing the driving and they would be together for several hours, most of that time in a cramped car. My, how the world can turn around, in only five short days.

Looking at the two of them, in the same room, at the same time, Mark could see the similarities. Same gray eyes, same dark brown hair, even the same twist to the smiles on their faces. He'd never even guessed. You could have knocked him over with a feather. "We've met, P. J., but I didn't even know you had a nephew."

5

The trip to Boulder was pleasant and Tony came across a startling realization as he drove his uncle and the others: Mark Howell was a nice guy. He was funny, energetic, and obviously very close to Uncle Phil. Suddenly, plans of retribution started fading away, like a foul stench will fade when forced to meet fast flowing air.

Unknown to Tony, Mark's thoughts were actually quite similar. He hadn't thought Tony capable of smiling without having his foot planted squarely on someone's throat. The world was simply too full of surprises. He looked over at Cassie, who was involved in a discussion of Stephen King's *Dark Tower* series with P. J. Again he was caught by how beautiful she was, the way her hair was highlighted by the sun and the way her skin had of almost glowing when she was involved in anything that made her happy.

Mark had been saving his money almost since the first day that he had started working, just for today. He was looking forward to blowing the whole wad on Cassie. He knew just what to get her too. There were bound to be at least three or four stands that dealt exclusively with autographed novels;

he'd get her a copy of the book of her choice and get himself a few as well. The list of authors he wanted signatures from was immense.

He felt the car turning and pulled himself away from his other thoughts. There it was, the Imperial Hotel, hosting the Third Annual Screamicon, with special Guest of Honor, P. J. Sanderson and a list of guests that stretched across three sheets of paper.

It was the biggest convention he'd seen since the last one he'd attended in San Diego. All around him were the lines of people preparing for one or another show, or waiting to buy their tickets for the convention. Mark had followed P. J.'s advice and all four of them had purchased tickets in advance (P. J. of course, didn't have to worry about that, he was a guest this year); the line they had to wait in was less than a twentieth the length of the one for those without the sense to pre-register. In only twenty minutes they were eagerly looking over the scheduled listings and seeking out the various attractions.

After the first hour the noise, the people and the entire building all seemed to blur. There was too much to see and too much to do. The time fairly flew by.

6

True to his word, Mark managed to blow every penny he had before the end of the convention. He was broke and delirious and weighted down with hard back copies of a dozen authors' novels for Cassie and himself. The only sad part for him, was that he couldn't find a hard back copy of *Stirrings* for P. J. to sign; he'd had to be happy with a paperback on that one.

Possibly the highlight of the convention had been when P. J., as the Guest of Honor, along with a few comic writers, had been on a two hour panel on breaking into the field; it changed Mark's life. By the time the panel was over, Mark had decided to write a novel and try to break into the field himself. P. J. applauded his enthusiasm and recommended not getting his hopes too far above his possible goals; he cautioned pessimism when it came to actually selling a story and warned that it had taken him almost four years to get his first story sold. Mark was undaunted and pointed out that he had a solid inside connection, in his stepfather. "Don't think that an inside connection alone will get you in," warned P. J. "If the company doesn't see you as a viable risk, they'll just say no and not all the whining and wheedling in the world will change their minds." Upon seeing the first signs of doubt crease his young friend's forehead, P. J. scolded himself quietly and remembered that Mark was essentially a mass of insecurities. "But, I have faith in you, Mark. If you really want it, you'll get it. It just might take a lot more work than you want to think about. I'll be of any assistance that I can, you know that, just don't expect miracles." Mark smiled again and P. J. knew that what he had said was true, he would help in any way he could. He'd grown to love the boy like a son.

7

By the time that Christmas had come and gone and the New Year had passed, Mark had learned the truth about writing a novel; it just wasn't as easy as it looked. But by Easter, his first novel had been submitted and accepted, by Ali Hathaway. Truth be told, the novel would have never been possible without the diligent and energetic P. J. to help him through the rough spots. Mark tried to insist on P. J. getting half of the credit, but the man would have none of it. "You wrote the story, you came up with the story, and you should get credit for the story. I just cleared away a few thousand run-on sentences and helped you stay in the proper tense. If you want, you can mention me in the dedication and give me a signed copy of the book," was the only answer he would get from the author and nothing could change the man's mind.

The dedication was another story entirely and he spent long grueling hours working over who should and shouldn't be considered, before coming down to Cassie, Joe and his Mom, Tyler and of course, P. J. Sanderson. As an afterthought, he threw in Tony.

The novel, called *When Stalks the Scarecrow*, was short by the standards of those he idolized. It was only three hundred and fifty pages, but it was, by Mark's standards, one hell of a lot of work. And he was damn proud of it. It was due to be published in September, just in time for the Halloween rush. At Joe's insistence, the advance payment was immediately put into the bank, for college (minus four hundred dollars, which was promptly blown on various books and dinner for a small herd of celebrators).

Mark felt that life was going very well indeed. He'd sold a novel; he was going steady with the most beautiful girl he'd ever met; he was now on good terms with Tony, who turned out to be a nice guy after all; his family was staying where they were and his mentor had now officially called him a writer. Not much was wrong with the world in Mark's eyes. Sadly, he'd forgotten the Fat Boy's number one rule; it could have prepared him for the events that were yet to come.

It could have prepared him for the murder.

8

Evan Wilde was not a sane man. He hadn't been for quite some time. Certainly not since his last three year trip to Ryker's up in New York. He had to admit that he'd certainly done enough to get himself there, what with the pimping and dealing that went on until he'd been nailed by an undercover cop.

He was a man with a purpose and his purpose was vengeance. Nobody in their right mind would have skipped out on payments to 'The Wildman,' but that was just precisely what Patrick Wilson had done. Not that Evan wasn't forgiving, he could have let the little pissant slide and waited patiently. If Wilson hadn't given him lip when he asked where his money was.

He knew the dork had been sampling too many of his own candies when Wilson had called him a "freaked out asshole," and could even have forgiven that, if he hadn't then threatened to kill Evan, if he ever saw him again. That was just pushing him too goddamn far. No More Mister Nice Guy, not this time. The real problem was that he needed to have Patrick alive if he was going to recoup his losses.

Evan had his sources, even in a little piece of shit town like Summitville—he knew just the ticket. Time to say good bye to one Tyler Wilson, little brother to a really stupid asshole, who didn't know when to shut his dumb fuck mouth. Evan smiled thinly as he pulled up in front of the Wilson house.

The place was huge, easily worth half a million or more in Denver. Evan marveled at how a shit head that lived in a place like this could possibly be dumb enough to skip his payments. Probably just did it for kicks. "Well, we'll give you some kicks asshole, hope you really like this one."

Four kids were coming around the corner of the house, "Like clock-work," he thought aloud. "Every day, like fuckin' clock-work." His informant had told him that the little brother and his friends went swimming every day, right after school and that they called it quits at five o'clock, religiously. That left over an hour before the parents came home from wherever the hell they went daily, and gave plenty of time for a hasty get away.

Casually, as if he'd been coming here every day for years, he got out of his Corvette. With the same practiced ease, he pulled out the sawed off shotgun and started to aim.

9

Mark was laughing, along with Tony and Cassie, at Tyler's latest antics. Today he was doing his impression of Mrs. Carlson, a teacher best known for her stuttering tirades, whenever she lost her temper, which was as often as once a period. Somehow he even made his thin face imitate the bloated features on what he liked to call her potato head. He had the curl of her flabby lip down and the way her right eyebrow ticked up and down. "Will y-y-you p-p-p-p-leeeeeaaasse be qu-qu-quui-et!" he howled shrilly, flapping his arms in pantomime of the genuine article. "This iss an imp-p-p-p-oortant quiz! Half of your grade d-d-d-d-de-pendss on these d-d-d-ddaily test scores!" The sad thing to Mark was that he didn't even have to exaggerate the stutter; whenever Carlson got angry, her lips just refused to listen to her.

When Mark saw the Corvette pull up, he was suitably impressed. Even in this town, a classic like that was enough to draw a person's eye. A '69 bubble back 'Vette was nothing to sneer at: drooling seemed infinitely more appropriate.

He was even considering going over to the driver when the man got out of his muscle car and expressing his appreciation, until he saw the driver. He looked feral, with hair that was groomed meticulously and a five o'clock shadow the same black color. He was dressed very well, but still gave off an air someone who liked to mess with people for the simple sake of messing with them; his immediate impression was of an inner city boy who had moved to the west, simply to avoid looking like an inner city boy. His eyes, even at a substantial distance, threatened a person with every jerky little move. Mark was fairly certain, that if he'd been an animal, he would have been born a badger, or a wolverine.

He bared his fangs only moments later, when Mark saw the sawed off shotgun being aimed in his general direction. Suddenly the car didn't seem all that nice, neither did the driver.

Mark reached over and pushed hard at Cassie, without even thinking about it. He tried to say something, anything to warn the others, but his mouth had gone dry and his tongue refused to work.

Cassie's sounds of protest over her rough treatment were drowned out by the report from the shotgun and Mark's world went red as the pellets tore across his chest and arm. The pain was blinding and he was vaguely aware of crying out as he fell towards to ground.

The sound of the first shot immediately got the attention of his friends, who stood absolutely still like birds mesmerized by a cobra. Mark was far too busy rolling on the ground, trying to put the fire in his chest and arm out to notice much of anything.

Mister Inner-city started to aim again as Mark became aware of the motion around him; motion caused not by his friends, but by the Folk. Cassie backed frantically away from the tiny creatures, thinking at first that they were rats, as they swarmed from the bushes near the house. Tony was staring down the barrel of a twelve gauge shotgun and was completely incapable of motion. *Who would have thought the barrel was so BIG from all the way over there?* And Tyler was looking at Mark, fascinated by the little creatures that covered him with Their own tiny forms, apparently intent on stopping the next round of shot with Their own bodies.

Evan 'Wildman' Wilde never even saw them coming. He was enjoying the look on Tony's face too much. Tony reminded him of about a hundred kids he'd run across and he was going to enjoy wiping his handsome rich-boy face right the fuck off of his skull.

His finger was starting to pull on the trigger when the first of the Folk made a spectacular leap and sank Its teeth into his testicles.

Evan Wilde screamed with the raw force of a hurricane as the pain ran straight to his brain. He looked down and pulled the renovated Winchester's trigger, simultaneously. Luck was with Tony and the Wildman's hand lifted away from him, as he pulled; the only casualty of the blast was a rather expensive storm window and a few photos on the mantel of the fireplace in the house's den.

Cassie and the rest looked on as Evan Wilde danced across the yard. The Folk rode him like a bucking horse, using Their claws and teeth for purchase, as he flailed wildly. As with many people who experience severe car wrecks, the four people watched intently, their minds absorbing every minute detail,

as the Folk tore the screaming man apart. They watched as he
finally fell to the ground and they watched as the tiny creatures literally dismembered him. The worst however, was the
mixture of the man's screams and the hissing laughter of the
creatures that worked him over; it was like the sound of a
world collapsing, Evan's world. The last they actually saw of
his face was the terrified expression of a man who couldn't
understand what he'd done wrong, who couldn't understand
why his life was leaking out of a thousand cuts, or why no one
would help him.

The creatures moved with frightening speed, tearing past
the startled foursome and into the woods, before any of them
could get a good long look. The sound of Their laughter faded
into the rustle of the wind and then was gone. The only evidence that They had been there was a rapidly cooling skeleton
covered with thinly shredded pieces of raw meat. For once,
even Tyler was speechless.

10

The wounds were painful, but minor, and Tim Posten pointed
out to Mark that he was remarkably lucky to be alive. "No
kiddin', I thought he'd blown my arm off. Ouch! Shit, that
hurts!" The paramedic laughed lightly at that and pulled the
last of the pellets free, dropping it into a small plastic bag,
along with seventeen others just like it.

"Hey, at least you can feel it. I've been known to do my
share of hunting and I've seen what this stuff'll do to a full-
grown deer. Trust me, you got off very lucky." He poured the
contents of one of several bottles of fluid over Mark's arm
and Mark practically howled at the chemical fire that danced
over his already aggravated nerves. "Now that I'll let you
slide on, shit's twice as foul as alcohol in the pain department.
But, it works."

Mark managed a smile and looked over at Tim Posten.
The man had sandy blond hair and twinkling eyes and made

him think of what Santa Claus must have looked like when he was younger, belly and all. He couldn't believe the luck of having a doctor living so close by and one that was willing to skip out on his date, a truly stunning woman at that, just to fix what was really a minor problem. Then again, it sure as hell hadn't looked minor. Mark's t-shirt was soaked through with blood, by the time the man had come running across the street with his bag. "Listen, thanks a lot, I mean I thought I was gonna die there."

Tim looked over at him and winked. "Hell of a way to impress the chicks, maybe you'll even score huh?" Mark blushed furiously and Tim patted him on his uninjured left shoulder. "Don't worry about it, I took this little oath, see, and it says I have to fix up macho men who step in front of loaded shot guns." Looking over at Cassie and then back to Mark, he grinned widely and thumped Mark on the knee. "Just name the first one after me, okay?"

He got up with that and started walking towards Sheriff Hanson and another man. Mark was sure there'd be hell to pay for this one. For reasons he couldn't place, he felt responsible for the corpse lying under a canvas cover not far away. The man with Hanson looked over at him, a puzzled look on his face.

11

Rick Lewis watched as Mark Howell came towards him. Next to him, Chuck Hanson tensed, ever so slightly; obviously Chuck hadn't yet broken himself of his natural dislike of strangers. He'd probably have reacted the same way if the boy headed their way had been six years old.

The boy looked familiar, but he couldn't place where from to save his life. He had cold blue eyes that seemed open and friendly, but at the same time seemed to hide dark secrets. His hair was moderately long and as dark as midnight. The most striking thing about him was the scar that ran across his right cheek and seemed to pull his face, even when relaxed, into a contemptuous sneer. It wasn't that the scar was overly prominent, it just seemed that way on a face so devoid of lines, almost devoid of emotion. The forensics specialist was fairly certain that he'd seen his face before, if only he could remember where...

The center of his attention looked directly at him and smiled sheepishly. "Hi, Doctor Lewis. I don't know if you remember me, I'm Mark Howell, you took out my stitches, last year."

Rick forced himself not to drop his jaw. He was stunned by the changes that six months had made on Mark: he'd lost easily twenty five pounds and whatever had been left to lose had distributed itself in the form of muscle, on a much taller boy then he remembered. About four inches taller; he was almost six feet in height now. Realizing that he was being rude, Rick finally forced his mouth to work, "Hi, yeah, of course I remember you. It's good to see you again."

He shook his head, it just couldn't be the same kid. Christ, the difference a few months could make in a pubescent. "Yeah, you're Joe's son. Looks like you got yourself patched up well enough. Hurt much?"

Mark looked uncomfortable and beside him, Rick could feel Chuck's attention switch over to the wounded teen. "Uh, not really, I guess I'm still having trouble getting used to bandages though. They make my skin feel like it's being stretched."

Mark looked over to Hanson and grinned sheepishly again. "You must be Sheriff Hanson, Tim told me you might need to speak with me." Tim, in the meantime, was looking over at the covered body with a mild interest.

Hanson looked down from his considerable height and tipped his ever-present cowboy hat in greeting. "If that's all right with you. I just need to hear your story on what happened over here." He looked around, at the other three teens and their parents. No surprise, the parents were all looking at

Mark with barely veiled suspicion. "We can wait," he paused as he continued looking around, "until your folks get here, if you want to."

Mark shrugged and immediately winced: a few of the small pellets had gone into muscle on their way in. "That's all right, Joe's probably still in the city and if I know Mom, she's still shopping for her art supplies. Ask away, I'm at your disposal."

Rick was having a little trouble with the way Mark talked; he didn't seem nervous, even shaken, by his injuries, or the corpse that lay just a few feet away. Little alarms were going off in his head. He studied the boy as furtively as he could, not wanting to give anything away. *There's something* wrong *with him. Something* very *wrong.*

Chuck Hanson had pulled out a small note pad and was writing down everything Mark said in a crisp, precise short hand, that Rick doubted anyone but the Sheriff could have hoped to understand. The Sheriff asked few questions, only asking for elaboration where it was necessary. In a matter of ten or so minutes, the Sheriff said his thanks and offered a squad car, should Mark feel he needed a lift home. Mark declined and waved to his friends before walking home. It was only when the boy was heading away, that the slightest jump in his step gave his nervousness away.

For reasons he would have been hard pressed to explain, Mark Howell made Rick uneasy. There was something not right about him. He didn't know what it was, but he suspected that the boy might have answers to a good deal of Rick's questions. Mark Howell was a youth who needed watching and Rick was certain that he would be watched, if not by him, then by the Sheriff.

12

Charles Emery Hanson was, by his very nature, a suspicious man. He was also a very subtle man; a talent that he made the most of, considering his line of work. Very few people knew him well enough to be able to say that he was subtle, cunning even. Doctor Richard Lewis was one of those very few.

He'd known Richard for a good number of years, since he'd gone off to college in Denver. When they'd first met, he had seen in Rick the potential friend that the man had later become. Richard had always been there, to help him with his mistakes and to solve the problems that Chuck just couldn't solve, few that they were. In all that time Richard had never asked for anything in return, until now.

"I can't put my finger on it, Chuck, but I just keep getting the feeling that Mark Howell is involved with the crap that's going on in this town." They'd had this conversation before, but the use of an actual name was a new element. Richard had pointed out the strange anomalies in the case of Tanya Billingsley and had pointed out that similar strange proteins could be found in minute traces in the blood all around Pete Larson, the boy that had been so savagely torn apart, last Halloween.

"So what the hell makes you think the Howell kid has anything to do with all of this?" Chuck looked over at him with brows lowered, a sign that he was angry or that he was thinking. The two expressions were completely interchangeable.

"Call it a hunch, okay? I just can't get away from the fact that he'd been seen arguing with Peter Larson the same night that Larson died. Or the fact that he was injured in a fight with Andy Phillips, the night that Phillips turned himself in for the murder of the Billingsley girl. It's nothing solid, but I think that he's involved."

"I looked over the bones of the guy who took a pot shot at Howell, Evan Wilde. I found traces of that protein again. Chuck, off the record, I have no idea where the hell that protein was produced. It defies all of the laws of nature." He looked genuinely puzzled, his brows knitted in concentration, as if even now he was trying to place where he could have seen the stuff before.

The sheriff sighed, wanting peace and quiet and getting strange stories from his friend instead. "How does it 'defy nature'? You never have answered that."

"I can identify it as a protein, that was easy enough." He looked over at Chuck, with something akin to fear in his eyes. "But I can't break it down any further; it doesn't seem to have any form of DNA configuration and the damn stuff still seems to have a life of its own, after several months worth of examination. Chuck, the stuff's still alive after almost seven months. Do you have any idea how rare that is? It hasn't had anything to eat, it hasn't decomposed, it hasn't multiplied, it hasn't even moved very much. But it's still alive on a molecular level and nothing has even attempted to infest it. If I can isolate what makes this stuff tick and where it comes from, I could be the most famous doctor since Pasteur."

There was the crux of the 'Protein Mystery'. Chuck wasn't stupid, not by anyone's standards, and he realized that his friend wasn't about to send the protein samples to another lab. Someone else might get the same ideas, might beat him to a discovery that could make or break him as a research specialist, which Chuck knew good and damned well was what Rick had always wanted to be. He'd only come to Summitville because Chuck had asked him to and pointed out that he'd have a great deal of time for research in a town where most of the illnesses were never worse that strep throat, and the vast majority of deaths were from natural causes. "So what do you think these proteins are? I mean they have to be related to something out there, don't they?"

Rick looked at him for several moments, long enough to make the sheriff uncomfortable. Chuck looked away and lit up a Camel unfiltered with his thick, yellow-stained fingers. When Rick finally started to talk, he looked back at his college roommate. "Chuck, I like to think of myself as a man of Science (You could hear the capital 'S' in the way he said it), I like to try to forget about ghosts and goblins and all that other shit that you hear about as a kid." Rick looked away from his friend and Chuck registered the uneasiness in the man's soul, as he continued, "If I didn't know that that kind of crap was for the birds, I'd think I was actually studying a physical example of ectoplasm." He looked over at Chuck again and silently begged his friend to laugh in his face, to get him away from the crazy thoughts that he was having. "Ectoplasm," he said soberly, "is the stuff that supernatural entities are supposed to build their bodies from. Entities like ghosts and goblins."

Chuck wanted desperately to laugh, but his friend's face, and the bodies he'd recently seen, and the haunted look in Andy Phillip's eyes as he made his terrified confession, took all of the humor out of the situation.

Unlike his friend the good doctor, Charles Emery Hanson had a healthy respect for those things that existed in darker corners of Man's history. He'd seen them before, when he was just a child himself; the night that his grandfather had come to say good-bye to him, four minutes before the phone call came and told his parents that his mother's father had died in his sleep. Died in the southern California home where he'd retired, several hundred miles away from Summitville, where Chuck was living at the time.

Chuck Hanson shivered and looked at his friend. They stared without words for a long time; neither could find the right words anyway. They were too involved in their individual thoughts.

Chapter Six

1

Tyler was having a great deal of trouble accepting what was happening in his world, or put another way, The World According To Ty was seriously fucked up. Things like what had happened that afternoon simply did not occur in Ty's World. He ran over the sequence of events again, paying attention to all of the little details that he had not consciously noted before.

Mark, Cassie and Tony had all come over to go swimming, as they did at least four times a week. Okay so far, no major problems, except maybe that Cassie was starting to look as often at Tony as she did at Mark and even that wasn't really a danger yet; nothing that would immediately surface and cause friction in their little group. Once again, Tyler's acid wit and beguiling charm had awed all around him and Tony had become a good deal less defensive when it came to his remarks, so he didn't lose teeth or hair as often as he used to.

So, that part of the day had gone properly and even school before that had been relatively tame. It was the shotgun that had started the world on its little spin into the Twilight Zone; shit like that just didn't happen in Summitville and certainly not to Tyler Wilson. The worst thing about that was that he'd seen the psycho before, in Denver, when his brother had taken him Christmas shopping. Patrick seemed to think Mister Twelve Gauge was an okay guy and he'd even seemed okay, when Patrick had introduced him.

So why was he taking up hunting and using Mark Howell as the catch of the day? Or, maybe he'd been aiming at Cassie, or at Tyler.

Tyler flopped over on the bed and turned face to face with the Halloween photograph that they had all posed for, along with that writer friend of Mark's, Sanderson. Ty looked closely at the photo, seeing the differences that had occurred in Mark since the shot had been taken; puberty was certainly being generous with his friend. My, my, how well Mark had filled out in such a short time. But, back to the problem at hand.

Even the gun-toting fruit loop wasn't that hard to swallow, shit like that happened all over this great country every day and in towns even smaller than this one. No, the really freaked out stuff started when he pulled the trigger. Tyler had seen the motion of Patrick's friend and even turned that way before the trigger was pulled. He would have called out to Cassie, but he didn't even have time to register what he'd seen, before Mark went into motion.

He'd befriended Mark on his first day in the town, even went and helped the Howells move in, just so he could get to know the new kid and warn him about the legendary Asshole Patrol—*the mostly deceased Asshole Patrol, mustn't forget about that little aspect of the picture*—before he had the displeasure of meeting them for himself. He had, truth be told, known him longer than anyone in town, excluding his parents. He'd learned all of Mark's characteristic motions and attitudes within three weeks; knowing how people worked was one of those special gifts that Ty had and tried not to abuse, though he often failed. Mark was nice, quiet, and clumsy. He was not overly perceptive, forceful, or blindingly fast on his feet; facts is facts, folks. But, when he moved, when he turned and knocked Cassie to the ground, he started into motion at the same time that the trigger on the shot gun was pulled; he stepped forward, knocked Cassie a good ten feet and was mostly turned towards the trigger man, before the blast of pellets hit. The look on his face, just before the fiery shot hit him was a look that Tyler would never forget. He'd thought Mark looked fearsome when Pete had racked him in the balls, but nothing like he had today. His face had seemed supernaturally mobile. The way his lips contorted, the way his eyes had almost seemed to flare with a light of their own, sent the chills through Tyler's heart.

Then the buck shot had slammed into Mark's arm and chest and the fearsome visage had magically transformed into his friend's face, contorted by white hot needles of pain, and he had fallen to the ground. Before Tyler could do anything at all, before he could make his brain and body work as one, those little things had come from everywhere. They shot out from under bushes, from up in the trees, even from the freaking sewer drain on the curb, and made the movements of Mark Howell look like a man swimming through tar.

Tony had been staring with great interest down the barrel of the illegal weapon, when the creatures made their move. Cassie was looking at the little things and at Mark, who had so rudely pushed her down to the ground, with confusion and terror; Tyler was fairly certain he heard her whisper "Rats, they're just rats," but he couldn't be one hundred percent certain. Tyler hadn't been so lucky. His quiet way of assessing everything, every iota of information, was as much a curse as a blessing. He'd seen the little monsters all too well, thank you very fucking much.

His biggest problem, was that he was absolutely certain that monsters had to be much larger than two or three inches in height. They always were in the movies, by God, and they should be in real life, if they had to show up. He couldn't stifle the panicky little giggle that erupted from his throat, as he remembered the tiny beasts. If they hadn't had such incredible ferocity, he could almost picture them being marketed as action figures for ten-year-olds, or as the newest item in the industry of home pets. Dammit, monsters should at least be tall enough to look frightening.

He remembered the creatures literally blanketing Mark, and had been about to try to save his friend, when the creatures looked up at him. Not all of them, just three or four, but the looks on their faces had convinced him that size really wasn't important when it came to monsters. That look had stunned him into immobility, that look had told him that he was already in a good deal of trouble and it would only get worse if he moved towards his friend. He got smart, he stayed right the hell where he was.

Having decided that he really didn't want to stare at the deadly little faces, he opted to remember the gunslinger; oh my, but wasn't *that* a mistake. He'd gotten more than an eye-ful of the creatures crawling all over Patrick's schizoid friend: he'd gotten a free look into the gates of hell. The sad thing, he mused, was that he couldn't even use that old "its only fake blood and latex" trick, this time. Nosiree, not when it ain't on a screen, not when you can see it with your own two myopic eyes, not when you can feel the little spritz of blood hit your hand; that took all the little mind guards down. The screams; nothing in all of Hollywood's studios sounded quite like the real thing, buddy. Nope. Not a Goddamn thing.

He lit one of Patrick's cigarettes, the machine rolled ones, not the hand rolled ones, and sucked the blue smoke into his lungs, stifling the urge to choke and spasm as it ticked the back of his throat. As always happened on the rare occasions that he snagged a stogie from his brother, his head went light and the room tilted ever so slightly. He allowed himself a few moments of non-thought, as he finished the cigarette.

He looked at the Halloween snapshot again and wondered just what the hell was happening to his friend. He wondered if he really knew Mark Howell at all; the thought scared him. He was used to reading people like books.

For now, he'd keep watching and then, maybe, he'd go look at some of those books at Sanderson's store. The special books, the ones that cost a small fortune. The ones that were supposed to be about real monsters in the real world. Maybe he'd find what he was looking for and maybe he'd understand the world again, the way he was supposed to.

He stared intently at the shot of the people he had come to treasure, in their fantasy get-ups, and focused on Jenny, in her tight, skimpy little Devil's suit. That was just fine, she was a stunning woman and well worth looking at and fantasizing about. Better the Devil you know.

2

P. J. Sanderson was rather surprised when he saw Tyler Wilson walk into the store, but at least it was a pleasant surprise. Not like hearing about Mark getting shot. The most surprising thing about the visit was that Tyler was nervous, fidgety, something that no one had ever been able to accuse the young man of. Pretending that nothing was wrong with the boy, P. J. smiled at him and waved quickly, before saving the last four pages that he had typed in the word processor's memory. "Tyler, my good man, how are you on this fine day?"

Tyler started guiltily and looked up at the author, where he sat at his writing station, which rested on a small island set about ten feet above the rest of the store and centered in the main room. "Hi, P. J., I was wondering if you could help me find something."

P. J. hid the frown of concern that threatened to pop up on his face, wondering if maybe the shooting incident earlier in the week had affected Tyler more than it seemed to have his nephew and his young friends. "Certainly, sir, your wish is my command. What are you looking for?"

"I, uh, I'm not certain," the boy started, pushing his thick glasses back into place. "Uh, Mark said you actually have some books you collected for your writing."

The boy looked down at his feet, uncertain how to proceed and P. J. started to truly worry; nothing ever made Tyler Wilson nervous, just as nothing ever stopped the sun from rising.

"Books on real magic, that you use for research," finished Tyler.

"Yes, that's very true. But, they're not for sale, Tyler, they're part of my own personal collection." The eyes behind the thick lenses hit him with an intensity that was completely unexpected. Whatever was wrong, it was apparently something that had shaken Tyler to the core of his being. P. J. practically ran down the stairs and gently forced the boy up to his little work alcove. After pouring them both a cup of strong coffee and diluting it with half a mug of cream, he nudged the youth's head up, until their eyes met.

"Tell me what's on your mind, Tyler." The expression on Tyler's face registered shock at the thought that his guard was so obviously down. P. J. looked him directly in the eye until he felt that the young man realized he could trust him, and then continued. "I won't tell a soul what's wrong, if that's what you want, but please, trust me. You should know me well enough through Mark, to know that I never break a trust."

Tyler looked him dead in the eye for almost a full minute before finally saying anything, and it was the look on his face, more than the words that he said, that chilled the author. "I think that there might be real monsters in the town and I think that they might be doing something to Mark." If he hadn't looked so very serious, P. J. might have laughed. Somehow, it just didn't seem very funny; he'd known Tyler for years and although it was true they had never been as close as he was to Mark, he knew the boy well enough to know that it wasn't the least bit amusing to him. That made the author curb the laughter and set aside his own beliefs about the reality that he lived in. Tyler didn't pull stupid jokes like that. He just wasn't a good enough actor.

P. J. listened earnestly to Tyler's suspicions, realizing soon enough the gravity of the situation. After they had finished their coffee, The author turned the sign at the front of his aged home and store to *closed* and the two set about looking through all of the ancient tomes and reference books. They had their work ahead of them: the collection of books was well over two hundred volumes and most of them were in either archaic English, or foreign languages that were equally out of use.

3

Tony tossed fitfully on the huge waterbed in his room, sleep refusing to come to him. After almost two hours in the dark, he finally gave up and struggled into a sitting position.

The day's events had just been too fucking weird. How the hell was he expected to sleep? Fortunately, tomorrow was a Saturday and he wouldn't have to deal with school. With a grunt, he stepped away from the bed and toward the door of his room. *Hopefully,* he thought, *a little work out will make me feel better.*

The Nautilus set-up was on par with any you could find at a fitness center and Tony made full use of it whenever he was too tense too sleep. Also, when he wanted to work out his problems in peace.

Oh, the problems were there in abundance. For starters, his master plan had backfired: he found both Tyler and Mark to be, if slightly nerdy, very nice people, with opinions and personalities that he had trouble disagreeing with; *dammit, why couldn't they have just stayed goof balls?* He also found that he was really starting to care about Cassie and her happiness, in ways that he had never expected; no misunderstanding, he still wanted to "jump her bones," as his father so quaintly put it, but he also wanted to be with her because she was an interesting and caring person.

He set the weights to two hundred pounds and started doing bench presses, already better than he had been doing only a month ago at one-sixty, but his goal was to reach three hundred pounds by the end of the year. He set his mind on automatic and started to think about his problems again.

The shooting had scared the hell out of him and filled his bladder to near over-flowing. The blurred flurry of rats afterward had nearly sent him screaming for the woods. He wondered if he would have handled being shot as well as Mark had, and suspected that he wouldn't have. The thought bothered him, but there it was; no getting away from it. What if Mark Howell was a better person than he was; what chance would he possibly have with Cassie, if that were the case? *Shit.*

He moved to the Life Cycle, setting it for maximum difficulty, and started on his thirty-minute ride, his legs already protesting the tortures ahead of them. Slowly he filled with a burning anger and the anger fueled his legs with all of the energy they could ever need. He held the anger closely, reveling in the raw power he felt from it. It was a good feeling.

By the time he had finished the Life Cycle and started on his pull-ups, the anger had bloomed into a full blown fury. He stepped away from the pull-up bar and slid his sinewy hands into the light gloves he always wore when he was working on the heavy bag. The bag took the pounding of its life for the next twenty minutes, until his sister, Lisa, came into the room.

Elizabeth Antoinette Scarrabelli, fraternal twin to Tony, was wearing a skimpy teddy rather than a full night gown and, he suspected, reveling in the knowledge that such garments on his sisters made him uncomfortable. He did his best not to stare as he continued pounding the canvas bag towards oblivion. After she had watched him for some five minutes, he could take it no longer and turned to face her. "What can I do for you?" The sarcasm was heavy in his voice: he considered this room his private domain and intensely disliked the interruption. Tony had never believed any of that crap about twins being linked, closer to each other than to others. He could barely tolerate the invasion of his domain and did not hesitate to let her know it. No love was lost between the two of them.

Lisa smiled dazzlingly and stated, "The question, bro,' is what can I do for you?"

Tony frowned, looking at his sister. "What do you mean?"

"You know what I mean," she answered. "You want Mark Howell away from your would-be love and you can't think of a thing to do about it." She paused dramatically and flicked her dark hair away from her eyes as she stared at him.

Tony hated the way she did that. It made him realize just how attractive she was and the thoughts he sometimes had about her sickened him. He snorted impatiently. "What the fuck are you getting at, Lisa?"

She pouted fetchingly and he clenched his jaws tightly in response. "I was just thinking that maybe we could help each other."

Here it came, the bartering; what would she want this time, his car?

"You like Cassie and I'm getting rather fond of the way your good friend Mark looks. So, maybe we could work out a plan that would get us what we both want."

Tony had to admit that his interest was definitely piqued.

"Well, what do you say, big brother, can we work together?"

Tony thought about that: if things worked out properly, no one had to get hurt, at least not very badly. He slipped the gloves off of his hands and set his heavily sweating body next to her scantily clad one. It was her turn to stir uncomfortably; flirtation was a game that two could play. "Tell me your plans, I'm all ears."

After over an hour of talking out details, the two went their separate ways, each to a separate room and each with thought of how soon they could alleviate the uncomfortable stirrings in their private parts.

4

Cassie couldn't sleep. She was too worried about Mark. All she could think about was looking over from where he'd pushed her, fully prepared to yell at him, and seeing his body twitch as blood exploded from his arm. Try as she might, she couldn't stop herself from feeling guilty; if he hadn't stepped up and pushed her, he wouldn't be hurt, lying at home with orders to avoid strenuous activities that involved the use of his arms. Activi ies like swimming and others that she tried not to ackno wledge—just as with her male counterpart, she was start ng to give serious thought to con-summating their relationship. For seven months now they had been dating, and the recent bouts of heavy petting were starting to affect her reasoning.

Swimming at Tyler's had become something of a torture: watching his muscular form—*and Tony's, at least be honest enough to admit it*—sail off of the diving board and just seeing him move with that graceful stride of his, were almost as bad as the damn petting.

Dammit, that was a big step to have to make; she liked the easy friendship they had and worried that would change. It almost always did in real life, or at least in real life according to the novels she read and the occasional nighttime soaps she watched with her mom. She had no personal experience. Mark was the first guy she'd ever gotten serious with. She needed to talk to someone, but she sure as hell couldn't talk to her mom and the only girl she knew who might have done the deed was Sandy; how the hell do you approach someone and ask? She could see it now, getting Sandy alone and asking her directly; "Sandy, did you and Pete ever go all the way, before he was torn apart by animals? I mean, did you have enough time to find out if it had changed your relationship with him, before he was dismembered?" Oh yeah, that would go over well and her problems would be over then. She doubted Mark would be all that eager, after Sandy had finished tearing her legs off and beating her severely with them. She chuckled at the image in her mind, of her standing a total of three feet in height, pushing herself on a skateboard, as she attended the Prom with Mark. *Well*, she thought, *at least the mouth would be at the right height.* That sent her off on another little set of chuckles, which turned into half tears, as she worried that maybe he would blame her for having been shot. She hadn't even called him to see how he was doing; it had been late when the thought crossed her mind and she was afraid that his parents would get pissed.

Thinking about it now, that seemed silly; Mark's parents never got upset when she called, they were always glad to hear her voice, always friendly when she dropped by. That sent her off on thoughts of how nasty her parents were about the whole thing. They had all but blamed Mark for the shooting, even though he had saved her life. Sometimes, she really hated her parents, like now. She would have a great deal of trouble forgiving the accusations that had come from them.

They all but came out and asked if he was forcing himself on her and she snorted quietly at the thought. Hell, she had practically had to force herself on him just to get a kiss, when they had first started dating, and holding hands always seemed like enough to keep him content. With that, she was right back where she had started, thinking about whether they should go all the way.

The answer was right there for her and she had finally solved the puzzle; he would wait, and patiently at that, until she was certain. Mark was like that, gentle and understanding. She smiled slightly as she closed her eyes, mind finally at peace.

Then she tossed and turned some more, wondering about whether or not she was ready.

5

Joe Howell felt impotent, filled with a unsettled worry about his son. Why the hell had some asshole shot at him, what had Mark done?

He knew it wasn't drugs—Mark showed none of the usual symptoms that came with serious drug use; he wasn't overly moody, he wasn't slipping in his school work—hell he was getting better in his scholastic achievements if anything. He hadn't been blowing wads of money, thinking about it; no more than he usually did on his hobbies and girlfriend. There were no small but expensive knick-knacks missing and the money in his wallet and in Jenny's purse never disappeared mysteriously. So why had the bastard shot at him?

Maybe, it had to do with Tyler's big brother, what was his name? Paul, Patrick, Peter, something with a "P" at the beginning; it had happened at Tyler's place and Joe still remembered the boy from the Halloween Carnival, how he had stumbled and slurred his words, and the glazed look in his eyes. He frowned to himself and decided that he would have to talk to Patrick, soon. And if that didn't produce answers, he'd just have to talk to the police. They had to have some kind of idea about what the hell was going on.

Beside him, Jenny rose from a light sleep and looked over at him, blurrily. He smiled down at her and reached out to gently stroke the side of her face; she smiled back and kissed the rough flesh of his knuckles, lightly. "S'matter, honey? Can't sleep?"

"Hmmn, thinking about Mark, hoping he's okay with what happened today."

She smiled at him and moved her hand under the sheets, to tickle his side, until he cracked a grin. "You worry too much, he's fine." She noticed the look of bewilderment on his face and kissed him lightly on the chest. "A mother knows her son," she assured him, as she moved her hand down lower, "Mark's a very strong young man, just like his stepfather."

She kissed his stomach and moved lower, pushing the bed-clothes out of her way. He hissed as she nipped at him playfully and forgot all about his son's troubles. They could wait. They could wait all night if they had to. He had other things to think about now.

6

After finally seeing the light go out in his parents' room, Mark stepped lightly to the front door and slipped out into the chill night air. He needed to think and he did that best out in the woods.

He paused on his way to look up at the window of Cassie's room in her parents house. Knowing that she was there made him feel better and he stared for some time before heading on his way.

He hesitated at the edge of the woods and held his watch out to catch the faint light of the moon. One-fifteen, plenty of time to go back in before the folks woke up; they always slept until ten on Saturdays. He slipped into the woods with ease, scarcely disturbing the mulched and rotted leaves on the way to his special spot. He wandered without real purpose and put his thoughts in order. He knew that what had happened today had nothing to do with him: he'd never seen the guy before. Probably just some sick bastard that got his kicks by fucking with people; Lord knew there were enough of them in the world.

He finally reached his destination, only ten minutes walk through the woods, almost a full hour later. No worries, no hurries. He idly picked at the scraggly grass growing near the rock where he normally sat and looked on, filled with happiness, as the Folk started scampering closer in towards him. He had been chatting with Them for several minutes, when They all looked in the direction that led towards his house and disappeared as suddenly as They had shown up.

It was then that he heard the sound of someone walking through the woods, heading in his direction. Mark was not so much scared as surprised by the unexpected sound; and he could almost hear that person's breathing as they came closer. With a small grin, he moved silently away from the flat stone and slid quietly behind a nearby oak tree. Slowly, the figure came closer.

In the nearly complete darkness, he waited and watched as the figure stopped near the stone and slowly walked a circuit around it. He was having great difficulty stifling the snickers that tried to erupt from within him. The figure slowly backed away from the stone, towards his hiding place, and he stepped directly into its path.

When she bumped into him, Cassie turned quickly and, seeing the dark shape before her, cut loose with a shriek of near-epic proportions. He smiled at her, beatifically, and said "Boo." She could have killed him when she realized who it was.

"Jesus! You scared the hell out of me!" She wanted to be angry, but that smile of his melted the anger like ice on a hot skillet. She managed to hold her glare for all of three seconds, heart racing the entire time, before she broke into a grin and started laughing with him. Before all was said and done, they were hugging each other and walking back to the stone.

"What brings you out here, at this late hour?" Mark looked at her with a blend of amusement and curiosity.

"I could ask you the same thing," she replied, as she wrapped her arms around his rib cage. He kissed her lightly on the top of her brow and enfolded her with his arms. "I was following you, silly. I thought you were sleepwalking." Close enough to the truth. She had also toyed with him meeting another girl, or maybe running away from home. Apparently it was none of the above. "So why are you here? Meeting another woman on the sly?" She tried to keep it light and pulled it off fairly well.

Mark looked down at her with that easy grin he'd developed of late and hugged her a little closer. "Not a chance in hell, you're almost too much to handle on your own." She pulled away from him in mock anger at the comment and he kissed her temple; she could almost feel his pulse in his lips. "No, I come out here a lot; it's where I go when I need to think, or just to get some fresh air."

She looked up into his eyes and tried to read what she saw there; for the first time, she couldn't. She had a brief flash of fear, where she thought that maybe she was with the wrong guy and then he smiled again and the Mark she knew was back. "Tonight it's just for the fresh air. I'm glad you showed up, I was just thinking how nice it would be to show you this place; it's so peaceful, solemn, like a church." The way he said it told her it was the truth and she looked around at the little area for the first time.

She could see his point, the place almost looked like it could be a church. The trees grew straight and proud, rising toward the clouds above as if in prayer. The ground was remarkably level, all the way to the path that had been worn over the last fifteen years by all of the children that opted in the nicer weather to walk home from the school, rather than take the school bus. And, the air smelled sweet with the remaining blooms of a dozen different flowers. All in all, it was almost a magical place; you could come here and forget that you had ever seen another person. Forget that you had responsibilities. "It really is a beautiful little place, how'd you ever find it?"

He chuckled deep in his chest and looked around himself, with a distant gaze. "I walk home sometimes, when I don't want to take the bus." Then he looked back over at her and said, "I guess you could say it found me." Seeing the confusion on her lovely face, he finished the thought, "This is where Tony and Pete and the rest of the guys landed on my back." He slid his hand down her back and patted the seat of her jeans briefly, before continuing; it was the closest he had ever come to a forward move. "Your derriere is resting just around where I split my face open, when Pete tackled me." The thought was vaguely repulsive and vaguely humorous at the same time, she would have been thoroughly repulsed, had it not been for the smile and the laughter in his voice.

"How can you stand it here? I thought it would have nothing but bad memories for you."

He looked at her and his smile changed, softened as he stared her in the eyes. "If that hadn't happened," he started his voice barely above a whisper, "Tyler would have never introduced us. I never would have had the nerve to talk to you first and when we ran into each other way back when, it would have just been 'oh, excuse me,' and you would have been out of my life." She couldn't quite look at it in the same light, but she understood what he meant; to clarify even further he said "I'd take a thousand injuries like that, Cassie, to be with you." The look in his eyes made hers want to water. She'd never realized how strongly he felt about her, he'd never put it into words before. "Cassie, I love you."

She had no answer to that. She still had to evaluate her feelings before she could say the same back. Instead, she hugged him fiercely and he returned the gesture. If she never said the words back, she knew he'd still feel the same way. It was almost scary the way he felt about her. Almost, hell. It *was* a little scary.

They were about to kiss, *like one of those mushy scenes in the movies,* she thought wildly, when they heard Tyler's scream, from off in the woods.

7

Tyler's plan, simply put, was to follow Mark. He had to know if Mark knew about the little monsters and see if he was being hurt by the creatures. Just because Cassie was out there too didn't mean that he was going to change those plans. Damn it, he was worried about his friend and he was determined to find out if he was in trouble.

What he hadn't counted on, was that the little creatures might take offense to his following Mark. He could hear Their whispered voices, calling out feverishly and he could also hear a strange noise that made him feel a little dizzy.

What he did not know, was that They wouldn't have hurt him at all, They simply meant to confuse his sense of direction, to scare him into running back home, out of the woods and away from Mark.

What They didn't know, was that Tyler needed those big thick lenses of his to see. They took them off of his face and threw them far away from where he stood, before he knew what the hell was happening. They also ensured that he would not see them, when They did it; the Folk were very good at not being seen.

So Tyler, believing that his glasses had simply fallen off, bent to the ground, trying desperately to find his them, un- aware that they were no longer in the vicinity. Confused by this strange behavior, the Folk touched his mind, with delicate mental fingers and discovered their error. This new knowl- edge brought with it the makings of a fine joke and the Folk love a good joke.

They retrieved the glasses and placed them just out of his reach. Naturally, he attempted to reach them just the same, becoming more and more frantic by the moment. They kept sliding them ever so slowly out of his reach. Tyler was already spooked, thinking about the very creatures that now, unknown to him, tormented him. The thought of Their little faces snarling at him gave him a case of the grade-A industrial strength heebie jeebies. Being in the woods, a place he had never been overly fond of, did nothing at all for his sense of well being. Add the darkness of the night to that and he was half a step away from a full scale panic attack.

When he accidentally knocked one of Them over, in his frantic search for his artificial eyes, It bit him, lightly, in warning. And It hissed.

We all have our deep-seated fears and you may rest assured, that the Folk know them all. Tyler was terrified of snakes; the thought of being bitten by one of the venomous little creatures, of rolling on the ground as his body filled with deadly poisons and bloated beyond recognition, was nearly enough to make him wet his pants. In a truly divine terror, Tyler shrieked in fear and started running. He ran over three of Them, in his haste to get himself to the hospital, and They were all quite taken aback by the speed with which the blind friend of the Chosen One moved. Right up to the moment that he tripped over a jutting root and slammed himself into the ground with enough force to break his nose and knock him unconscious.

Oh, how They laughed at that one, until the slightly more sober ones, Those still pushing Themselves out of the blind giant's footprints, pointed out that the Chosen would be very angry indeed, should he find out what They had done. In the distance, They could hear the thunderous steps of the One, and his bellowing cries indicated the worry he felt over the blind one's dilemma. They quickly retrieved the seeing device, placed it near the unconscious form of the Chosen's friend and ran like the wind to ensure no sign of their involvement.

They chastised the biting one, as They raced through the woods, but not too harshly—it had been funny, and He had been run over by the blind one. In moments, the sound of Their laughter had faded to naught. This was definitely a joke that They would remember for a long, long time.

Even the Folk make mistakes, the wind whispered. Ooops.

8

When Tyler woke up, he found himself facing a broad back, that undulated in place, before him. It took him a moment, to realize that he was being carried over someone's shoulder. He started struggling frantically, thinking that he had, perhaps, been kidnapped and that he would be ransomed and then shot in the head and left in the woods, his body to be found some year, by a red neck hunter and his pack of huntin' dawgs. He stopped thrashing when he heard Cassie's voice above and behind him, telling him to calm down. He almost sobbed with joy when he saw the vague image of his beloved glasses in her hand. Never, he swore silently, would he complain about their need again.

Mark grunted and set Tyler down on his two none-too-steady feet. The grin he flashed at Ty apologized for the inconvenience and queried as to why he was in the woods so late at night, simultaneously. "Ty, for such a skinny guy, you weigh a ton." Mark rubbed at his lower back and grimaced. "My spine may never be the same."

Tyler grinned and lightly punched Mark on the shoulder, switching targets when he remembered the bandages on Mark's right side. He was a good sport and obviously felt that whatever Ty's reasons for being in the woods, they were his own. Not so Cassie. She put her hands on her well formed hips and stared him in the eyes, with exasperation written on her face. "What were you doing out here in the woods? I thought you hated the woods."

Tyler grinned sheepishly, flushing crimson and 'fessed up. He went on, with his usual accentuations and expansions, to tell of his being lost in the woods and panicking when he dropped his glasses. By the time he was done, all was forgiven. He also assured them that his nose wasn't a serious problem: "Damn thing breaks at the drop of a hat, has ever since good ol' Tony broke it in the fifth grade." He then regaled them with the story of why good ol' Tony had felt it necessary. on that long ago date, to cave his face in. They settled at the edge of the woods for over an hour and whisper-talked about a dozen things, never really getting back to the issue of why he followed Mark, for which he was grateful. He was, and had always been, a lousy liar. The Old Tyler Charm had saved his ass again. It was almost dawn, by the time they got home.

It was several hours later that Cassie said her good byes and headed for the airport in Denver. Her father had awakened her at nine o'clock, to tell her that her grandmother had passed away in the night. They had to go to Florida and settle the funeral arrangements. The look on Mark's face when they parted was almost enough to break her heart.

She promised to be back as soon as possible, and lamented that Tyler's late night accident had stopped her from carrying out her plans; she didn't know how long it would take her to build up the courage to offer herself to Mark again.

Chapter Seven

1

Mark was having a particularly shitty day. Tyler's gift for gab had failed him when his parents had seen his face, which bore a strong resemblance to a raccoon's, and they had grounded him for the weekend. Cassie's grandmother had died and she had to leave town for at least a week despite confessing, when he offered his condolences, that she hardly knew the woman and found it difficult to mourn her. Tony was in Boulder. P. J. was in New York, having finally admitted that he and Ali had become something of an item, and to top it off, Mark was now suffering from his first-ever case of writer's block. He'd given up drawing, because it just didn't do anything for him anymore, and the folks were going shopping in the city and then out to dinner with Joe's boss, Rob. He was, in short, alone and painfully aware of it.

After mulling over this fact for just a little over an hour, Mark pulled on his jogging shoes and took to the road. A little jogging was good for the soul if not the soles.

After seven months of steady jogging and swimming, Mark had built up a level of endurance that he would have never dreamt possible before he moved to town. He now used that stamina to his advantage and took the three-mile route into the town proper.

He spent most of the afternoon in the town's only cinema watching the latest in Sci-fi/monster movies; it was a sequel to an earlier movie starring his all time favorite brick wall, Arnold. The movie was good and full of action, but not quite on par with its predecessor. After the movie, he started wandering around the town and basically enjoying the fairly pleasant weather.

The day promised nothing but boredom—at least until Tony's twin sister showed up.

2

Lisa had worked hard to locate Mark and finally she had him in her sights. She had spotted him going into the Stardust Theater and had immediately driven home to prepare; a quick shower, some make-up and her tightest jean-and-tee-shirt combination, and she was ready to move in for the kill.

Lisa had been waiting for quite some time to get him away from the group he hung around with and today looked like a golden opportunity. Tony had been forced to go into Boulder with her father and she'd taken a message meant for him, which she "accidentally" forgot to give him. She was sorry for Cassie, about her grandmother and all of that, but she was also glad to have her out of town. It would be ever so difficult to get close to Mark if Cassie was draped over his arm.

She couldn't even say what exactly made him so attractive to her unless it was the way he had stood up to Tony, something that absolutely no one in the school had ever been willing to do. That and the fact that he had shaped up very nicely after he had lost a little weight. He just seemed like the best the town had to offer. Lord knew she was sick to death of Tommy Blake and his constant attempts to get into her pants; the only other real options were Jerry Sanders (who was even worse than Tommy, if Sandy could be believed), and Patrick Wilson. Thanks, but no. She'd already dated most of the guys that were worth dating and had found them wanting; she was rapidly running out of options in the crappy little town of Summitville.

Mind set, she started walking towards him and turned her head so that he couldn't see past her sunglasses that she was watching him. Mark had his mind elsewhere and wasn't really paying attention to where he was going. This, she decided, was going all too well. It almost took all of the fun out of it. Almost.

Having played this game before, she waited for just the right moment, when Mark's gaze was far away from her and darted into his path. He walked right into her and with a great deal more force then she had intended. He quickly caught her, using both of his muscular arms, and set her back on her feet. Just as she was about to give her heartfelt thanks, he turned away from her and slammed his fist into the brick wall beside him. It was that, or he would have lashed out at her. Better his hand stinging a little than the guilt he'd have felt if he actually hit another person.

His teeth were clamped tightly together and she heard the whispered profanity escape his lips. It was then that she remembered his injured arm. She mentally chalked up her first strike and rested her manicured hands on his back, lightly. "Oh, Mark, I'm so sorry," she twisted her face into the proper look of concern and batted her dark lashes at him. "I didn't see you. Gawd, I'm such a clumsy idiot."

His look of pain and anger faded and he smiled weakly. "No, I'm sorry. I wasn't paying attention to where I was going."

Lisa shared three classes with Mark and had always thought the modesty he showed in the classes was for the teacher's benefit; the look on his face and the way that he said what he said made her rapidly reevaluate her opinion. He was sweet and as God was her witness, he was shy.

"Are you okay?" he asked.

She laughed lightly and decided that she was definitely going to enjoy this. "Shouldn't I be asking you that?" She looked pointedly at his shoulder and bicep, where the thick gauze of his dressings could still be seen through his shirt. He shrugged, careful to use only his left shoulder, and blushed at the attention he was getting. Mind in overdrive, she smiled sweetly, "How can I make it up to you?" Then she smiled a little broader and wrapped her arms around his uninjured bicep. *Big arms, I wonder if everything else is as big?* "I know, let me buy you a late lunch, or an early dinner." Over Mark's protests, she dragged him over to Wing Pu's Chinese Garden, and armed with Daddy's American Express, got to know her latest victim a little better.

3

The food had been wonderful and the company even better. It was just what he had needed to get over his little case of the ho-hums. By the time they had finished eating and left the tiny restaurant, Mark had decided he liked Lisa, a lot. He studied her face and body, as she leaned against her car and offered to give him a ride home. She had full, bow-shaped lips and a delicate aquiline nose, along with dark brown eyes you could lose yourself in; all of that in a heart shaped face surrounded by wave after wave of thick, lightly curled brown hair. Like her brother, she was "built like a Brick Shit-house," to use Tyler's favorite term for any person with phenomenal proportions; the difference, of course, was that her body was built phenomenally for a member of the opposite sex, more attuned to thoughts of pleasure than of pain.

Pulling himself back to reality, he remembered her invitation and, realizing that they had somehow managed to spend almost three hours in the restaurant, readily agreed. She flashed him another incredible smile and moved to unlock his door. She dropped the keys and with painstakingly slow moves, bent to retrieve them. This motion caused definite stirrings in Mark and he guiltily thought of Cassie, as he enjoyed the view.

Her car, like Tony's, was a Camaro and the latest model, no less. It was red inside and out, with crushed velvet seats and a stereo system that was almost worth dying for. She looked at him and flashed a seductive smile in his direction. "Feel like going straight home, or would you like to cruise around for awhile?"

The question and the look both threw him and he could feel himself flush slightly, before he responded. "Uh, sure, I'm not in any hurry to get anywhere." His mind was telling him things he should seriously consider and his conscience was trying desperately to remind him of Cassie. His mind was winning the battle, no contest.

She drove the car around the town a couple of times, pointing out the different sights and giving him the first actual tour of the town that he had ever received. She also gave him a thousand little hints that she might be interested in more than just his friendship. His mind flashed the irritating question to him several times, before he got the courage to mumble it under his breath. "Where the hell were you, eight months ago?" He had mumbled the question and didn't expect an answer, but he suspected that he had gotten one anyway when she pulled the car off of the road, not far from the school.

Before he knew what the hell was happening, they were walking hand in hand towards the woods.

4

This was going even better than she had expected; there was a chemistry between the two of them that she found very exciting. Even when he was looking away from her she could feel his eyes on her and the thought of feeling his hands on her in a short while got her hot. It hadn't been in her plans to go anywhere near this far, but she didn't mind the idea at all. Lisa was very glad that she'd had the foresight to lift several of Tony's condoms.

They trekked through the woods, walking slowly and talking very little, save when he'd point out something that she would never have noticed on her own; certain plants that bloomed only at night, or the sounds of various animals that roamed only after the sun had set. He showed her a new perspective on the woods that raised not only her appreciation of his intellect, but also her appreciation of the woods' natural beauty. She was rapidly beginning to understand what it was that Cassie saw in Mark Howell and with that understanding, she realized her main purpose for setting out to break them apart. She had been jealous of their relationship, and the fact that none of hers ever seemed to work out simply emphasized the point. She hoped that things would be as good between Mark and her. He was an extraordinary person.

He seemed to know these woods like the back of his hand and knew every spot to step where he would make the least noise. The clouds of the night before had passed away and the moon shone down upon them, illuminating little but highlighting much. She looked over towards him and had the momentary thought, brought on by the gliding and silent steps and the pale silvery moonlight, that she was walking hand in hand with a ghost. He smiled at her and drove the brief flash of fear away. She pulled closer to him and felt the securit' of his arm wrapping around her.

He turned suddenly and ushered her through the woods in another direction. Lisa felt the ground start to rise gently and after a while, realized that they were almost all the way to Lake Overtree. She hadn't realized how deep into the woods they had gone.

Overtree rose gracefully away from the small place where Summitville rested, locked in place and guarded by the foothills of the Rockies that completely engulfed the town. Overtree also separated the town from the rest of the world, as Interstate Seventy was on the other side of the lake and the only way into Summitville was by following the winding access road that lay hidden between the aspen and oak trees. The only sign that led to the town was completely hidden, overgrown years ago by the trees.

Most people forgot that the lake was there until somebody brought it up in conversation; the fish that hid within its depths seemed reluctant to be caught, even at the best of times, and as a result it had never become popular even within the town itself. Boating was completely out of the question, there were far too many places where the rocks hid mere inches under the murky green waters.

From where they now stood Lisa could see the moon reflected off of the lake's water, which ran almost parallel in height to where they were. It was beautiful. Not knowing what to say in light of the panorama, she hugged Mark tightly in lieu of opening her mouth and ruining the majesty of the scene. Mark's response was to lean over and kiss her lightly on the lips.

She responded immediately, feeling herself grow excited as he pushed past her lips with his tongue. They locked together running their hands over one another, caressing and fondling. The sound of her tiny groans urged him on and the eager motions he made caused her to moan even louder.

After several minutes of heavy petting he suddenly pulled away, a pained look on his face. Quietly, he slipped back from her, ignoring her questioning stare. Mark turned his back to her. She covered herself, rubbing her arms over her body to keep her warmth, and waited until he finally turned to face her.

He tried to look stern, resolute and managed only to look sad and wounded. "Lisa, I'm sorry, but I can't do this. It isn't right."

"Why?" she demanded, half angry, half confused. "What did I do wrong?"

He shrugged his shoulders, flashed a grimace of pain as he was again reminded of his injury. Sheepishly, he tried to form the words that would make sense of what he was feeling. "It's not you, dammit, it's me." He looked into her eyes with a nearly feverish intensity and explained, "I'm in love with Cassie and I couldn't live with myself if I hurt her. I'm sorry. I really am, but that's how I feel and I can't do this. Not with you. Hell, not with anybody, if it's not Cassie."

Lisa stared at him and understood perfectly what he had said. Decided in that moment that an apology wasn't anywhere near good enough. She hauled her arm back to Texas and cut loose with a vicious right hook across his face. Tears of hurt and humiliation threatened to erupt, complementing the shame and rage that darkened her beautiful face, and she turned and stomped off towards her car.

She looked back at Mark and saw the look of quiet grief on his own face. At that moment he looked like a girl, the way the darkness hid his body, the way his full lips trembled at the edge of a pout. For some reason, possibly the way he shook his head, almost as if he just knew he was dreaming the whole thing, she walked back to him.

They stared at each other in silence, each wanting to say something and neither of them knowing how. After a timeless little span of seconds, they hugged lightly. He smiled that wonderful smile of his again and kissed her forehead. "Thanks for understanding." She smiled briefly and caressed the side of his face.

They walked hand in hand back to her car and briefly kissed goodbye to what might have been.

When he finally got home, she called him on the phone and asked if he had Tyler's phone number. He gave it to her.

5

Tommy Blake's rage went beyond merely monumental, it went all the way to god-like. Lisa'd dumped him and she was making it clear to everyone at the school that he was essentially a prick with hands. This would not do, hell no, not at all. There was, of course, the fact that she was Tony's sister to take into consideration, so he couldn't take out the rage on her. But he definitely needed someone to take it out on.

That was when he saw the bitch standing with Tyler Wilson, of all people. She looked his way and immediately ignored him and whispered something to Tyler that made the little faggot look in his direction and laugh. He felt the urge to break the little shit in half and headed in that direction. Tyler wasn't laughing anymore, he was looking kind of green, and that made the smile come back to Tommy. Like Tony, Tommy had a very nasty smile when he wanted to. Understanding that Tommy was smaller than Tony, one would also do well to understand that Tommy tried all that much harder, as a way of compensating. Tommy was on literally all of the major sports teams in the school and had lettered in most. Tommy had also spent practically all of his summers in Denver, where his cousin and he attended karate classes together, classes taught by none other than Tommy's Uncle Bill. Tommy had his black belt and had had it for well over two years. He practiced regularly.

Tyler knew all about Tommy's history and knew that he was a dead man, just as soon as Tommy caught up with him. With a dazzling and buck-toothed smile at Lisa and a hearty "Gotta go, love to the kids, Marge," he tucked his books up to his rib cage, pushed his glasses back into place and ran like hell. He amazed himself by reaching all new speed records. Had Coach Malloy seen him just then, he'd have drafted him on the spot. Tyler shot through the crowded hallways, weaving madly between the groups of students ambling slowly towards their classes, or just having conversations with the people in their clique. Many of the students and not a few of the teachers took passing interest in the event and most of them wondered idly just who Tyler had pissed off this time.

No one saw Tommy following him, because Tommy had long ago learned all of Ty's escape routes and was in the process of heading him off at the proverbial pass. It was just before the start of third period and Tyler had a science class in Mr. Hinkley's room, all the way on the other side of the school; Tommy was fairly certain he could beat the little prick down there, it was just a matter of speed. Along the way, he gathered Jerry Sanders and the ever unpopular 'Goose' Brundvandt. Goose was always eager to help, but was generally unpopular, because he'd never figured out the use of deodorant and had a tendency to save showering for special occasions, like Christmas and maybe his birthday. People had a tendency to think of "Pig Pen" from Charles Shultz's Peanuts comic strip when they first met Goose.

6

Tyler was definitely not having a very good Monday. So far, he'd already pissed off two teachers with his mouth, and had, for reasons unknown to him, managed to send Tommy Blake into a frenzy; it wasn't that he didn't like sending the ape into an occasional rage, he just liked to understand why.

Rounding the bend into the west wing of the school, he managed to slam into Sue Talbot and knock her sprawling, a sensation that he honestly wished he'd had time to enjoy— the girl was stacked. Over her extremely loud protests, he called an apology and kept moving. Sunday, now there had been a day to remember. He'd gotten a long list of messages when he finally got home from P. J.'s, *a brief guilty flash there but he'd had to lie to Mark, he had to research the damn books with P. J., it was for Mark's own good* and surprise, surprise, they had all been from Lisa Scarrabelli, the hottest little number in the school—with the possible exception of Tracy Steiner, who was known to sleep with any man at the drop of a hat, though Tyler had to admit he'd never had any success and he'd dropped a hell of a load of hats! Seemed she just wanted to talk and could she come over for a while? Hell yes! Four lovely hours, spent easing her troubled soul and looking at her chest as frequently as possible; and as a reward, he got a hug and a kiss from her, which was, to date, an all time record for physical contact with females other than his mother in the Ty-Man's life.

Then, just when it was all going so very nicely today, Tommy—new king of the Asshole Patrol, since Tony had decided to abdicate—takes it into his mind to rearrange Tyler's body, free of charge but not free of pain. Ain't life a scream?

He was almost all the way to Hinkley The Herniated's class, when the walking trash-heap known as Goose stepped into his way. Goose was fairly tall and as angular as Tyler himself, but was also known to lift tanks in an attempt to build a better bicep. He was really remarkably strong, both physically and in the olfactory sense of the word. Ty was having none of it. He lowered his head, tensed his toothpick neck and head butted the man into next week. Ty was later told by Stan Martin, a sub-freshman, who was eagerly working on becoming the next Tyler of good ol' Westphalen High, that it was a sight to see, he literally ran up the man's torso and over his head and landed on his feet without missing a beat. That was when he saw the rest of the Goon Platoon standing in front of the open door leading to Hinkley's classroom.

Never one to be slow in thought, Tyler tossed his books at Jerry's head and saw the goof ball duck from the high velocity missiles (said missiles then scattered themselves all over the interior of Hinkley's room, actually startling the man into a state of semiconsciousness). Simultaneous with that action, Tyler sped up and ran straight at Tommy.

Tommy stood his ground and tensed for the collision; no way was he going to get bowled over by a dweeb like Wilson. Tyler, naturally, had no intentions of slamming into Tommy; what works with the sewage man seldom works with slabs of concrete. Instead, he waited until he was almost within arm's reach of the resident psychopath and dove towards the ground.

It should be noted at this point, that Principle Sam (The Ham) Watkins was known to be slightly anal retentive when it came to filth of any kind. He had a staff of four janitors working at the school, having worked the financial reports with enough finesse, that three of the fine gentlemen in question never even showed up on the annual and quarterly reports to the county education system. These fine upstanding men were paid well to keep the school clean and through the remarkable level of fear the old Ham managed to inspire, did it damn well. You could, though to date no one had, eat off of the floors, at least until the end of the first period. This particular wing of the school was normally handled by Sam's very favorite janitor, Otis. Otis believed that the best way to keep a floor clean was to wax it once a week, which he did, at the end of the school day, every Friday afternoon. The floors in the west wing were just slightly easier to walk on than ice and were wonderful for sliding on.

Tyler shot like a bullet between Tommy's braced legs and because he was there any way, slowed himself slightly with a vicious fist to Tommy's crotch. He did not, however, slow himself enough to avoid crashing merrily into the first three rows of desks, sending pencils, paper and pupils flying in the process.

Tyler was mostly unscathed and certainly in better shape that he would have been had Tommy and friends had a chance to dance the Watusi on his face.

Tommy was not nearly as lucky; he had after all been struck at velocity in his testicles. By the time Hinkley had staggered over to him, he was curled into a fetal position, loudly moaning out his pain for the entire classroom to hear. After the class had finally put two and two together and realized that Tyler was the victor, a good portion of them burst into a combination of laughter, applause, and snide jeers directed towards Tommy, that was as beautiful as the finest music ever performed to Tyler's friction burned ears.

Hinkley looked down at the convulsing Tommy and asked him sharply, "Were you chasing that boy?" while pointing his finger in Ty's general direction.

Tommy responded with, "Urnk," while his comrade in arms, Jerry, beat a hasty retreat.

"Why were you chasing that poor boy, what did he ever do to you?" was the next question aimed at Tommy.

Ever quick to get into a teacher's good graces, he responded promptly with "Ooolk."

Well, enough was enough. Hinkley immediately called at the top of his lungs for Coach Malloy who, fortunately, was in the process of trying to locate Tyler before he had to scrape him off of the ground with a spatula.

That boy's mouth was going to be the end of him yet; Malloy still remembered the year Tyler first came to school and had to be driven home every day to avoid the literal line of kids outside waiting for a chance to crack his skull. As Tyler's folks both kept busy schedules, Malloy had taken the task of driving him home upon his own weary shoulders. It avoided having to testify in juvenile court as to why the seventy or so people should not be thrown in prison for manslaughter. He was more than willing to drag Tommy away, after a quick smile and wink towards Tyler who, though he would never admit it, was his favorite student, not just of this year, but of his entire academic career.

Tyler reveled in the praise of his fellow students the rest of the day and was the first one on the bus just as soon as the bell rang. As always, life was good to Tyler, if in a way that was as crazy as his own mouth.

7

Mark spent his Monday in a blue funk that reminded him of the same color funk he'd been in the day before. This was unfortunate, because the reason for his funk happened to be what had happened the day before yesterday, when he had cheated on Cassie. Mark had a tendency to flog himself mercilessly when it came to his guilty feelings. The fact that Cassie had yet to call was definitely not making him feel any better.

He thought about her and his heart broke. He felt like the junkies always looked in the movies when they couldn't get their fix; his insides had jellied and he couldn't think about anything else.

He managed to tolerate all of his classes and to survive the monotony of his life by thinking about her smile. If he had to go through too much more of this, he was certain that his brain would explode into a thousand little bits and leak out of his ears. He was fairly certain that it was already too late for his heart, which he was convinced had stopped beating at least two hours earlier.

Also, he knew what was on Tony's mind and he couldn't blame his one-time worst enemy for wanting to steal Cassie away from him. In his present state of mind, he felt that he didn't deserve to be with her, she was too wonderful to be stuck with a loser like him.

All that any of these thoughts did was make the whole matter worse and unfortunately, they were all that he could think about.

He missed the bus home, lost as he was in his own private hell of guilt and depression. He walked without thought and They watched him, afraid to show up too soon and worried about what could be bothering the One so very much. They whispered to each other, trying to decide what They should do; They had been having this problem for the last three days.

He was all but lost to Them and They couldn't understand why. It had all started with the dark-haired girl, that was the only certainty that They had. The worst thing, was that They couldn't decide if she was friend or foe. One moment, she had been caressing the One in a way which They knew He enjoyed, the next, she hit Him in the mouth. Then, just when They had decided she must die, she and He had had some sort of reconciliation. All They wanted to know, was just what the devil was going on. It was all very confusing.

They watched and waited. Sooner or later, He would come to be comforted and when that happened, They would be there. He was still necessary. For now. They still loved Him. For now.

As They had predicted, the One showed himself in the sacred place. He talked, They listened; He cried, They soothed. He slept and dreamt of making love to His one and only, They made the changes in Him that They had to make.

8

On Thursday afternoon as Mark was climbing out of the school bus, Cassie was waiting for him. He could have cried when he finally saw her face; for Mark it seemed as if years had passed.

Both stood completely still, looking at each other over the distance of several feet until the bus was gone, and then they fairly flew into each other's arms. When they pulled apart from each other, Cassie looked slightly puzzled and couldn't understand why. Something felt wrong to her, just slightly off kilter.

After convincing her to go with him for a walk in the woods, Mark told her about the preceding Saturday night.

At first she was too stunned to speak and then she was furious. She screamed at him and called him names and even came damn close to knocking his teeth down his throat. She swore she would never speak to him again and she stormed away. And he took it all, he deserved nothing but her condemnation and he knew it.

The sun had long since set before he bothered to move. When he did move, it was with a determined walk and a deep scowl across his face.

He'd heard about Tommy's latest attempt to devastate Tyler and Tommy seemed as good a way to vent his steam as any. For the first time in his life, Mark knew why people from time to time took out their frustrations on others, people who had nothing to do with the problem.

Just as They had been changing his body, They had been changing his mind, and now was the time for the first real fruits of Their labors to show the scar They had left on his personality; it was Mark Howell that set out that night to find Tommy Blake, but it was a different Mark Howell than the one who had come into the town of Summitville almost a year ago. Very different indeed.

As he walked through the woods heading towards the school he had left earlier in the day, The Folk gathered around him and rushed through the woods to watch the creation They had been working on. They were certain that a fine time would be had by all.

9

Cassie was furious and more than a little saddened by Mark's betrayal. After spending so much time getting to know each other, Mark had pulled this crap and destroyed the fragile trust that the two of them had shared. Now, storming through the woods, all that she could think of was the fact that he had all but slept with Lisa Scarrabelli; the fact that he had confessed his indiscretions did nothing to soothe the wounds to her ego.

Hurt and angry and confused, Cassie did as she had always done when the world slapped her down; she ran to Tyler. She didn't concern herself with the fact that he was a close friend to Mark; she knew that he would listen, he always had. He always would. That was simply what best friends did.

Trying to find him at home had done no good whatsoever and now she jogged the distance to the Basilisk, where his mother had said he was spending a great deal of his free time. Her frantic state of mind threw off her ability to breathe properly and she was forced to stop just before the front door and catch her breath.

She looked at the huge old house with the same mixture of feelings that she always had; awe at its stunning landscaping and more than a little dread at the thought of passing the unique statuary that P. J. had placed around the premises. The creatures that seemed to peer around trees and look out from beneath the crawl space made her want to shudder. Roughly carved as they were, they all seemed to have a life of their own. She could easily imagine the various gargoyles and ghouls sneaking away from the house late at night and going to find flesh to feast on.

Pushing away the morbid thoughts, she forced herself into the sanctuary of the store and was relieved to find P. J. and Tyler looking over at her with mild surprise and more than a touch of concern. Ty frowned and for the first time it occurred to her that she might be interfering in something that was private. Then Ty smiled and she realized that all was well with the world. Tyler Wilson was here and if anyone could drive the demons away, it was him.

"Cassie, babe, how are you?" The concern ran across his face, so much like an open book to her, and she realized that she was supposed to be in mourning for her Grandmother. "You holdin' up okay?" Tyler ran over to her and gave her a brief hug with his reed-thin arms; she hugged back ferociously and felt better for it. Tyler looked away from her, over to P. J., and said that he'd be back in a little while. P. J. was anything but slow and nodded once, a sad smile on his face, before going back to the enormous stack of moldy books in front of him.

Tyler casually wrapped an arm around her shoulders and she realized numbly that he too was in a serious growth spurt, he was almost as tall as she was once again. She waved and smiled her thanks to the author, as they slipped outside.

They walked in silence for a little while, until they came upon a clearing near one of the dozens of tiny creeks that trickled through the woods. Tyler cleared the dust and leaves off a couple of the larger rocks and settled her down upon one of them before perching on the other just off to her right.

"So," his face shifted into his The Doctor Is In look and he pushed his thick glasses back into place. "Are you going to tell me what's wrong, or are we going to play twenty questions?" The smile he flashed took any possible hurt from the words and looking at him, she felt the sting of tears starting in her eyes.

Before she knew what was happening, she started blurting out the words. "Mark went into the woods with Lisa the very same night that I went to bury my Grammy. He went into the woods with her and they almost screwed. I thought he cared for me, I thought he was special. I thought he was going to be the one, the one I gave myself to." She felt the tears flowing with greater force and closed her eyes, covering her face with her hands as she finally let the impact of her Grandmother's death and her betrayal by Mark sink in. It couldn't have been a second later that she felt Tyler's thin body and arms crush against her. He pulled her close with remarkable strength and forced her to accept the comfort of his friendship. She cried, hormones and grief gathering together in strength and assaulting her as a hurricane batters a rowboat adrift at sea. She mourned the loss of her Grandmother; she mourned the loss of the innocence that had marked her relationship with Mark and she mourned the fact that childhood ends, replaced by the bitter cynicism of puberty.

Through it all, Tyler, who knew of all these things, held her and whispered gentle assurances and proved once again that he was the finest friend a girl could ask for. She realized that he too was crying, mourning with her the pains of a broken heart.

When she was finally done crying, he pulled the button up shirt off of his back, leaving behind a tee shirt that was in desperate need of bleaching and offered his dress shirt to her as a make-shift hanky. She accepted gratefully and he stroked her long hair and rubbed lightly at the tension that had developed in her neck and shoulders.

Finally, he sat next to her and folded her hand into a tight grasp, pulling it towards his chest. They sat for several moments in the silence of the woods, listening to the birds chirrup and the occasional hiss of a car going down Third Avenue, hidden away by the trees.

Then he looked at her and said, "Would you like to hear the whole story now, or would you rather wait for the TV movie?"

Cassie looked over at her friend and saw the gentle admonition on his angular face. "What do you mean, 'the whole story?' Mark told me himself."

Tyler grinned that ridiculous grin of his and shook his head sadly. "Since when have you ever known Mark to have the slightest clue as to what was going on around him?" She wanted to protest, to defend him, despite what he had done, but Tyler held up his hand, signaling for her to stop before she got started. "Mark never noticed that you were looking at him almost as much as he was looking at you. Mark never noticed that the Asshole Patrol had it out for him in a bigger way than they did for other kids, and Mark never noticed that Tony Scarrabelli was the biggest homophobe this planet has ever seen." He pushed his glasses back into place again and frowned at her, defying her to deny any of the things that he had just said; she couldn't, they were all the truth.

"Mark never noticed that his own face is more that a little effeminate; you put him in a dress with falsies and the guys would go wild. Mark just doesn't think that way, he's too busy think about other things, like horror novels," Tyler leered at her and winked evilly, "and getting into your very shapely pants." That did it, she stood up, ready to tear into him for the comment and he looked at her, with enough force behind the stare, to stagger her. "Sit down! I'm not finished yet." Shocked by the anger in his voice, she sat.

"I'm not saying anything bad about Mark. Hell, I happen to think he's a very nice guy, I'm just saying that he's never been what you would call quick on the pick-up."

Tyler turned away from her for a moment and then looked at her with a forgiving smile. "I think you're tops, you know that. But, I have to say some of the same things about you." Again, he held up the cautionary hand and again she waited for a further explanation.

"What I'm trying to get across to you, is that I knew he was about to get into trouble and if you'd been paying attention, you would have too."

He shrugged his shoulders and looked her in the eye as he sat in front of her on the rock and pulled her hands to him. "Lisa's been looking at him like he was fresh meat, for weeks."

"No. I would have noticed, I would have spotted that." Her protests were, to be kind, weak.

Tyler grinned like the Cheshire Cat and shook his head gently. "No doubt. Just like you noticed that Tony's been looking at you like a starving man looks at a roast beef sandwich." She stared at him, certain that he'd lost his mind and he continued undaunted. "So suddenly, the guy that's been trashing Mark since his first day in school, the guy that's been out for my blood since the third grade, got a conscience? Wake up, Cassie! He's been wanting to jump you for the last two years!"

Cassie decided to get to the heart of this and get to it fast, before he said something that she couldn't deny and that she really didn't want to hear. "Well, so what if he has? I didn't go off into the woods with him, did I?" She was feeling damn triumphant about her little retort, until Tyler asked her the question that she'd been dreading.

Looking her in the eyes, with perceptions as sharp as a hunting hawk, he asked, "Are you saying you wouldn't?" She had no answer to that and he clarified, making sure that she saw his point. "Are you actually saying that if Tony Scarrabelli was innocently walking in the woods with you and kissed you on your lips, that you wouldn't be sorely tempted to let it go farther? You know better," he chastised softly. "I've seen the way you watch him when we're at the pool. It's not a one-way street."

She didn't know what to say, she was torn by her anger and her guilt; Tyler often had that effect when it came to solving differences. Tyler opted to have mercy on her and told the rest of the story. "I got a call on Sunday morning. Lisa Scarrabelli. She wanted someone to talk to and she found me." He looked away for a moment, muttering something about the enormous number of attractive females that called on him for advice, but never for anything else, and then turned back to her. Cassie felt a brief flash of guilt about that, too. "She admitted to me that she all but raped him. That's between you and me, I gave her my word that I wouldn't tell anyone and I wouldn't have, if it wasn't so important to you. I'm trusting in you to leave well enough alone and not go beat the shit out of her or anything." She stared at him for several seconds and finally nodded her agreement. "Everybody was out doing their own thing and she saw an opportunity to add one more to her list of broken hearts." Cassie recalled all too well the way she used to lead Tyler around and was amazed at the lack of bitterness he seemed to feel about the whole situation. "Mark was pretty much all for it at first, but he decided he couldn't go through with it. He said it would be wrong, because of the way he felt about you."

He looked her in the eye again and refused to let her look away. "Cassie, he's a guy and not exactly a guy that's used to being shown affection, except from his mom, maybe. Take it from someone that people only now and then consider to be among the same species; once the hormones kick in, it's damn near impossible to tell them to shut up." He smiled again and broke the spell that he seemed to have had over her. He was just Tyler again, not a mesmerist with supernatural powers. "He stopped himself and he left her in the woods and he told you all about the whole thing. He had some dirty thoughts, but he didn't do anything all that horrible. He stopped because he loves you. He doesn't love Lisa. It's just that simple."

Cassie stood in silence for a long time and Tyler held her hands in his throughout the drawn out silence, reading her face and wanting to know what she decided. Finally, she smiled and looked at him with guilt on her face. "Guess I overreacted huh?"

Tyler smiled at her and patted her hands. "Not at all, make him squirm for awhile. He deserves it for playing around on you. But, when you think he's suffered enough, accept his apologies." He winked again, with a mischievous smirk on his face. "And let him know that if he does it again, you'll tear his balls off." He looked towards the road and the Basilisk. "Screw all the sayings you hear, 'Forgive but never forget,' that's my motto."

10

It was Saturday by the time she finally decided he had suffered enough. He was so grateful that he insisted on taking her to the movies and to dinner. The movie was good, the dinner was okay and the hugs and talking were wonderful. She was glad that they were back together. She was ecstatic.

That same Saturday, Mr. and Mrs. Arnold Blake reported their son Tommy missing. Sheriff Charles Hanson stated that he would keep a look out and prayed the boy was all right. It would be over a month before his body was found.

The clouds that built that night were black and threatening and promised a hellish storm indeed. Mark and Cassie never even noticed; they had eyes only for each other. Mark gave her a passionate goodnight kiss and slowly walked towards his home as the first fat drops started to fall and had only just made it inside, when the first lick of lightning kissed the surface of the lake. Had it struck him in the head he wouldn't have even noticed, save to think that it could never compare to the kiss of the girl he loved.

Chapter Eight

1

Life went fairly smoothly for a while. Most of the town's gossip mongers had moved from stories and fictions about Tommy Blake's disappearance—the boy had moved to L.A. and was going to be an actor, the boy was in trouble with the law and planned to leave town, the boy could no longer stand the abuse his parents heaped on him, sexual abuse at that—and found other juicier things to whisper about. School was in its last two weeks and Mark was more in love with Cassie than he had been before. Fortunately, the feeling was returned. It was almost as if they were locked together by chains, so seldom were they seen apart. The coming summer held great promise, a potential to spend every available moment together.

Lisa soon grew away from her infatuation, to one that she found too silly to even contemplate; she had strong suspicions that she was falling for Tyler, in whom she saw many of the same qualities that she had seen in Mark. Rather than suffer the shocked stares of her peers, she simply went back to another flame, one she hadn't devastated for a few years, and put thoughts of Mark and Tyler on the back burner.

Tyler continued in his normal way, assaulting the guilty and innocent alike with his tongue and running for dear life a few moments later. If he had any feelings about the relationship between Mark and Cassie, he kept them to himself, never the one to admit to anything that vaguely resembled jealousy. In reference to Lisa, he could see the way she looked at him and after a few hours of worry, decided it was best to let her make her own decisions. This wise choice had been made several times in the past about other girls who momentarily opted to look past the Face That Time Destroyed (as he liked to put it, when no one was around to hear) and he suspected that nothing would change; she would go on dating the morons that he had to endure and he would fantasize about crawling all over her ripe little body. Tyler had an annoying tendency to be overly critical which, sadly, was the wise thing for him to do at the age of sixteen.

In the meantime, Phillip James Sanderson spent his time looking over his collection of rare occult books for some hint or clue about what might be happening in Summitville. P. J. spent a great deal of time trying to figure out just which book to look in and he looked with a fervor, because he seemed to recall something very similar to what Tyler had described to him, but he couldn't for the life of him remember where. Frankly, he'd read the damn books so very long ago and had both written and read so much popular horror fiction, that he no longer was even certain that he had read the description in one of his collections of antique books.

Patrick Wilson was still the number one source of chemical escape in Summitville, but he was easing out of it gradually and paid his new supplier on time, religiously; he was stoned, but not stupid and when he read the name of the mysterious shotgun slinger, in the newspaper, he took the hint that maybe it was time to give college some serious contemplation. Some place private, like Alaska. He was also giving serious contemplation to just saying NO to drugs. He kept flashing back to the horrible trip he had recently been forced to endure, revolving around Mark and Tommy. The thought of it was enough to send the chills through his body.

Joe managed to find enough spare time in the day to worry about Mark and to marvel at how he'd changed since they had moved into the small town. His son (never his stepson anymore) had become a man almost overnight and he thanked God that he'd been around to see it.

Jennifer Howell continued to sell her artwork and to spend time with her husband and son. Of all the people in the town she seemed the least disturbed by bad emotions, little ever seemed to faze her. It wasn't that she was unaware of the things that went on around her, both good and bad, it was simply that she refused to let anything get her down. It was just that trait that made her fast friends wherever she lived, even in a town as paranoid about strangers as Summitville. It was just that trait that had attracted Joe to her in the first place. Much to her husband's perpetual delight, she continued to have a voracious sexual appetite.

Tony Scarrabelli, on the other hand, openly accepted what Cassie had to say about her feelings for Mark, but refused to acknowledge them in his heart. He was absolutely convinced that he loved her and to prove to her that she loved him he went out with every girl he could get his hands on. He felt that by making her jealous enough, he could win her love. Not even Tyler could convince him otherwise.

Rick Lewis and Chuck Hanson still looked for clues, anything that would tell them what had happened to the missing and murdered of the town, a task made more difficult by the acts of random violence that add to the number of deaths in even the smallest town. Both had become somewhat paranoid as time went on. Both still believed, without a single solid lead, that Mark Howell was responsible in some way. Both were, of course, quite right.

Without a body, the Blakes kept up a nightly vigil, hoping that their son would write to them or, even better, come home. They refused to accept that their precious boy could possibly be dead. He was all that they had.

Antoinette and Raphael Scarrabelli pretended to be civil to one another, barely. Antoinette went "shopping" in Denver almost daily. Raphael didn't have to go as far, he was engaged in a ridiculously clichéd relationship with the maid. He never questioned his wife's trips to the city and she never questioned the frequent bonuses that he awarded Sally. She did, however, take every opportunity to verbally attack the maid about her lack of cleaning prowess.

And, Tyler Wilson finally managed to convince Cassie's parents to at least meet Mark Howell before making a judgment. For reasons known only to themselves, they took Tyler at his word about the shooting a while back and finally understood that Mark had actually saved their little Cassandra's life, getting himself wounded in the process. Tyler actually wrote the date down on his computer journal; it was one of his greatest triumphs ever. For her part, Cassie tried to swallow the knowledge that her parents put more trust in Tyler than they did in her.

2

The dinner meeting was set for the Friday night before the final week of school and all in all, it went fairly well. Clifford and Anita Monroe had decided to reserve judgment (again, at Tyler's request) until after they had met Mark and they were suitably impressed by his manners. To make the night go down a little easier, the Monroes had invited along Tyler, who was remarkably well behaved in their presence, and he managed to point out all of Mark's best attributes in a subtle way that any who truly knew him would have recognized. Mark sounded like a demigod before the dessert was served and could have probably asked for and received their blessings, if he had decided then and there to ask for Cassie's hand in marriage.

Cassie's parents proved to be something of a surprise in their own right. They were not at all the ogres that Mark had envisioned them to be. Cliff, (just call me Cliff, young man, my father was Mister Monroe) proved to be intelligent and charming and had the easy good looks and manners of a man bred to be healthy and wealthy. Mark imagined that dinner with the Kennedys would be something like the dinner he was served that night and he had little doubt that the man who had fathered the girl he loved was probably on good terms with the Kennedys and the Rockefellers and the Vanderbilts, Et Al. Anita (Annie, dear, call me Annie) was almost as beautiful as her daughter and carried herself with the same delicate grace. It was obvious that they cared greatly for their only daughter and seeing as he felt the same way himself, Mark forgave all trespasses against him.

As always, meeting the parents of one of his friends was extremely unsettling; he always expected them to be as young as his mother was. Mark was, thankfully, always quick to hide the shock he felt and in this case, the shock was minimal. He guessed that neither of her parents were much above the mid-thirties mark.

The conversations lasted until almost midnight as the Monroes subtly grilled Mark on where he had lived and what his plans for the future were. They were a little disappointed that he wanted to be a writer, (Don't you feel that the entertainment industry would be difficult to break into, Mark?) until they heard that he had already sold one novel and was planning to write another one over the summer. They were also quite surprised to hear that he still intended to go to college, despite his early success. His response to the surprise they showed was "I can only learn to do what I'm already doing better than I'm doing it now. And that way, if the writing ever dries up and fades away, I'll have something to fall back on." To him, it was the only sensible thing to do; to them, it was a sign that the boy was not planning to waste his life on empty dreams.

Tyler almost stood and applauded at the end of the little speech.

Over brandy and cigars (Cliff insisted that a meal was not finished until after brandy and cigars), the three men talked about politics and other subjects in Cliff's den, while Cassie grilled her mother for her impression of Mark. When at last it was time for the dinner and meeting to be over with, Cassie walked outside with the two males in the world that meant as much to her as her father, and said her goodbyes. To Tyler, she gave a fierce hug and a kiss on the lips that left her young friend speechless. To Mark, she smiled and gave him a quick hug, knowing that her parents would be watching from somewhere in the house. Both men smiled lovingly at her as they left.

Cassie went back inside, assured that she could now speak Mark's name without fear of a nasty little argument breaking out. She was very happy about the situation and again indebted forever to Tyler, who always seemed to have the right words to say and a shoulder to lean on.

3

Tyler and Mark walked over to Tyler's house on the next street and enjoyed the late night spring air. The breeze was a gentle kiss on the skin and the temperature was just chilled enough for them to be glad of the late night brandy.

They had walked just under half of the distance, when Mark turned to Tyler and rested a hand on his friend's shoulder. Tyler looked into his friend's eyes and realized that Mark was more than a little buzzed as a result of the potent liquor they had consumed. "Listen, I know I've already said it, but thanks. I don't think her parents would have ever given me a chance, if it wasn't for you."

Tyler looked back at him and beamed happily. "Shit, I still owe you for the scar you got on my account. I'd do anything for you, you're a hell of a guy." The words were true, but only brought on by alcohol; the kinds of words he'd regret if he remembered the whole thing tomorrow.

Mark looked slightly taken aback by the comment and then he smiled shyly. Tyler was surprised by the honesty on his friend's face and the slight break in his voice when he responded. "You're a good friend, Ty, probably the best friend I've ever had." Before Tyler could come up with the proper sarcastic response, Mark continued. "If every person in the world had one friend like you, there'd never be another reason for a person to kill himself." Mark turned away and Tyler could see his throat working, he realized that Mark was trying to hold back tears.

Tyler looked at his friend for several moments and then gently laid his bony hand on Mark's shoulder. "Hey, c'mon, this is me, Tyler, tell me what's wrong."

Mark turned towards him then and he saw the tears that fell freely from his friend's eyes. Tyler was almost shocked by the tears and he felt his heart break a little. "Ty, I'm scared, man. I-I think maybe I did something really bad. But I can't be sure."

Tyler pulled the larger boy to him and hugged him awkwardly, ashamed of the little part of himself that worried about somebody seeing them in the position they were in; embarrassed to show his affection to somebody for the first time in his life. After a few minutes, when Mark was finished crying on his shoulder, he gently pulled his friend towards the massive structure he called a home. They didn't speak at all as Tyler led Mark into the house and past the dark living room, down to the rec room his father had furnished with every conceivable way to amuse oneself.

They sat in silence for some time and then Tyler got up and poured them each a soda, ignoring the need for ice in them, and handed one to Mark. "So, tell me what you think you did. Maybe I can give you some help."

Mark looked at him for a long time, seemingly weighing whether or not he could trust Tyler with so dark a secret. Finally, he decided that he could and looked away, unable to face his best friend as he made his confession. "I think that maybe I killed Tommy Blake."

Tyler sat in stunned silence as alarm bells rang in his mind. Now just how the hell was he supposed to handle this one? Jesus, wasn't life already complicated enough? "Shit, Mark, that's fucking serious. Don't joke about that kind of thing, okay?"

Mark looked up at last and the sorrow on his face spoke volumes. He pulled at his own hair, not hard, but hard enough to hurt. "I'm not joking, Tyler. I wish the hell I was, but I'm not." Tyler watched as Mark clenched and unclenched his fists, again and again. He knew the danger signs in Mark well enough to know that his friend was ready to destroy anything that crossed his path. The thought was not conducive to his own stability. With sudden inspiration, Tyler stood up and walked over to where the gymnasium part of the rec room lay, hidden in the shadows.

The rec room was sound-proofed, a bit of foresight on his father's part as he knew that sooner or later his sons would want to have parties and he valued his sleep too much to have to listen to them. He also valued his sanity enough not to say no, when they asked. Tyler's father was not the strictest man; he could even have been said to be rather lacking in the discipline department.

Ty pulled hard at the heavy bag on the floor and finally managed to place it on the hook that hung from the ceiling. He grabbed the light gloves and walked back over to Mark, where he sat with his head in his hands. "Here, put these on."

"What? Why?"

Tyler mock-scowled and pushed the gloves into Mark's lap. "Don't argue with me, put the damn things on. You need to vent some steam and I don't want it vented on me."

Mark put the gloves on and Tyler pointed to the heavy bag. Tyler quickly adjusted the anchoring chain, giving the bag almost no slack, as it was hung from the ceiling and now chained to the floor. "Now, I'm going to step away from the bag and you can whack away at it as you tell me what's on your mind."

So saying Tyler stepped back and Mark looked skeptically at the punching bag. "You want me to hit this?"

"No, I want you to French kiss it. Of course, I want you to hit it. That's what it's there for. And get that goofy look off of your face; I told you to hit it and I mean *hit it*, trust me, it's very therapeutic."

Mark shook his head and took a halfhearted swing that barely grazed the bag. Tyler groaned in disgust and looked him in the face. "Y'mother can hit a bag harder than that. Tell me your story and hit the bag, I'll be right here listening, but you're too goddamn tense to just sit there."

Mark finally caught on and started telling his tale, punctuating words with a savage strike to the bag. "Remember how Cassie and I had that big fight a couple of weeks ago?" Mark hit the bag, which let out a satisfying "*Whump*" with each strike. "Well, we had that fight because of Lisa Scarrabelli. *Whump* I guess you already know about that, don't you?" *Whump* He acknowledged Ty's nod and continued. "Well, I got angry, mostly with myself I guess, *Whump* when Cassie walked away from me."

He stalled in his conversation, spending several minutes doing nothing but taking swings at the bag, strikes that got progressively harder. "Well, I got to thinking about how Tommy had been giving you grief at school, *Whump* and I decided to have a talk with him. *Whump* I never expected to get into a fight with him, but he sorta makes it easy to want to fight." Mark paused long enough in the swings and in his story, to remove his dress shirt and tie and coat. The gloves went back on and Tyler marveled at the sight of Mark's body; he didn't look any larger exactly, just firmer than he had before. Tyler imagined the muscles in his friend's body were almost like steel.

"I told him I'd heard about what he tried to do, *Whump* and he said that it was your fault, that you made Lisa break up with him. *Whump* Well, I told him that was a bunch of shit and said that she had been considering breaking up with him for a long time, *Whump* that's what she told me, when she took me out to dinner, back when you got grounded. *Whump* He started calling me a liar and calling me names. *Whump* I thought about how he'd helped get me trashed last year *WHUMP* and I started getting really angry. I started calling him names back." *WHUMP!* Tyler noticed the increase in force that Mark was using on the bag and actually worried briefly that his father would be awakened. He decided it was okay, because his father was on the third floor and they were in the basement. Otherwise, he would have made Mark stop.

"He hit me, Tyler. *WHUMP* He hauled off with his fist and knocked me on my ass. I never even saw it coming.

WHUMP And when I tried to get up, *WHA WHUMP* he kicked me in my stomach. I thought I was going to spit blood."

Mark hit the bag in a flurry of punches that seemed to Tyler to be too fast for the human eye to catch. Tyler guessed that if he'd hit it one more time, the canvas would tear open, spilling out sand. In his mind's eye, he pictured what that same savage assault would have done if it had connected with, oh, say, Tommy Blake's rib cage. He felt rather queasy at the image.

"I don't really remember anything after that, I just sort of blacked out. I didn't even give it another thought, until I heard that Tommy didn't show up at school. I thought maybe I'd managed to get in a few good ones and he was hurt bad enough to stay at home. Ty, I was hoping that I'd hurt him that bad." Mark looked at him, desperately hoping that he was making his point. "What if I did? What if I killed him?"

Mark pulled the gloves off of his hands and Tyler could see the red knuckles of his fists. He looked up and saw Mark's face crack, like fine porcelain dropped from the top of the house. "Ty, I'm scared. I don't remember."

Mark's whole body seemed to sag then and he started crying openly. Again, Tyler pulled him close and let his friend cry. "It's gonna be okay, Mark. It's not something that you'd do. I know you, you'd never throw the first punch." Mark looked at him, his chest hitching desperately to grab more air. Tyler looked at him and led him back to the couch.

"Are you so sure, Tyler? Do you really believe that I couldn't?"

Tyler forced himself to look in his friend's face, as he said he was certain. His mind was thinking back to the look on Mark's face when he shoved Cassie out of the way of the buck-shot, that only Mark seemed able to perceive as it flew towards her: the look of a wild beast, barely hidden by the thin veneer of a man's face. Inside, he wasn't as certain as he said he was. Inside, he prayed desperately that he would never get on Mark's bad side, and chastised himself for the doubts he had. "'Course I'm sure. Relax, I'll help you figure out what the hell happened."

Again, silence fell for several minutes and then Mark looked over at him. "I wish I was so sure. I can almost feel the changes going on in my body. I don't really look any different, but I feel different. Does that make any sense?"

"Yeah, that happens to everybody when puberty hits. Hormone rush from hell, man."

Mark looked at him for a minute and then turned away from him for a moment or two, before starting to speak again. "Do you remember when I got my contact lenses, a couple of weeks after we met?"

Tyler frowned for a second and then recalled the lenses almost as thick as his own, that Mark used to wear. "Yeah, you stood around all day, freaking 'cause you could see more of what was off to your sides. But what's that got to do with anything?"

Mark looked at him with a vaguely puzzled expression that scarcely hid the fact that he was looking inward, rather than at Tyler. "My vision was almost as bad as yours, Ty. Except I didn't have any astigmatism." Mark focused on Tyler completely and Tyler felt the intensity of his gaze. "Ty, I'm not wearing my contacts. I haven't needed them for over a month. Have you ever known puberty to fix the eyesight of someone who was legally blind without glasses?"

Tyler had no answer for that one, his mind was too busy refusing to believe what he'd just heard. No, he'd never heard of any such thing.

4

Patrick crept up the hallway and slid gracefully up the stairs to his own room. The last thing he needed was for Tyler to find out he had been eavesdropping on a private conversation. And he most certainly didn't want Mark to find out.

He hadn't planned on listening in, it just sort of happened. He'd just been doing his own thing and heading down the stairs for his stash in the rec room and he heard the voices through the crack in the door. Well, hell folks, the story he heard had just been too damn good to ignore.

And it had also been too damn scary to ignore. It brought back to mind the things he thought he'd seen in the woods the other day. Little things, that jumped and danced in a frenzy of excitement while Tommy and Mark had it out on the football field at the school.

The field was where he always made his deliveries: it was close to the woods in case the Sheriff should show and it was pretty much neutral territory; no muss, no fuss and he was on the way home faster than a cobra could strike. He had been on his way to make a delivery to Tommy, one of his few remaining customers, when he'd seen Mark come out of the woods, walking like a man with a mission.

He'd known Mark almost as long as Tyler had. He was no where near as close to him, but he knew him. Or at least he'd thought he knew him, until he saw him come out of the woods that day. At first he thought it was the drugs playing with his mind and then he *knew* it was the drugs playing with his mind. Mark was easily three or four inches taller than he remembered him being, and seeing as he'd last seen him only a few months ago, that was a hell of a lot of growth.

But it was more than that, Mark looked meaner than it was possible for Mark to look. He walked stiff backed, like a dog getting ready for a fight and his upper lip had pulled away from his teeth, a sneer of contempt for the guy he was about to face. He looked like he'd have fun taking on a couple of drill sergeants and maybe the Dallas Cowboys; worse still, he looked like he would have a hell of a chance of winning. It was as much in the way he carried himself, as it was in the way he had changed physically. Everybody changes at that age, Patrick himself had looked an awful lot like Tyler once upon a time, but the changes in personality, in the way he walked and the way he looked at people, it just wasn't right.

If he hadn't known better, he'd have thought that Mark was soaring on PCP. Patrick had watched a guy heavy into that kind of shit go berserk once. That had been the first time he'd considered giving up drugs. This skinny little guy, name of Stan Powers, had just gone nuts and started swinging his little fists with enough power to drop the Wildman's personal assistant with one punch; a guy that had outweighed him by at least seventy-five pounds of solid muscle. Then he'd really gone nuts. Stan tore through the room like a fucking tornado and no amount of talk had come anywhere near to calming him down. Patrick had watched the whole thing from behind a sofa, he'd seen Stan knock over tables and people like they were balloons; he'd seen Stan break his own fists against one of the walls and keep going like it was nothing at all. He'd watched numbly, as Stan drove his already pulped right hand into the television set, breaking the glass of the screen and electrocuting himself.

What he'd seen when he was out on the field that night had been much worse. If he hadn't been so deep into an acid dream at that time, he might have believed it.

When he was safely in his room and had the door closed and locked, he reached into his closet, feeling for the hole he'd cut into the wall behind and above the closet's shelf and pulled out his .357 Magnum. He'd never had reason to fire it and he doubted that he ever would, but he loaded it with bullets just the same. If he ever saw Mark coming at him the way he'd come at Tommy Blake that day, he'd be ready. Not all the drugs in the world would stop a round from this baby.

5

The last day of school finally came and, after what seemed a few lifetimes, the final bell of the year echoed shrilly through the hallways. As the last bell rang, the halls of Charles S.

Westphalen High, exploded with frenetic noise and the bodies of teenagers, free at last to do as they pleased, at least until August crept around again.

Mark was introduced that day to a Summitville tradition; the rolling of the school. After living under the iron rule of Samuel Watkins for the majority of the year, a man who felt that chewing gum in class was tantamount to murder and should be punishable by death, the students all gathered together, free from his tyrannical rule and proceeded to toss roll after roll of toilet paper high into the air and across the school's facade, roof and greenery. It was a day that they all dreamed of, secure in the knowledge that no harm would befall them as long as they didn't pull any offense too serious, like spray-painting anything, or worse. To ensure that they behaved themselves, Deputy Sheriff Alan Fisk and the Big Man himself, Chuck Hanson, watched with amused grins from the sidelines. Sam the Ham had long since given up on anything that even vaguely resembled resistance to the notion and normally sat back at his desk and lit a fat and foul scented cigar, the better to enjoy the show. If anyone could be said to take it poorly, it was the staff of janitors, who really couldn't complain too much, as they had done the very same thing in their day.

Mark found the idea of rolling the school and not getting in trouble very strange, but considering some of the things he'd known people in the big cities he'd lived in to get away with, simply opted to enjoy himself. Twenty dollars worth of facial-quality paper later, he decided that he rather liked the tradition. But, nothing surprised him as much as when Sheriff Hanson asked for volunteers to help in the clean up and most of the students actually stayed to help. Cassie and Tyler had opted to help, so he did the same. Seeing their decision, Tony joined in as well. Around five-thirty, the majority of the clean up was done and they all wandered away in small clusters, laughing and saying good bye to those they most likely wouldn't see until the next school year. Mark was touched and pleased by the number of people who said such good-byes to him, as well as the number who wanted him to sign their annuals; it was the first time in his life that he signed more year books than he had fingers on his left hand. He and his closest friends were joined by eight others and all of them took off for the center of town where most of the freed youths would spend the better part of the summer, talking about nothing of great import and being seen with those they cared for most in the world, their friends (friends being ever so much more important in the late teens than family).

As night fell full and proper in the hot, dry summer air, the informal and unofficial party dispersed and most went their own ways. Each knew that by this time next year their status could have changed completely. They could be low man on the totem of inner school society, but for the present time they were all freed of the status they struggled to achieve in the school and they could all be themselves. In more than one case, people who had ignored long-time friends rekindled the camaraderie that they had known the summer before, without so much as batting an eye about the entire situation. The rules were gone and the freedom to just be themselves had come back, however briefly, to remind one and all that life was for the living, life was for the young. And they were all so young that summer—younger than they ever would be again.

As happened every time the school year ended, a few of the more daring, (normally the seniors, who would be heading away from their hometown when the holiday ended, possibly never to return) remembered Lake Overtree and decided that the time was right for a dip in the tepid lake's refreshing waters. Preferably a dip that involved no clothing and a partner of the opposite sex. This year was nearly a record for the number of people who attended, finding their own spot on the lake's shore; a spot with enough secrecy to allow their natural urges to take over should their partner's be willing, but close enough to others to allow voices to carry and the occasional view of other people, the better to remember that you weren't really all alone in the dark woods where Stoney Miles still roamed looking to catch you with his wife, or any female he might mistake for her.

As many people showed this year with bathing suits as did without. Among those who had garments were Tyler, Tony, Cassie, Mark, Lisa, Sandy and another six people, to make an even dozen. Somehow Tyler and Lisa ended up paired together and, somehow, neither of them seemed to mind. Somehow, the rest of the group lost track of them a good while later and somehow, they never seemed to mention the fact to one another. Tony, complete with Sue Talbot on his arm, also disappeared, but he made good and damn sure that Cassie knew where he was going and what he planned to do. She pretended not to be a little bit jealous of the fact and Mark pretended not to notice her jealousy.

Jack Watkins and Kathy Olsen, seniors who were at last free of the high school and both eagerly awaiting their letters of acceptance from the University in Denver, found a favorite spot of theirs from the year before and they took full advantage of the area, kissing and holding one another when they weren't in the process of laughingly trying to drown each other in the waters of Overtree. They had grown up near each other and had been an item through most of their time at Westphalen. They fully expected to go to school together at the university and they planned on coming home when they had graduated and marrying. They had already picked names for the children they planned to share. Their love, they were certain, would stand the test of time with ease. That their futures were intertwined was the one thing that both were absolutely certain of and their certainty was as strong as the faith that many hold in the Lord above them. Where many of their peers had gone to the lake believing that they may never see their present partner again after the summer ended, believing that this would be their last real chance to hold and share intimate feelings with the one beside them, Jack and Kathy felt no such pressures. They simply enjoyed one another's company, prepared to face whatever the future might hold for them as one spirit in two bodies.

Even the faith of the strongest is tested from time to time. And so it was that Kathy and Jack's resolve was tested, when, after four years of waiting, Kathy agreed to consummate their relationship. All was well, until they had finished and were in the process of stepping out of the lake's waters. (Kathy was absolutely convinced, thanks to her girlfriend Marilee, that the waters took the sting away from losing your virginity. As was normally the case, Marilee had no idea in hell what she was talking about and she would have to let her dear friend know that, if she decided to confide in her again. But the pain had been worth it, she had made Jack happy and she had enjoyed it herself, after the initial sting.) They were in the process of stepping back to the muddy shore, when Jack cut his foot open on something in a plastic bag.

With a hearty yelp of pain, he hobbled on one foot and promptly fell on his bare ass in the waters, leaving Kathy in the awkward position of trying to ensure that he was unharmed, while trying not to laugh at the stupid look on his face.

He came out of the water howling and holding on to his ass cheek, as if he'd been stung by an angry hornet. More than slightly embarrassed, Kathy studied the wound on his injured posterior and was glad it had happened to his back-side and not his front. It looked for all the world as if he'd sat on a knife. After she helped him out of the waters, where he quickly put on his clothes, she reached around at the spot where he'd cut himself and found the heavy plastic garbage bag that he had stepped and then sat on. It took all of her strength to pull the package from the waters to the shore, but she managed.

Just as quickly as he had, she got dressed and the two of them took off for the Summitville Emergency clinic, because despite the rather humorous location, they feared that Jack might need stitches. They took the bag with them and never even bothered to look inside; it stank something fierce and they threw it in the trunk, after the fifteen-minute hike back to the school's parking lot.

At the clinic, Doctor Richard Lewis tried his best not to laugh out loud, and took a look at the wound. When he asked if they knew what he'd cut himself on, Kathy immediately explained about the bag and with the help of one of the interns, hauled the soggy mass into the clinic.

Rick took one whiff of the waterlogged black lump and set it aside. He pulled on gloves, and got out the sponges for scrubbing. The wounds were deep, and the shit Jack had cut himself on was exactly the sort of stuff that could lead to dangerous infections. As the young man yiped, groaned and all but howled, Rick inspected the deep cut and cleansed the wound on Jack Wallace's derriere and applied a thick layer of gauze; telling the young man to wait while he made a phone call.

Ten minutes later, Sheriff Hanson stepped into the room and asked questions of the two young lovers for over an hour. Finally, Kathy agreed to show him the exact spot where the package had been located. But he refused to answer her questions as to why, simply saying that it was official police business. Jack went home a short while later and heard from Kathy after the Sheriff dropped her off as he had promised.

What the two of them found out the next day was just exactly why the doctor had been so thorough in the cleansing of the wound and just exactly what they had hauled to the clinic with them. They had gone the entire night unaware of the fact that they had found a portion of the mortal remains of Tommy Blake, primarily, the upper torso region. The sheriff found three more bags in the same basic area, one with his arms, one with his legs and one with his head, which apparently warranted a bag all its own. They'd have both slept better if they'd never heard of the bags' contents.

It took a while for Rick Lewis to realize which part of Tommy was which. Whoever had killed him had made certain to break every single bone in his body, with the single exception of those in his head. In a moment of near hysteria, Rick pointed out to his college roommate that if the look on the corpse's face was any indication, the victim had been alive for the vast majority of the bone breaking.

Had Hanson been a softer man, he would have lost his three-chili-dog lunch, much as Rick had, when the realization came to him. Chuck considered shock to be a luxury. He did, however, find it to be very peculiar that the fish had refused to partake of the flesh left in the waters for them. The bags had all been torn and they would have had ample opportunity. After he'd listened to all that Rick had to say, Chuck nodded and, looking a mite on the pale side, excused himself.

When the chili-dogs had finished freeing themselves of his stomach, he broke the law and lit himself a cigarette. When he was finished, he had another. When he came out of the rest room, walking through the virtual cloud of nicotine that flowed freely from the enclosed space, he ignored Rick's shocked stare and lit two more. Rick Lewis hated smoking and always had, since he lost his father to cancer. Today was an exception. Despite the coughing fit, he'd never loved the idea as much. He decided that the next body he found was going to start him on being a regular smoker and to prove his point, asked Chuck for another, right after he'd analyzed the protein traces that he found inside the cranium of the dear departed. Chuck gave the cigarette willingly and smiled as he looked out of the morgue's window. The smile would have scared away the Bogey Man.

Less than an hour later, Alan Fisk was assigned to watch Mark Howell. He'd be relieved some eight hours later by the part time deputy, Pat Whalen.

At eight in the morning, the day after the tail was assigned, Mark Howell turned himself in. It should have made Chuck Hanson's life easier. It didn't.

Chapter Nine

1

Chuck Hanson looked at Mark Howell and saw not an evil mass murderer, but a scared and confused young man. He would have preferred the mass murderer; it would have made his life ever so much easier.

He sat down at his desk and lit one of his patented hand rolled cigarettes and turned his predatory eyes towards Mark. Mark looked back at him and trembled. *Whatever else the boy might be,* he thought, *he sure as shit ain't a killer.*

"I understand you might know something about what happened to the Blake boy," he started, his voice a deep rumble in his barrel chest. "You want to tell me what that might be?"

Mark looked the Sheriff dead in the eye and with a trembling lower lip and a voice that cracked like thin ice responded. "I think I might have killed him, but I don't remember it."

Through the open doorway he could hear the sounds of his two town drunks screaming their protests at the cruel mistreatment they suffered in the arms of the law. Along with the original town drunk, Sam Posten, they now had the nightly pleasure of William Phillips' presence. The man had taken to drinking heavily when he heard about his son's suicide and nothing on this earth seemed strong enough to stop his need for liquor. He'd lost his job, his wife and about fifty pounds so far and Chuck couldn't think of anything that would change the trend he was on. He felt sorry for the man, but refused to let him wander around the town nightly. If only for the man's own safety he ended up with Will in his jail until ten in the morning, almost religiously.

Hanson lowered his head for a moment and rubbed at his temples. He absolutely hated days like this one; nothing ever

seemed to come easily. Every fiber of his being screamed that
Mark had something to do with the murders and he knew it
wasn't just his paranoia about strangers. Rick, a stranger in
town himself, felt the same way. "So, why don't you tell me
what you know or think you know and I'll see if it matches up
with what we know."

Mark proceeded to tell him about the confrontation with
Tommy Blake, leaving out only the reason that he went in
search of him that day. Chuck, for his part, asked him questions about when the incident had occurred, what he had been
wearing and whether or not he'd had any weapons with him.

Mark was rather shocked and even a mite indignant at
the thought that he might resort to a weapon and went about
explaining as much (but very diplomatically, as the Sheriff
was still a giant in comparison, despite his recent growth
spurts.). The Sheriff held up a hand and explained the line
of questioning, in a round about way. "I didn't mean to hurt
your pride, boy, I'm just doing my job. I can't divulge any
details, but I feel fairly safe in saying that if you weren't
using any weapons, you wouldn't have stood a chance in hell
against the Blake boy."

Once that would have been a relief to Mark. Now, he was
again mildly hurt by the comment. Hanson cautioned listening before taking anything the wrong way and continued.
"Tommy Blake was a black-belt in Tae Kwon Do, certified
and registered. He was practicing his kicks and punches around
the same time he was learning to walk. Most likely, no one
without the element of surprise would have been able to drop
him in hand to hand combat, 'cept maybe somebody like his
uncle, the man that taught him."

Hanson excused himself and picked up the phone, rapidly
dialing a number that he must've memorized. He turned his
back on Mark and talked in a low quiet tone to whoever was
on the other end of the line; Mark could hear the sounds, but
not quite make out the words. After almost ten minutes, the
sheriff hung up and turned back to him. "I was just talking to

Doc Lewis, I believe you know him, worked on your stitches awhile ago if I remember right. Anyway, he's also a qualified forensics doctor and I've been taking advantage of that, so I can get quick responses about what killed people in this area. Now, I won't tell you what was done to Tommy Blake, but I have been assured by the doctor that nobody could have done anything like what was done to that poor boy without a great deal of heavy equipment, or at least a few dozen dogs."

Mark looked puzzled by that and reminded the man that he didn't own a dog. "I know that Mark." He pinned Mark in place with a look. "I know a great deal about you. It's my job to learn about everyone that moves into *my* town." The way he emphasized the "MY" in his last comment hit Mark well and he swallowed any discomfort he felt about the man looking into his past. Obviously, Charles Hanson took his responsibilities to heart. "I know where you went to school and I know where you've lived. See, I thought long and hard about you moving to town and all the things that have happened since then." Mark didn't quite know whether or not he liked where the conversation was going. Wisely, he kept his mouth shut. "I've been watching you and I've been watching your folks. Before you go and take that the wrong way, I'll remind you that it's my job to keep the peace in this town and I take it very seriously. I'd watch anyone who came to Summitville the same way.

"What I'm getting at, is that I don't believe you have it in you to do the kind of damage that was done to Tommy Blake, or to Pete Larson. I still don't quite understand what happened on the day you got shot, but I imagine that was just one of those things that never really gets explained. All I know is that you couldn't have been responsible for that one either. Personally, I think you've been listening to the wrong voices in this town, the ones that take offense at you and yours moving here in the first place."

The sheriff leaned forward, close enough to Mark that he could smell the tobacco on his breath. "I'm a very thorough

man. I know approximately what time you went home that
night, because you told me. I know about what time Tommy
Blake died, because of what Rick Lewis told me and because
he was seen with other people before he disappeared. To a
degree, those times coincide. But not to a big enough degree.
Not only do I think you don't have it in you to kill a man, I
know you couldn't have killed Tommy Blake. Hell, you're
lucky he didn't cave your chest in when he kicked you."

They sat in silence for a few minutes and Hanson could
almost see the gears in the kid's head going around as he absorbed what he'd been told.

Finally Mark stood up and held his hand out for Hanson;
who, suppressing a smile at the solemn look on the boy's face,
took his sweaty palm firmly in his own and shook it. He
thanked the sheriff for his time and for the information and
Hanson would have sworn that he looked ten years younger
when he finally left the office.

Then Hanson reflected on what Rick Lewis had told him
about the fluid found in each case and thought about the time
his grandfather had visited him, after he had already died, and
suppressed a shudder. He didn't bother to tell his deputies
that they could come in from watching Mark Howell; he felt
that the extra watch couldn't hurt.

"Back to square one," he sighed, never realizing that the
sweat he wiped from his hand onto his pants leg, held traces
of a strange protein that Rick Lewis would have recognized in
a heartbeat.

2

Mark was feeling a world and a half better as he left for Red
Oaks. All of his doubts had been crushed by the simple and
direct manner in which the sheriff had assured him. He forced
himself not to think about the way in which Tommy must've
died and he forced himself not to think about the last comment the man had made to him. The one about caved-in rib

cages. Instead he thought of Cassie and the world brightened of its own accord.

He carefully pulled onto Third Avenue, avoiding the black Mustang that was taking the corner at the same time and pumping his legs as hard and as fast as he could. His trusty old bike took the torture with a minimum of protest and he felt the exhilaration that always accompanied a high-speed charge down the long stretch of road. The first mile disappeared under the Schwinn's tires in near record time.

As summer was officially here, he stopped well before his subdivision and decided to pay a visit to P. J. He pulled his bike off the main road and into the long driveway that stopped at the Basilisk. As he headed towards the glass front doors, Mark paused to study the statuary, marveling at the crude beauty that he could see in each of them. *One day*, he thought, *I'm going to own a house just like this one.*

The ideas for stories were already whirling through his head, calling sometimes softly and sometimes with great force, demanding his attention now that he no longer feared for his sanity. The answer had been right in front of him the entire time and he had never even noticed; it was obvious to him in hindsight that Tommy must've knocked him into unconsciousness when he planted the kick in his stomach. The killer may have been very close to him, but he wasn't the killer himself. Equilibrium had been returned and he accepted the peace it offered, eagerly.

When he pushed the door open, he was surprised to see Tyler, looking over books with P. J. The two of them practically jumped out of their seats as they spotted him and then relaxed noticeably, but with an effort. "Hi guys," Mark called, "I was up and thought I'd stop by, see if you needed any help." This last called directly to P. J., who beamed winningly and told him to come on over, despite the quickly concealed look of terror that crossed Ty's face.

"We've been looking over my old research books, trying to find a reference to some little creatures that haunt the forests at night, something like goblins, or gremlins. I know I have a book on the damned things, but I just can't find it anywhere."

Mark flashed his easy-going grin and walked over to the small island where his friends waited. "Have you looked over your inventory sheets? I thought you'd categorized and cross referenced what was in each of the books."

P. J. frowned sheepishly and Tyler shot a death-glare at him, as he confessed. "I lost them. I haven't been able to find the damned things in the last three months."

It was Mark's turn to receive the evil eye when he walked over to P. J.'s filing cabinet and almost without bothering to look, pulled a computer disk from one of the files. "It's under 'I,' for 'inventory.' You asked me to file all of this months ago; I took the liberty of cleaning up your files when I did." He looked at the two scowling men before him and laughed easily. "Hey, I can't help it if you're a slob. I just did what I was told."

P. J. mumbled his thanks under his breath, and went directly to his word processor. He booted up the necessary file and started looking. After a moment he shut the computer back down and found what he was looking for in a book that both of them had overlooked several times.

Mark looked at the two of them and was glad that both Tyler and P. J. had found someone to kill time with. It gave him more free time for his own writing and for Cassie. After a few more minutes and a quick conversation off to the side, where he told a very relieved Tyler about his visit to the sheriff's office and the resulting revelations, he said his good-byes and went to see if Cassie was busy.

He was in too good a mood to notice the strange looks his two friends had exchanged. The sun was high in the sky, the girl he loved was close enough that he would be with her in mere minutes and his mind was finally processing raw ideas, converting them into a coherent pattern that he would spend a good portion of his night working on putting into words.

He was in too good a mood to even wonder why the Mustang he'd noticed after leaving the sheriff's office was still following him.

3

Tyler looked over at P. J. steadily, not talking, just staring, until the writer finally looked up at him with an exasperated sigh.

"Have I suddenly grown some unusual feature that you find fascinating, or are you glaring at me for another reason?"

"You told him what we were doing! What are you, nuts?" Tyler pushed his battered lenses back in place and continued. "What if he'd decided to stay, help us look for the information? What the hell would we have done then?"

P. J. looked at Tyler with amusement and then knocked his hard knuckles against the youth's brow. "Hello? Is anyone home?" Tyler pulled back with a shocked look on his face—for just a second he'd had a flash of when Tony had done the same thing to him, way back in the fifth grade; the difference was that Tony had used a locker door, rather than his knuckles. "Of course, I told him what we're doing. Why on earth shouldn't I?"

"Well, maybe because if he does have little monsters running around to protect him, they'd take what we're doing as a threat against him?" Tyler looked triumphant, certain that his comment had made a telling blow against his latest victim.

P. J. smiled thinly and arched both of his eyebrows, as he fired his retort. "Why? As far as Mark knows, you're just helping me research a story."

Tyler cracked his knuckles, preparing for a solid fight. Ah, the challenges that a sharp opponent brought always made a victory ever so much sweeter. "I—" He shut his mouth, suddenly feeling the full weight of the author's remark. His mouth tried to work, but his brain wasn't having anything to do with it. He closed his eyes momentarily and forced his brain to come up with a proper comeback. Finally, it did. "Touché, I hadn't thought of that."

P. J. smirked victoriously and patted him on the head. "I was a champion debater in college. You're ever so good, Tyler my lad, but I've taken on the best and won."

Tyler scowled, trying to convince himself it was just a case of hating a poor winner, rather than his being a poor loser. His host was pouring them both mugs of coffee, something Tyler would never have expected to gain a liking for until he had met the man, when he asked another question. "So, what did you find on your disk, that we hadn't located in that book?"

"Not a single solitary thing." Tyler looked over puzzled by the answer and after the appropriate dramatic pause, got an answer to his unspoken question. "I simply felt that, in acting like I had found what was necessary, I could get to the problem at hand without our friend making it even more difficult."

"Which problem would that be?" Tyler asked.

The writer set down the coffee and took a sip of his overly sweetened brew, before responding. "The fact that three of my books are missing," Tyler watched as the man's eyebrows pulled down in a frown. "And the fact that one of those books is one that I fear we've been looking for."

The two sat in silence for several moments, as the talented writer tried to put into words an event that he'd never written about. "You see, Tyler, I have a suspicion that I know what it is that is haunting dear Mark and that I may very well be the cause of the problem." Looking into the writer's eyes, Tyler felt himself grow cold and wondered if it was a tale that he wanted to hear.

"So, why don't you tell me a story?"

4

Jennifer Howell reclined on the back porch of her home, tanning her body in the sun's warm light. Today, she'd decided some hours ago, was a day made for tanning. She sipped at her iced tea, sweetened with honey, never with sugar, and flipped the page in the murder mystery she had been reading.

She was fairly certain she knew who was responsible, but she refused to allow herself the pleasure of going to the last few pages and finding out the easy way. By reading the book all the way through she got to read all of the dirty scenes—they were all but a trademark of this particular author.

She listened to the door open in the front of the house and decided that it wasn't worth the trouble to make herself decent. If it was Mark, he'd seen her in her birthday suit before and it wouldn't bother her at all. If it was Joe, all the better.

It was Mark; he walked out onto the porch only moments later and looked at his mother intensely. Suddenly she felt naked, as she never had before her son in the past. The reason was obvious and she marveled that she hadn't seen it before. He had literally become, save for the scar on his right cheek, the spitting image of his father. She flushed at the thoughts that raced through her mind and flushed twice as hard when she recognized the look in Mark's eye that said he was thinking along the same lines. After a pregnant pause, he turned his head away and she covered herself with her towel.

"Um, sorry, I was just going to let you know that I'll be over at Cassie's." There was a thickness in his voice that she'd never heard there before and she finally noticed on a conscious level that his voice had gotten a good deal deeper in the last few months.

Jenny looked at her son and smiled, keeping her voice light. "I should have put up a sign, imagine how embarrassed I'd have been if Tyler had been with you." That seemed to break the tension in him: he was probably picturing Ty's eyes leaping out of his skull. "So, when will you be back, should I save dinner for you?"

"Um, probably not, I'll scrounge up something when I get home." Mark was turning away when she called him back and he looked down at her uncomfortably.

Jenny smiled her brightest 'Mom' smile and beckoned him to sit next to her. He did. "The folks are going to be coming down in a couple of weeks. I thought you'd like to have a little advance warning, a chance to prepare Cassie for when they meet her. You know that as soon as they hear about her, they'll want her over here for dinner."

Mark positively beamed at the thought and said he would prepare Cassie for the meeting. As he stood up, Jenny looked at how tall her son had become and stood with him, careful to keep the towel from falling off of her body. With a quick peck on each cheek, she dismissed her son. He was off to find true love and she knew how very important that was in this world. After all was said and done, she was glad that she'd opted to keep him, rather than abandon her baby to strangers who could have none of their own. Mark was more than just her son, he was her memories; Jenny Howell could never give up her memories, not the good, not the bad. They were hers.

She stretched the towel out beside her on the recliner and turned on to her stomach. She did her best not to think of the man who was Mark's father. Like always, she almost succeeded. Joe would be home soon and she wanted to look her best for him; she wanted to make her husband as happy as he made her. That was even more important than memories.

Finally, she decided that she needed a treat and confirmed her suspicions about whodunit. She was right, the author was predictable and safe, just the way she liked her writers to be. The way she liked her men to be.

5

Alan Fisk left his car parked at the edge of the Red Oaks subdivision and found a good hill from which to watch the Howell boy on his route through the area. Normally, he would have found the work dreadfully boring, as he had for most of the day, but from his vantage point, he had a good clean shot of the kid's mother and his binoculars picked up details very well. He couldn't see writing this part down in his report; somehow he doubted that his wife Donna would see the humor in the situation.

Donna was a wonderful woman, but she was hardly a ravishing beauty. And since the stork had delivered the second rug-rat, she had really put on the weight. He loved Donna with all of his heart, but she just didn't have a figure like the woman he was looking at. Probably never would again.

He waited a few extra minutes enjoying the sights, before he started sweeping the area with his field glasses. While he'd been ogling the momma cat, the baby cat had left the premises. There! Already on the next street.

He watched silently as the boy walked over to the Monroe house, and thinking about the two women that lived there, Alan wished he was ten years older or younger. There were two women he would have loved to know better. He mused over the likelihood of the two ever wanting anything to do with a low-income deputy and did his best to think of other things before he got himself depressed.

After the boy had been in the house for about ten minutes, he and the Monroe girl stepped back into the rapidly warming daylight. They walked together like two young people in love; slowly, hand in hand, with no place special to go as long as they were with each other. Alan longed for the days when his life had been that free and easy.

Alan found himself hoping that the sheriff was wrong, that the young man down in the subdivision had nothing to do with the murders; but then, Alan always hoped that no one was guilty, it was one of his flaws. He thought back to when Andy Phillips had burst into the sheriff's office, so long ago now, and felt himself fill with pity for the dead boy. Even realizing that the kid had done wrong, the tormented shrieks from the holding cell had filled Alan with an overwhelming sense of sadness. No one should suffer as the Phillips kid obviously had.

That train of thought eventually detoured as he watched the two young lovers walk into the woods, closing in on the question of what could have scared the poor slob so much. As always the thought of personal fears sent his mind running to his own worst nightmare; Stoney Miles. Everyone in the town knew the story of Stoney, and Alan was one of many who would swear that they had seen his mad specter running through these very woods. It had been a long time ago, when he was only ten years old, but he would never for as long as he lived forget the sight of that blistered festering smile, or the burnt skull that gleamed under what was left of the man's steely gray hair. Or the hatchet that had still glistened with the blood of Stoney's victims, decades after the man had died in the fire that killed Summit Town. Stoney Miles was Alan's worst fear, a dead man with a murderous penchant. How the hell could somebody catch a dead man?

Such thoughts put the fear of God into Alan. Momma Fisk had done one hell of a job raising a superstitious coward. With a sigh, he realized that he'd let the Howell boy out of his sight again. Grumbling faintly to himself, Alan lowered his binoculars and started off into the woods; there'd be hell to pay if he let the kid get away, but then, who was going to tell? Certainly not him.

6

They had walked in silence for almost ten minutes, when Cassie spoke aloud, "So, what do you want to do today? Movie? Lunch? Wild passionate sex?"

Mark practically gagged, feeling that his mind was making up the words. He looked over at her and saw the teasing gleam in her eyes. He smiled back and responded that all of the above sounded wonderful. "But, because I'm such a wonderful guy, I'll let you decide."

Cassie smiled wickedly and pulled him close for a passionate kiss. She chided herself silently as she enjoyed the sensation and then responded. "Hmm, let's try lunch and a movie." As always, Mark smiled in return and nodded his agreement. She felt slightly like a tease, but he knew as well as she did that they would proceed when the time was right.

Their walk to town was slow and they meandered through the woods in no particular hurry to get anywhere. From time to time, Mark would look over towards where Third Avenue stretched off to their left and he would frown. Finally having decided that enough was enough, she asked him what was so interesting. He took a few moments to prepare the words, before responding. "If I didn't know better, I'd think we were being followed."

"What do you mean?" For some reason she found herself very nervous at the concept, though for the life of her, she couldn't think of why. She wouldn't allow her self to consciously think about it, but it was there, a whisper in the back of her brain, just the same: *Tanya was followed once and the same guy followed me!*

Mark pointed over to the street and stopped moving. As they both looked where he had pointed, they saw a battered old black Mustang cruise at a pace just above idle, slowly coming around the bend in the road. "There, see? Whoever it is, he's been following me for a long time." He frowned, momentarily lost in thought. "Since about eight o'clock this morning."

Upon seeing the car, Cassie felt much better. "Oh, jeez, you had me a little scared for a while. That's just Alan Fisk." Seeing the blank look on his face, she added: "The sheriff's deputy, he's probably just doing the rounds over here, since they found—since Pete's body was located."

Mark looked over at her, with a strange expression; it looked like equal parts of fear, anger, and relief. "Oh," he said, "if that's all you think it is."

In the woods, she could practically hear the cessation of sound; all of the animals stopped their natural buzzing, chirping, and chattering, as if they were waiting for something. *Well, MY broker is Merrill Lynch and he says...* She started feeling edgy and Mark grew silent for a moment. The whole world seemed to be waiting for something that she was unaware of. She felt like she had said something horribly embarrassing in church, as if she had screamed out loud, to be heard over the crowd in one of those sudden moments when everyone stops talking at the same time.

"Mark, is something wrong?" She was worried by the look he threw her for about three seconds. Then he smiled openly and she knew everything would be all right.

"No, I guess I'm just being paranoid, I mean, except for you and Tyler and maybe a few others, I've kind of gotten the impression that nobody here really trusts me." He looked at her, trying to see if she understood what he was trying to say. Apparently he realized that she did, because he continued. He told her about his visit to the sheriff's office and about what had happened between Tommy and himself, so long ago. Then, he added, "I guess the sheriff knows what he's talking about. I just wondered if maybe he had the deputy following me because he thought I was lying." He looked worried and then he looked very sad and then he brightened again and she would have been amused by the sudden rapid changes in his expression, if she hadn't been reeling mentally from what he had just told her. "I guess you're right though, maybe he's just looking out for us, seeing us going through the woods and all."

Cassie smiled at him, finally realizing that there was simply no way that her Mark could kill a person, let alone Tommy Blake. She wrapped her arms around his neck, giving him a strong hug, to say without words that she loved him and that everything was okay. He hugged her back, running his hands lightly over her back and sending shivers of pleasure through her. When she looked past Mark, towards the road, she suddenly saw the Mustang accelerate. It was gone around the next bend before she could even comment. They held each other for a slow eternity and then forced themselves to separate before lunch and a movie were over-ridden by other desires. She flashed her beau a grin of challenge. "If you can beat me in a race to the theater, we'll see about that third option." He grinned at her and both of them ran as fast as they could.

She won, but just barely. She had the impression along the way that if he'd put his mind to it, Mark Howell could have left her stranded in the woods, watching a trail of dried leaf dust and dirt trace through the air, where he'd been only seconds before. She thrilled to think of just how far he'd come with his running and did her best to stifle the thoughts of how powerful a lover he would be. She was mildly disappointed that he hadn't tried harder.

7

Alan knew as he came around the gentle curve in the road, that the Howell kid had spotted him. The kid had been pointing in his direction as he came around the road's bend. To try and dispel the belief that he was trailing the kid, he sped up and away from them.

Chuck, he decided, would not be pleased. He was on his way to the office, to let Hanson know that he'd been spotted, when he saw the sudden explosion of birds from the woods on the other side of town.

For reasons he couldn't quite place, the sight unsettled him. He skipped past the offices and went in the direction of the sudden flight. Because the town was so ridiculously small, he knew that the detour wouldn't take but about ten minutes; he was at the approximate spot in only five.

The woods looked perfectly normal, but there was something wrong. It took him almost a full minute of thought to realize what it was; there was absolutely no sound except for his breathing and the gentle sigh of the woods. No crickets or cicadas making a noise to tell everything within a quarter mile where they were; no frogs, calling for a mate to come and seduce them. It wasn't a natural silence and Alan was made uneasy by the lack of nature's symphonic rhythm. He was actually backing towards his car, when he saw them.

Somehow, Mark Howell and Cassie Monroe had beaten him out here. His mind refused to accept the knowledge, it wouldn't sink in, no matter how badly he wanted it to. No way, could they have come the six miles involved, on foot, in the sloping wooded area, not in the time it had taken him by car. But there they were, holding each other and peeling their clothes away.

The thought of a little voyeuristic fun took all of his quiet fear away and he slipped silently out of the car, glad that he had thought to bring his binoculars with him. He watched as they stood together, holding each other tenderly, their bodies tanned a golden color and their hands roaming each other, exploring, while his heart stuttered excitedly in his chest.

Mark lay Cassie on the ground and stood over her, his hard body gleaming with a light sheen of sweat in the dry Colorado summer. He moved his field glasses down slightly, to concentrate on Cassie's form and marveled at the supple, sinuous girl-woman that writhed in anticipation of her lover. He longed to be down there with her, longed to be in the boy's place; both in time and in lack of responsibility. He crushed the guilty rush of thoughts that tried to remind him of Donna and focused the binoculars to give him a clear shot of the two forms.

Before his eyes, the girl's features changed, twisted and ran and in less than the span of one heartbeat, she had become Donna Fisk. Not as she looked now, but as she had looked six years ago, when he had first made love to her; with firm heavy breasts and luscious wide hips, her chestnut hair spilling across the ground.

Donna beckoned to Mark Howell with her arms and he dropped to his knees before her, gripping her breasts in his powerful hands. He heard her moan, as she hadn't moaned to him in a long while.

Alan Fisk felt his blood pounding in his temples, as he dropped the binoculars from hands gone suddenly cold and numb. With a strangled cry of rage, he started forward, intent on wringing the life from the boy he was supposed to be watching. He never looked past where the boy was roughly pleasuring his very own wife. "That sumbitch," he spat venomously. "That sumbitch!" He broke into a full run, crossing the distance between him and his intended victim in a matter of less than a minute. He hadn't felt this kind of anger in a long, long time.

He felt himself growling, a primal fire burning in his chest, feeding him the raw strength to pull his target's face off. He hit his young opponent with all of his strength and velocity in combination, knocking the boy off of his wife, who screamed shrilly at the sight of him.

He grabbed a handful of Mark Howell's hair and physically lifted him into a standing position, pulling back his free hard, prepared to send a devastating blow into the little punk's throat.

The man of about fifty that he held up smiled through burnt, peeling lips and blew a kiss at him. Alan felt his whole body freeze, all of the anger that had propelled him this far going away like a wisp of fog in the brightest sunlight; replaced by cold hard fear, as he looked into the one remaining eye of Stoney Miles.

Stoney pulled him into a ferocious bear hug and stared at him with mild amusement in his one good eye. The other socket spilled a foul, thick, yellow pus that dribbled down onto Alan's shirt. Alan screamed as loudly as he could and fought for dear life to break the grip of iron that Stoney held him with.

He looked around himself, trying to find a weapon, his revolver forgotten. To his left and behind him, the young and shapely Donna laughed at him, seeing his predicament. With a new strength, fueled by anger, shame, and fear, he swung his knee into Stoney's crotch and felt the satisfying release of his pinned arms. Stoney was bent almost double over and Alan took full advantage, swinging his joined fists into the side of the evil bastard's head and watching as he staggered and fell to the ground. He kicked and stomped and jumped up and down on the stunned man, reveling in the sensation of bones breaking under the force of his assault. With a cry of triumph, he drove his foot through the demon's back and felt the spine snap.

Breathing heavily, he looked around for his wife and saw instead, Stoney Miles, axe in hand, where his Donna should have been. He looked down at the pulped mass at his feet and saw chestnut hair, sheened lightly with crimson, resting under his black boot. With a dawning sense of terror, he looked back over at the specter with its axe. Stoney's hair was steely gray, in the places where it still hung on his burnt scalp.

He looked down again, at the shattered features of his wife, a woman that he had from time to time hated and always loved. He made not a single sound as he felt the first blow of the hatchet against his chest. Alan's body took a long time to die, but his mind and soul had died already; finally having realized that it wasn't just the form of his wife, but her lovely and patient spirit that he had crushed under his bloody heels.

8

They laughed, and the creatures that, unlike the birds, had stayed motionless in the hopes of being unseen ran from their hiding spots, their instincts telling them that the Folk were in rare form that day. The Folk finished their grisly work and separated from the dreams and nightmares that They had stolen from Alan Fisk. The battered body of his wife faded into a clear fluid, as They reshaped Themselves into a form They found more acceptable. Stoney too, went back into the separate forms of over one hundred of the Folk.

The one who liked to watch had frightened the Chosen, and that was all it took. They needed little as an excuse. This one had meant nothing to the One and so there had been no need for caution. With a malicious dance around the deputy's mortal remains, They celebrated victory. And then, They ran through the woods, sighing that the fun had not lasted, but certain that more fun was sure to come. The Chosen seemed to draw trouble like a magnet; that was one of the reasons that They liked Him so much.

"Soon," They whispered, "Soon the time of change will be complete. Soon, we will be free of this love." The love had been so tiring. They loved Him still, but not for much longer. He would soon have served His purpose, He would soon be able to defend himself. That was what mattered now.

Chapter Ten

1

Patrick sat alone in his room and shivered in the noonday heat. He shook not with the cold, but with fear; the kind of numbing whispery fear that holds tightly to your insides and freezes your blood when you hear the slightest sound that is out of place.

He knew now that it hadn't been the drugs, he knew that what he'd seen had been terribly real. Unlike the strange visions he often had when in a chemical stupor, he knew that these visions could kill him as easily as they had killed Tommy.

He had watched from his safe vantage point as Tommy had assaulted Mark and he had watched with all of the passion of a lover. Patrick didn't like to do violence, but he liked to watch others do it; he loved the sounds of someone getting hurt. He throve on the high pitched squeals of some macho bastard getting hurt so badly that he screamed like a girl; it was like revenge for all the times in the past, when it had been him doing the screaming.

Like his younger brother, Patrick had had more than his share of enemies in school before he suddenly bloomed, putting muscle on as if by magic. His father had been that way as well and he suspected the same lay somewhere ahead for Tyler. Unlike his younger brother, however, he had never had the rapier wit to cut his opponents even as they blasted him into a semi-conscious stupor with their fists. *Maybe, if I had*, he thought, *I wouldn't have started dealing drugs.*

Becoming Summitvilles' local dealer had started because he needed an angle, a way to save himself from those of his peers who found it necessary to pound anyone even remotely different into a new shape, rather than just let them alone.

After he had found a few patsies to buy the drugs, he had found a few allies to assist him whenever someone wanted to trash him. It was a simple equation: if they hurt Patrick, they hurt the supply of party-favors; without party-favors there was no fun. Patrick had never dealt for profit, only for cost. He had dealt to save his face.

He envied his brother the strength to manage without such tricks. But he did not envy his brother the friend he had in Mark Howell. Closing his eyes, he saw a crazy unfolding of events that just didn't make any sense. He watched from the sidelines as Mark Howell stormed across the foot ball field, hell bent and determined to get Tommy to lay off of Patrick's little brother, once and for all. Part of him had been happy that Tyler had such a friend, part jealous that he couldn't do a better job of protecting Tyler himself.

He'd listened to the names called by both parties and felt himself get excited, knowing that a fight would be breaking out in only a few minutes at most.

Then he'd seen Tommy Blake spin a roundhouse kick into Mark's jaw and he'd seen Mark go down like a sack of potatoes. He'd seen the following seven kicks and punches, each faster than the last, that literally knocked Mark all over the fucking field. He knew that Mark was going to die, murdered by a bastard that would feel almost no remorse for the action, for trying to stop Tyler's endless persecution.

He'd actually been steeling himself to break up the fight when Mark got back up. He'd had what seemed like a long time to study the damage that had befallen his brother's friend; Mark had teeth broken off and missing, he had a nose that had been crushed by a solid kick in his face and he was bleeding in several places. His jaw didn't fit his face right anymore, it hung at a twisted angle.

All of that changed so quickly that he still had trouble believing it wasn't a bad trip. Mark had stood perfectly still and his body and features had run like hot wax. His teeth reformed, literally flying back into position like a film in reverse, lifting from wherever they had spilled and sealing themselves into their proper places. His nose, a ruined bloody mess, reformed on his face as perfect and straight as it had ever been. His fractured jaw slid back into the proper place with a sound like two rocks grinding together. The blood disappeared from his clothing, leaving only the dirt and grass stains behind.

If that hadn't been enough, Mark continued to change. His mouth reshaped itself from the base of his jaw on up to his nose. It grew wider, the muscles bulging outward with a sickening hissing noise. His arms elongated, stretching in length even as extra muscle came from nowhere, helping them maintain their original width. His fingers grew longer as well, sprouting thick and wickedly sharp nails in the process. His torso, already powerful in dimension, expanded outward in a way that was almost comical to watch; it had made Patrick thick of the old Bugs Bunny cartoons, where the Wascally Wabbit would go against the enormous wrestler/boxer who, when he flexed, popped muscles on his muscles. Only, this wasn't a cartoon and he was definitely not in the theater or at home watching television. The worst part was the look in Mark's eyes, during and after the transformation. As it occurred, Mark looked terrified, ready to scream in horror at what was happening to his body, almost as if it wasn't him doing it. Then the metamorphosis was completed: his skin had become scaly under its stretched outer-layer and the blood in between his skin and the scales, ruptured from its vessels, turned him a grotesque crimson. His eyes changed; no longer frightened by what had happened, they looked terribly amused. Like someone hiding in a monster suit where they had forgotten to do any work to the eyes, they shone their normal brilliant blue and laugh-lines showed themselves with crystal clarity.

Then the Mark-thing had screamed its rage and Tommy, poor Tommy, who always thought that the world revolved around him, had screamed just like a girl. Patrick was disgusted to remember the joy he got out of that shriek. Tommy tried to get away, but the Mark Monster was simply too fast, too strong. It grabbed him up by his throat and held him as if he weighed less than a baseball. He couldn't remember clearly—by then, he'd felt the keen thrill of terror gripping his own heart, but Patrick thought he saw one finger reach through the flesh of Tommy's neck as if it was just colored air and pull something free from the inside. There was no blood, no wound, but something was pulled away from his neck. It must have been Tommy's vocal cords, because after that, the only sound his one-time customer could make was a whistling little squeak, like a dog's chew-toy.

He watched, enthralled, as the Mark-beast systematically started tearing the clothes away from Tommy and then started tweeking his toes. *This little piggy went to market and this little piggy stayed home!* The thought had him giggling madly, and Patrick had to bite the inside of his mouth to stop from doubling over and laughing out loud. Every toe that was tweaked made a sound like someone bending a green stick beyond the point of its endurance; he heard the little snaps from his hiding place a full twenty feet away in the bleachers.

Patrick observed the entire incident in muted fascination, as the Markstrosity moved from the toes up, taking its time about the situation and chuckling like a river after torrential rains, the whole time. Tommy remained conscious for most of it; and when he passed out, the grinning thing that had been Mark Howell waited patiently until he stirred into consciousness again. Then it started on a new bone, careful not to kill its toy.

He must have made some kind of sound—some noise louder than the hysterical, half-giggles he'd been holding back—because the Markstrosity looked up and their eyes locked over the distance, as if the shadows hid nothing. Then it winked at him.

As it turned away, it gestured to indicate that Patrick should clean up the mess it had made; too stunned to think, he almost did. He pulled trash-bags from the storage space under the bleachers—Malloy never locked the damn thing, he said if someone needed cleaning supplies that badly, they could have them. To the town's credit, until Patrick himself, nobody ever had. He walked over to what was left of his client and, seeing it clearly, he ran for dear life, swearing he would never drop acid again. To that very day, he hadn't.

The worst part was yet to come, however, when he almost ran into Mark in the woods. He hadn't thought about it as he ran, he'd just run. In the same direction that Mark had. He spotted the thing that Mark had become, falling to its knees in front of a large rock—and stared in amazement as it literally dropped what seemed like millions of little creatures from its body. Each of the tiny ones looked enough like the big one to make him think of the pictures he'd seen in biology; pictures of a mother spider carrying her countless legions of young on her broad back, where they would crawl all over her and each other without the least bit of concern for any of the siblings they stepped on.

The little ones noticed him and fell to the ground laughing as they would at the best joke they had ever heard, shrieking little laughs that sounded all too human for comfort. Some of them got up after their belly laughs and darted into the surrounding woods towards the school. Others caressed the unconscious form of Mark Howell—who looked perfectly normal again, as if the creatures had been inside of him, like an allergic reaction that swells some poor soul like water in a balloon and now the reaction was over and he was just Mark again—and cooing to him like a lover, running their sharp little claws over his body and through his hair. Mark moaned as if he was in the arms of a voluptuous, voracious woman, and the bulge in his jeans was painfully obvious.

Patrick lost it then and there: somehow he managed to get home with only a few scratches on his arms and face, no worse for wear. He knew that he would never go into the woods again.

He had honestly convinced himself that it had all been a bad trip and he still never meant to touch the shit again. He'd believed that he could live safe with the knowledge that the only thing screwed up was his own brain, until Jack Watkins had told him about the body that was found at the lake, found when he cut his foot on something in a plastic bag, just like the ones that he'd dropped next to the body of poor Tommy Blake. He wondered briefly how the bags had gotten from the school to the lake. He prayed fervently that the water had washed his fingerprints from the plastic; he prayed for that almost as much as he prayed never to see Mark again.

As with all people, many a prayer seems to be ignored. The water had indeed washed away the fingerprints on the bags, but as for Mark, it was a small town and the fates had other plans.

2

P. J. reached into his breast pocket and produced a cigarette from a crumpled pack that rested there. Tyler was taken aback. He'd never known the man to smoke and he'd known P. J. for quite some time.

"When did you start smoking?"

"About twenty years ago," the writer responded as he struck a match and brought the flame to the tobacco stick's tip. He looked at Tyler and grimaced. "I quit ten years ago, never thought I'd be doing this to myself again." The man started coughing violently and continued until Tyler brought him a glass of cold water. He nodded his thanks and gulped it down eagerly. Then, with a look of pure disgust on his face, he crushed the cigarette out. "To hell with it, I think I'll just stay quit."

The man looked everywhere but at Tyler for several minutes. Tyler, with his normal patience, waited through the silence knowing that P. J. needed to sort out his thoughts. Finally, P. J. Sanderson looked at his young friend. "So, you want to hear a story."

"The best way to start, I imagine, is at the beginning." He took another sip of water and rubbed futilely at his temples, trying to get rid of the tension threatening to crush his skull.

"Once upon a time," he began, his rich voice modulating as if he were talking of a story that had no great purpose save to amuse. "When I was a much younger lad, I found a book, on these very premises."

"My grandfather purchased this house back in nineteen forty-seven. He moved here because he wanted to escape the troubles he felt brewing in the big cities, the growing crime rate, mostly. Well, my father and his young wife moved with him. They had no money and my grandfather told them that they could stay with him until they got on their feet. I might add that the town was only a little smaller in those days than it is now. No building had been done in this town for many a year and the old man opted to buy a house that was, even in those days, remarkably cheap." He looked at Tyler briefly and a hint of amusement touched his eyes for just that moment. "The house had something of a reputation in town, as a haunted dwelling."

He watched the dawning realization in Tyler's eyes and nodded his affirmation of what was on the boy's mind. "Yes, this very dwelling belonged, a long, long time ago, to one Albert Miles. A fact that most in this day and age have forgotten about. A fact that I knew nothing of until I was almost fifteen years of age."

"I was born in this house and so was my sister Antoinette, who is now married to Tony's father, though I suspect, not very happily. But all of that is an aside. Back to the story."

"When I was fifteen I finally decided, aided by some less than gentle prodding on my father's part, that it was time to give the attic a proper cleaning. It seems that the people who had been living in this house had had no belief in throwing away what was no longer to be used. They simply tossed it all into the growing piles of relics that rested in the attic. It would have taken me about two months, after school and on the weekends, to clear out that monstrous attic by myself. Luckily, I had assistance. My one true friend in town, Alex Harris; a boy who had moved to Summitville only a few months earlier."

"Alex was a voracious reader, who still managed to look like a dark-haired god. He was funny, friendly, and adventurous. I was none of those things. For some reason, he took me under his wing and allowed me the pleasure of his company and protection from the many who wanted to tear my head off." Again the writer paused in his narration and looked at Tyler with a haunted sort of happiness, "Oh yes, my fine friend, my mouth was almost as deadly as your own in its time."

"Anyway, it was Alex that found the book. I believe it was buried under a thick pile of clothes, in the very farthest corner of the attic, in an old steamer trunk, that had definitely had its better days in the last century. Being the adventurous type, he set the book in a special spot and we went back to putting the finishing touches on the cleaning, which at that point was mostly opening the attic's windows and tossing all of the garbage out for collection when we were done. It was easier than hauling all of it down several flights of stairs.

"We looked the book over and while we could read some of the words, most were beyond us. It had been written in an odd mixture of Celtic and old English and it was a mystery to our young minds. Never one to be pushed away by troubles, Alex set off and actually found books at the Denver library that allowed us to translate the cursed tome. It was fascinating reading, I assure you.

"The book was a book of dark magic, a history of the sordid past that this town never knew Stoney Miles was involved in. The man was decidedly foul. He had written stories of events that would turn your most devout pacifists into a hanging mob were they to know what he had done. He talked not only of events, mind you, but of the secrets that he'd learned in traveling a good portion of the world. Secrets I dare say he would have been better off without."

"Being fifteen and as enthralled with monsters then as I am now, I initially found the book fascinating. I later forgot about it. Alex found the book to be irresistible. He spent almost the rest of that month looking over the passages that had been written down, trying to translate every story completely. Many of the words in the book were beyond his comprehension. I believe that they may have been written in a third language, one that may not even be remembered to mankind. Or, possibly they were written in a code that only a few would know. Anything is possible; for all I know they were simply misspelled, but I doubted it even then. You see the book was written on soft leather, with odd rusty colored ink. Perhaps it was human flesh and blood. I certainly took many of my descriptions of the books in *Stirrings* from what I remembered of that particular tome of horrors."

"There were whole sections of that book that contained nothing but what looked like magical spells, and being the adventurous type, Alex convinced me to join him in the woods; to try to perform the rites for ourselves, just to see if they would really work. I hesitated at first, but Alex had always been able to sway me from what my own heart knew to be right. It was done on Halloween day, for flavor, not because it was necessary. And as it was the proper season, we brought our girlfriends with us on that day, certain that the attempt would excite them as much as it did us. We were right, they did enjoy the show as much as we did, not that it mattered in the long run, because nothing seemed to happen. We tried, and when we failed, we tried again. Nothing seemed to work you see, because at least one portion of each incantation was written in that damnable code. I grew bored with the entire thing, but Alex was insistent, he fairly demanded that we try them all. I didn't want to lose my only real friend, so I went along with him. Several of the spells required blood, and since neither of us wanted to be the donor, we took the blood from one of the chickens that was in the refrigerator and used it in substitution."

Tyler frowned deeply at the thought of where the story was leading. "Where did you say you did the magic spells?"

P. J. smiled again, "You are the perceptive one, Tyler, I have to give you that. We performed the acts that the spells demanded in the woods, somewhere around where you now have your home. At a guess, I would say somewhere between where your home lies and where the school is."

"If my theory is correct, and I fear that it most likely is, Mark may have cut his face on the very stone we used as our sacrificial altar. I can't be certain. I know the stone he was injured with was considerably smaller than our makeshift altar. I also know that the stone was gone when I went back to the woods a week later. We're talking about a stone over four feet in length, mind you. It just couldn't be found, and I looked."

"I should also add a few more facts to this tale. The blood required was to be virginal and again I remind you, that we had two more people with us on that little trip. Two young ladies who, like me, felt that it might be fun and even a little risque, to perform the secret rites. They were Anita Van Der Graff and Susan Hailey. Oh, and Antoinette was there too."

"Yes, I thought you might well recognize the names, they are after all, the mothers of you and Cassie Monroe."

"Alex moved away that very week. His father had been in a car accident around the same time we were performing our magic spells. His mother showed the next day, coming in from California. They left almost as soon as she got into town. I don't think he ever even really said goodbye, I just remember going to his house, a few days before school was to start again, and realizing that he was gone. He and his mother and his little brother had left Summitville; I never heard from him again."

Tyler gave the author credit; he told a story almost as well as he wrote one. But the writer hadn't finished his tale, not quite. "I have tried from time to time, to remember if anything strange happened on that day and most of the time, I say to myself that nothing did. But, from time to time, I could almost swear a wind picked up, a wind that was warm, sweet, and smelled strongly of summer time. But, that doesn't make any sense to me. No summer breeze has ever blown in

Colorado on the last day of October." He paused momentarily, reaching for the cigarettes that he had just sworn off of again. When he offered, Tyler took one as well. "At least no natural wind—which brings us back around to that damnable book and to the spells we cast that day, a very long time ago. And to Mark."

"I asked your mother once, some ten or eleven years ago now, when I had the pleasure of her company as she tried to sell me Tupperware, if she remembered that day. She said that she did not. Cassie's mother was an even bigger surprise to me, because when I had occasion to ask her if she remembered, she had not only forgotten about that Halloween day, she had forgotten about Alex Harris as well, and the two of them had dated for some time, almost half a year as I recall."

The author sighed heavily and pulled himself from the bittersweet past with an almost visible effort. "I miss those days, Tyler. The whole world seemed more colorful back then. I suspect growing up pulls the colors away from you, as the time runs past; I should do my best to avoid that if I were you."

And then, P. J., who had seemed to age as he spoke of the events, grew back to himself and smiled as warmly as he almost always did and Tyler felt the spell of his storytelling crumble away. "So, it would seem to me, my fine young friend, that we should find that book and see if we can help poor Mark out of any possible supernatural dilemma he might be in." They divided the likely areas of the store and started to search.

3

Tony was in a foul mood again, frustrated and bitter at the lack of progress in his attempts to win Cassie's heart. The girls he'd been dating hadn't been working out. None seemed able to compare to the image he had planted in his mind of how perfect Cassie must surely be. The thought of her was enough to make him smile on a bad day, or make him scowl when he had thought all was right with the world. He tried his best to hide the feelings, but knew as well as the next person that it wasn't working very well.

Now, just to add to his delight, he was on his way to Tyler's and they were all going swimming. Today he was prepared—he had brought another person with him, Lisa. If he had to be miserable in the company of someone he loved who was inaccessible, by God, he wouldn't be alone. He could watch as Tyler stared, squirmed, and tried to relax around his sister. And squirm he would. If her suit were any skimpier, she could have been in a Playboy magazine as the centerfold. Petty? Yes, but he no longer cared.

Lisa, it seemed, was up to her old tricks again, leading the poor guy around with nothing more than a smile, and he had fallen for it, hook, line, and sinker. They had gone off into the woods a few weeks back, on the night that school had ended, and almost everyone had assumed that something was going to happen. Tony knew better; she was leading him around because it was easy, it made her feel good and because she needed someone who would listen to all of her problems. Tyler always had time to listen to someone's problems, even when he knew that he should avoid that person.

He had no doubt that Ty knew better than to see his sister—the anguish was visible even through the thin veneer of happiness that Tyler always wore. Tony wondered what it was about the male of the species that made them such gluttons for punishment, and then decided it was most likely the lump of flesh that dangled between their legs.

He smiled wryly at the thought and Lisa looked over at him from where she sat in the passenger's seat. He turned slightly and smiled at her. They each understood the other's reason for going to Tyler's pool and they understood without a single word having to pass between them; they were, after all, fraternal twins. As often as not, they could guess what the other was thinking, though both would deny it vehemently.

Tony pulled to the curb in front of Ty's home, puzzled by the large number of cars before the monster of a house. He and Lisa got out of the car and were walking towards it when Tyler popped his head out the front door and waved them in.

Tyler was wearing his usual baggy cutoffs and a white tee shirt that had probably never been used before—he couldn't have looked any more different from Tony if he'd tried. Tony was wearing the same swim suit he wore during the school year, something just slightly larger than a G-string. Like his sister, he wore burgundy, a color that was an excellent contrast to their matching tans. Both of them had well-defined bodies and had no hesitation to flaunt them—*Must be dressing up for the special guest,* Tony thought with a guilty smile, *poor sonuvabitch.* Tony felt himself growing guilty about asking if Lisa could come along; Tyler didn't deserve the pain that her presence would cause him.

Lisa smiled warmly at Tyler and Tony watched the way his entire body tensed with the desire to hold her in his arms. He was feeling worse about this by the second. "Tonio, Lisa, come on in! The others are all here. I figured we'd go ahead and make a full scale party of the day." They followed their host and exchanged puzzled looks.

When they entered the poolroom they showed their astonishment clearly; the entire room was festooned with streamers of paper and with balloons. All the way across the pool, from wall to wall, was a huge hand-painted banner, garishly colored, with the legend "HAPPY BIRTHDAY LISA and TONY !!!!" written across it. Inside the room, along with the decorations, were easily two dozen classmates and their Uncle Phil. Flashbulbs exploded like blazing blue suns, leaving spots of darkness in their eyes, as they heard the triumphant cry of *"Surprise!"* escape from over a score of mouths. Tony looked stupidly at the assembled people and slowly grinned. Lisa, for her part, squealed with delight and threw her arms around Tyler, who, to his credit, managed not to break into a thousand anguished pieces at the contact.

Tony found himself in a better mood in next to no time. Tyler had managed a surprise party well in advance of the actual date for their birthday, but that was all right; they could wait the fourteen days for the family's celebration.

Mark and Cassie were there and held to each other like Siamese twins, but with the other females there, he would manage. It was Tyler he felt for; the guy had set this whole thing up and after the initial hug, Lisa went about the room as if he didn't even exist, flirting with the other guys and ignoring all that Tyler had done for them. Tyler however, never lost his smile, strained though it was. If he had felt justified, Tony would have torn her apart; but he knew that he himself was less than innocent in the game of using people.

Uncle Phil was as friendly as ever, but he looked tired, as if he hadn't been sleeping properly for quite a while. It hurt Tony to see the man in pain. He had always been at least as much a parent as his real folks were.

Later, he promised himself, he would get to the root of what the problem was. For now he had important things to do, like showing Cassie that he didn't care if she preferred Mark, by keeping himself busy with every free female in the room.

Sadly, he realized that he was hurting Mark in the process of avoiding Cassie, but some things were simply unavoidable. He thought back to the times before he and Mark had become friends and shook his head to realize that he had been the source of so much grief for the guy. Perhaps in the future, if he really tried, he could avoid that kind of mistake. Perhaps.

He wondered idly where Patrick was. Normally he would be at any function that could be called a party and he'd be having a good time and getting almost as many laughs as his hyperactive brother. Today, he was nowhere to be seen. The party got into full swing a little over an hour later. Most everybody was in the pool and those that weren't were trying to sneak a drink past the hawkish eyes of P. J. Sanderson. They never had a chance—as soon as they looked even slightly suspicious he was right there smiling politely, looking slightly apologetic and plucking the liquor out of their hands. Tyler explained to Mark and Tony as they finished a race across the small lake of a pool, that the only way to have the party was to have a chaperon; P. J. had volunteered. Tony noticed that P. J. was smoking again and *knew* something was definitely wrong, but whatever it was could wait at least a little while.

Cassie and Lisa had apparently gotten over any differences that they might have had and were surrounded by a gaggle of other bathing beauties (and some not so beautiful, Tony allowed) talking no doubt about the small herd of guys at the other side of the party. The guys, of course, were eagerly returning the gossip in their own way. Tyler ran about the room with a nervous energy, making sure that everything was perfect; except for the few disgruntled would-be drinkers, everyone was having a great time.

Everyone except for Tyler. He hid it well, but Tony had learned a few things about how Tyler worked on the inside since they had buried the hatchet. Mark had also noticed and looked less than pleased, to put it nicely. When Ty was on the other side of the pool, he got right to the point. "What's with Lisa," he asked. "It's like she's trying to fuck with Ty's mind. If she didn't even know him, she'd be friendlier than she's being."

Tony looked back at him and shook his head. "I really don't know," he lied, "I guess she just doesn't realize what she's doing."

Mark looked over at her again and his face grew slightly stormy. He sank under the water for a moment and came back up flinging his hair out of his eyes. Tony hadn't noticed how long Mark's hair had gotten until he saw him soaking wet; he didn't like the look on Mark, it made him look almost pretty. The effect was unsettling.

Mark looked over at him again. After several moments of treading water he asked, "Look, do you mind if I talk to her? I want to see if she could go a little easier on him, at least tell him that she's not interested." Tony was silent for a minute, trying to decide if that would be a wise thing to do. Mark decided to press the point. "I just think Tyler deserves better. You know how he feels about her." His words were half question and half demand.

Tony had to agree with Mark on that point and nodded his assent. Mark flashed his even white teeth and sank under the waters like a hungry shark. Tony watched, amused, as Mark moved quickly and quietly across the pool's length. Cassie yelped as he went past her and Tony cracked a smile of his own. Mark talked to the girl they both felt so strongly for and she looked at him as if he'd lost his mind. They whispered for a few minutes, all the time with Tony watching intently, staring at Cassie's angelic face, until finally, Cassie broke away from Mark and headed for Lisa. Mark shot across the pool's bottom again, heading back in Tony's direction.

He came out of the water, not even breathing hard from lack of oxygen, and explained that Cassie was going to do the talking. Tony bit his tongue on the questions as to why; he already knew what had almost occurred between his sister and his friend. Lisa couldn't keep something like that a secret from him. He smiled and watched as the two girls got out of the pool, walking a safe distance from the rest of the group. When Tyler started in their direction, he was appalled. Tony thumped Mark lightly in the chest and pointed. "Yo, Mark. Red alert, man."

"Oh shit. This ain't gonna be pretty."

A moment later, P. J. stood in front of Tyler and redirected their friend, heading in the opposite direction with him. They would have thought the action a coincidence if he hadn't winked at them as he went past.

Lisa and Cassie spoke for several minutes, angry expressions changing to hurt, changing to anger again and finally transforming into smiles and laughter. They had no idea what she had said to Lisa, but whatever it was had worked. Lisa was moving across the room in a beeline for Tyler. A moment later, she walked outside with him, disappearing for a long time.

When they showed back up, Tyler looked confused and Lisa looked content. Mark and Tony looked at each other, sharing a puzzled *who the hell can say* look and went about their water sports.

4

Cassie and Lisa walked together through the woods behind Tyler's house. As a result of Tony's friendship and the odd times when he would bring Lisa along, they had started to become friends. Neither had really expected it to happen, not with what had almost happened between Mark and Lisa, but they had managed to do it just the same. They had a lot in common, aside from just being female and teens. They liked the same kind of music (Bowie was without a doubt, the best looking man either of them could think of in the music industry and both admitted to more than one sexual fantasy about him), they had similar tastes in movies and in books and of course, they agreed vehemently on men. The talk at the pool had helped to cement their friendship; they had finally gotten all of the walls between them torn asunder and could now begin to build a trusting relationship.   --

Cassie had hit the nail on the head when it came to observations about how Lisa felt about Tyler. She liked him more than just a lot and she wanted to see if they had any kind of chance at a relationship, but she also had a few problems with his looks. Cassie clarified that as well: he was twice as skinny as a beanpole and had more grease on his face than a pizza has cheese. It was only when she felt herself starting to take offense at the comment, that Lisa realized just how right Cassie was. She really did have feelings for him.

She took the advice that Cassie had to give; she dragged Tyler outside and told him how she felt, cautioning him that it would take her awhile to really sort everything out in her mind. Tyler nodded and said that she could take her time, his schedule was clear for about the next century or so. He made her laugh and that was a big boon. Now all she had to do was avoid the head games she had been playing on him and sort out her real feelings. That was what she was trying to do now, with Cassie along for support and advice. Cassie hadn't said a word so far, she'd just been there. Lisa was grateful to her.

"Mark and Tony asked me what we'd talked about," Cassie said, startling Lisa half out of her swimsuit.

"What did you tell them?"

Cassie smiled maliciously and Lisa waited, knowing in advance that it would likely be something about it being none of their damn business. "I told them exactly what my mother told me to tell guys who were too curious. 'Girl stuff'. You should have seen the looks on their faces."

Lisa chuckled at that one; she'd used it more than a few times herself. They continued in silence and Lisa decided that Cassie should go into psychoanalysis as a profession. Either that, or she could be a talk show host. Lisa looked over at the girl who was so different from her in appearance—slimmer and more athletic, with eyes and hair a thousand shades lighter and freckled skin as pale as cream, except where the summer sun had given a light bronze coating—and she wondered how it was that they could have so much in common. She decided at last that some things shouldn't be questioned, some things should simply be.

5

Patrick sat in his room watching the two girls step out from the pool area, into the warm summer's light and he admired the way their bodies shifted. He'd spent the last seven days practically locked into his room afraid that he might run across Mark if he left. Afraid that Mark might decide to remove the one witness to his crime.

He was startled by the sound of someone knocking on his door. He blushed at the yelp that escaped past his lips. After a few silent seconds, he called for his visitor to come in. It was Tony.

"Hey, Tony, what's up?"

Tony frowned slightly, looking at the mess that his room had become. "I was gonna ask you the same thing, man. Where you been hiding yourself?"

He motioned for Tony to have a seat and after kicking a small pile of dirty clothes off of a chair, Tony did. "I've been feeling kinda weird, guy. I—" He didn't know what to say, he couldn't just blurt out that he'd seen Mark turn into a monster, Tony would be the very first one to say that he'd been tripping.

He shook his head and finally said, "I've just been recovering from a bad trip. I think I'm gonna stay away from that shit from now on." Tony looked puzzled and he knew his friend was asking politely for all of the juicy details.

Patrick couldn't get his mind to function, it just refused to work. Every time he thought he'd come up with something that would work as an answer to the look in his friend's eyes, he found himself needing to tell somebody, anybody, what he'd seen. Finally, unable to stand the silence anymore, he blurted out his story, pausing often and shaking at the memory. Tony asked few questions, but those he did ask were direct and to the point.

After the story was told, they looked away from each other, lost in their separate thoughts.

"Maybe," Tony started. "Maybe you saw Mark out in the woods and you saw somebody kill T-Tommy and you just fantasized the rest of it." He started again, before Patrick could come up with a solid counter argument. "You said yourself you were tripping and you were over twenty feet away in an area that was dark. How could you have seen everything as clearly as all that?"

Tony had a point— he had been a distance away and he had been tripping and it had been dark. Patrick lost himself in thought for a good span of time and finally Tony spoke one last time.

"Look, Ty's got a lot of people over here and I know that Mark's here too." Patrick must have looked as panicked as he was, because Tony immediately stood up and made calming motions with his hands. "Relax, there are a lot of people down there and I'll be there too. Even if he is a monster, and I don't think that he is, he wouldn't be stupid enough to do anything there." He paused a moment, to let all of that sink in. "Come on down with me, talk to him and see if he says anything weird. If he does, I'll take you to the sheriff myself."

Patrick thought about that and after ten strained minutes of silence, he nodded his agreement. Tony practically had to shield him with his body. When they got there, the party was still going strong and Tyler and Mark were engaged in a water-wrestling match. Patrick nodded to all of the people he recognized and stared at Mark in cold dread, trying not to let it show. It must've shown anyway, because Tony kept muttering reassuring words to him.

When Ty and Mark finally stopped wrestling and swam over to the side, Mark was as nice and friendly as he'd ever been. Patrick stared at his eyes and face, trying to find any sign of duplicity, but to no avail. Finally he allowed himself to relax a bit and made a mental note to thank Tony later, when the crowds had all gone home.

By the time that the girls had finished their walk through the shallowest part of the woods, Patrick was enjoying himself for the first time in over a month. He left only once, to run to his room, change into his swim suit and flush every last illegal substance that he had hidden in the house down the bathroom toilet.

6

They watched the two females walking and probed delicately at the edges of their minds. They talked and whispered to each other and one of the bolder ones made a suggestion. The rest listened intently and finally, They decided. Perhaps, the idea had merit. But They would have to wait. Tired as They were, They had all the time in the world.

They looked at the two, recognizing them as the two They had seen The One with. Would one of these be the Chosen's Mate?

They watched. They waited. They whispered suggestions, there was much fun to be had, the females could ensure that fun.

7

It was early the next morning when Tyler and Mark finally had time to be alone, to talk as they seldom seemed to manage to anymore. The morning was a little chilly but neither bothered with coats; in another hour it would be warm enough to make the coats a hindrance.

"How'd it go between you and Lisa?"

"Mmmm. It was different. It was definitely different." Tyler paused, momentarily ignoring Mark's quizzical look and started kicking at a stray rock on the street. "She said she thinks she likes me, but not to take it the wrong way. When I asked her to clarify that statement, she said she hadn't decided if she likes me and I shouldn't get my hopes up or anything." Tyler looked at his friend, with solid confusion in his eyes. "Mark, what the hell am I supposed to make of that kind of crap? Why can't anyone ever tell you straight out how they feel?"

Mark smiled gently and for just a second, Tyler saw a pudgy bespectacled boy no taller than he was, reflected in the eyes of the young, scar-faced man that stood next to him; it was almost enough to break his heart. "I don't think we're supposed to have any easy answers; I guess God figures if we have to work harder for it, we'll appreciate it more." He too grew silent, reflective. They walked in silence for a long time, almost all the way into the town proper, before either of them spoke again.

Mark said; "Do you love her?"

Tyler thought hard on that one. "No, but I think I could love her. See what I mean?"

"Yeah." He paused a while longer, trying to decide how to word the whole thing. "Maybe that's the way she feels about you. Maybe it's because you never let anyone see what's going on inside of you, that she can't really decide."

"How do you mean?" Tyler pushed his glasses back in place and wiped a sweaty hand across his sweaty forehead, irritated at the perspiration running down the inside of his lenses.

Mark looked over with a puzzling smile on his face, a smirk that seemed to acknowledge Tyler's having secrets that he didn't want to reveal and, at the same time, seemed to forgive Tyler for those secrets. Mark's friendship was one of the few things he truly treasured. Until he'd gone to P. J. Sanderson there had been no secrets between them, they'd been soulmates. Now so much was changing, so very fast. He wished the world would slow down again, give him a chance to catch his breath; somehow he doubted he'd have that luxury.

He'd had a strange talk not long ago with his father, a man who never seemed to have any problems that were too big, and he'd expressed that sentiment. His father had laughed lightly and at the same time, managed to look heartbroken. His mouth had smiled and his eyes had looked ready to shed a thousand tears of sorrow, presumably because his youngest son was in the process of growing up.

The man had stepped away from his chair for a moment and come back with two small glasses of brandy. He knew his father always saved the liquor for special occasions and had been touched when he had handed one to him. Like an obedient son, he sipped at the warm glass of furnace flames and forced himself not to hack out a cough as it scalded his insides. His father smiled again and he saw a great deal of pride in that smile. Then the man held up his glass in salute.

"Son, I want to congratulate you on getting this far. Lord knows your mother and I had our doubts, what with that mouth of yours." He gentled the words with the affectionate tone in his rich deep voice. "I know you can't help it, but that mouth can be lethal. Now, my son comes to me talking about how fast the world is moving, which is to me at least, a sign you are growing up. Not all the height in the world could be a better convincer." The man chuckled throatily and pushed his glasses back up on his round and crinkly face, but they were the good crinkles, the kind you get from having paused many times to laugh, or enjoy the sunset. "I want to give you one little bit of advice, Tyler and I don't suppose you're going to like it very much, but it's a fact and you'd do well to remember it." He paused once more, trying to look serious and failing and Tyler loved him more then, than at any time he could clearly recall; he suspected that if his father died tomorrow, he'd choose to remember him in that one moment of time. "Son, you just said that the world is going too fast for your liking and I reckon that that's the truth, it does speed up something fierce." His father's face grew mischievous and a certain light glowed in his eyes. "This is my advice to you; find a grip and hold on tight. The sonuvabitch never slows, it just keeps getting faster and faster." Having said his piece, he touched the tip of his brandy snifter to Tyler's and tossed back the remaining brandy. Tyler thought his father's face was going to catch fire in that moment, it turned red enough to glow. Taking his father's lead, he tossed his own back and proceeded to cough hard enough to send his glasses sailing towards the floor.

Mark's voice brought him back to the present. "I mean, that you hide behind your mouth, just like Tony hides behind his fists. People get a little scared to talk to you, Tyler, they're afraid you'll tear 'em a new asshole."

Tyler hated it when someone, anyone, pointed out a flaw in his personality; not because he didn't want to know about them, but because someone had learned to know him too well for comfort. He realized that Mark was right, but how could he change from being what he was? He asked the question of Mark, who smiled sadly and shook his head. "You have to trust someone, like I trust you and Cassie; believe me, I know it's not easy, but you have to trust them if you want them to trust you."

The conversation ended then, they had reached their destination. The cinema was playing a new sequel to an old horror movie. Typical Hollywood fare about a madman who just wouldn't die. It was a serial movie, same plot, new faces and new death scenes. For a change, the movie was better than they had expected.

Mark treated, which was damn decent of him considering that they were joined by Cassie and Lisa—Cassie had spent the night at Lisa's and they had spent a great deal of time talking about boys and getting to know each other better. Tony hadn't slept a wink—he spent the entire night in his work out room.

It would always be one of Tyler's fondest memories, the way that Mark laughed on that day, with all of the enthusiasm of a five year old, able to relax and trust in the world, that all would turn okay in the long run.

Chapter Eleven

1

It was almost three weeks to the day after Alan Fisk disappeared that his mortal remains were found. His Mustang had been located easily enough, it was right were he'd left it, on the other side of the town from where Mark Howell lived. Jeremy and Joshua Grunewald were the unfortunate boys who found what was left of him. They had been playing in the woods against their mother's strict rules and ran across the ant covered remains while playing cops and robbers. At the ages of seven and six respectively, they didn't bother to look too closely before running home with their screams carrying before them. It was the last time they ever went into the woods without permission.

Chuck Hanson was nearly blinded by his grief; as annoying as Alan could be, he'd loved him like a brother. Donna was inconsolable; she'd cried on Chuck's shoulder for well over an hour and he had to admit that he'd joined her for a good portion of that time. She would be taken care of; the extremely large life insurance policy that the town provided for its law enforcers would see to that. If she didn't go crazy buying new things that she didn't need, Donna would never have to work. But, to tell the truth, he hoped she would, because it was too easy to picture her turning into a couch potato of epic proportions.

Rick Lewis was shocked by the state of the body and spent almost seventeen hours in intense examination of the deputy's corpse before he came to Hanson, bleary eyed from lack of sleep and made his report. "Alan Fisk died as a result of over thirty blows to the chest and genitals, from a dull and over-sized bladed weapon. The type of weapon is unidentifiable,

as there are no traces of any foreign substance that could con-
ceivably have cleaved him open in that way. The wounds would
appear to be similar to those made by a very big hatchet. There
are indications of extreme shock, brought on by fear. He never
removed his revolver; it was never fired. Going by the larval
infestation of the body, both the age of the current maggots
and the evidence of previous generations, I'm going to say the
approximate time of death was between three and five p.m.
on Saturday three weeks ago. Variable for time of death could
be one day in either direction."

Chuck looked at his friend and told him to sit down. "Now
what aren't you telling me? What else did you find?"

Rick rubbed at the bridge of his nose, groaning at the
thoughts that ran through him. "I found more of that crap in
his chest, at the genitals, and on his hands." He looked at the
sheriff with genuine fear in his eyes, he looked to the sheriff
like a man on the edge. "Chuck, this shit is really starting to
scare me. It's bad when the only death in a town this size that
isn't involved comes from a ninety year old man keeling over
at the top of his stairs."

"Still can't figure this stuff out? What makes it tick?"

Rick's face contorted in frustration and he slapped his
hand against the desk with a sound like a kettle drum. Chuck
flinched. "It doesn't make any goddamn sense!" he roared,
his face turning red as his blood pressure skyrocketed.
"Nothing seems to hurt this shit! It doesn't dry up and
blow away, it doesn't decompose, it doesn't even smell like
anything, for God's sake! Chuck, this stuff defies every
damn rule of nature."

Chuck Hanson sat in silence, waiting patiently until Rick
had calmed down enough for him to speak rationally. "I want
you to send a sample of it to the labs in Denver."

Rick looked at him, with shock and outrage warring on his
face. He was ready to tell his college room-mate to go to hell,
until he realized that Chuck had given him a considerable
amount of time, based on their friendship alone.

His expression softened and sadly he nodded. "Yeah, maybe they can figure out what it is, maybe I should send it to the fucking Parapsychology departments, too."

Hanson smiled thinly and nodded his head. "Maybe you should at that."

"You're not serious." It wasn't a question.

Chuck Hanson's face reddened and Rick remembered the one other time he'd seen his roomie's face change to that particular shade and the resulting four hospital beds that had ended up occupied. He held his hands up, signaling his understanding and made it clear that he didn't necessarily agree.

"You don't have to agree, Rick, but you said yourself that this stuff defies nature. What the hell can it hurt?"

"No argument there, Chief. You win."

Hanson stood, and from his standing position, Rick was reminded that the sheriff was a monster of a man. Then Hanson walked over to a framed picture that showed him and one of the previous Mayors and Alan Fisk standing together at a Christmas party. He gently touched the face of Alan in the photograph and turned slowly back towards Rick. "I want this person, Rick. I want this person in a bad way. The longer I have to wait, the worse it's going to be." He then pulled his old battered hat from the hat-rack near the door and walked away without a word. Rick would stay for awhile, answer the phones should there be a call; it was after three in the morning and he didn't expect any, but he knew that Chuck needed to walk, to think and to plan. He would wait. That's what friends were for and it would start their friendship on the way to what it had been before the murders had started.

Maybe, just maybe, he could reaffirm the bond that they had shared since college. Maybe he could make up for his lack of forethought when it came to being a coroner. He should have sent the samples off a long time ago; it was what his job required. He wondered if any lives would have been saved if he had followed the proper procedures.

2

The dreams ran through his slumbering skull, like a freight train rampaging through its station never having applied its brakes. P. J. Sanderson didn't moan in his sleep, he howled.

In his dreams, nightmares really, P. J. saw Alex Harris, his best friend in the whole world and he saw the little boy that was with Alex; the boy who looked so very much like his friend, if his friend was only three years old. What was his little brother's name? Why couldn't he remember and why was it so important? In the dreams, they walked through the woods and he heard the voices of the girls; knew who they were, even though he couldn't see them.

Susan and Annie were beautiful and they drew his eyes like moths to a flame. He stared at them as if they were all that mattered. They talked animatedly, laughing and shuddering, as the six of them walked through the woods.

Susan was glorious, like a delicate flower kissed by the dawn's first light; in her he could see the features that would be changed, diluted, in her offspring. *How sad*, he thought through the murky depths of his dream, *that she never had any daughters*. His dream self was confused on many levels, it was almost as if he was seeing the future; how could he know that she wouldn't have daughters? Susan's eyes were as dark as the night and her hair was the color of honey in the moonlight and he loved her with all of his young heart, as only a man-child of fifteen could love. Her eyes glowed with affection, hungry to make the world a better place, eager to bring a smile to anyone's face no matter how forlorn. Perhaps that was why they went so well together; for he was a sad and lonely old man, even at the age of fifteen. Oh, how often he'd longed to hold her, to feel the enthusiasm for life that seemed to flow from her as if it were the sweetest and purest of waters. He tried so hard to put her on a pedestal and she always managed to step away from that notion, to make him realize that she was only human, too. Without Alex to encourage him, he'd never have had the courage to even speak to her; he thanked God above for his friendship with Alex.

Anita looked so much like her daughter that seeing the younger girl always brought back the bittersweet memories of Anita and Alex together. Here his dream self wondered again; How could he possibly know of a young girl named Cassie? He shook the puzzling thought away and looked over at his sister, her proximity almost enough to ruin the day, but not quite. She was beautiful in her own right, but to acknowledge that was taboo. Antoinette was his sister, she was never to be beautiful to him.

He turned to look at his friend, a man still trapped by youth, forced to endure the prison of school and the rules of his father for a short time more. The dark hair that fell from his crown was like a curtain of finest silk. The light blue of his eyes was a stunning contrast to that hair and to his coppery skin. He was as much like a god as the girls were like goddesses. He loved him too, but in a different way.

Alex's little brother? Ah, there was a strange one, trying so hard to be like his sibling, failing so completely. In looks he was identical, in action and gesture he was completely different: fear of this wondrous world marred his beauty, even at his young age. Where Alex was godlike, his tiny imitator was roughly sculptured of clay, marred with the scrapes and bruises of a thousand falls to the ground. Had he been larger, he likely would have done himself serious harm by now. The tiny Harris looked around with large glassy eyes, seeking the insidious form of Stoney Miles, kept calm only by the reassuring presence of his sworn protector, Alex. Only by seeing the child, could he understand why Alex would spend any time at all with someone as graceless and useless as he himself was.

The scene should have been a happy one, but it sent chills of fear through his dream-self. A sense of great foreboding crept through him, bringing with it the puzzling sensation of having been through all of this before. He couldn't fathom the dread that filled him, until he saw the book, the moldering mass of pages that Alex held so tightly in his free arm, as if its protection meant as much as the protection of his brother. The sight of that book brought with it the recognition of a danger greater than any he'd ever known. Still, he could find no voice for his fears; he was trapped in a body that moved of its own accord, moved with the certainty that to be elsewhere was to lose the friendship of Alex. The thought was enough to send tremors through his heart.

They wound through the darkening trees, a chill coming forward to remind them that the sun would soon set, that winter was on its way and would be here all too soon, ready to annihilate the days of swimming at Overtree and the stolen kisses that so often occurred there. The wind whispered promises of snow and the crisp tang of burning wood to keep them safe until the next spring. In the distance, approaching rapidly, their destination; the slab of stone that looked so like an altar.

It promised to be a most unusual Halloween. Despite his fears, he felt the muscles of his body tense in anticipation.

The stone stood all alone, without so much as a single spare chip of granite to show that it was a natural formation; that was what made it so interesting to Alex. Did the Indians perform sacrilegious rites in this very place? Was this then the altar to some ancient gods that had long since faded from Man's past? Had this stone known the taste of sweet virgin's blood in its distant history? And if so, did it remember the taste after all this time? Its black and gray surface glowed dully in the setting sun and one could almost see its smile, at the thought of having a new sacrifice after so many millennia.

The dream progressed, as dreams so often will, at a terrifying pace. The motions and gestures were made by Alex, as the others looked on. His voice thundered in the shade of trees that were like as not as old as the stone around which they stood guard. It was fun at first and then the strange things started to happen.

The sky grew dark in a matter of minutes, not with the easy pace of sunset, but with the frantic threat of rain or snow, as the clouds scudded across the roof of the world. The winds increased and they shrieked rather than whispered. The scents of autumn changed, growing stronger with the smell of burning and then replaced by the smells of early spring after a rainfall. For only one moment, the dreaming P. J. saw his friends replaced by sinister replicas; their bodies became angular and their faces grew cruel; their motions were not those of children frightened, but rather the moves and gestures of demons cavorting, lusting for the taste of young and tender flesh.

Then the little brother of his best friend Alex, fell forward, almost as if he'd been pushed; caught himself on the altar stone and screamed in anguish and horror, as the sharp edge that none had noticed sliced through his delicate skin and cut him to the bone.

In his dream, he saw the child's flesh ripple, as tiny creatures as small as the three-year-old's hands, flowed into the toddler's body like air flows into a balloon. He watched in terror as the moving lumps bloated the little brother's form and filled him beyond the breaking point. The pudgy child danced as if scalded by hot water and expanded in height and width, screams pouring from a mouth distended horrifically. He cringed and closed his eyes, fully expecting to see the child torn asunder by the pressure of an infinite flow of possessors; fully expecting the remains of the exploding form to bathe him in a rotten stench. Then it was over.

When he opened his eyes, mere seconds later, Alex was holding the hand of his tiny sibling, pressing kisses on the minuscule scratch where the screaming wound had been a moment before. The little brother sniffled and tried to smile bravely in the glow of the setting sun.

So they left the make-believe altar of gods long dead and wended their way through the woods, Alex holding onto the hand of his brother, Anita and Susan walking with P. J., talking about how neat it was and how glad they were that nothing had happened. Antoinette was no longer in the dream, she had disappeared. P. J. couldn't keep his eyes off of the miniature form of Alex's brother, who walked so gracefully, seeming to float above the ground, where he couldn't possibly get hurt. Oh, how he looked towards his older brother, with eyes that once had worshiped and now seemed to mock. And oh, how powerful the gaze of the three year old boy, who stared at P. J. for just the briefest of moments and said without words that he knew what the friend of his brother had seen. And threatened the direst of consequences, should a word be spoken, and stared with eyes a thousand years too old to be held in so cherubic a face.

The dream changed, as dreams so often do and in his sleep, the author of many best sellers relaxed. This was a much better dream, a dream of love and kisses, stolen from his Susan, his goddess, his love. Replaced later by the face of another, darker, lover whose name he swore never to recall.

3

Tyler stared at himself in the bathroom mirror and groaned at the sight before him. He had become the acne king in the eight hours that he spent sleeping. He brushed diligently at the taste of burnt concrete in his mouth and wondered what he and P. J. would do if they couldn't find the damned book again. They had only looked over the man's house from top to bottom about a zillion times.

He almost choked on his rinse water, as Patrick slammed his fist into the door of the bathroom. "Get the hell out of there Ty, other people live here too, y'know!"

Tyler groaned. He didn't know what his brother had been up to for the last few weeks, but whatever had him in such a funk was obviously no longer bothering him. "Shit, hold on to your ass, Patsy, I'm almost done." He looked at his face carefully, ignoring the glaring red zits in his attempt to see if any facial hair had shown yet. It hadn't.

Out he went, past his brother who looked about as lively as Boris Karloff in The Mummy. He scratched idly, as he stumbled up to his room, dragging his comb through hair that was already being attacked by the grease in his scalp. After finally gathering the energy to pull on jeans and a light shirt, he walked toward the front door.

P. J. was already outside waiting for him. He scowled as the man smiled sunnily in his direction. "Good morning young Master Wilson! May I say how fine you're looking on this bright and cheerful day. My, but it does this old heart good to see the beaming face of youth up and about at this early hour."

Tyler slid into the two-seater and groaned audibly; the man was playing another of those groups he listened to so endlessly and if Tyler had to listen to them too much longer, he was going to develop a taste for them. Today it was the Moody Blues, singing about the acid guru being dead. "Why must I always endure this music," Tyler asked by way of greeting. "Why can't you listen to something a bit more upbeat or even remotely modern, like Pearl Jam, or even Fat Boy Slim?"

P. J. looked over at him, a smile taking ten years from his face and replied, "I could always pull out a Bay City Rollers tape, or perhaps The Monkees are more to your liking?" He smiled as he started for the dashboard and Tyler immediately blocked his hand.

"No! That's all right, I can deal with this. Honest."

"Well, if you're certain. I'm almost positive I have a Beach Boys tape in here somewhere."

"I'm sure, but thanks just the same." He knew the man was deadly serious; he wouldn't hesitate to find something even more obnoxious. He could have shouted for joy when they finally reached the Basilisk. Inside he normally had a television running the latest video releases and that was certainly preferable to hearing anymore of the ancient hits of the distant past; he wondered how his parents must've felt when they were forced to listen to the big band music of their folks. It couldn't have been as bad as this.

They went into the store and P. J. sat down wearily at his desk, looking over the notes that he had written for today's plans. Without consulting his young friend, he studied the page before him for several minutes. Then, "I think it must've been stolen from me. I can't imagine who would want the damn thing, but I am certain it can't be in the store."

"Who the hell would have stolen it? You said yourself that it's not even worth that much, except to a historian maybe."

"I was wondering about that myself, I just can't see Mark having any need for it. It's not at all like him to do such a thing. Besides, I never gave him a key to the collectibles."

Tyler frowned and looked around at the glass case from which they'd pulled all of the books. "Well, who did you give a copy of the keys to?"

P. J. looked over at Tyler and then looked away from him. "I've only ever made one spare copy of the key and I gave that to Tony. He worked here last summer, before I hired Mark. But, he's my nephew and I just can't see him stealing anything from me. It's not at all like him, not with the huge allowance he's given by his father."

Tyler looked at him for a long time, trying to find a way to point out that the man's blood relative was less than a saint; finally he decided to ask a question of his own in response. "Why did he need a job here, if his allowance is so big?"

P. J. looked over at Tyler and frowned at the honestly placed question. "I don't believe I ever gave that much thought. I'd just assumed that he wanted something to keep him busy a few days every week." He looked around the room and his face grew cloudy. Tyler could see in that brief moment why Mark was always worried about being on time; the man looked like he could break a statue just by looking at it. "Well, why don't I give him a call and we'll see if he has any clue as to where those books might be." The tone was light and friendly, but the look on his face promised a solid answer, or a reason for his nephew to continue living on this world.

4

While P. J. and Tyler where trying to locate Tony, Cassie and Mark were enjoying a fine lunch in Denver, with Jenny, Joe and Jenny's parents. They had only just arrived and as Jenny had predicted, decided to stay in Denver proper, certain that they would only get in the way despite the numerous protests to the contrary. Emily Gallagher was a sweet woman, with a face as round as a basketball and a body to match. If you looked carefully, you could see where Jenny had gotten her looks; she had the same features and even the same kind of hair, all made a caricature by age and weight. Still, she knew how to dress well and how to minimize her own girth. She was also one of the nicest women that Cassie had ever met. From the moment that the two of them had first met, they had hit it off beautifully. The woman's bubbly personality and throaty laugh made it easy to understand why Mark cared so deeply for her.

Walter Gallagher was a different story entirely; he was not as round as his wife, nor was he as energetic. He was fifty-seven and wore each and every year as if it were a scar. His hair was mostly gone, save for a fine white misting on the back of his head. His face was craggy with wrinkles and his nose had thinned to the point where it looked like the beak on a vulture. His only saving grace was the love he obviously felt for his family, even Joe. His smile, when he chose to use it, made him look like a man of thirty. Sadly, he seldom chose to smile at anything; his was the face of a man who had suffered too many hardships. Cassie liked him anyway.

The Gallagher's seemed to feel the same way about her, they doted and reaffirmed a thousand times that her lunch was to her liking; assuring her that if it was not, they would have it sent back immediately. They asked questions of how she and Mark had met and they asked questions of what her plans for the future were. She silently thanked Mark for the advance warning on their arrival.

For all the time they spent doting on her, they spent twice as long on Mark. No sooner had they met at the restaurant, than Emily had practically broken into tears over the scar on Mark's face. Mark, naturally, turned a remarkable shade of crimson, as he tried desperately to convince his grandmother that there was nothing wrong about the scar and that it did not hurt.

Cassie suspected that it would be a long week's visit. Walter Gallagher spent a great deal of time staring at his grandson, as often as not seeming to be lost in his thoughts. No one seemed to notice his spans of silence, save Cassie and Jenny.

By the time they finally departed, with the Gallaghers staying in Denver but promising to drop by the next day, it was almost time for dinner. They opted to make a night of it and after talking to her parents, Cassie and the Howells spent the remainder of the evening at a fine little restaurant and then at the movies. They were still in the theater when the shit hit the fan in Summitville.

5

Tony Scarrabelli got off of the phone, with cold sweat running freely across his brow; Uncle Phil hadn't believed him and was right not to. He knew exactly where the missing books were. He was the one that had stolen them.

When Phil called, the tone of his voice had started Tony well on the track of knowing that he was in deep shit. By he time the call was over, he knew that he had to get the books back. A task that was easier said that done. He had given the books to Patrick Wilson in lieu of the one hundred dollars that he had owed him, back pay on several narcotic delights that he had purchased fully aware that he couldn't pay for them. He'd gotten the job with his uncle to earn spare money, but that money disappeared as quickly as it fell into his hands; money had that tendency when in his possession.

Now his problems were threefold. One, he had to get the books back from Patrick, assuming that he could get the owed money gathered together. Two, he had to get the books back to his uncle. And three, he had to get his own fat out of the fire. This was not starting off to be a good day.

Hopping into the Camaro, he revved the engine until it had become a screaming banshee and popped the clutch, rocketing into the street and barely missing a collision with Mister Merriwether's mail truck. He waved an apology to the old man and ripped across town. He had to get hold of Patrick, as soon as possible. The implied threat in his uncle's voice was enough to send shivers through Tony. He still recalled with crystal clarity the one time his father and uncle had gotten into a fight and how his quiet and retiring uncle had beaten the living snot out of his old man. He didn't remember the reasons for the fight, but he remembered how the fight had ended well enough. He had little doubt that the same speeding fists could and would collide with his own skull, if Uncle Phil ever found out the truth.

The thought was not precisely conducive to caution in driving. He'd kill Patrick if he'd sold the books; that much he promised himself: he wouldn't go down alone.

6

Patrick, for his part, was patiently explaining over his private line, that he no longer dabbled in the illegal trades which had saved his hide so many times. Dave Brundvandt didn't want to hear it. And that, friends and neighbors, was very bad news.

Dave was from the part of Summitville that was only half in jest called the slums. It wasn't that the houses in the area were bad, it was simply that they weren't as well kept as they once had been and the people that lived in them couldn't afford to change the situation. The Brundvandt clan lived in one of the nicer houses in the area, meaning that they still insisted on picking the garbage off of their front steps and managed to repair the roof with shingles instead of plywood; they made enough money to live on. Most of the people living in that part of the town managed to keep a roof over their heads by spending far too much money on their property taxes to allow them any luxuries, such as air conditioning in the summer and heating in the winter. The luckier ones normally managed to scrounge enough scrap wood to keep the fireplaces burning.

Just when the separation in the two sides of town had occurred was not a well-documented fact. It just seemed to start in the fifties, as a slight decrease in the upkeep of a few houses, and slowly descend into a less dignified squalor in the entire area as the years went on.

Dave Brundvandt was one of the few who always managed to have enough money to pay for his recreational habit and Patrick was wise enough to avoid asking where he got the money. He tried to explain why he wasn't dealing anymore. Dave wasn't in the mood to listen calmly.

"I don't care," the voice grumbled through the phone. "I want my shit and you said you'd have it. If you're goin' back on your word with me, things are going to get really ugly, Pat."

"Dave, you're not listening, man. I can't deal anymore. I already kissed all my connections bye bye. Even if I wanted to get the stuff for you, and believe me I do—I can't. These guys aren't like you and me, these guys don't just say, 'Sure, one more small deal, for old times sake.' They don't deal in anything but large quantities."

There was a long pause on the other end of the line and Patrick could almost see the thick eyebrows of Dave Brundvandt knitting together in thought. The breathing sounds made him uncomfortably aware that his customer was still on the line and most likely displeased with the present situation. "Look," Patrick started, "I'll give you a name in Denver, maybe you can pick up my slack, even turn a profit and start the business for yourself." It was the last thing that Patrick wanted, but he thought the alternatives less than pleasant to contemplate. Dave didn't normally cause the same amount of grief as some of the other people at Good Ol' Westphalen High, but when he decided that it was time to lay a hurt on someone, he did a fine job of it.

After almost a full minute of silence, Dave agreed to Patrick's idea. The catch was that he wanted his good buddy Pat to come with him when he met the man in Denver. Patrick had lived too long to say no.

Tony missed Patrick by less than three minutes and for the first time in almost six months gave the idea of doing extreme injury to another person serious thought.

He knew most of the people that Patrick associated with and spent a good portion of his day trying to locate him. As the fruitless search continued, he grew more and more sullen; the day was rapidly going from just bad to really shitty.

7

The Folk watched in wry humor as the car carrying Chuck Hanson made another pass near Their woods. They knew the sheriff by sight and knew what he and his friend the doctor had in mind. The thought brought Them great amusement; They had not had a good battle of wits in all too long.

Perhaps, They mused, it would do the sheriff good to see Them in person, something tangible for him to hunt. The idea sent shivers of delight and anticipation through Them. The Chosen was away, guarded as always by a few of Their number, and They were rapidly growing bored with this world; it was always so painfully mundane, lacking in the colors and sights that made Their own home so lovely. There was no challenge here that was worthy of Their notice and They thrived on a good challenge.

Without a conscious decision having been reached, They started forming bodies, coming out of the hiding places that They had established in the dim past, before Man had really even come to this land. They decided in the long run to give the man a fighting chance, a hint or two as strategically placed as any piece on a chessboard. A brief scare and then a clue, that would get the man thinking; and that was really all it would take—the man was sharp in thought and good at puzzles. Maybe, just maybe, They chittered, he will even surprise us.

8

Chuck was not having a good day and had not been having anything remotely like a good day in the last ten months. It ate him up inside to think about the people he had let down. The people of the town counted on him to ensure their safety and prevent the loss of lives. It sounded hokey, he was the first to admit that, but damn it, he really wanted to protect them.

Chuck hadn't had a serious relationship with any woman in the town, or elsewhere for that matter, since he had taken the job of sheriff; he found a great deal of emotional comfort in his duties. Certainly, he had the same physical needs as anyone else in the world and now and then he would get together with Antoinette Scarrabelli and take care of those needs. The woman was a freakin' nympho and if she could be believed, her husband was about as satisfying in bed as an overcooked spaghetti noodle. But he had no emotional needs that were left unanswered by his job as the town's protector. He needed the position of sheriff as much as he needed the air he breathed. The thought of failing in that position was the equivalent of failing in a marriage to him. He hated failure.

The need to put a stop to whatever the hell was going on in his town was as strong as any urge that he had ever experienced, mental or physical. The need to hurt whatever was doing his town harm, was almost as strong. He was the first to admit to himself that he was becoming obsessed.

It was as he was rounding the bend on Third Avenue, coming towards town, with the Basilisk ahead of him as a marker, that They made Their move. Alan Fisk stood on the edge of the road, looking pale and sickly and holding his

Join the Leisure Horror Book Club and
GET 2 FREE BOOKS NOW—
An $11.98 value!

— Yes! I want to subscribe to — the Leisure Horror Book Club.

Please send me my **2 FREE BOOKS**. I have enclosed $2.00 for shipping/handling. Each month I'll receive the two newest Leisure Horror selections to preview for 10 days. If I decide to keep them, I will pay the Special Members Only discounted price of just $4.25 each, a total of $8.50, plus $2.00 shipping/handling. This is a **SAVINGS OF AT LEAST $3.48** off the bookstore price. There is no minimum number of books I must buy and I may cancel the program at any time. In any case, the **2 FREE BOOKS** are mine to keep.

— *Not available in Canada.* —

NAME: _____

ADDRESS: _____

CITY: _____ STATE: _____

COUNTRY: _____ ZIP: _____

TELEPHONE: _____

E-MAIL: _____

SIGNATURE: _____

thumb out waiting for a car to stop and give him a lift. Chuck stopped. Not so much out of a need to give his dead friend a lift, as the need to gawk at him while his heart stuttered fearfully in his chest.

Alan sauntered casually to the side of the car and before Chuck could get his brain back into a functioning gear, slid into the passenger's seat, through the closed and locked door. The sheriff stared fish-eyed at his deceased deputy and the man stared back, eyes equally round and watery. "Chuck, you gotta listen to me. It's in the woods, not far from Overtree."

Hanson tried to force himself out of the driver's side door, neglecting in his panic to open the door first; despite his size and strength, the stubborn hatch remained closed. "Ahhhhhhhh."

"Chuck, listen to me. It's in the woods, not far from Overtree. It's bad Chuck, it's really bad. I can't say what it is, but it'll only get worse if you don't stop it." The specter stared at him, trying to discern if what it had said was getting through to him. Sadly, it shook its faintly translucent head. "You ask Tony Scarrabelli, he can tell you what's going on. He knows what's happening. It's all his fault, you ask him. You'll see."

Chuck almost screamed when the fading hand reached out to caress his skin. The ghost mouthed words without sound as it dissolved into nothingness. The words might have been "Good bye" but he couldn't be certain.

He sat stock still for almost five minutes, the words of his deputy ringing in his ears and the sight of his friend's ghost burning on his optic nerves. After that timeless five minutes he broke down in tears, partly of rage, partly of grief, mostly of confusion. When he had regained himself, he cautiously drove over to Rick's house and when his friend opened the door, he stepped inside without a word. The thought of being alone was too much to bear. He knew before the day was through, he'd be paging Antoinette on her beeper number. He would need the emotionless comfort she offered, if he hoped to keep his sanity.

9

They laughed and laughed, kicking Their feet in the air and
howling Their joy into the winds. They would remember the
look in his eyes for a long time to come and Their brethren
would be envious of Their ingenuity.

It was the thought of Tony Scarrabelli, being watched and
stalked by the lethal man They had just scared so easily, that
gave Them the greatest joy. As with the One, They both liked
and hated the one called Tony. Like the Chosen, They had
forgiven past trespasses against Their love, but They had not
forgotten them. The day was looking brighter by the minute
and They could hardly wait to decide who was next on Their
list. Perhaps the Author, a few false hints would do wonders
when it came to sending him in the wrong direction; They had
no fear of Hanson, but the Author was closer to being right
than They wanted to think about.

Yes, They decided, the Author would be next. And They
knew just the way to take care of the problem; it would be a
jest worthy of the last one. The very best part was that the
Author would only find out about it second hand, if he ever
found out about it at all.

10

The car hummed like a gentle breeze and he would have it no
other way. If it could actually be said that he had any friends,
they could have told you that John Crowley was a man who
needed his world in perfect order. They would have even gone
so far as to say that he was a man that would go to any length
at all to ensure that his world maintained that perfect order.

He had no friends to say such things about him, he was
far too busy for friends. He looked in the rear view mirror
and studied his own face for a moment. His eyes, he decided, were too close together behind his round rimless

glasses. His nose was almost hawkish. His hair was too thin and refused to stay where he wanted it to. But, it was his teeth that annoyed him the most: he thought of himself as horse-faced, with over sized incisors trying to force their way past his thin lips. Over all, he also felt that he was far too skinny.

Had he had any friends, they would have also pointed out that John Crowley was overly critical of himself. While he was not a paragon of good looks by any means, neither was he ugly. He was simply plain.

He looked away from the mirror and tuned in another station on the Lamborghini's radio; try though he might, he hadn't been able to find a classic rock station since he had entered the state of Colorado. He was fairly certain that if he heard another country song he would go insane. After almost a full minute of turning the dial fruitlessly, he decided that it was hopeless and turned the noise off. That was all right, it wasn't that much farther.

He slowed as the almost hidden access road came into view and with a cautious look over his shoulder, took the sharp right onto the only road that led to Summitville. He grinned from his average face and whistled tunelessly from between his teeth. "Just a few more miles, Johnny me lad, and then we can fix this little problem." The words came out cheerfully, between the tuneless little whistling noises he made; they came out as cheerfully as the smile on his face.

Had he had any friends, they could have told anyone curious enough to ask to get the hell out of John Crowley's way when he smiled like that. They could have pointed out that his sunny little all-is-right-with-the-world smile normally meant that the shit was about to hit the fan.

Those same friends would have been more than glad to let everyone know that John Crowley was possibly the meanest sonuvabitch ever to be born. Upon seeing the man, those who had been warned would have chuckled at the very thought. Right before he started breaking bones.

Jonathan Crowley focused his attention for a second; reality warped around him and the Lamborghini shifted forms, blurring, stretching, changing color, until it looked like and drove like a second hand Ford station wagon.

"I haven't seen you in a lo-ong time, Philly." Crowley smiled, reminiscing about the past. "My, my, my, won't you be surprised." He whistled a little longer, almost frowning. "I guess I should have killed you the first time. Some people never learn."

Jonathan Crowley's laughter was a twisted maniacal thing. Had he had any friends, they could have told you to get away and pray that he never saw you again. That laughter was a sure sign of the worst kind of trouble. The words would have been wasted. Anyone hearing that laugh would long since have run away.

Chapter Twelve

1

Summitville carried the same signs of civilization as any town worth its weight in earthworms: it had a McDonald's, a Kentucky Fried Chicken, and, of course, a Pizza Hut. Without those three important elements, the town would have been less than a speck on the map. It also had that other important claim to fame, a bar on the edge of the town where the working class townspeople came to relax after too many hours of manual labor.

As has already been pointed out, Summitville didn't take to strangers well. So, naturally, the first place that John Crowley ended up was at Dino's Bar and Grill. With his grin firmly in place, John stepped out of the Lamborghini-cum-Ford LTD and shook his head sadly. He would have told anyone who wanted to know that he had been in a hundred towns with bars that looked exactly like this one, with its neon signs and its slat board walls and the driveway made of one hundred percent pure gravel, with a seasoning of broken glass to add to the potential tire damage. The others had not all shared the dubious name of Dino's Bar and Grill, but the names were normally just as unimaginative. Naturally, it came with the same assortment of beat-up pick up trucks and trashed Mustangs with rebuilt engines. The only places for drinking that he hated more were the ever present and equally obnoxious yuppie bars in southern California. Here he stood out like a black man at a Ku Klux Klan rally. He wouldn't have had it any other way.

In his line of work the most important person to meet in any given town, was The Law. Call it a Marshall, or a Sheriff, or even a Constable, every town of this size had at least one person who was simply The Law. Look at The Law, see what shape The Law was in and you could tell how bad off the town was.

The catch was, you couldn't let The Law know that you were studying how it looked, so you normally ended up getting yourself in some minor trouble in order to satisfy yourself. With his looks and the looks of his clothes—the pressed blue jeans complete with creases and the Izod dress shirt and penny loafers, Crowley doubted it would be very difficult. Carefully putting his glasses away, he stepped towards the door of Dino's, bracing himself for yet another bout of Country Western Music.

As soon as he stepped inside he knew he'd have no trouble meeting The Law. As he walked towards the bar, he could feel the eyes of every person following him.

Just to add to the fun, he called loudly enough for the whole bar to hear when he ordered a Perrier with a twist of lime...

2

As it turned out, it was not the sheriff who answered the call from Dino's, it was one of his deputies, a relative newcomer to law enforcement, Dave Palance. Dave was only recently out of college and had heard horror stories about how ugly bar brawls could get. He'd never doubted that the tales were true, but he had never really been prepared for the actual sight, either. No sooner did he open the door to his cruiser than the sounds of violence hit his ears. The most noticeable sound was of a man screaming in pain. He called in to let Stacy Calhoun know what was going on and she chuckled throatily. "If you're at Dino's, you'll get used to it," she replied fondly. It was then that he remembered she used to work at the bar herself, when she was working her way through college. Dino was her mother. He never had gotten up the courage to ask how the poor woman had gotten stuck with such a name: Stacy's legendary temper preceded her and he had no desire to get on her bad side.

The trick, he decided, was to look confident. He was a figure of authority in the county now, not just Bubba Palance's son. Every one in town was simply going to have to learn that. If the lesson was a hard one to learn, well then, he'd just have to be firm in his resolve as he was busting heads. He hitched his size twenty-eight pants up to their proper position and walked towards the door of Dino's, scolding his traitorous knees for the way they insisted on shaking. Forcing himself to look mean, he stepped past the threshold and into Dino's.

Mike Byrne was the first sight to meet his eyes; the man was leaning against the wall opposite him, holding his right hand in his left, cradling the swollen pulped fingers and whimpering softly. Dave was fairly certain that it had been Mike he heard screaming a moment before. Slowly, he let his eyes roam over the rest of the establishment. Just as slowly, his eyes widened in awe of the devastation. William Phillips, father of the late Andy Phillips, was unconscious on the floor, a line of blood running from his nose to leak across his ear. His nose looked more like a bulldog's than anything else, which was saying quite a bit when Dave considered its normal hawkish profile. The rest of the usual crowd was still on their feet, surrounding a man that Dave had never seen before.

The stranger was grinning ear to ear, ignoring the busted lip on his face. The grin was decidedly nasty, promising without the need for words to destroy every one of the men surrounding him. Looking at the lean athletic build on the man, Dave could understand why the men seemed hesitant to do anything. The looks they gave back seemed made up equally of anger and wary respect.

Just before Dave was finally ready to announce himself, the stranger launched himself at Dwayne Reinfeldt, one of the most notorious brawlers in town. Apparently the men had already exchanged blows, if the swelling eye on Dwayne was any indication.

Dwayne was ready for the attack: he planted a left hook across the stranger's jaw that snapped the man's head back and sent him stumbling after it. Dave was now convinced that the newcomer was a lunatic: he was still smiling when he came back for more. Dwayne never had a chance. The mystery man ducked under his right arm and used his own right hook to return the damage Dwayne had inflicted a second ago. The people surrounding the two men hastily backed up as Dwayne pushed between them and grabbed for a pool cue from one of the now-forgotten billiards tables. Dave was preparing for a warning shot from his pistol—the Sheriff insisted that each man carry only blanks in the first three chambers of their revolver for just such ludicrous situations—when the stranger broad-sided Dwayne. The cue was dropped before the fight could get to the level of lethal weapons or assault with intent to kill. Dave was very happy about the change of tides: he couldn't remember if he'd been spinning the cylinder on his pistol or not and knew that he'd have been in deep shit if he'd blown a hole in Dino's roof. He was already chastising himself for what the sheriff had chastised him for a thousand times; his service revolver was not to be played with and he swore to himself that it would never happen again.

The sound of Dwayne's unconscious body crashing into the pool table was enough to pull the deputy out of his guilty thoughts, as he came back to the real world he saw the burly man fall to the ground, a beefy pile of loose bones and bloodied teeth.

Somewhere along the way, somebody had noticed the deputy, as well as the deputy's hand, which was now resting on his pistol. The area around the victor of the battle had been cleared entirely. Dave realized that he was now the center of every single person's attention.

Before a word could be spoken, Dino popped up from behind the bar with a ferocious scowl scrawled across her broad face. Meaty hands placed on even meatier hips, she glared venomously around the room and finally locked eyes with Dave. In a panic, he tried to make himself invisible, realizing sadly that it was far too late for that. "Well," demanded the barrel-shaped woman on the other side of the room, her raspy voice striking fear into the deputy's heart. "What the hell are you waiting for? Arrest 'em all!"

Heart too low in his stomach for health, the deputy looked towards the roof and prayed for a miracle, anything to avoid having to arrest all of these men. A miracle showed itself to him, in the form of Chuck Hanson. Dave decided that God had a twisted sense of humor in that moment and knew in his soul that today the joke was on him.

3

Lisa was most of the way to Tyler's home when her tire blew. She held the wheel tightly and gently pumped the brakes on her car as she pulled over to the edge of the road, cursing fiercely all the way. After the argument she and Tyler had just had, she didn't need anything else going wrong.

Tyler was acting like a little boy; ignoring her phone calls and acting like the search for some stupid book was more important than being with her. Well, she had had more than enough of that and she intended to let him know it. She cared about him, suspected that she might even be falling for him, but she wasn't going to tolerate his treating her like shit just because he couldn't find a book. Nossiree, that wouldn't do at all.

With a sigh of epic proportions, she switched on her hazard lights and stepped out of the car. Happily, her father hadn't hesitated to put a little extra money into buying a real spare for her car, instead of one of those cheap little donut tires most companies now used. After fighting for several minutes with her trunk key and then with the spare tire and jack, Lisa set about actually replacing the shredded mess that was once her right front tire.

Lisa was not a horribly physical person, nor was she gifted with a great amount of patience. After about five minutes of struggling with the lug nuts and getting absolutely nowhere, she threw the tire iron away from her and crossed her arms for a proper pout. The day just kept getting worse and worse.

It took only a second or so to realize that the tire iron hadn't made a clanking sound after she tossed it. Confusion getting the best of her, she turned in the direction of her ill timed toss and saw the dark figure of Mark Howell standing not four feet behind her to the right. He was holding her tire iron in his hand and smiling brightly in the twilight. "Lose something?"

Lisa let slip a little squeak of fright, before she could stop herself. "What are you doing here? I thought you were off in Denver!"

Mark's smile increased in wattage as he came over to where she squatted next to the treacherous tire and helped her stand using his free hand. As always, his touch left her feeling slightly weak-kneed and she immediately chastised herself for the thoughts running through her mind. Oddly, the look on Mark's handsome face seemed to reflect the thoughts she was having, or maybe it was just the way the scar on his face made his mouth smirk. He brushed back a stray lock of hair, as he replied to her question with a laugh. "We just got back. I saw the lights from my little spot in the woods and figured I'd see what was going on. Looks like this is my chance to help a lovely damsel in distress," He winked slowly, as his grin increased again. "I never could resist a damsel in distress."

Lisa was fairly certain she was reading the look on his face properly at this point and she frowned slightly, puzzled by the way he was acting. Mark was, as far as she could tell, head over heels in love with Cassie. Mark simply didn't have it in him to play the field. He had even had a chance at this particular field once and passed it by. So what the hell was going through his mind now? As if reading her mind, he smiled broadly and responded to her unasked question.

"Cassie had to get home, her folks left a message on the machine. I'm too bored to rest and when I saw your little problem, I thought I'd come and help." He flashed that impish smile of his again, "Unless you'd rather fix the tire on your own…"

Shifting her mind away from his smile and thoughts of what might be going on in his head, Lisa hastily assured Mark that she had no desire to try her luck any longer with the thrice damned invention of torment. He bowed mockingly and waited until she was out of the way before starting on the stubborn lug nuts from hell.

Despite her affections for Tyler, Lisa couldn't help but admire the cords of muscle on Mark's shoulders and neck, the way that they rippled as he flexed in combat with the stubborn bits of metal. She still couldn't quite understand the odd mix of feelings whenever she was close to him. Lust was obviously a heavy influence, but at the same time, she saw in him the exact same kindness she saw in Tyler. If only Tyler looked that good.

It only took him five minutes to accomplish the task she had failed to even get started in twice that time. After he had settled the traitorous tire in the trunk's resting spot and had replaced the tire-jack in the proper location, he once again turned into a shy and awkward young man.

Her heart went out to him, the way he stared while trying so hard not to, the way he blushed whenever their eyes met for more than a split second. She had long ago forgiven that awkward night in the past, but it was still obvious that he hadn't. He looked like a puppy dog that had been caught piddling on the carpet when he noticed her stare; she turned her eyes away, more to let him gather his thoughts than because she herself was in any way embarrassed.

"Uh, well, I guess I better get home." The words were directed towards her, but his gaze was aimed directly at the ground beneath his feet.

"Can I give you a lift?"

"No, thanks. I think I'll go into the woods, do a little walking around." He managed to look at her for just a second, before turning away. "See ya 'round."

She couldn't help herself, she just couldn't stand to see him looking so dejected. Lisa ran forward, managing to get in front of Mark and, as he looked up in surprise, threw her arms around his neck. He stiffened for a moment, as if struggling not to run and then relaxed, patting her back affectionately. "Thanks for the help, Mark. I don't know what I would have done without you."

"N-no problem." She felt the warmth of his breath on her neck and ear and felt her knees trying to go all watery. Against all common sense, she turned her head up to look him in the eyes, a small part of her wondering if he would ever stop growing—the first time they'd actually kissed they were much closer to the same height—then she lightly placed her lips against his. He responded with unexpected passion.

His hands ran across her back, his tongue danced teasingly across her teeth, his arms surrounded her like two iron bars sheathed in a thin layer of flesh. She pulled back, trying to resist what she was feeling, trying hard to think about Tyler and even Cassie. Mark leaned forward as much as she pulled back.

Frantically, she pulled her head back from his, literally gasping for breath. "Mark, no, we shouldn't be doing this." Before she could continue, he lowered his head, nibbled lightly at her neck. She pushed against him with both hands, having absolutely no effect whatsoever on his oral examination of her nape. She was rapidly getting angry, thoughts of Cassie and Tyler washing away what had been the start of passion moments ago. Once it wouldn't have mattered, now it bothered her a great deal. She realized in a far distant part of her mind just how much she had changed in the last few months, how good Tyler had been to her; how, even after all that had happened, Cassie had accepted her as a friend, and she didn't want to betray those trusts.

Lisa started actually beating against his chest and would have tried to knee him in the groin, had he not maneuvered himself so that his crotch was turned away from her. In response, his powerful arms reached lower than they had before as he grabbed her buttocks in both hands, squeezing hard enough to cause pain.

Lisa pulled her hand back as far as she could, determined to strike him in the nose or jaw, to get him to stop immediately at any cost. But, all power left her arm when she looked at his face. The features were the same she had seen a hundred times before, the same she had studied intently when she first thought about getting to know him better, but the expression on all of those almost girlish features was like nothing she'd ever expected to see on Mark Howell's face.

He looked utterly insane, a grin of raw viciousness spread across his sensuous lips, his nostrils flared like those of an animal sniffing for its prey. But his eyes, God above, his eyes burned with a hideous strength, an elemental power that promised to destroy her. If she had ever doubted that the eyes were the mirror to the soul, she doubted no longer. She was certain that she had just seen the true soul of Mark Howell staring at her and she was equally certain that his soul was as empty of kindness as the cold depths of outer space.

She tried to scream, but as she sucked in a breath for just that reason, one of Mark's hands slapped across her mouth, successfully stopping the sound and breaking the full skin of her lower lip. As she felt his free arm wrap around her waist and felt the ease with which she was lifted off of the ground, she had serious doubts about whether or not she would live through the night.

Later, after a seemingly endless trek through the woods, as she felt the clothes literally torn from her body, she fought again until she was pounded in the face by Mark's fist for her trouble. Most of her mind was filled with pain, the desire to escape the torment that ran through her entire body. The smaller parts, as yet distanced from the searing agonies, wondered if it would ever stop, if she would ever see her family again and how she could have ever cared for the fiend that was doing this to her.

Eventually, her mind just refused to think anymore. But it took a long, long time.

4

Chuck Hanson had heard the stranger's story, had heard it collaborated by Dino, whom he knew to be a reliable source, but he had trouble believing the words.

Oh, he understood as well as anyone that Summitville took automatic offense to any stranger in town and he understood well enough that every one of the locals involved could have started the fight. That wasn't the problem. It was just the thought of this well dressed stranger taking out most of his assailants that he had trouble swallowing. That the man was athletic was obvious by the way his clothes fit him; that he was capable was obvious by the end results of the fight. But, he was almost disgustingly polite. As a general rule, Chuck Hanson found polite people to be…well, wimpy; Clark Kents, not Supermen.

The man, John Crowley, was nothing but helpful, going so far as to offer to pay for any and all damages done to Dino's place in the fight, but something about him just didn't quite ring true. He swallowed the thought as he turned to ask the man a few more questions.

"How long you in town for, Mister Crowley?"

The man shrugged, looking a little dazed as the adrenaline wore off in his system. "I honestly don't know, I'm just here to visit an old friend, P. J. Sanderson. He gave me a call not long ago and I finally had a chance to join him up here. Seems like it's been forever since we had a chance to talk. I'm guessing maybe about a month or so." Again that oddly friendly smile peeked from his face, just a hint of amusement to go along with the cheerful words.

Hanson thought about that for a minute or so before adding, "What is it that you do, Mister Crowley? Not too many people have that kind of free time these days."

Crowley grinned ear to ear, a light, mischievous twinkle striking his eyes. "I must confess, Sheriff, I'm just a filthy stinkin' rich dilettante. Mostly, I enjoy the sights and pretend to paint. Big inheritance and no desire to make it bigger."

Hanson decided then and there that the man would need watching; something in the way the words rolled off of his tongue was simply too practiced, as if he'd used the exact same line in every town he came to for the last five years. He brushed a stray lock of hair from his eyes and nodded at the man still smiling at him. "I appreciate your help, Mister Crowley. If you want to file charges on any of these boys I'll be glad to be of assistance."

Crowley's face twisted for a moment, the mischief replaced by serious thought. "I don't think that will be necessary, Sheriff." His grin came back, twisting upward on the left side of his face and becoming more a smirk than anything else. He shifted his eyes to where the men sat nursing wounded arms and egos. "I imagine they've already been taught a lesson."

That was when Dino barged into the conversation, her gravelly voice catching the attention of every person in the room. "They damn well better have," she started, glaring balefully at the group of men who now looked rather sheepish about the whole incident. "'Cause if it happens again, I'll press charges! You already got half the damages added to your tabs, boys and you will pay the tabs..." Hanson grimaced, knowing that the incident was far from over in Dino's eyes and knowing that until the tabs were paid in full, he'd keep hearing about it.

Just once, he thought to himself, *I'd like to see someone other that Dino get in the last word...*

5

William Phillips was feeling sober, a condition he tried hard to avoid these days. Sober was bad enough, but the constant throbbing in his nose simply added to his overall discomfort. He grimaced in reflection, still shocked by how quickly the stranger had sent him into unconsciousness. He hadn't even gotten in one good lick before the man was all over him like stink on shit. Three rapid-fire shots to his face and he was down for the count. The scary part was, he just knew the man had been holding back. The thought made him shiver inwardly, sending images of what his face would look like now if the man hadn't gone easy on him.

Probably like Andy's had, on the few occasions he'd let himself cut loose on the boy... His mind did a flip-flop at the thought of his only child, now dead for almost nine months. He longed for a drink. The thought of his son did that to him these days and he thought about his son an awful lot. The wounds just wouldn't go away; the disgrace of finding out what his son had done, compounded by the creeping guilt that told him he was to blame. He should have spent more time with the boy, he should have explained things to his son more carefully, he should have been sterner, and he should have been kinder to the boy... The thoughts simply wouldn't leave him alone.

Myra didn't make it any easier; she'd been the first to lay the blame on him. That they'd been in love once was still a thought that hurt, but somehow the love had faded, replaced by a bitter melancholy that stood as a wall between them. William Phillips longed for the past to return, the past that had always seemed so bright and hopeful.

Those were the thoughts that insisted on coursing through his brain, round and round in a never-ending circular argument, as he drove down the winding stretch of Third Street. Those thoughts were just coming back to his sobriety and desire for that condition to be gone, when he hit the naked and screaming Lisa Scarrabelli as she ran across the road in a blind panic.

6

Time went very slowly for Lisa after the first assault. She lay in a dazed pain-filled stupor for a span that could have been minutes or hours. The assaults just kept coming. It wasn't very long before her entire body felt wrapped in a blanket of hot iron that pulsed as wildly as her heart beat.

Slowly, very slowly indeed, she became aware of the absence of new aches, the absence of Mark's continuing efforts on her body. It was rather like being under water with weights attached to her body and then having the weights removed; she felt herself float back towards the real world as if from the bottom of a very deep lake. In a short time she became aware of how cold she was, an odd thought considering the time of year.

It was still dark out, something she considered to be a plus. One small part of her mind realized, in a distant voice, that being seen in public as she was would be socially incorrect. Most of her couldn't have cared less.

What had actually occurred here, in the woods, was finally starting to sink in when she heard the voices. They were familiar voices, tone and meter she had grown to know over the last few months: the deep melodic rumble of Mark's voice interwoven with the higher lighter clipped notes of Cassie's. It took less than a second for the full implication of what those voices meant to sink into her tortured mind. Fear, like a rabid dog, leapt at her throat and sank its chilling fangs deep into her, locking vocal cords that otherwise would have sent the shrieks of a mad woman echoing through the woods. With less sound then she would normally have managed, she scrabbled frantically to her feet and started to run.

From a distance, she heard the voice of her tormentor, so full of innocent concern that she almost stopped her dash away from him. "Lisa? Lisa, is that you? Are you all right?" His voice was joined by Cassie's, as the sounds of pursuit started.

The footsteps gained on her easily; the sound of brittle twigs and crumbling leaves being pushed away by his powerful strides coming closer with every step she took. Two semicoherent thoughts raced briefly to the surface of her mind only to be slammed back down by the fear that now overwhelmed her: "Mark never makes that much noise...what's wrong with him?" and "When did he learn to run so fast?"

Even in her tortured state, she could hear the second set of steps, the steps of her friend, Cassie, falling back from those of her tormentor.

With a desperate burst of speed, she forced herself to gain distance, forced her legs to piston and pump as they never had before. Lisa felt no pain from the thorns and branches that lashed against her flesh, drawing welts and blood both. She never felt the rocks that sliced through the soles of her feet. She felt only the terror of pursuit, the stark cold certainty that the man following her would never let her go, would use her again and again for as long as they both lived.

Elation started to mingle with the fear when Lisa realized that he was no longer gaining on her. She looked over her bruised shoulder only briefly, to reconfirm what her ears were telling her, that he had stopped chasing her. He stood stock still, almost a hundred feet back, his right arm held out, as if to ask her to see reason, to come back and tell him what was wrong. She almost laughed at the look of fear and dawning realization on his face; probably would have laughed, had it not been for the look of growing horror on Cassie's face where she stood only a few feet behind him—and the sudden light from behind her coming towards her at a speed that was utterly inhuman.

From the woods, she heard the mingled sound of Mark and Cassie screaming out in denial and, with a certain sickening dread, turned to look at the light. Lisa Scarrabelli finally noticed that she stood on asphalt at the same time that her mind took in the dark shape with burning eyes set low to the ground. She thought about the shape for only a second before her brain supplied the last words she would manage for quite a while. "Oh, it's a car."

Perhaps Lisa would have preferred to die right then, perhaps she would have wished to avoid the car altogether; either way the choice wasn't hers to make. The car hit her at a speed far too fast for the road. The impact lifted her one hundred and twenty-three pound body off the ground as if she weighed less than a balloon in a strong wind. She never felt the metal bumper collapse against her thigh even as the bone shattered; she never felt the windshield explode against her face and skull; she never felt her flesh tear against the vinyl roof of the old Impala. She was unconscious when her back slid over the rear of the car. She didn't have to see the tarmac rush forward to eagerly shatter her ribcage and spine. The last irony would probably have done permanent damage to her battered ego; she never realized that her own car was only twenty or so feet from where she finally skidded to a halt.

She never saw how quickly Mark stopped at her side, afraid to move her broken but breathing body. She never saw the look of insane rage that crossed his face as he looked towards the Impala where it stopped almost a football field away.

But Cassie did. It was a look she would never be able to drive from her mind.

7

They watched from the sidelines, even hiding Themselves from Him. Terror rippled through Their bodies. This wasn't supposed to happen; it was just a joke. They had meant to have a good laugh at the expense of the girl who had so frustrated Him, at the expense of the Writer, but *never*, *NEVER* at the expense of *Him*.

They watched from a distance as the Chosen One approached the car that had struck the girl. The other humans would never understand if he did the man harm, the humans wouldn't realize that Their strength was also His strength. With desperate speed, They sang to Him, calming the passionate fires that They had instilled for His own protection. It was not easy; They struggled to make Him obey, chilled for the first time in memory by His strength of will. "Soon," They whispered in the silent tongue. "Soon, he will be Yours, but You must wait, until all is quiet again." Slowly He calmed and They sighed with relief. The Mate of the Chosen had already opened the silent car near Their victim. She held a box for talking from within and They sensed that she called those who could help on the device. Carefully, quietly, They touched the one They had hurt so much and they slid beneath her broken skin, making changes and fixing what They could. She would live, of that They were certain. She had to live, on that They all agreed. She held Their progeny, Their only other hope, the only chance They had, should the Chosen prove too strong to finish bending.

Shivering in the night's heat, They conferred. Accusations would have to wait; for now They had to work even faster than They had desired.

Just as They felt all would be well, one of the Watchers approached. In a frenzy of fear the Watcher explained that the Hunter had returned. The woods shivered in fright as the ambulance pulled to a stop. The winds screamed in terror as the attendants took care of Lisa Scarrabelli's battered form. The Hunter was back; the very thought terrified Them. He had been gone so long. They had hoped to never see him again. The Folk scattered throughout the town of Summitville, trembling with terror and anxiety; each knew now that the Hunter had returned, each knew that Their lives could end in a matter of minutes if the Hunter spotted Them.

This changed everything. The Hunter wouldn't just destroy Them—he might destroy the Chosen, or the Chosen's Mate, or even the whole town, if he so desired. They had to find the Hunter and soon, if They hoped to bring the Masters forth. They had to find the Hunter and kill him, before he became aware of Them; They prayed it was not already too late.

Chapter Thirteen

1

A week passed in which everything proceeded in the way that life should; peacefully. With the exception of Lisa's hospitalization, the world was mundane. Mark's grandparents left earlier than expected, apparently opting to try their luck at a little gambling down Vegas way and life returned fully to the norm, except in the cases of Lisa, her family, and Tyler.

There is such a thing as simply giving up, shutting away all that matters and all that hurts in an effort to stop the soul numbing agony that life has thrown in your direction. Tyler had decided that giving up was the best way to take life after his first visit with the breathing, battered mannequin that had been Lisa.

The shock was too heavy for anyone to notice at first. Everyone that was close to him was experiencing their own pain. But, as is all too frequently the case, Lisa had started to show small signs of recovery. Virtually everyone who was close to her was ecstatic to hear the news; Tyler was totally unaffected. Tyler no longer smiled, not even the sad little smiles he used to give when he was hurting deep inside. He no longer seemed to have the energy to get out of bed before noon; it was as if he was the one who had been hit by the car.

Truth be told, his body was fine. It was his heart that had been shattered once too often. Mark tried to comfort him, Cassie tried to comfort him, all to no avail. He staggered through his days watching all of the shows that used to have him roaring with laughter and now did nothing for him. He lived by habit, not desire.

William Phillips was in the county jail for several days before being released. The blood tests were enough to convict him of driving under the influence and his license had been taken away on at least a temporary basis. That was just as well in his eyes, he had no desire to get behind the wheel ever again. Nothing changed when it came to his drinking, however. He simply stayed at home to get drunk; leading to violent arguments with his wife of eighteen years and finally culminating in her moving out to stay with her brother's family in Boulder. Less than two weeks later, William ended his life in a less dramatic way than that of his son; he suffocated in his own vomit while sleeping off his latest drunken stupor.

Chuck Hanson marked the case closed and even attended the funeral. Aside from Lisa Scarrabelli's family and the minister, he stood alone as the body was lowered into the ground.

That was the only case of violent crime, intentional or not, that Hanson managed to close during the summer. The strain of his job had started to show itself in the way he walked and in the haggard expression that always showed on his face. Although no one showed it in their talks with him, or even in their faces when he was around, he knew that the town was losing their faith in the man they had elected to protect them.

Rick Lewis for his part had sent the samples to every government agency he could think of as well as to several different colleges in the area. The results had not to date been conclusive. The only positive response he had received had been from one of the parapsychology departments that said it showed all of the properties inherent in the few documented cases of ectoplasmic activity and offered to send someone to aid in any way possible. Rick was so desperate for any solid evidence that he actually took them up on their offer. The psychologist that joined him had a list of credentials as long as her name, Jaquelyn Fitzgerald Rosenquist. Had she been less of a fanatic about the supernatural they would have gotten along better. As it stood, they could tolerate each other and he did appreciate the help.

With her, Jackie—a name she insisted on despite Rick's belief that she looked more like a Jaquelyn—brought several thousand dollars worth of monitoring equipment; machinery she was sure would be of use to them later on despite its occupying over half his office's free space. He would have been able to label her a kook with greater ease if she hadn't proven to be a veritable font of knowledge on damn near every case in history that couldn't be explained away easily.

Her knowledge was more useful than they had expected, when she managed to put the finger on Jonathan Crowley as a parapsychologist who had been quite the figure of attention in the early part of the Eighties.

The day had been stretched to its limits and the sun was setting when Chuck Hanson mentioned the name in passing. Chuck had just stopped by for the seventh time in as many hours to see if their had been any progress on the joint analysis of the "Goop," as he had taken to calling it, and mentioned briefly that he had spotted Crowley skulking around in the old cemetery at the heart of town, the cemetery that contained the earthly remains of the town's founders and the marker for Stoney Miles.

The name Crowley had perked Jackie's attention immediately and she smiled as she asked, "Which Crowley, Alastair or Jonathan?"

Hanson looked at her with his head tilted, as if he were listening for a distant sound in the woods at night and replied with the proper name. "Well, I guess maybe we are on to something out here, after all." The prospect made her high cheekboned face seem almost girlish. Her smile was as radiant as the early morning sun and as eager as a starving man's at the sight of a Thanksgiving spread.

Both men looked at her with puzzled expressions, silently asking her to continue. After a moment of calculating the looks they exchanged, she finally realized that they had no idea who Crowley was. The concept obviously shocked her.

"I thought everybody knew who John Crowley was! Why, he's one of the most important men in the field of parapsychology, or he was, until he went into retirement." She looked

at them to see if that had helped. It hadn't. "Jonathan Crowley
was the first man to document and record a full figured appa-
rition," she explained patiently, as if to mentally slow children. "His use of Kirlian photography in a house reported to
be haunted was a simply amazing break-through. The man
should have gotten a Nobel Prize for his work."

The two men stared at Jackie as if she had grown an
extra nose on her face. She fidgeted for a moment and then
tried to shrug off everything she had just said. "Naturally
the laymen refused to believe that it was anything but a hoax,
but all the experts in the field agreed that there was simply
no way he could have superimposed the image of that girl
onto the film. No way at all." She fought the urge to check
her face for extra nostrils and finally let loose with a sigh of
epic proportions. "Will you please tell me why you're staring
at me that way?"

That was all it took: the two men smiled and Jackie realized that her chances of leaving this room anytime in the near
future were absolutely non-existent.

2

Tony had all but forgotten about his uncle's damned books, the
last few weeks having been completely occupied with worrying over his sister. The books were really the last thing he
could have given a good goddamn about, until he saw Patrick
Wilson and Tyler step into the hospital room. Patrick was
dressed with his usual care, hair just so and blue jeans pressed
and creased; Tyler looked like he hadn't showered in about a
month, which was fairly close to the truth.

He studied Tyler closely and knew where it counted that
Tyler was grievously wounded by the injuries that had befallen
Lisa. He knew in an instant that the only reason Tyler was
here was because his brother had forced him to be here. Tyler
really looked like shit: his face was pale and listless, his eyes
were downcast and stared straight into the ground as if they

were glued into an unmoving position; they shone in the pale
light of the hospital room, looking more like glass orbs than
like part of a human being. Tyler's clothes looked like they
had been slept in, wrinkles upon wrinkles, like old parchment
that had been badly misused. Patrick smiled wanly, hoping
that Tony would read his meaning from the look in his eyes;
Could we leave them alone together for a few minutes? Tony nodded
and stood aside, watching as Patrick forced his brother to sit
next to Lisa and look at her.

Lisa had looked better in the past, when half of her face
hadn't been covered in scabrous growth that looked all too
much like the dirt of the grave and when her eyes had opened
and looked at people and acknowledged that they were there.
What wasn't covered in bandages or stuffed with tubes on her
body looked too pale for life, too fragile for the world they
were all living in. As long as he lived, Tony would never forget the look of raw anguish on Tyler's face as he and Patrick
stepped away from the bed and out of the room. Tyler looked
like a man whose entire life had been one injury after another;
he looked like a man who had suffered a fatal blow and still
couldn't manage to die.

Deep inside of his soul, Tony wondered how many of those
injuries he had caused to fall on Tyler's shoulders. He suspected that he knew the answer. It was an answer he didn't
like. The kind that, if examined in close detail, would make
him realize just how small a person he really was.

Outside of the room, the two young men stood in uncomfortable silence for several minutes, staring anywhere but at
each other. Finally, just for something to talk about, Tony
brought up the books.

Patrick stared at him blankly for a few seconds before finally understanding what it was that Tony was talking about.
When he finally did understand, he confessed to a lack of
knowledge to the whereabouts of the old tomes. Seeing the
expression on Tony's face, he quickly promised to find them
as soon as he got home.

They stood in silence for almost thirty more minutes, before Tyler came out of the room in which Lisa lay in deathless sleep. He looked better.

Not healthy by any stretch of the imagination, but better just the same. As if a weight had been lifted off of his soul. He even managed a tentative smile at Tony, which Tony forced himself to return, before walking slope-shouldered away from the room.

3

Mark and Cassie held the kiss for a long time before calling it a night. The movie had been fun, the dinner enjoyable and the walk home relaxing, but the night was growing old and Cassie's curfew still stood at eleven o'clock. Sometimes Mark couldn't help but wonder if the curfew would have been lifted for a local boy like Tony. Most of his mind told him that the answer would have been no, but there was still that part that acknowledged the lack of enthusiasm on the part of Cassie's parents, at her dating an outsider like him. Try as he might, as nice as he might be, her parents refused to look at him as anything but a stranger. He should, he supposed, be used to that by now; he had been the stranger all his life.

He was less of one here, he realized that, but he was still a stranger. Just a stranger with friends. Friends. He pondered the power that one syllable word had over him, as he wandered seemingly without direction into the woods.

As he entered the forest, Lake Overtree a distant glimmering jewel suspended halfway between earth and the heavens, the reality of his friends came back to him. With each step he took he remembered more of the Folk in the woods, Their tender caresses and the love that They felt for him. Every tree he passed was like another loving parent, giving him the full memory of his secret friends as if They were giving him a precious garment to shield him from the cold realities of the world.

No matter that Cassie's parents disliked him, he had more love than any person could ever need waiting in the clearing just ahead. He had pleasant memories by the dozen and more of the same to come, in his little private spot in the woods. He felt the troubles and worries of the day fade away from his soul the closer he came to his destination.

There, the stone that was more comfortable than any bed could ever hope to be. There, the trees that held the Summer's heat at bay with their shading. There, his friends.

He could cry when he saw Them; no creature was ever meant to be so very beautiful. The way Their delicate wings rustled lightly in the gentle breeze, the way the stars were reflected in Their almond eyes. How could God have created such things of beauty, only to hide Them from all the world?

They danced with joy to see him again; some lifting into the air to hover around his head, others swarming over the ground around him, plucking delicately at his clothes or caressing the exposed flesh on his body, leaving pleasant little tingles where Their skin contacted his.

He smiled rapturously, allowing the Folk to guide him to his place on the stone. He told Them of his day, feeling Their grief over the horrid fate that had befallen Lisa. They laughed to hear of the movie he had seen, lost in wonder at the thought of the worlds beyond the stars and They crooned with delight to hear how well he and his beloved Cassie enjoyed each other's company.

He smiled in turn, when They whispered the secrets of nature in his ear; how the Robin's eggs had finally hatched, how the Wolf had passed through Their glen just today and paused to greet them, he shared Their grief in hearing that the Old Owl had passed from life today, leaving the world just a little colder for his passing.

He lay his head down upon the stone, feeling Their loving caresses and hearing Their gentle words, a perfect lullaby by which to sleep. As he slept, he dreamt. He dreamt of perfect days, days when all was right in the world and all the little pains of life were sloughed away like water from a duck's back. He dreamt of Cassie's slow approach, her perfect body gleaming palely in the moon's faint glow. He dreamt of kissing her delicate skin, the sweet taste of her flesh upon his lips. He dreamt of her caresses, of their passionate love-making, of the days when all the world would realize as he already did, that they were meant to be together, forever.

As he lay sleeping, lost in a world of dreams, They reached towards him and into him, making the necessary changes. Their time was almost upon Them.

4

Cassie stirred in Her sleep, moaning with suppressed passion. They had to be very careful with the ways in which They altered Her; She was not as completely under Their spell as was the Chosen. She might awaken abruptly if They were careless, She might see Them before They were ready to be seen by Her. Slowly, with great delicacy, They made the changes.

"Soon," They whispered in her mind, "Soon all will be ready."

The changes in the Mate were not as severe as the changes that were needed in the Chosen; They could take Their time with Her. The worst of it was the changes in Her mind; She had a much more fearsome will than had the Chosen. She liked Herself the way She was, that always made it harder to perform the Changes...

5

Crowley walked down the road, whistling tunelessly between his teeth and knowing that his life could well depend on the next few moments. He hated it when people followed him, especially when he couldn't figure out who the followers were. The moon, directly above him, striking his crown of hair made him look older, the light changing the bland brown to something closer to its true color. The shadows that covered his face made the hollows of his cheeks seem more like the high proud cheekbones of a skull minus flesh; made the thin hawkish nose hide itself when viewed from the front. The over all effect was slightly sinister. He smiled at the thought.

He listened carefully, seemingly indifferent to the slight scuffling noises from behind him. Unless one knew him well, he would seem completely at ease, ignorant of his pursuer. No one alive knew him that well.

With casual easy moves, he picked a handful of gravel from the side of the road, looking at the sky and tossing the small stones at easy targets, normally missing them. He kept the larger stones in his jean pocket, secreting them there, using a few old tricks he'd learned from an even older prestidigitator. By the time he'd gathered the third handful, he was ready to do battle. Just the same, he kept walking, gathering stones, tossing them at targets and missing for the most part. He hated missing, especially when the targets were so damned easy to hit. Still, he mused, it'd be a shame to drive off what was hunting him before he'd had a chance to view it properly.

After another ten or so minutes of playing with his opponent, he decided it was time to change tactics. With the same casual whistle from the teeth, the same slow, easy stride, he looked for the right place to make his move. Just ahead was the spot he needed: a little puddle of darkness that was ideal for his purposes.

He counted to ten, pacing himself to make it take that long, and stepped from the road. The footsteps from behind him faltered almost immediately, grinding to a complete stop in a matter of five paces.

He could envision the sudden paranoia, the cold certainty that something had gone horribly wrong that must now be on his tracker's face. The whistling was gone, the man was gone, not even a leaf disturbed to show where he might have gone into the woods. Crowley had to bite lightly at his lips to prevent snickering.

Slowly the footsteps started up again and in less then a minute, he saw the powerful figure of Sheriff Hanson walk into view. He was impressed. The man had sounded much lighter than he should have. Crowley had almost convinced himself that he was being followed by a girl; perhaps that silly little parapsychologist that they had imported from out of town.

He notched his respect level for the sheriff up one more spot. The man could probably sneak up on a deer. But then, deer were, to his experience, almost as deaf as humans.

Crowley waited patiently until the man had passed him by about fifty yards and then he started to follow after him. Hanson continued on his little trek for easily half a mile before deciding that his prey had eluded him.

Cursing under his breath, the sheriff turned back towards his car, ready to call it a night. The sight of Crowley directly behind him damn near caused him to shit his pants. "Jeezus Christ!"

Crowley smiled thinly, doing absolutely nothing to help Hanson's heart go back to its regular pace. "I don't believe," the man stated dryly, "That I've ever answered to that particular name." He crossed his arms casually, looking at the sheriff with a devilish twinkle in his eye, "Was there something you wanted to ask me, Sheriff Hanson, or were you, perhaps, following me with some diabolical scheme in mind?"

At the look of shock still on his erstwhile pursuer's face, Crowley laughed out loud. It was not a pleasant laugh, despite Crowley's being so very pleased with himself.

Crowley then grinned, patting the sheriff on the back, fondly. "Well, come on then, I imagine this is something we should discuss like adults, hmm? Perhaps over coffee?"

Hanson decided to play it the way Crowley wanted it played. Not because it was the proper thing to do, or because he'd been caught in the act of tailing the man, but because he hadn't even heard a single footstep from behind. After sixteen years as an officer of the law, he hoped and prayed that he was only losing his hearing; because if it wasn't his hearing, he'd have to fear it was his mind. That thought was almost as scary as the man walking next to him. Almost.

6

The sun was set to rise in little over an hour and Hanson had just finished filling Crowley in on all of the nasty little details that he had; he wondered if the man would have believed him, if not for the confirming voices of Rick Lewis and Jackie Rosenquist. Normally, he suspected that even with the addition of two doctors the information would have been ignored or scoffed at by a person; Crowley was anything but normal.

The man grinned ear to ear, looking for all the world like the cat that had swallowed the canary. Hanson still couldn't bring himself to like the man. Crowley gave him a terminal case of the creeps. Jonathan Crowley leaned back in the battered wooden chair from Deputy Alan Fisk's desk and placed his muscular arms behind his head. Hanson managed not to hit him in the face with an effort; he was the first person to use that chair since Alan's bizarre death and the look he'd given Hanson when he so casually pulled it away from the desk seemed to goad and ask for violence. The look practically screamed the challenge, *"Well, its not like the old corpse has any use for the damn thing, is it Chuckie-boy, hunh?"* Chuck forced his hands not to ball into fists. If the man took that as a threat, the sheriff would be forced to back the threat up and he wasn't certain that he was up to it. Damn, but the man scared the hell out of him. There was no one thing about him that could be said to be wrong; his face wasn't deformed, his teeth didn't have sharp points, his eyes didn't burn with the fires of hell or anything like that, but he was scary just the same.

Jackie Rosenquist didn't seem to think so; Hanson would have bet money that if he so much as crooked a finger in her direction, the woman would have crawled into bed with Crowley right then and there. The smile on her face and the moist glow in her eyes all but promised to give him endless pleasures if he but asked. Crowley didn't seem to notice, or if he noticed, he didn't seem to care. Crowley was staring at Lewis with amused eyes, like a man waiting for the punch line to a very long and humorous joke.

"So," Crowley started, "what made you wait so long before trying parapsychology as an answer?" The tone of voice was off-hand, casual. But, there was an underlying sound of threat to the question, a subliminal warning not to step too hard on any toes.

Rick seemed not to notice. He shrugged his shoulders as his reached for his coffee cup. "I was trying to find the answers all on my own. I figured it was something that could win big awards if I found some new and unique natural enzyme. I wasn't really thinking at all, I guess." Hanson was stunned. Never in a million years would he have expected so straightforward an answer. Rick never admitted to being wrong, unless he was pinned to the wall either figuratively or literally. Now, as if it were no great admission, he stated the cold facts almost as casually as Crowley had asked the question. While he sat with his jaw all but hanging open, Rick continued with his answer. "Tell the truth, I probably still would be trying it on my own, if Chuck hadn't opened my eyes to the lack of progress I'd been making."

He sounded almost too at ease, he could have been discussing the weather with a good friend. To Hanson, he acted like a man drugged, which simply wasn't possible. He knew Rick better than that. With a small shrug, he put the information in his mental To Be Filed Drawer and listened for what was next.

Crowley smiled thinly, showing obvious disapproval for Lewis' attitude and responded, "How many lives do you suppose that might have cost you? Hmm? Two, three? What a waste."

Hanson started to defend his friend, setting himself to bark angrily at this stranger to his town. One look from Crowley quieted his anger before it could erupt from his throat. *Yep*, he thought, *I'm scared in a big way. No doubt, no lack of explanation, no fuckin' way. This man scares me.*

Crowley stood up, walking over to the map of the county on the wall not far from where he'd been seated. "Sheriff Hanson, would you mind locating the spots where you found the different bodies for me?" he asked, gesturing at the map with a simple sweep of his hand. Hating himself for it, Hanson stepped forward and made light pencil marks at all of the proper locations.

Crowley stared for a long time, looking for all the world as if he were contemplating which tie to wear with which suit. He nodded a few times and pointed to where the sheriff had indicated the remains of Pete Larson. "Here's where the Larson kid died," his finger drew a line to where Andy Phillips had hidden the body of Tanya Roberts. "Here's where the Phillips boy told you to find the body." He looked for a moment longer, before moving his hand again, this time he moved it to Lake Overtree. "Over here you found the Blake boy," his hand moved on one last time. "And here is where the one that is still alive got...injured. Scarrabelli wasn't it?" He acknowledged Hanson's nod with a nod of his own and jabbed his finger harshly at a small area of buildings on the map. "What are these, houses?"

"Yeah, the Red Oaks subdivision." Before he said another word, before Crowley had a chance to respond, Hanson realized what the man was leading up to. His eyes must have shown his shock, because Crowley nodded like a teacher to a slow student finally seeing the answer to a painfully simple question.

"Just so, Sheriff Hanson, just so. The subdivision is right in the center of this little storm of activity. You even had one unexplained death in the complex proper, did you not? Evan Wilder, I believe you said, rats or something..." Hanson stared at the man as if he'd lost his mind; Lewis and his new partner simply stared, awestruck. "I suspect the answer to your questions lies somewhere near this complex. Can you tell me who lives in there?" Hanson nodded, numb at the thought that he could have missed so obvious a picture.

The sheriff sorted through file after file pulling every name that he could think of that belonged in the Red Oaks complex. As he did so, he answered easily two dozen questions about various residents; did they know any of the victims? Naturally, it was a small community. Did they have any reason to wish the victims harm? In a few cases, probably, but nothing solid. Did the sheriff think any of the people capable of murder? Oh, yes. He could think of one or two. And the one that finally seemed to strike a memory or two; were any of the residents new to town?

Mark Howell's name popped up like a rabid jack in the box. There had been rumors about how the boy had managed to get that nasty scar on his face, rumors about some of the school toughs taking a walk with him after school. There was bad blood between him and at least one other boy, enough that Howell had come to explain what he thought he might have had to do with the boy's disappearance and death; Hanson remembered dismissing the idea a ludicrous at the time, but then again, there seemed to be more connections between him and most of the people who had ended up dead. The only exceptions would seem to be the deputy—Hanson choked for a moment on that one—and Evan Wilder. The Sheriff even had a newspaper shot of the boy and his parents, kept on file since the family had moved into town. Bill Waldsburg over at the Summitville Press made it a habit to get a shot of any newborns or strangers moving into town, it helped fill space on his little monthly rag. Bill hadn't covered any of the murders; his was a *good* news magazine; nothing sour for the people of Summitville, that was for the real papers.

The picture was over a year old and Hanson noted that the boy looked a lot different these days, taller and a good deal less pudgy. He explained about the scar on his face, from a fall in the woods, the boy had claimed. That garnered an in-depth explanation from Rick, who had been the one to attend to

Howell on both the occasion of his facial injury and the day that he got himself shot by Wilder.

Through it all Crowley listened intently, asking questions only when necessary. He gleaned from the discussions that Howell was an only child and that he had most likely been assaulted in the woods the day his face had been injured; the boy's parents had been utterly convinced of it. The boy had refused to give names; saying only that it was something he could handle on his own.

After a good while of such conversation, the bleary-eyed sheriff pointed out that there was absolutely no solid evidence of any wrong-doing on Mark's part; in fact, the boy had almost always been out of town or with other people during the occurrences. Crowley seemed entirely undaunted, pointing out that if, in fact, the cause were paranormal in origin, the boy could have been in Texas with a thousand witnesses and still be responsible for a crime that took place in Summitville.

Hanson frowned over that one. "I don't quite get you. How could he have influence over events here if he's off doing whatever with whomever in another area entirely? Are you trying to tell me that Mark Howell is a Voodoo doctor or something?"

Crowley grinned that dangerous grin of his, the one that made him look like a wolf with bared fangs, and responded as if he were talking about the way that birds migrate, or some other mundane and essentially useless subject. "Not at all, Sheriff. I seriously doubt that the young man would even be aware of his involvement." When the sheriff and Rick Lewis both looked at him in bewilderment, he continued. "It sounds more like a case of poltergeist activity, or even a case of demonic possession than it does like a conscious effort to get rid of his enemies. If that is the case, the Howell boy is as much a victim as anyone else." Crowley thought for a few minutes while those around him stared at the floor or the walls or anywhere that was not Crowley. The man was compelling, seductively fascinating to observe, but he was also scary in a way that could not be defined. He was a man that just gave off bad vibes, the kind that made people think of someone stepping on their grave.

When he spoke again, the sudden sound startled all of his listeners. "Do you know who he hangs around with? Who his good friends are, maybe even a girl friend?"

Without warning, the memory of his own little visit from a ghost popped into his mind; the name that his dead deputy had spoken fairly leapt past his lips before he could stop the words. "Tony Scarrabelli. The...The ghost of my deputy Alan, he told me that Tony Scarrabelli was at fault. I'd forgotten all about it until just now." He looked down at the ground. "At least I'd been trying to."

Crowley looked at him as if he were looking at a lab specimen that didn't agree with his stomach. Abruptly he stood, looking around for the briefest of moments before starting towards the door. "Well then, I believe I'll have a chat with the boy."

Hanson watched him leave, a large part of him relieved to see him gone. But a larger part of him, a part he would never really let see the light of day, had other thoughts. That hidden part was convinced that Crowley meant serious trouble and whispered in his mind's ear to look out.

Because, whether he liked it or not, there seemed to be a new sheriff in town and there didn't seem to be a damn thing that Chuck Hanson could do about it.

6

P. J. absolutely hated hospitals. The only thing he could think that he possibly hated more was sick people. The exception being his niece. It hurt him to look at her, lying so thin and wasted on the bed with tubes and tape and bandages covering most of her angelic face. P. J. desperately wished to hear her voice again; even if it was just to hear her bitch about her father.

It wasn't going to happen; he knew it deep in his heart, the same way that a mother knows her son won't come back from the front in a war. It made no sense—her vital signs had actually showed small signs of improvement—but he knew she would never be the girl that she had been. It must have shown on his face, because Cassie was there in a flash, hugging him fiercely and murmuring nonsensical platitudes meant to give him some kind of comfort, some sense of hope. The words failed, but he forced a slight smile to show his appreciation just the same.

Mark was bitterly silent in the corner, fidgety and almost angry at the still figure on the bed, as if she were to blame for what had been done to her. P. J. knew that wasn't really the case, just as he knew that all of Mark's anger was directed at whomever it was that had done this to his niece. Mark wanted desperately to find the man responsible for the latest development, just as P. J. himself longed to find him.

She might recover enough to awaken from the coma; it looked better and better for a full recovery almost daily. But the pregnancy was a very different story; abortion was completely out of the question, too many risks in her present state. The shock to her system would like as not kill her.

Tony had gone over the edge upon hearing the news, as had Antoinette and Rafael. The other girls had seemed shocked, but remained, for the most part, lost in their own lives. Antoinette hadn't done a very good job of raising her other children; she had never seemed to care before the twins were born. The others didn't matter the same way as the twins did. The twins were all the children she had room for in her heart. Sometimes, P. J. really hated his sister.

Cassie held onto him as if to keep him from blowing away in the wind, and he was grateful for the aid. He leaned ever so slightly forward and ran his hand over the unmarred portion of his niece's face, hoping against hope that she would recover soon. Knowing that she wouldn't. Not fully, not with the baby of a rapist growing inside of her.

The thoughts he had were as depressing as the lyrics from one of his old favorites; like Mick Jagger, he wanted the world painted black. Looking over at the young man he almost wished were his son, P. J. realized that Mark had different lyrics in mind; he wanted it all painted red. Blood red. He suppressed a shudder at the thought, all the while wondering what was happening to his young friend. Just when had he developed that sneer of hatred and contempt? Just when had he started looking through people when he spoke to them instead of looking at them? He looked at the scar on Mark Howell's face and again suppressed a shudder; he suspected he knew and he feared that it would soon be too late to save his friend's life, to say nothing of his sanity, his soul.

Slowly they left the room, with Mark taking up the rear, as if he were daring anything or anyone to touch anyone else that he cared about. Most who saw him got out of his way. For a boy just turned sixteen, he looked powerful and intimidating. P. J. prayed that no one would cross his path, but he knew just the same that someone would. A deep sense of dread filled P. J. Sanderson to overflowing. He didn't know where, he didn't know when, but he suspected that before long, the plans of something otherworldly would lead Mark into a confrontation. He thought about the past and prayed he was wrong.

7

Tony couldn't hold the anger; it slipped away from him like a lost dream. All he could feel was shame; shame that his sister had been so injured and he had not been there to protect her. Why? Because while she was being raped, impregnated, he was looking for a book, the same book he now held in his hands. He longed to tear it to shreds, but the energy refused to hold, shame sapped him of all strength.

Besides, it was his uncle's. He could never do anything to hurt his uncle, not in a million years. He'd already hurt the man enough when he stole the damned thing.

He looked at the book closely, squinting to keep the sun's glare from blinding him; his shades were in his car and his car was at the house. He'd felt like walking today. The book was bound in fine grain leather, dyed to the color of rust with some primitive dye that smelled like leather, dust, and age. He stopped to caress the supple cover, then pulled the book open to a random page, looking at the odd writing style, the language he couldn't hope to read, with letters in its alphabet that simply didn't exist in this modern age. He guessed that the old tome was worth a pretty penny, but he couldn't understand the need his uncle felt to have the book immediately. He shrugged lightly, guessing that the damn thing was research for yet another of his uncle's books. Maybe he needed to write, needed to write in the same way that Tony needed his anger, as a way of escaping the pain and frustration that tore into him more with each step. He wished his uncle the best of luck with whatever his need, he hoped his luck was better than the luck of his nephew, the loser, the one who watched while everyone he loved died or left or was injured by fate. He tossed the book casually in the air, unaware of the man that followed him, unaware of Them and the way that They watched the man, fear trembling in Their bodies.

"*Soon*," They whispered, "*Soon We shall destroy him.*" The wind in the woods howled as if with the laughter of mad men, mocking the courage in Their voices. "*But not today…Soon.*" They silenced Themselves, remaining as still as statues, when They noticed the Hunter cocking his head, as if he had heard something, in the woods. The thought terrified Them: he shouldn't be that powerful, he hadn't been when last They had met.

8

Tyler watched from his window as life proceeded without him; he had always known that it would, but now he had his confirmation.

"Useless," he whispered through vocal cords made strange by lack of use. "I'm utterly useless." With the weight of the world on his shoulders, he forced himself up from the too soft recliner in which he had spent the majority of the last week. He felt greasy from the lack of proper grooming and he knew his deodorant had died at least three days ago. Scratching at his chin, idly surprised by the stubble he found there, he made his way, slowly, towards the bathroom and the promise of a shower. It wasn't so much that he cared if he was clean; it was more that the smell emanating from his body had started to become a distraction to his moping.

Tyler was certain that he could have taken the entire situation with a light heart if she'd just dumped him and gone on her way; he was more than halfway expecting her do just that, even when they were on a date and having a great time. But, to lose his heart's most recent flame because some asshole in a car couldn't hold his liquor? No. That he could not tolerate. He set the water in the shower as hot as he could physically tolerate and stepped into the ferocious torrent. The scalding fluid felt more likely to burn the filth away than to wash it off; he didn't care.

A small part of his mind, the part that had, until recently, been giving him directions, protested his apathy. He did his best to ignore it. It said: "*What about Mark? Aren't you supposed to be stopping whatever it is that's happening to him?*"

Tyler replied with, "Who gives a fuck?"

It called back, "*Isn't he your best friend?*"

"No, he's Cassie's best friend."

"*Then who is your best friend?*"

"I don't have one. I don't have any friends."

In response to that last remark, the tiny almost silenced part of his brain decided to make him see reason. With a sudden fight for control over the depression that had taken hold of the rest of him, Tyler's cynicism forced his eyes open, making him shriek with the sudden pain of too hot, soapy water running into his eyes. Anger and depression fought a savage battle for Tyler's soul and for the first time in his life, anger won. Tyler was tired of getting the shit beat out of him by life. Really, really tired of having to put up with that kind of shit. Standing taller than he had in…well, forever, really, Tyler stepped from the shower and looked at his soaking wet steaming figure in the fogged mirror. With the condensation in his way, he could almost consider himself to be attractive, in a geeky kind of way, but attractive nonetheless.

He toweled himself off vigorously, promising himself that he would not tolerate the blues in his soul any longer. He felt better than he had in days. He even went all out and blow-dried his hair. After discarding the filthy blue robe that had been his clothing for the last three days, Tyler got himself dressed in his best jeans and a plaid shirt he had never taken out of its original shrink-wrap. He slid into a pair of boots that he almost never bothered with, jet black and glossy enough to reflect his face. He put on his coke bottle glasses and looked again at himself in the mirror. His figure had filled out slightly over the course of the summer and he looked almost human, in his own estimation. He studied his face with careful scrutiny and then pulled back with a look of contempt. "Still too many zits, Tyler-me-lad and you still look like shit." The morning's ritual over with, he picked up the phone and started dialing P. J.'s phone-number. Time to get back on with the process of living. No more time for moping around the house.

Sometimes, just sometimes, Tyler was almost convinced that he was a madman; every time he decided to get good and depressed, something stopped him. Nine out of ten times, that something was the face he saw in the mirror.

9

P. J. and Tyler were now at the Basilisk, sitting down and talking animatedly about what to do with what they normally called the "Mark Situation," when Tony arrived with the book in his hand. P. J.'s eyes flew open wide, as he saw the binding on the book. With eager fingers he all but ripped the tome from his nephew's hands, frantically scanning the pages.

"It's so nice to see you, too, Uncle Phil." Tony regretted the words, as he saw the man's eyes turn away from the book and lock onto his.

"Where did you find it, Tony?" The voice was casual, but Tony knew better than to think he was in the clear; in a matter of an instant all of his problems were forgotten save that his uncle was very upset.

"Uh, I loaned it to Patrick. I guess I'd forgotten about it. Sorry." The words sounded like a lie to his own ears, he knew they wouldn't cut the mustard with his mother's only sibling. He felt his face redden as the man studied him.

"Hmm. Well, we'll discuss this at a more appropriate time. Perhaps we should leave your parents out of this one. I don't think they'd take well to your relieving me of my three-hundred year old rare books."

"Thanks, Uncle Phil, I really am sorry."

The man nodded, apparently satisfied. "You didn't by chance read this book, did you?" Again the casual voice, too casual to Tony's sensitive ears.

"No, just looked at some of the illustrations. Weird stuff."

"I should say so." P. J. Sanderson walked slowly towards the island in the center of his bookstore, carefully flipping the pages of the old musty volume as he went. It seemed that he had lost interest in Tony, for the moment at least.

Tyler looked past the author, nodding a hello to Tony, who responded in like.

Tyler looked at the writer, studied him briefly and looked over to where Tony was standing near the front door. "Maybe you should fill him in, P. J., maybe he can help." Tyler wasn't in the mood to watch anyone squirm, not even an old enemy like Tony. He just wanted this done.

P. J. Sanderson looked up from the book, then glanced quickly over at his nephew before turning to lock gazes with

Tyler. Finally, after what seemed like around a hundred years, he nodded. "Come over here, Tony. Let's see if your imagination is suitably primed for the telling of an old story." Tony stepped up to the island, smiling his thanks at Tyler for getting him off of the hot seat.

Tony was about to reply, when the voice came from the front of the store, "Well, I don't know about your young friend, Philly, but I'm always in the mood for a good ghost story." All of them looked over at the same time, startled by the sound of a cold, empty voice where there should not have been one; the bell connected to the door had not rung, an impossibility that had never before occurred.

There, leaning against the threshold on the interior of the store stood Jonathan Crowley. His arms were crossed casually over his chest and the thin smile on his lips was equal parts cruelty and amusement. He stared directly over at P. J., only moving his eyes away from the author's face to acknowledge the book in his hands. Phillip Sanderson swallowed hard at the dry lump that had suddenly formed in the back of his throat. His eyes flew wide with a dawning horrific recognition, even as his unexpected guest walked confidently towards the island's stairs. Even looking up at the three of them, he was a scary figure. "Long time no see, Philly." The voice was icy, mocking and challenging, but confident that the challenge would go unaccepted. "Read any good books lately?"

Chapter Fourteen

1

Mark leaned against the wall of the high school, empty and desolate now that school was out. He imagined that the hollow shell, now emptied of all life, felt a great deal like he was feeling right then. Try though he might, Mark could not understand what his world had become. Nobody was acting the way that they should and he couldn't decide if it was he that had changed, or the rest of the world.

Kicking at a stone that had indignantly sat itself near his feet, Mark almost wished that he was still the new kid. Relationships were so much more awkward than he had always assumed them to be; friends, girlfriends, parents, even enemies, none of it was easy to comprehend. When the hell did the good times start and just when were the bad times supposed to end?

He pushed himself free of the faded brick wall and, hands in pockets, walked towards the closest wire-meshed window. Through the crosshatches, all he could see was an endless, empty hallway stretching quietly through the gloom. The summer was almost over, the nights already turning chill and the thought of returning to the school-day routine sent almost forgotten but all too familiar chills through his spine. His reflection in the dusty glass looked haunted. He turned away before he could spend too much time thinking about that look.

Quite naturally, his thoughts gravitated towards Cassie; her lovely eyes and her perfect smile. Again he was astounded that she could find anything about him attractive. Sure, he'd lost some weight and put on some muscle, but he was hardly a fascinating person for all of that. His conversations normally revolved around his dreams of tomorrow, when he would be the next great author of the world, and his dreams were hardly as dust before the glory that was Cassie. No comparison.

Unpleasantly, his mind also turned towards Lisa Scarrabelli and the dreams he was having about her almost nightly. The dreams both excited and repulsed him: they had to do with her rape. They normally started with the memory of her running towards the road and him trying to catch her before it was too late, but they always ended with her pinned under his body, pleading through tear-stained eyes while he pounded into her mercilessly. Sometimes, he woke up whimpering, knowing in some strange way that he really was responsible for all that had happened to her. Just as often, he awoke with a fading smile on his face and a painful erection demanding his immediate attention. That always led his thoughts back to Cassie. The part of himself that he liked to deny was telling Mark that it was time to take action, even if she wasn't ready. He tried to brush that attitude aside, certain that only his raging pubescent hormones were responsible, but now and again the thoughts refused to leave him for hours at a time. The darker part of him wanted to do to her what had been done to Lisa, both in his dreams and in reality. No, he would never let himself hurt her in that way, never. Sometimes, however, his loins were sorely tempted to try.

The sun was setting behind the trees near Lake Overtree and Mark knew that he would have to get home soon. Of all things, Joe was actually worrying about him. The thought of Joe even acknowledging his existence was still too new to Mark to allow him to fully comprehend the concept of Joe actually caring about what he did with his spare time. Yet another brick in the Great Wall of Confusion that surrounded Mark on all sides these days.

With a sigh, Mark started towards the road home. He had no desire to be in the woods today. Today was one of those ever so rare occasions where the thought of running through the forest or stopping at the rock caused him to feel uneasy, almost afraid. He didn't like to think about it, so he shoved the feelings away, back inside their special cubby-hole. Hitting the road at a full run, Mark pushed himself to his limits again, straining his muscles and stretching for that extra inch in every stride. Running made him feel alive and as often as not was all he needed to do these days to feel better about everything. Had Chuck Hanson been sitting in his car, radar aimed at the trim and muscular figure darting down the road, he would have been forced to pull Mark Howell over and give him a ticket for speeding. The speed limit on this stretch of Third Street was clearly set at 45 miles per hour. Mark was exceeding the limit by at least fifteen miles per hour. The muscles in his body moved with fluid precision, and Mark Howell ran down the road at speeds that simply weren't possible.

2

While Mark was busy feeling sorry for himself, the town of Summitville was learning about itself in a thousand small ways, as many towns are wont to do. Cassie Monroe, for instance, was learning more about her parents than she had ever wanted to. Cassie was learning that despite everything he had done for her, every little way in which Mark cared for her, her parents still didn't trust him. The point was made painfully clear, when her father started discussing just what their plans for her future were; not surprisingly, at least in hindsight, those plans made no mention of what Cassie herself desired out of life.

Cassie, sadly realizing that her one-time dream of being a professional gymnast had withered into dust even as her body blossomed, had moved her goals towards other things. Cassie wanted to be a writer, she wanted to be a doctor, she wanted to be a housewife, and she wanted to be a thousand different things. Writer always came back up to the forefront, though. She realized as well as anyone that the desire came partially from her association with P. J. Sanderson, as well as from her association with Mark, but the dream was still a valid one in her eyes. Where the hell did her parents get off wrangling her towards a law degree, especially when they were doing it without her consent? Damn it, they were talking as if she wasn't even in the room. Cassie knew better than to argue the point with them. Frankly, it just wouldn't do her the least bit of good. Even when she tried to explain herself, it was brushed off as if she had suggested going to the movies or perhaps even going on a picnic as a family group. Nosiree, none of that nonsense, this family unit was as dysfunctional as any she had ever come across. Dad worked, Mom worked, Cassie did as she was told. Now and then, she wished her parents were a little less normal, not quite the picture perfect Yuppies that they had turned out to be.

Now and then, she wished she had the strength to change them. She almost opened her mouth, she almost told them that she would make up her own damn mind as to what she would do with her own damn life and if they didn't like it, they could eagerly go to Hell. Almost—because to have actually said it would bring about disfavor and disfavor brought about punishment. Not punishment like she knew some kids had to endure, nothing physical, but punishment in the form of silence, in the form of rejection from the rare moments of affection permitted in the Monroe household. She crept off to her room instead, wishing with all of her heart that Mark was there to hold.

Mark didn't show up. She didn't call him and he never pushed his affections towards her by showing up without being invited, it just wasn't something he could do. So instead, she took a nap. She was doing that a lot these days, almost everyday as a matter of fact. One thing about the naps, the one thing that made it safe to get sleepy whenever she was sad or angry; she always had the nicest dreams about Mark while she slept.

Dreams of love and dreams of passion where she was always safe in his arms. Lately, the Folk had been forced to work almost continuously to make the changes necessary in Cassie. They didn't mind. They were almost done now.

3

Joe and Jenny Howell were watching the news and getting more depressed by the moment as a result. Nothing pleasant ever seemed to occur anymore. Not in Summitville, not in Denver, not it seemed, anywhere on the whole freaking planet. Jenny watched her husband grow more and more sour by the minute and finally turned the television off.

When Joe started to protest, she smiled demurely and then kissed him on the side of his mouth. Joe was, by his own estimation, not the brightest guy on the planet, but he wasn't stupid either. He got the hint and he took the hint. Inside of twenty minutes, all of his worries over Mark were gone from his mind.

That was just fine with Jenny, in fact that was why she had decided it was time for a little whoopee in the first place. In her mind, she heard the voices continue their promises, "*Soon Jennifer, very soon...*"

4

Over at the Basilisk, three men stood warily watching another who scared them all on a primal level. P. J. was quite literally too scared to move, even to think, looking at the man before him. Nothing about him had changed in the last twenty-three years, nothing. He was the same height, build, even hair color as P. J. had remembered. That really didn't surprise him, at least not in his heart, where it counted. The dreams he had been having about this man, well, let's be honest here, the nightmares he had been having about this man for the last two-decades-and-change years pretty much assured that he would know every detail of his face. Unlike most of his dreams, the details never seemed to fade when it came to Crowley.

For Tyler and Tony, it was more along the lines of the hairs rising on the backs of their necks, a vague unease caused by his presence, like the feeling of having someone walk across their final resting place and then having that someone point to the spot, look them in the eyes and say, *"Here, good buddy, right fuckin' here. That's where you're going to be planted. Would you like me to tell you when and how you get here?"*

Crowley simply stared at P. J. Sanderson, as if they were the very best of friends and the author had just told him a mildly humorous joke. The smile was casual and friendly, not at all the sort of thing that should make a person nervous, until you looked closely at his eyes. There was something there, something very unpleasant; a light that reflected towards you from no definable source, or perhaps it was not reflected at all, that bone white light, perhaps it came from inside of his eyes...

With a cat's grace, Crowley moved closer to the three nervous men, approaching his good buddies for a pleasant conversation, or at worst a ghost story told around the campfire, late at night when a spectral cloud smudges the light from a moon that stares down on all below without interest. Nothing to be afraid of, not here and just how the hell are you guys doin'? He pulled the last chair out from under the table in the store's island and, turning it around, sat down easily. Never in the entire span of time, did his eyes leave P. J.'s. He didn't even seem to blink.

"Tell me a story, Philly, tell me a good one, better than that shit you call fiction. Tell me a real story, one that counts." The voice spoke in silken tones, like the sound made when a spider spins its web, amplified just enough for them all to hear him speak.

P. J. swallowed hard, his throat clicking dryly. He would have given every cent he ever made, just to look away from those cold hard eyes. "O-Okay, listen closely folks. This is a story I've never told, except in bits and pieces, and I never want to tell it again. So just listen, no questions." He hesitated there, praying for some intervention that would stop the memories from coming together. None came.

"Once upon a time, in this very town, there lived a man."

5

The man's name was Stoney Miles—well, Albert really, but every one called him Stoney. Stoney was the kind of person that everybody liked, because Stoney always knew just the right things to say, in order to assure everyone that he was likeable.

Only a few people knew the truth about Stoney, and only one of them lived in town. That one was his wife, Jillian Wadsworth Miles. Jillian was as easily tricked as the rest of the world by the quick smile and the pleasant conversations that Stoney had had with her—she was so taken in fact, that she actually married him against her family's protests. Contrary to popular belief, that wasn't the kind of thing that happened every day in England. To avoid the problems that the marriage incurred, the young couple moved to the colonies, the United States.

They started in Boston and later, after they had gathered a very large sum of money, they moved here. Nobody knew why, not even Jillian. Stoney never volunteered information to anyone, at least not information that could be considered important.

And here, P.J. paused for a moment, looking puzzled. Tyler had to shake his head, jarred back to reality by the change in the author's voice.

Even in the book that was just returned to me, Stoney never tells why he came here, save that the Stone could be found in this vicinity. He always wrote down the name with a capital letter at the beginning, so I have always assumed it was a proper title, at least in his eyes.

But I digress, the subject of this tale is the kind of man that Stoney was, later I'll tell of the Stone and Stoney's search for it.

Albert Miles was a man who needed to own things—be it a house, a horse and carriage, or even a person, Stoney had to own things. One of the possessions he was most proud of, was his wife. Stoney wooed her, seduced her away from the security of her upper-class family and then possessed her entirely. What never seemed to cross his mind, was that she might not want to be possessed. Jillian learned over the course of time to hate her husband. She learned that once an item was in his possession, he really no longer cared for it. She had her son, of course, but a son's affections are decidedly different from a husband's. She needed more than a smile and a hug. Like most every creature, she had desires that needed to be sated. That was where Abraham Smythe entered the scene. Everyone knows the silly old legends about their lover's tryst and I won't bore you with the details, suffice to say that the legends had their foundings in truth.

What the stories can't tell you, is that Smythe had plans to run away with Jillian, to start a new life in another part of the country. They planned to take the child together and make for California, where the gold was supposed to be easy to find and where riches were but a day's labor away. Abraham Smythe must have told someone, somewhere in town about his plans; because that someone told Stoney and Stoney went to find Smythe.

He killed him and yes, he also killed Jillian. He carved the flesh off of both of the bodies and left them to die in each other's arms. The stories told around the campfires come Halloween don't mention that part, or the truth of what he did to his son, either. Yes, his son was found in the well and he was found alive, cold and shaken, but alive. But he was found with one finger from each hand removed and the hair cut away from his head, another little part of the tale that is missing.

Joshua Miles was taken in by the Smythe family, because some thought he was the son of Abraham Smythe. So what's wrong with this picture? As I said before, Stoney came into the village of Summit Town with his wife and his son.

Joshua was his second child by Jillian, not his first. Nowhere in the old battered legends about Stoney Miles does the mention of two children come into play. But there was another child, I know that for a fact. I can even tell you what happened to him: he was sacrificed, on a large stone in the woods near where Summit Town once stood. How do I know this? Well, Stoney talked all about it, in the diary he kept, the one now in my hands. The entry basically says that Stoney had found the Stone of his family, and in the traditions of his family, he had surrendered his first born child to the Stone, in order to prepare the way. He never clarifies just who or what he is preparing the way for, even in his own private journals. Stoney had a tendency to keep secrets. If the tale is told, then it is in one of the parts of this journal that makes no sense, written in a gibberish code with no clear pattern that I could discern. That is the first part of my story. The prelude, if you will.

The rest of the story takes place only a handful of years ago, at least by my reckoning. I was fifteen then. I never had a great number of friends, like another young man I can think of. While I had lived here all of my life, I really never fit in Summitville; to be honest, that has never really changed. One must often work very hard to make friends and I lacked Stoney's innate ability to hide my opinions from those around me. My mouth, like a certain young man named Wilson that lives in this town, was simply too large to be tolerated by others in town. Those I knew I wished I hadn't had the pleasure of meeting, as often as not.

There was one exception to the rule. There are always exceptions to the rules. In my case, the exception was a new boy in town, Alex Harris. Summitville almost never gets new kids, or as I have heard them called, "Fresh Meat."

When Alex came to town, the local welcoming committee took a fancy to laying verbal abuses upon him without end. Alex took them all in stride, as if nothing in this world could hurt him. I took them in stride too—they were only words, nothing as serious as what was done to Mark when he came here.

Tony flinched at the comment, but nobody but Jonathan Crowley noticed.

The part about the whole thing that shamed me, was that Alex ended up coming to my rescue on one of the occasions where my mouth got the better of my common sense. Alex wasn't a unstoppable juggernaut, he wasn't even above average in height or in muscle tone, but I always seem to remember him that way. What he lacked in size he made up for in speed and prowess. He fought like a madman, taking ridiculous risks and somehow getting away with it, as well as dodging nearly every punch thrown at him by the local bully squad. I still remember the look on Chuck Hanson's face, when Alex shot a knee into his testicles and followed through with an elbow to the side of his head. Yes, the very same Chuck Hanson who is now the sheriff in town. He was a wild one as a youth, always instigating the fights and normally winning them. Chuck lived in the slums back then, that part of town delegated to the poor of Summitville. Not that they were slums then, anymore than they are slums now, but the name always stuck just the same. Everyone talked down about the people that lived there, except for Chuck— no one ever said a word about Chuck, they were all too scared.

Anyhow, when the fight was over and Alex was helping me to my feet, I'd learned a lesson about friendship, and I had learned it from a stranger. I never minded my own business when it came to the underdog again. I suppose that's why I decided to be Alex's friend. He was the only person who was more of an underdog than I was. No, maybe it was simply because he would let me be his friend. I don't know.

Summer came not long after that and we went about enjoying the summer as much as we could, often burdened by Alex's little brother...for the life of me, I can never remember his name. The little boy was almost a tragedy, he looked so much like Alex, but he had none of the grace or confidence of his older brother. He was possibly the most awkward child I ever saw. Everyday it was a surprise to see how he had injured himself. One day a scraped knee, the next a bruised forearm, Alex used to say that he had "the grace of a gazelle, with four broken legs." Sometimes I was honestly surprised that the child managed to live through the day.

That boy worshipped Alex and Alex in turn seemed to worship him. Anything that happened to his little brother sent Alex to his side instantly. The slightest scratch and Alex was there to make it all better. It was like his little brother was all he had room in his heart to love and he was going to make certain that his heart never got broken.

It was a good summer, lots of swimming at Overtree, lots of wrestling in the woods with the girls that found us attractive, even time for the ever popular ghost stories around the campfire. I felt like that summer would never end, like I had all the time in the world to be popular with Alex, Susan and Anita as my friends. I was wrong, nothing is forever in this world, certainly not the friends we have and certainly not the summers. But maybe they could have been, if not for the book.

It's just a collection of Stoney Miles' thoughts, almost a diary, but some of the book, a small part really, holds rituals. Alex was fascinated by the entire thing, loved the idea of performing these rituals like a seance at Halloween. That was even the day he picked for us to perform one, Halloween. I've never believed in magic, at least not the type that calls demons from the bowels of hell and such nonsense. But I was willing to believe in it that day. I really can't remember all that happened, sometimes its like a part of that day is gone for me and sometimes it's like a flash from a dream that fades if you focus on it. All I can say for certain is that things were different afterwards. No one acted like they had before. I had a small gathering of friends that I held dear to me before that Halloween day and afterwards we just drifted apart. The ones who had meant the most to me during that summer vacation were all just strangers I'd pass a smile with by Christmas.

Susan and Antoinette had always been the best of friends until then, and then none of it seemed to matter to them; they broke away from a life-long friendship and found other people to call by that special title. The only other person I'd ever had a chance to grow truly close to seemed only a shadow of what he had been, drained of all vitality, a god whose feet were clay. The only person who seemed better off for the experience, was Alex's little brother. During the days that followed, before Alex and his family moved away from Summitville, I saw his brother again. He looked sturdier somehow, as if at three years of age, he had found the purpose for his existence. He was also as graceful a child as I have ever seen, no longer getting injured or even stumbling any more.

Mostly, I remember the look he gave me on all three of those occasions. It was a warning to be quiet, a warning to be careful of what I said and a promise to hurt me, all rolled into the eyes of a three year old boy. It was amazing how frightening he managed to be, it was amazing how frightened I was. I hope I never see a child that young with a stride so purposeful again, it intimidated me. It terrified me because he was a little boy with a very important mission in his heart and no little boy should have so much weight on his shoulders, no matter how sturdy he seems to be.

6

"I've only ever seen a look that was even close to his haunted, terrifying look in the eyes of one other boy, a boy who was injured in the woods near here. He told me that he had cut his face on a stone, in a part of the woods between his school and his home, when four or five boys, all bigger than he was, beat him into the ground." P. J. Sanderson looked around the room, finally free of whatever Crowley had done to him, finally able to look at the other people around him.

"That boy told me that he would handle his beating by himself and in that moment, when I saw that same haunted look in his eyes, I believed him."

"I had no doubt in my mind that Mark Howell would do exactly as he promised and I fear he already has, on most of the boys that hurt him." P. J. Sanderson looked his nephew straight in the eyes and Tony grew cold under the rage focused there, a rage his uncle had never before shown to him. "Of course, times and people change and I suppose that there might yet be a chance he'll forgive the one that got away."

Across the table from P. J., Jonathan Crowley clapped his hands in the unearthly silence, a smile perched sardonically on his lips. He stood up then, towering over the writer and plucked the book from Sanderson's hands. "A delightful story, Philly, a true treat." He scanned the book quickly, flicking pages with hardly a glance at their contents. When he had found what he wanted, he shoved the book in P. J.'s face. "Is this the ritual your little friend called out that night? Don't tell me you don't remember, Phil, I hate liars."

P. J. nodded his affirmation.

"Well, well, well, that does make this a nasty thing you've called forward, provided that your friend even managed to pronounce the words properly." He folded a corner of the page over and grinned down at the man before him as he tucked the book under his arm. "Let's get down to business here, Philly. The way I see it, you're responsible for this mess, you let him read the damned thing. So, what're we going to do about this nastiness?" The last was as much a rhetorical question as it was an actual question waiting for an answer. No one seemed to have the vaguest clue how to respond.

Crowley leaned in close to the writer, sneering down on the man who visibly quaked before him. "Well, let's just say I have a few ideas that might prove helpful."

7

While Summitville's only famous resident was telling a story that made him afraid, made him never want to remember his past, Rick Lewis was sleeping. Next to him, not more than a hand away, Jaquelyn Fitzgerald Rosenquist slept too. For her, the images that slumber inescapably brought where far more pleasurable. Rick was dreaming about Mark Howell and in those dreams the two of them discussed any number of subjects, calmly and clearly. Most of the subjects were the victims of something not quite within Rick's view; something that was watching him and that he could almost see out of the corner of his eye.

Try though he might, he couldn't quite turn his head enough to see it clearly.

He could feel the presence near by, its attention on him like a bitingly cold breath of winter air from the mountain tops that embraced Summitville. He could sense the way in which it studied him and he could feel its malignancy. *Cancer*, he thought. *It's like a Cancer that wants to grow, wants to devour me and all of the people around me.*

Mark looked over at him, smiling pleasantly. "You're right, Doctor Lewis, that's exactly what it wants, but it can't. Not yet. It needs me to do something first." Mark smiled at Rick, a sad smile that was almost hidden by his conversational voice. "It needs me to finish changing and after that, it just needs a little time. Then, when it's had that time, everything here will go away."

Rick wanted desperately to speak, but the little things were stopping him, little things he hadn't even noticed before. They were everywhere now, climbing over the remains of Pete Larson, Tommy Blake, and Tanya Billingsley. Others were present as well, but none he could recognize, none that he himself had ever witnessed. He couldn't see them very clearly, they kept trying to change shape, as if they were looking for the right form.

"Don't worry, Doctor Lewis, They won't hurt you." Lewis looked over towards Mark Howell and started with fascination and fear. Something was happening to the boy, right before his eyes. Marks skin was blistering, blisters that looked like fresh burns from hot grease, save the color was wrong; the blisters were the color of corruption, blendings of green and gray, yellow and black, not colors that refreshed or looked healthy, but faded, worn with eons of waiting.

Rick felt magnetized by the sight, as the blistered patches of flesh covered over the healthy tan on Mark's body, growing larger in size and number. "They never hurt anyone, so long as no one hurts me. I like to think of Them as my defense system, a way of protecting myself from the things that have happened to me in the past." The ulcerated flesh covered him now, festering and all but boiling over him.

Somehow, the face hidden by the foul miasma managed to convey a frown of puzzlement. "I don't think They'd look at it the same way, but that's okay. As long as They'll protect me, I don't have to worry about it. They're my friends, Doctor. Do you know how hard it is to find friends in this world, ones that won't hurt you?" Pustules erupted on Mark's swollen form, spilling a hellish scent of mold and decay into the air.

"It's harder than you think. I got lucky. They found Me." The piercing shriek of Rick's alarm clock stopped him from hearing what Mark would have said next. Richard Lewis had never before been so grateful for its interruption.

8

Patrick Wilson was suffering from nightmares as well, but his came for him while he was awake. Dave Brundvandt was making an unexpected house call. Patrick was scared; Dave had a way of explaining his problems with his fists and Patrick had a strong allergy to physical pain.

"Look, Dave. I told you before that I'd set you up with the guys to buy from, I never said I'd do anything more than that." Brundvandt's expression told him that excuses weren't going to cut it this time.

"Pat, we made a deal a good while back and I always kept my half of the bargain. I want my shit. Now." It wasn't the size of

Dave Brundvandt that carried strength, it was the seriousness of his words. No inflection, no reaction, just a steady monotone.

"Shit Dave, what the hell do you want from me? I took you to Denver, I introduced you to all the right people. I told you then that I couldn't do anything else for you. Don't take this the wrong way, but are you thick or what?" That almost got a flicker of reaction from Dave. Patrick was doing his best to get through, but Jesus Christ, the guy wasn't listening.

"You told me all that before and now I'm telling you, I don't have the time for this. Those friends of yours said they won't do business with me. So I'll do business with you." That was just about it then, *no* wasn't going to make a difference with Dave. Patrick started mentally covering the people who owed him favors. The list was surprisingly short and none of the favors were big enough to get rid of Brundvandt easily.

"Leave it be, Dave. I don't do that anymore. I'm not going to start all over again just to satisfy you. Go find a new connection. Better still, straighten out your mind and get a fucking job."

"Okay, one more time. Get me the shit. Get it by tomorrow, or else."

"'Or else' what? You'll shoot me? Get real. Get a life. And while you're at it, get the fuck out of my face."

Dave Brundvandt stared at Patrick Wilson for a long time, neither one of them giving an inch. It took a while, but Dave finally stepped back, nodded once and turned away. Patrick tried hard to convince himself that everything was finally over. It didn't work.

With a sigh, he stepped back into the house and closed the door. Standing behind him was his father. For most of his life, Patrick had seen his father as a good man with no anger in his body. He never punished Patrick or Tyler, he just explained why it was wrong to do certain things, like pulling the cat's tail or lifting a candy bar from the counter at the store. It was Mom who did the punishing, Dad just explained the reasons for the punishment.

The thunderous look on his father's face let Patrick know that today would be different. Today, Dad would be doing a lot more than explaining. Samuel Wilson reached for his son faster than Patrick would have ever thought possible. The hand that struck Patrick across the face was anything but the hand of his father; it was more akin to the hand of God.

Patrick looked fearfully at his father as the man forced him against the wall. "Drugs?" Just one word, but the voice wasn't even like his dad's. It was like Clint Eastwood in Hollywood makeup, a prosthetic dad face that couldn't hide the squinty eyes and gravelly whisper.

"Dad! I...uhm. I think we need to talk."

Samuel Wilson pivoted at the waist and put his whole body into the swing that sent Patrick into the other wall of the hallway. The plasterboard wall gave slightly at the impact leaving a dent in the cheery plum and pink stripes. Patrick was stunned by both the impact and by the source of impact. Never, never in his whole fucking life, had his father hit him. Patrick couldn't think, couldn't breathe. He knew deep inside that he had just crossed over a line not meant to be crossed. He could think of no words to soothe the man coming towards him. The capacity for speech had left him completely when he saw his father start loosening his belt.

9

Chuck Hanson stared at the snow on his television screen without acknowledging that his cable had gone out. His mind was too occupied with fear. It wasn't the type of fear that grips a person into paralysis, it was the kind that nibbles at all of your foundations for belief. Too much little shit that didn't add up.

Alan Fisk was dead. Dead Alan Fisk had told him that Tony Scarrabelli was responsible for everything that was wrong. No sir. Didn't add up.

Dead Alan Fisk had told him it was in the woods near Overtree. What was in the woods near Overtree, the answer?

The goddam questions? Yet another body? Nope. No way was he going into the woods.

Jonathan Crowley, a man four inches shorter and half his weight, was scaring the hell out of him. Why? Chuck never thought of himself as a hero, but he sure as hell wasn't a coward.

Rick Lewis, long time friend and all around good guy, was letting him down. Rick couldn't find the answers that Chuck needed and that was bad. If Rick couldn't, with a degree in Pathology, what the hell chance did he have? All Rick had had time for today was trying to stare up that Jackie girl's skirt, and Chuck resented that too.

The people around town weren't looking at him like he was something special anymore. Something was going down that shouldn't be and he wasn't getting the answers fast enough for them. People were dying. Looks like Chuckie can't handle it anymore, time to get someone new in here. Everything in his gut pointed to the new kid, Mark Howell, but there was no solid proof. Was that just the old paranoia about strangers, or was it something real? He just didn't know.

More and more Alan's dead voice told him that it was time to go look in the woods. More and more he tried to ignore that voice. More and more he couldn't. Alan had been a good kid, if a little thick sometimes, and Alan had died in the woods near Overtree. What if he'd seen something? What if it was so big it was worth coming back from the dead for?

Chuck Hanson stared at the snow on his Panasonic's screen, not noticing that his cable had gone out. In his hands he held his service revolver, its weight a strong reassurance that he was still in control. He had to go to the woods. Every time that thought crossed his mind, the gun seemed less substantial.

10

In the woods near Lake Overtree, the Folk gathered together. Time was growing shorter and the Hunter was getting closer. The world was not working as They would have liked. The

Chosen had picked this time, of all possible times, to be obstinate. They had wonders waiting for Him, if only He would let Them finish Their work. Even the Chosen's Mate was starting to come around, bit by little bit. On her They could force the Changes. But on the Chosen? No. Too risky.

So much could go wrong. The Chosen had to be willing in order to avoid potential catastrophe. Nearby, the stone shifted fitfully, bulging and growing in ways that were never meant to be seen by living things. What had once appeared to be a buried rock was now closer to a Cadillac in size. The woods pulsed with the Stone's impatience. Animals started moving on, the sure knowledge that the worst was yet to come propelling them from their havens.

As the Stone changed its shape, so too did the Folk. They grew static, fluctuating fitfully with the whims of the creatures around them.

Chapter Fifteen

1

Later that same night, Samuel Wilson lay in his bed wondering just where he had gone wrong. He'd always tried his best to be a loving father and role model. Now, to find out what his son had been doing for three years…well, it was enough to make him want to cry.

The reasons for his son dealing drugs had not escaped him either; he wasn't stupid enough to think the boy would have risked prison just for kicks. How in the name of God was he supposed to punish the boy for protecting himself in the only way he could think of? The thoughts of what he had almost done to Patrick were enough to make Samuel sick. He'd long ago promised himself that he would never punish his son in anything remotely resembling the way his father had punished him. Barring rape or murder, Sam couldn't come up with a single crime that deserved physical reprimands.

Thank God for Susan. If she hadn't heard the sounds of poor Patrick hitting the wall he would likely have skinned the boy. He turned his head to study Susan's body under the sheets. She was more than he deserved. A sad little smile creased a face made for larger grins as he hoisted himself out of the bed. He was calmer now, more able to speak rationally with his son. Now was as good a time as Sam was likely to find for apologizing for his behavior. For all the good it would do—Patrick would never see him in the same way again. How could he?

He walked barefoot through the plush peach carpet in the hallway, treading as lightly as he could to avoid waking Susan or Tyler. It was only a dozen feet to Patrick's room, but it seemed a much greater distance. How could he expect Patrick to forgive him, when he couldn't even forgive himself?

The door to Patrick's room was unlocked, but Samuel Wilson knocked lightly anyway. His first born was old enough to have earned his privacy, even if he had been dealing in narcotics. No response. He knocked once more with a little more force, not much, as he still feared waking Susan.

Nothing. All of the worst case scenarios started running through his mind. Patrick dead with slashed open wrists and a pool of drying crimson soaking into the carpet around him. Patrick lying face up in the bed, a puddle of bile blocking his oxygen starved lungs. A dozen more ways to end one's own life flickered painfully through his skull. With a heartfelt prayer and closed eyes, Samuel Wilson eased the door to his son's private sanctum open. When he finally pried his eyes open far enough to see the room, Samuel Wilson shed a silent tear of relief. His little Patrick was asleep, snoring softly. Tomorrow. Tomorrow was soon enough for the man to man talk he had in mind.

Samuel Wilson crept slowly back to his own room, relieved of his fears for his son. If nothing had happened by now, nothing was likely to happen at all. The talk would still occur, but not now. Tomorrow, after he had spent time thinking carefully on the words he would say. When he could be properly prepared for any contingency and he was calmer still than he was now.

Samuel Wilson drifted into his sleep peacefully as the luminous clock face registered the new day's beginning, unaware that Tyler had yet to come home.

2

Patrick waited until he heard his father snoring. No way was he heading out after curfew with the man conscious. Not after today. After he had heard the familiar growling sound for a good fifteen minutes, he slipped his fully clothed body from under his blankets and scurried out of his room.

Somewhere out there was his little brother. Tyler needed him. He knew Tyler well enough to know that he wasn't just imagining things: Tyler was never late getting home. Tyler had a good deal more sense than his older sibling. All he could think of was what he had seen Mark Howell do in the woods so long ago. Even knowing that it had been a hallucination didn't make the thoughts any easier to deal with. Tyler was in trouble, nothing else mattered.

Patrick knew every sound his home made and avoided the front door because of the squeaks from the hinges. The kitchen door was his safest bet and getting out was easy enough. It was colder than he'd expected and Patrick cursed himself for not pulling out a sweatshirt at the very least. Worry over his brother made Patrick's senses sharp. He moved as quietly as he could towards Mark Howell's house, then thought better of the idea. Tony had told him that Mark was okay, but Tony wasn't the brightest guy Patrick had ever met either. Maybe it was just leftover anxiety from a very bad mind trip, but he'd avoid Mark Howell for as long as he could.

Cassie's place looked like a mausoleum this late at night and Patrick was forced to go back to the house for his car after checking the Monroe place. Mom and Dad would be sound asleep, and even if they weren't he'd just roll the car down the hill before starting the engine. Easy as pie he thought, and why shouldn't he? Patrick had done this a hundred times in the past.

Rolling the car took more out of him than he had expected; his rib cage was bruised from his earlier impact with the wall. He wondered if his father had broken anything, then he shrugged the idea off. Everyone in the movies always whimpered too much when they broke something. If they couldn't handle the pain, he sure as hell wouldn't be able to.

It had been a long while since he'd hit the roads this late at night. Patrick had forgotten how dark the night could be. Clouds obscured the moon and the only real source he had for seeing anything at all was his car's headlights. The Honda's

high beams revealed only the road ahead and the trees on either side. No Tyler walking home from wherever he had gone,
no clues to easily point the way to his brother. Just road that
curved gently and trees that swayed in a wind that was growing stronger by the minute. The Basilisk. Tyler hung out there
a lot these days. Patrick pulled up in front of the stout old
house just a short while later. The lights were off. Damn,
where the hell was Tyler? Never, never late. Tyler was the
one who always got home with a half hour to spare.

He'd try Tony's place—if he had no luck there, then Tyler
would have to save his own ass. Patrick was tired and the day
had drained him of any extra reserves of energy a long while
back. Tony lived on the other side of town. The Scarrabelli's
just weren't the type to give up the old ancestral home, thus
they lived in the part of town that really was a part of the
town. Red Oaks was a good three quarters of a mile from the
Basilisk and that was a good mile and a half out of Summitville
proper. No big deal if you had a car, but Tyler didn't. Tyler
had to walk unless Tony gave him a lift home.

More and more, Patrick felt the niggling little worries about
his brother growing into serious worries. Too many people
had died in recent months for him to remain comfortable.
Without conscious thought, his pressure on the Honda's gas
pedal started to slowly increase.

3

In his own eyes, Tyler was taking the ongoing one-on-one conversation with Crowley, outside the Basilisk, remarkably well.
He had yet to wet his pants. It was two o'clock in the morning, Tyler had been up since ten A.M. yesterday, and here he
was having pleasant conversation with a mad man.

If you'd asked Tyler his opinions of the man, he would
have been at a total lack for words. The guy looked like anyone you'd find on the street, but it was like he was wearing his
average-guy face as a mask or something. He was too extreme

to be an average guy, too intense in a way that made Tyler uncomfortable. He looked at everyone like he knew just what they were thinking and he found their thoughts to be amusingly suspect. Tyler didn't know if he should be worried or pissed off.

For the last three hours, he'd been having a long talk about Mark and Tony with Jonathan Crowley. He didn't really want to have the discussion, but he had the uneasy feeling that just leaving was an option he should not give consideration in a serious way. So far he'd been asked just about every question in the book, and while Crowley was thinking of another dozen or so, Tyler decided to turn the tables on his interviewer.

"Okay. I've answered your questions, now you get to answer a few of mine." That wasn't so bad, almost sounded authoritative.

Crowley raised his left eyebrow and curled the right side of his mouth into a smirking half grin. The over all effect made his face seem extremely lopsided. "Fair enough. I can spare a few minutes. Ask away."

"My, how magnanimous. For starters, where do you know P. J. from?"

Crowley smiled openly at that one, you could just see that he knew it was going to be the first question. Tyler decided to be angry. "I met your famous author back when he was going to college. He had a little problem going on with a demon he'd managed to summon. Seems he's always pulling that kind of shit. Next question?"

"Demon?"

"Yeah, y'know, fire? Brimstone and horns?"

"You're kidding me."

"Yes actually, the little beasty was more like a poltergeist really, not a solid visible manifestation." Tyler looked at the man as if he'd lost a few marbles in the last couple of minutes. The man's responding look didn't give any reassurance.

"What, you hunt demons for a living or something?"

"No. Not just demons. Too limiting."

"Right. Sure. You betcha."

"Hey, you asked."

Tyler had to give him that point; it was a small point, but it was significant enough. "So what brings you to Summitville? Did you just find out about this on your own or what?"

Crowley pinched his nose between his forefinger and thumb and rubbed for a moment. His hand blocked most of his face and Tyler couldn't tell if he was smiling or not.

"No, Tyler. I was called. There are rules you couldn't hope to understand and I have to follow them. One of those rules says I have to be called. P. J. Sanderson is the one who called me. And just to put your mind at ease, he used the phone. In no way shape or form was I summoned by magic. Got a goddamn phone call at three o'clock in the morning and I got in my nice expensive car and I drove from California all the way out to this little shithole of a town because I was called."

Tyler looked on at the man for a minute without saying a word. He didn't think the man had said so much on any given subject at once in the entire amount of time they had been speaking. It was also the first time he sounded like it wasn't all a great big joke. "Sorry, I didn't mean to offend."

"No and I'm sure you never mean to offend, Tyler. That's one of the big differences between us."

Tyler stared at the man for a moment, Crowley stared back and then abruptly looked away. "So why do you do it? Why do you hunt monsters if it bothers you so much? I mean, there have got to be better career opportunities out there."

Crowley smiled at that last little comment. It was the first and only real smile Tyler ever saw on the man's face. For just the briefest of seconds, he thought he saw the real man behind the average-guy mask. What he saw made him just a little nervous.

"Tyler, I wish I could give you more of an answer than I can. Let's just say it goes back to those rules I told you about, and an old family obligation."

Crowley reached out a hand and slapped Tyler lightly on the shoulder, almost in a friendly fashion. "Thanks for your help, Tyler. I really needed the information and I really didn't need the grief of putting up with Philly."

"No problem. Just do yourself a favor and try to relax, okay?"

Crowley snorted abruptly. "Sure. You too, kid." He turned away from Tyler and headed back towards town as the first glimmer of distant headlights started glowing around the edge of the road in the distance. Tyler recognized the battered front end of his brother's car and waved his arms in the air to catch Patrick's attention. In the distance, the car started to brake, slowing gradually.

"Hey Tyler." He turned back towards Crowley when he heard his name called. Crowley was standing almost a hundred feet away already and the man had just been walking at a normal pace. He should have still been within ten feet of Tyler. "I'm only going to say it once, and if you quote me I'll deny it." Crowley looked him in the eyes and for an instant he seemed like he was right next to Tyler instead of a score of yards away. "I'm sorry for what I might have to do here. I'm sorry for the people who'll get hurt." The sound of Patrick's car running into the gravel on the side of the road took away the last words that Crowley said. Tyler didn't hear them. A sickening dread in the pit of his stomach made him think they were something along the lines of "But mostly I'm sorry for what it'll all do to you."

Spiders where slithering under his skin by the time Patrick reached him. Crowley was nowhere in sight. Tyler let Patrick lead him to the car, all the time nodding politely to the statements that Patrick kept making. Things like "Are you okay?" and "It'll be all right" with the occasional "Man, Dad's gonna have a fit."

Tyler went home with Patrick and they managed to sneak into the house without waking up their parents. Patrick slept easily with the knowledge that his little brother was safe and in bed. Tyler tossed under his covers. Sleep wasn't going to come easy. For some reason, the apologies from Crowley scared him more than anything else that had happened recently.

4

Mark Howell came fully awake at the sound of his mother entering his room. She crept in as quietly as she could, but to him her footsteps sounded like a giant striding through the forest. He kept his eyes closed and forced his body to remain still. He knew it was his mother by the smell of her perfume and the way in which her feet struck the carpeted floor. These days he always seemed to know who was near him.

It wasn't something he thought about, but his senses were all much sharper than they used to be. His sense of touch was sensitive enough that he found himself stroking a variety of objects whenever he was thinking; the textures he encountered were endlessly fascinating. These days he could easily have distinguished between different types of wine ... and to this day he had never tasted any. He never allowed himself to think about how heightened his perceptions were.

It was almost as if he was afraid to think along those lines. Afraid he might really start to think about all of the changes he had gone through, not just the physical ones, but the mental as well. No, not a subject he relished.

Above him, Jenny Howell stared down at her son. She lightly reached out and touched his face, running one finger lightly over the faded scar that snaked across his cheek. He could feel her smile in the darkness. She pulled his tumbled blankets back over his shoulders, perhaps afraid that he would catch a cold as he always had when he was younger. She needn't have worried, Mark never got sick these days.

One last touch on the side of his head as she dragged her fingers across his hair and she was gone. The whole thing had taken only a few seconds, but Mark held the memory of those seconds as closely as he could. His mother's touch was still reassuring at the age of sixteen, possibly more now than ever. Knowing that she cared enough to visit his room nightly and reassure herself that he was still all right, that was his mom's daily allowance of serious affection. She seemed to have a problem with showing her feelings, almost as if she felt the distance between them was a way of acknowledging to herself that she was still young.

Mark didn't mind. She was still young and she needed to have a certain amount of freedom from her son and her obligations to him. He'd seen kids his age with mothers that worried themselves into ulcers over every day things like a scraped knee or a black eye. He believed that seeing his mother that way would have killed him. At the age of sixteen, the last thing Mark wanted was a doting mother. If she was the type to worry too much, he would never be able to go to the woods.

Even now the woods seemed to call him. Not in words so much as waves of feeling, but they called just the same. He would go tomorrow, maybe the day after. More important than the woods was the need to see Cassie. Being with Cassie was like being alive, and allowed him to study her with his senses. Study and memorize, against the day when they would inevitably be separated. It was only a matter of time before Joe got the wandering blues and decided to move on. Mark hoped it would be a while yet, just long enough for his book to come out and for him to make a deal with P. J. Mark never intended to move again if he could avoid it. Summitville was home now. Summitville was the only home he'd ever known.

Mark prayed that Joe wanted to stay long enough. Mark had grown to like Joe in the last few months and really didn't want to see anything happen to him. Mark drifted off to sleep then, content in the knowledge that Joe would either stay in Summitville or Joe would no longer be a problem. The thoughts didn't really register in his fading consciousness, they simply seemed a part of a distant dream. The only person or thought of any real importance in this world was Cassie. In his dreams she came closer, clothed only in the flesh that nature provided. The dream was wonderful, as always. So why was it that he kept hearing another familiar voice, Lisa's, screaming and begging him to stop before it was too late? It took serious effort, but eventually he managed to block out her screams for help. There was nothing he could do for her. She was already beyond his reach.

Lisa faded away to whispers in the presence of Cassie. Soon even the whispers disappeared. Had Jennifer Howell picked that moment to visit her only son's room, she might have been surprised by the smile on his face. Or by the tears that flowed from his tightly closed eyes.

5

The sun was finally rising above the tops of the trees when Chuck Hanson reached the woods. Hanson was glad for that; it had been a long time since he had been in the woods at all and he was terrified of getting lost out here. Even with the dawn's light filtering down to the ground at his feet, the woods looked dark and menacing.

Born and raised in Summitville, Chuck still thought of the woods as a nasty place, a place full of secrets best left untouched. Chuck had worked the family farm when he was a boy growing up and the only trees there had been in his father's feeble attempts at an orchard—if seven trees placed here and there without any thought to pattern could be called an orchard. He could never remember a single apple growing on any of those seven trees, but he could remember the one that sprouted near his tree house.

The thought of that old fort was bittersweet, bringing memories of playing there when he was nine and ten years old and hanging around with Philly Sanderson and Sam Wilson. Back then they had all been friends. It was high school that had destroyed that friendship; for some reason he just hadn't fit in anymore after the age of twelve. That was all in the past now, years gone by. He was surprised to find the memory still held feelings after so long a time.

When the time had come for Chuck to go to college, he even attended the same university as Sam and Philly. All of them managed to make their own groups of friends, but now and then, he'd spot one of the others on the campus and wish he could go back to the age of ten again. Time hadn't healed the wounds of his separation from his childhood friends at all. It had just built up a thick callus, a scab too hard to be broken by any of them. He wondered if they ever missed that friendship as much as he did whenever he saw them.

Hell, both of them had more money coming in a month than he made in a year. What was to miss? He chided himself for the uncharitable thoughts, but they remained just the same. The only time Sam ever spoke to him was to tell him something was wrong somewhere near Red Oaks, a busted light on a street lamp or maybe a kid playing his car radio too loud for Sam's delicate ears.

P. J. was different though, P. J. had at least made a few attempts at pleasant conversation with Chuck since they had both moved back home. Much as Chuck was lamenting the loss of that friendship at the moment, he always seemed content to brush away those efforts on Philly's part when they were happening.

Maybe that was resentment on his part. It was hard to take a man who called himself by initials and made millions every year very seriously when you were staring him in the face. It was hard to accept that the taxes his old friend now paid were more than he himself earned in a year. Maybe it went deeper even than that. Philly had come home to a family that already had money enough to allow him his dreams as a writer; Chuck came home to a family that resented his not wanting to stay on the farm. His dad had never come right out and said anything, but the resentment had been obvious from his first day on the job as deputy sheriff.

Chuck had managed his revenge for the resentment well enough: when his folks passed away he had sold most of the farm's land to the Brundvandts next door and left the remaining parcel with its small farmhouse to grow weeded over. He still liked going past the old place now and then, just to see how the deterioration was coming along. Sometimes he hated himself for enjoying those little visits.

His parents just hadn't understood his need to preserve Summitville as it was, not let it become another ski town that lived for four months of the year and died the rest of the time. Chuck had always taken the nickname Chief very seriously. He felt the need to keep the peace and keep out the riffraff that would have let his hometown become another Breckenridge or even worse another Aspen. Chuck Hanson wanted his family to grow up in the same world that he had, providing he ever got around to a family. He wanted more than anything else to keep his town pure. To keep the people of Summitville safe from the changes going on all around them was the one thing that Sheriff Chuck Hanson believed in. For him, the protection of Summitville was more than a job, it was almost a religion.

Hanson was drawn out of his reverie by the certain feeling that something was horribly wrong with the woods around him. He couldn't place what it was, but there was definitely something out of place. He stopped walking and started concentrating on his surroundings. The leaves on the trees were still glistening with droplets of morning dew, the mulch beneath his feet was wet enough to allow the dampness to edge though the leather of his boots. The only sounds he heard was his own breathing and the wind through the branches rattling like a dying man's last breath.

No animals. Not even a cricket could be heard chirping away for its mate. Shit. That just wasn't the way a stretch of woods this size was supposed to sound. He drew a tight breath and held it for several seconds, hoping to hear more than just the cold wind's hiss. Nothing. Damn, but this was starting to make his balls shrivel up.

"What the hell's goin' on out here?" he asked, just for the pleasure of a voice, any voice. Looking around in a slow circle, he spotted a clearing over near the bottom of Overtree's incline. It had been a few decades since he had been in the woods, but he just didn't like the way this was looking at all. That clearing hadn't been there before. He would have remembered an area that large that stood alone. Even Chuck had brought a girl or two out here for sneaking kisses and hugs when he was younger and that clearing would have been a perfect place for such nocturnal activities.

It took a long while for him to gather up the courage to go forward into the silent woods. Eventually he decided it was time to look the clearing over. Chuck Hanson started walking towards the last minutes of his life, pausing only long enough to light a cigarette.

6

Starting her day off right was always a pleasure for Cassie. And the first part of starting the day off right was a shower, breakfast and a cup of hot tea. She'd tried starting off with coffee once and had almost retched on the bitter flavor. After she had taken care of the morning's essentials, Cassie traded her robe for her running outfit and waited for Mark to show up.

When Mark arrived his predictable five minutes late, she ignored the frosty glares of her mother and father, waved a goodbye to them and ran out to meet her beau. Mark flashed a smile meant for her alone, one that she returned as the two of them started on their run. Once upon a time it had been difficult for Mark to match Cassie's pace; these days the opposite was true. His long powerful gait was effortless and far quicker than it used to be. Cassie liked that, the challenge of keeping up with Mark added a sense of friendly competition that Cassie missed from the days in the gymnastics classes. By the time they had passed the Basilisk and were getting ready to turn back the other way, Cassie realized that he actually was holding back for her, almost as if he were walking with a toddler.

When they had finished their morning run, Mark looked at Cassie's house and risked a quick peck on the cheek. They were going to meet again after showering. Today's agenda included going back to Mark's and working on a new idea for a collaborative book. It was best to leave the writing at Mark's for fear her parents would go through the ceiling in a fit of rage. Maybe if the story could be accepted by a publisher, she could tell her parents about her plans. It was safer that way; she had suspicions her mom and dad wouldn't hesitate to send her off to a private school in Denver, the type used for disciplinary problems, if she didn't have proof that she could make a living as a writer.

Cassie showered quickly and got ready to meet with Mark. They were already on chapter 8 in the outline of the book and so far it read well in her eyes. It was possibly a bit clichéd to write a book about a haunted house, but the story had a few good twists in her opinion.

Lately, Cassie had become a bit more optimistic about the story, or maybe she was just optimistic about writing the story with Mark. Either way she was happy.

Twenty minutes later she was on her way, unaware that a stranger in town was watching her every move. Jonathan Crowley looked at the girl as she jogged by and followed. He needed confirmation on his suspicions before he made any moves.

7

Breakfast had been awkward. Jackie ate in embarrassed silence and Rick couldn't think of any way to break that silence. In a fit of desperation, he mentioned Crowley. "How old is Jonathan Crowley? He didn't look much over thirty-five."

Jackie looked his way and he could see her gratitude for any safe subject. Neither of them had really intended to go to bed together, it had just sort of happened—and neither of them had thought about protection until well after the fact. "I think he's somewhere in his fifties, but you're right, he just doesn't look that old."

"Well preserved man."

"Actually, I was wondering if that might be his son or something, the man I heard about was more...I dunno, scholarly is the best word I can think of. He was the type to always have a book in his face and a pocket protector in his shirt, if you catch my meaning."

Rick thought about that for a few moments, yes, he could see her point. "You thinking maybe he's an impostor?"

Jackie frowned in thought and shook her head. "No. Or if he is, he's a very knowledgeable one. He works with the same techniques that Will—he's my old professor—said Crowley used. Lots of questions and research before he even considered looking into a case. God, the man was accused more than once of trying to spend university funds to research a new book or something instead of actually investigating the 'scene of the crime,' as it were."

"This Will, would he recognize Crowley if he saw him?"

"Sure, Crowley was his teacher." She looked ready to ask why and then the comment sank in. "Oh. You want me to call Will?"

"Would you?" Rick put on his best puppy dog face and after a second's hesitation, Jackie gave in and nodded.

"Okay, but only under one condition."

"Name it. Anything I can do."

"Get that stupid look off of your face."

Yep, he thought as he made a dead pan face, nodding solemnly. *Gets 'em every time.*

8

P. J. and Tyler got together a little after one in the afternoon. Neither of them really knew what to do about what was happening, now that Crowley was in town. Tyler told P. J. everything that Crowley had asked and most of the answers he had given, leaving out the answers to his queries on how Crowley had met the author. P. J. nodded several times and sipped at his coffee. The author looked drained by his meeting of the night before. Tyler sympathized.

P. J. started the conversation rolling again after pouring them both another cup of the powerful black coffee. Both of them needed any stimulation they could get. "He took the book with him. That son of a bitch took the shitting book with him. And I let him. Christ, I'm a coward at heart I suppose."

Tyler shook his head and grinned weakly. "No, just smarter than you give yourself credit for. Man scared the pee outta me without even trying. There's something unnatural about him."

P. J. nodded absently, eyes focused on the cup of steaming coffee in his hands. "You may be right about that. I met him twenty-two years ago and he doesn't look a day older now than he did then. Our Mister Crowley is a very strange man and I wish to hell that he would just leave. I don't think he plans to work this out in a way that you or I would approve of."

Tyler had to know. He could not take Crowley's word for it. "How did you meet him?"

P. J. Sanderson closed his eyes for just a moment then, sagging down in his chair before he straightened himself up and looked at Tyler again. "I played with things best left alone. I didn't believe that magic was a real thing and I really don't know if I believe it now, not even after all that has happened."

"When I finally decided that I wanted to write in the horror field, I decided that I would gather a few old books on the subject, just so I could have reference materials at my disposal. It took a fair amount of looking and some of the books cost me a small fortune, but I felt it was best to have the sources and they fascinated me. One of the books I ran across was written entirely in Latin and seemed to be a thesis on Demonology, complete with recipes for summoning some of the lesser demons. Well, never one to pass by a quick chill, I found one that sounded fairly uncomplicated. Nothing happened after the summoning. At least not at first."

"About a week after the summoning attempt, I noticed a few odd things going on in the dormitory where I lived. Odd areas where the heating seemed to fail, the occasional item missing, nothing serious.

"Then one day, about a month later, when I had all but forgotten about the book, Jonathan Crowley showed up at the door. Seemed a nice enough man, asked if he could speak to our dorm mother, Mrs. Arbinger. Well, not knowing any better, I got her."

"She seemed very happy to see him and I was asked to leave them to talk in peace. I had midterms coming up soon and I needed the time to study. I never thought a thing about it. Not until I woke up at three in the morning with Crowley standing over my bed, pointing a finger in my face. The man was furious. He called me a dozen names the likes of which should not be repeated to young man of your age, or to a man of any age, and demanded to know why I had summoned a demon."

"I laughed at him, I thought he was joking or drunk. He was very serious and very sober. He slapped me several times, just to make sure he had my attention, and then he pointed to a corner of the room. Crowley said a few words that sounded similar to the ones I had spoken a month earlier and before my eyes a hazy glow started in the corner where he had been pointing. 'There! That is what you summoned!' he screamed in my face. The shape was entirely wrong for a human being, entirely wrong for any living thing I've run across. It looked like a lump of shit with mouths and eyes spread over its surface. I couldn't breathe. With another few words in what I like to call Pidgin Latin he made the thing just sort of blink out of existence, rather like turning off a television."

"After he was finished, he told me I had Mrs. Arbinger to thank for my life. He said if she hadn't called him the creature would have destroyed me by the end of one year. I hadn't bound it properly into servitude. Just to ensure that I was listening he slapped me again."

"He ranted about killing me himself, saying that I would come to no good. He said he'd seen my type before, that my type never listened. I bawled my eyes out, the man was scary even then. Finally he dusted me off, even gave me a tissue to blow my nose and said that he would let me live. I would have cried from relief then, but I was still afraid he'd hit me some more."

"The last thing he did was tell me a phone number to call if I ever got into any trouble again, or if I thought that there was someone in trouble." P. J. shook his head in wonder, eyes widening with a realization. "Do you know, I never even considered calling him until you told me about Mark. I'd actually forgotten all about the incident until then. I never wrote the number he gave me down, I just remembered it when I thought I might need to call him. Lord, I wish I had never remembered the number at all."

The silence between them grew again, Tyler leaning back to digest what he'd heard and P. J. Sanderson remembering more than he wanted to about his college years. They sat in the still bookstore for a long while, lost in their own thoughts.

9

It was well after dinnertime and the two nurses on duty were off taking a coffee break in the small lounge the clinic provided. There wasn't much to do…they only had two patients and both were sleeping soundly. Old Mister Kelley was only in for observation to make sure his concussion didn't lead to serious complications. Alice and Terry were certain that he'd be fine, it wasn't the first time he'd dropped the hood of that old truck on his head and it wouldn't be the last.

The only good news in Mr. Kelley's case was that his head was harder than one of his wife's pound cakes and both of the nurses were convinced that Emma Kelley's pound cakes could dent cement from a height of three feet.

The other case was that poor Scarrabelli girl, and the good news there was that she was starting to show signs of recovering. Now and then they'd find she had moved in her sleep or that she had even managed to turn on her side. They both kept their fingers crossed for her. She was such a pretty little girl and wasn't it just horrible to think someone in Summitville could do such a thing?

Alice and Terry were far too busy chatting about a hundred patients they had seen in the past to notice the visitor going into Lisa Scarrabelli's room. That was just fine with Jonathan Crowley. What he wanted to do here was none of their business anyway. Some things require privacy.

10

Tony Scarrabelli didn't believe in telepathy. In Tony's world if you could not touch it taste it or feel it, it simply did not exist. Tony had a lot to learn about life at the age of sixteen.

Tony was doing what he always did when he was stressed out, he was pumping iron. At the time of his precognitive flash, he was bench pressing his free weights with a full two hundred and twenty-five pounds. Anyone watching would have thought he'd had a sudden cramp, the way he threw his weights backwards and screamed, looked as if he might even have torn a muscle.

The weights hit the floor and shook the room as Tony rolled off of the bench with his hands covering his head. The work out room was gone, all he could see was Jonathan Crowley reaching out with his hands and the acoustic tiles above his body. He'd seen tiles like those just yesterday: they covered the ceiling in his sister's room at the clinic. The images left as unexpectedly as they had arrived, leaving only a blue afterimage when he closed his eyes, as if he had been looking at the sun.

Tony didn't take the time to tell anyone anything. He just stormed up the stairs, knocking his sister Amelia to the floor and grabbed the keys to his Camaro. He ignored Amy's protests and stepped over her prone body, taking the stairs two and three at a time.

Outside, he ignored his overheated body's response to the chill air and pulled the car door open with enough force to rock the vehicle. By the time he had pulled the car out of the driveway, his father was screaming for him to get the hell back over to the house and apologize to his sister. If Tony noticed he gave no sign to his father. Gravel flipped through the air behind him as he forced the gas pedal as far down as he could. He fervently hoped the stones took a shining to his father's face. The clinic was only a mile and a half away and Tony made the distance in record time.

Alice, the larger of the two nurses, tried to stop him as he entered the clinic, tried to explain that visiting hours were over and he would have to come back tomorrow. Tony Scarrabelli shoved her hard enough to knock her on her overripe ass. Her squeal of indignation fell on deaf ears.

Room number three. The door was closed. They never closed the doors to the occupied rooms, instead they dimmed the lights in the hallways at ten o'clock.

On more occasions than most of his close friends could count, those that were still alive anyway, Tony had lost his temper and gone into a fit of rage that was almost unholy to watch. Tonight was no exception. Tony didn't bother with trying the knob on room three, he just slammed his full adrenalized body into the plywood as hard as he could.

The door hadn't been locked. Jonathan Crowley saw no need to bother, he could handle the nurses if they interfered.

Tony's momentum carried him all the way to where Crowley stood leaning over his sister and he used the force of his entry to his best advantage, whipping his fist into the side of the startled man's head.

Crowley's head and neck twisted around towards his right shoulder and soon his body was obliged to follow. He spun half of a full circle and landed on his left shoulder and arm against the edge of Lisa's hospital bed. He managed to hold the awkward stance with his left arm supporting his body weight for all of a second before he crashed on the floor, eyes showing only white.

Tony reached down and grabbed his prone opponent, growling audibly like a rabid dog. Before he could do more than heave the man into a standing position, Crowley was all over him.

Tony wasn't used to losing in a fight, especially not one where he got in the first punch. Crowley brought both fists together into Tony's solar plexus and head-butted him in the face at the same time; Tony felt his nose mash in as if it were made of cardboard. That took all the fight out of Tony; he wasn't prepared for much of anything with tears flooding his eyes and the taste of blood and snot filling his mouth. Crowley didn't let up, he threw somewhere between twelve and three thousand more punches into Tony. It was probably only twelve, but it felt closer to the three thousand mark.

Tony cut his chin on impact with the floor and lost part of his right incisor as a bonus. He wanted to get up and take the fucker *down*. It wasn't meant to be. His best efforts looked like a turtle trying to right itself after some sadistic five-year-old set it on its back. Crowley kicked him in the face for good measure.

In the distance, padded by the ringing in his ears, he could have sworn he heard Lisa's voice. It sounded like she was begging Crowley to stop. The world grew fuzzy and gray. Then it disappeared all together.

11

When Tony was next aware of anything, it was the sound of Dr. Lewis' voice coming from over on his left. When he could finally focus his eyes, he saw Dr. Lewis looking down at him. The good doctor was an okay guy, but seeing him that close up was more than Tony could stomach. He closed his eyes, turned his head and puked on the side of the bed. Soon he felt the strong hands of Doctor Lewis holding him in place as he started to fall from the bed. He wondered just when Lewis had grown two extra hands. At least he didn't have to hit the floor. From Tony's perspective it looked like one hell of a long fall.

He closed his eyes again and fell asleep.

12

Tony finally reached full consciousness the next morning. Much as he desired a few more hours of sleep, the sound of his parents' happy tears tore his rest away from him. Why were they crying?

Tony opened his eyes and sat up on his bed at the clinic; he was feeling better this time around, the room only turned a little instead of spinning. Nausea forced him to close his eyes again, but only briefly.

Tyler's voice right next to him brought about a smile. "Hey, it's alive. Tony, jeez you look awful, guy. How're you feeling?"

Tony opened his eyes to Tyler looking at him from a few feet away. Behind him were Mark and Cassie. Near the door was Rick Lewis with a woman he'd never seen before.

Across the room, both of his parents were smiling uncertainly. So was Lisa from her hospital bed.

Getting out of bed was a task that was almost too much for Tony. He had aches all over his body and his head throbbed with every pulse that ran through him. Twice, he had to grab hold of Mark in order to avoid falling over. Mark was always right there to help.

Eventually he made it to where his sister lay on the bed. She had never looked more beautiful; pale and thin, face covered with the gray glue residue of her bandages and peppered with a few ugly brown scabs. The sight was enough to make him cry.

Lisa cried with him, holding her fraternal twin in her wasted arms. Everyone had the decency to leave the room for a short while. Neither of them talked, they just held each other, as a thousand thoughts ran through their minds.

In the clinic's waiting room, Dave Palance was doing his best to interrogate Jonathan Crowley. Crowley seemed perfectly willing to answer any and all of Dave's questions—it was just that Dave was having a horrible time coming up with any while the man smiled at him.

Crowley broke the smile just long enough to ask a question of his own, before bringing the grin back to his face. "Deputy Palance, are you going to press charges against me? Or am I free to go?" Dave couldn't think of an answer to that one; he was just trying to hold the guy until Stacy could get hold of Chuck Hanson. So far, Hanson wasn't answering on his radio or answering his phone. Crowley turned up the juice on that smirk running across his face and called the deputy's mind back to the subject at hand. "Deputy? I really do have things to take care of. Am I free to go?"

Dave ruminated on the question for about half a second before turning his eyes away from the man in front of him. "Sure thing, Mister Crowley. Just do us both a favor and don't leave town. Okay?"

Crowley patted the deputy's hand like a man consoling his son. "Nothing to worry about there, Deputy Palance." He winked slowly at the astonished man. Dave started as if a bee had stung him. "I wouldn't dream of going anywhere. This town seems to be where everything is happening. And I like to be where the action is as they say."

Dave was glad to see him gone. There was something decidedly unfriendly about the man and Dave had seen what he did to people when he was feeling unfriendly. The Scarrabelli kid looked worse than anyone who was up at Dino's that first night of Crowley's stay in town.

Dave was at a loss when it came to what to do next; he'd already talked to Lisa Scarrabelli and to Crowley. Maybe he should get Tony Scarrabelli's story, while it was still fresh in his mind. He headed towards the room where both of the siblings and a great deal of other people were crowded together. Where the hell was Hanson when you needed him? He always took care of this kind of crap himself.

13

Crowley left the Summitville Clinic with his trademark smile plastered to his face. The smile slipped when he heard the voice of Tyler Wilson behind him. "Thanks, Mister Crowley."

Crowley turned to face the boy, the smile slowly returning, but a little weaker. "What for Tyler? I was just asking the girl a few questions."

Tyler flashed a quick grin of his own at that. "Yeah. Probably. But thanks anyway."

Crowley shook his head, a frown forming on his face. "I don't get you, Tyler. You're thanking me for something that just happened. Why?"

Tyler looked at the ground, his face unreadable.

"Ah," Crowley started. "Now I begin to see the picture. She's someone special, isn't she?" Tyler nodded quickly, almost guiltily. "Well then, you are welcome."

As Crowley made to turn away, Tyler grabbed the man by his arm. It could be opened for debate as to whether or not that was a foolish move; Crowley turned back to face him with a curious look.

"What did she tell you?" Tyler asked. "Did she tell you who did it?" Crowley looked at Tyler without speaking for a very long time. Finally he nodded. "Tell me who it was." It was not a request.

Crowley looked at Tyler, looked at the rage and frustration welling behind the boy's eyes. "No. You really don't want to know that, Tyler." To Tyler, he sounded almost sad. "Sometimes, its best not to know. Let's just say it was a stranger and leave it at that."

"She'll tell me herself, I know how to ask questions, but I wanted to do it without hurting her." The boy's voice was tight, barely a whisper. "Please answer me, I don't want to have to ask her."

Crowley shook his head. "You never take no for an answer, do you Tyler?"

"Not as a general rule, no."

Crowley looked at the boy for a very short time and the turned away again. "Learn to accept no, Tyler. Sometimes it's the only answer someone is willing to give." He turned back to Tyler's petulant face, his smile back in full force. "And don't bother asking Ms. Scarrabelli. I made sure she wouldn't remember. It's best that way."

Tyler turned crimson, his whole body shaking with barely contained rage. "You son of a bitch. I'll find out with or without you. You just watch, asshole."

Jonathan Crowley rocked back on his heels as if someone had slapped him. In a heartbeat his hand was back to deliver a punishing slap to Tyler's face. Tyler's eye grew wide, but he held his ground. Crowley's hand went back to his side. "All right. You win, Tyler, I'll tell you what she said." Tyler did not look victorious, he looked afraid. "She told me it was Mark Howell that raped her. She told me he raped her in every way possible. She told me it felt like it went on for hours. Is that what you wanted to hear?"

Tyler fell to his knees, all color drained from his face.

Crowley knelt beside him and placed a hand on Tyler's shoulder. Tyler tried to shake the hand away, but it maintained its grip just the same. Finally he was forced to look Crowley in the face. "Tyler, I've looked at the sheriff's report on the rape. Lisa was found by Mark Howell and Cassandra Monroe. They had been together all night. They had been in Denver until twenty minutes before they found her. They even had four adult witnesses to confirm where they were. Your sheriff was very thorough in his questioning. It couldn't have been your friend Mark. It was either someone who looked like him, or she doesn't remember it properly."

Crowley helped Tyler to his feet. The boy's face had lit up with a vague sense of renewed hope. His eyes begged for further reassurance. Crowley could give him none. "I didn't think the girl would want to remember what she'd had done to her. I know I wouldn't if I was in her place. Don't tell her who it was. Just be there if she needs someone to talk to."

Crowley turned away and Tyler let him. Tyler wanted to say something, almost anything at that moment. The words refused to come. He watched as Crowley walked away. He didn't know whether to hate the man for telling him, or to love the man for letting Lisa have her life back. In the end, he went back in to be with Lisa.

Chapter Sixteen

1

Jennifer Howell pulled her Volkswagen Rabbit into the small parking lot on Main Street's right hand side and parked. It was too late in the day to go into Denver and still be home by the time Joe arrived, so Marty's would have to do. Marty's Art Mart didn't have a very large supply of quality art products that she could use, but Marty had the sense to at least fully stock his place with the charcoals and paper that she needed to complete the rough drafts for The Bunny's Big Day. From her own point of view, the story was a waste of paper, but the money for her work was just as spendable as it would be on a good tale and it was just a children's book after all.

Jenny gave contemplation to maybe writing a few children's books of her own as she walked into Marty's. Marty waved and smiled from where he sat behind the counter, Jenny waved back as she headed for the pencil selections. Normally Marty flirted incessantly, but today he was stuck on the phone, making an order apparently. Jenny was glad of that; the man was a pig. The bell above Marty's door jangled as another customer walked in. Jenny paid no attention. Like most newcomers to Summitville, she had learned quickly that the average citizen in town had no desire to speak with someone who had not been born there. She plucked several pencils from their neat little containers and headed towards the art paper in the next aisle.

Jenny almost walked into the man standing in front of the Bristol board. "Sorry," she mumbled as she reached for the largest size Marty kept in stock.

A hand landed on the paper even as she touched its edge. She looked up, startled by the sudden appearance of the obstacle. Jonathan Crowley smiled in her face. "No problem.

Oh, I'm sorry. Did you want this pad?" The voice was pleasant and apologetic. Jonathan Crowley held the pad of paper out to her, and she took it quickly.

"Thanks." The man made her nervous. Jenny found herself looking towards Marty for comfort, but his back was turned towards her as he looked over the papers in his hand, mumbling into the phone.

"Is it just a hobby, or are you a professional artist?"

"A little of both, really. I make some side money doing illustrations for children's books and the occasional science fiction or horror magazine."

"Which do you prefer, the kiddie books or the horror stuff?"

Jenny felt herself relax. The man was just making pleasant conversation. *Christ,* she thought, *I'm acting as bad as the town folk around here.* The poor guy was obviously a stranger in town and she was damned if she'd simply give him the brush off like so many people had done to her when she first got here. "Actually, I think I prefer the horror and science fiction. More interesting than drawing bunnies and ducks all day long."

Jonathan Crowley laughed pleasantly and was rewarded with a smile from Jenny. "I can certainly understand that. You can only draw so many cutesy animals before you want to start drawing them as road kill."

"Are you an artist Mister...?"

"Oh, sorry. I'm Jonathan Crowley, and you are?"

"Jenny Howell. Nice to meet you. Are you an artist, Jonathan?"

Jonathan Crowley smiled bashfully and shook his head. "No, I am just an admirer of the ones who actually have talent. Say, did I ever see any of your work in Phantasma?"

Jenny brightened immediately. She had worked on several issues of that little magazine before it went under. "You might have, any particular issue come to mind?"

"Yeah, there was this one issue with P. J. Sanderson, had a really nice double page spread that went with the title of his novella. What was the name of that...? Oh yeah, *The Stained Window*. That's what it was called."

Jenny smiled even wider and the man reciprocated as she spoke. "Yes! I did that one a long time ago! I'm flattered that you remembered."

"Oh, it couldn't have been that long ago, I mean how old are you, twenty-four, maybe twenty six?" That brought a flush of pleasure to her face. "Oh, I'm being rude, I always forget you're not supposed to ask a lady her age."

"I'm a little older than I look, flatterer. But thanks for the compliment." She felt fifteen again. It had been a long time since anyone had flirted with her so well, instead of just leering like Marty behind the counter. It was nice to be flirted with; she was only thirty-one, but sometimes she felt worlds older with only Joe and Mark around to talk to. "So, what do you do for a living Mister Crowley?"

"Please, keep it to Jonathan, Mister Crowley was my father. I do freelance reviews for a couple of literary magazines and sometimes even for the Syndicated Press. That's actually one of the reasons I'm here, I met Phil Sanderson at a convention a few years ago and I thought I might try my luck with an interview."

Jenny's pulse raced a little quicker, as she thought of her son's upcoming book. "Really? You know we have another writer here in town. Mark Howell. His first novel is due out at the end of September. I bet he'd love to meet you."

"Mark Howell? Don't tell me a pretty young woman like you is already married?" The wink he threw took the dangers of this becoming an actual pass instead of just harmless flirtation out of the air. Jenny smiled and tapped him on the arm.

"Yes I am married, but Mark's my son, not my husband."

Crowley's jaw dropped in astonishment. "Your son? What is he, a child prodigy in literature?"

"No," Jenny laughed, "actually you might say he's the protegé of your friend Mr. Sanderson. I saw the original draft of what he wrote and I can say in all honesty the book would never have had a chance if it hadn't been for P. J. The man is practically a saint with the amount of time that he spends with Mark."

Somehow the art supplies got left behind as the couple walked out of Marty's Art Mart. Inside of twenty minutes they were chatting pleasantly about where they had grown up and what it was like where they were now. Inside of an hour, Jonathan Crowley had been invited to dinner at the Howell residence.

2

Rick Lewis hated William DeSilva the moment he laid eyes on him, but he hid it as well as he could. The man positively screamed "academic snob" in the way he acted and dressed. His hair was swept back in a swirling mass that looked like a lion's mane and his clothes looked like they were fresh out of the most recent issue of GQ magazine.

Jackie was obviously infatuated with him and although he had no delusions of their accidental one night stand becoming a long term relationship, the way she swooned when the man approached made Rick want to scream. His ego was small enough in this little town without the one woman he'd had sex with in the last two years stepping towards another man as if he was chopped liver.

Just to add to Rick's discomfort, the son of a bitch was incredibly nice. He was all too eager to help and all too eager to meet Jonathan Crowley. "If he is my old teacher, I'd like to see him again. If he isn't, at least it was worth the effort. The man simply seemed to drop off the face of the earth a few years ago."

"Well, I don't even know how to contact him, but hopefully he'll show up. He was here just yesterday and I imagine he'll pop back around to see Lisa Scarrabelli or maybe her brother." Jackie had explained about the unfortunate accident that Tony's face had experienced on their way over to the clinic.

"Well, frankly from what I've heard about the man, I'd have to guess that he isn't my old teacher." William DeSilva frowned as he pulled his Meerschaum pipe from inside his jacket. Sheer willpower allowed Rick not to fall to the ground laughing. *Of course, naturally he'd have a Meerschaum! God help me, I bet he drinks only cognac!* With an effort, Rick managed to ask him why he believed this couldn't be the man. "Well, its not the sort of thing I usually think about when it comes to John, but he always walked with a cane."

Rick looked over quizzically and finally asked the question that silence demanded. "Why was that?"

"The old boy had a false right leg. Lost it in Korea I believe."

"Yeah, I'd say that eliminates his being your professor from college, Will. I'm sorry to have bothered you with all of this."

"Nonsense. No bother at all. Gets me out of that stuffy old classroom for the day and I get to spend a little time with one of my favorite students." He smiled at Jackie and Jackie smiled back. Rick gave serious contemplation to throwing up.

Well, wouldn't Chuck be glad to hear about this. The man wasn't a renowned specialist in the occult after all. Rick frowned at the thought. He hadn't heard from Chuck Hanson in over fifteen hours and lately that was something of a record. He made a mental note to call Chuck later, right after he lost the good professor.

3

Jonathan Crowley beamed across the dinner table at Mark Howell. Mark smiled back and then quickly looked back at his spaghetti dinner. The man was making him nervous. Just as quickly, Crowley looked over at Joe Howell and winked slyly. "Handsome lad you have there, Joe. Must make you proud to be a father, what with him already having sold a novel."

Joe smiled back, always eager to entertain a well known or even little known book reviewer to whom he could send copies of the books he published. "Well, I really can't take much of the credit, Jenny here did all of the raising. I normally didn't have a chance to spend too much time with Mark while he was doing most of his growing."

Joe looked over at Mark, hating himself for the truth in those words. Mark busily played with his food, pushing piles of pasta from one spot to another. Apparently Jenny's prize catch of the day noticed, because he broke in just before the moment could become awkward. Joe thanked him silently. "Mark, why don't you tell me a little bit about your novel? Who knows, I might even be able to give it a good review in *Fangoria*."

That got the boy's attention. Mark lit up like a bonfire and started talking about the novel. Jonathan Crowley listened and even asked questions in all the right places. Joe looked over at Jenny and smiled. She smiled back and the two of them did that 'parental conversation without words' trick that so many long time couples seemed able to do. He told her what a wonderful thing she had done for building their son's morale and she told him that she knew she had done a wonderful thing while suggesting that he get the man's address so he could send him advance copies of the books that were published in his department.

The night went on until, before anyone really knew it, it was just before midnight and Jonathan said he had to leave. Mark ran upstairs to get a Xerox copy of his novel in its proposal form for Crowley. Joe took that moment to thank him for his time and trouble. "Mark really needed the morale boost, he's been in a daze for the last couple of weeks."

"It's my pleasure, Joe. Besides, I may just be reviewing the first in the next wave of new authors. Who can tell?" After getting the copy from Mark, Jonathan said his good byes. He shook hands with Mark and Joe both and received a hug and a kiss on the cheek from Jenny.

After he had left, Mark chatted excitedly with both of his parents about how great it would be, if he could just get a good review in Fangoria. P. J. had told him how important it was to get good reviews in magazines, especially genre magazines, if you were working in a specific genre. Joe and Jenny both gave him congratulations and warnings not to get too excited, but the warnings bounced off him like bullets off Superman. Nothing could bring him down now. Nothing in this world.

4

P. J. wasn't really surprised to see Jonathan Crowley sitting next to his bed. Scared, but not surprised. As he sat up and turned on the light, Crowley handed him a cup of coffee, just the way he liked it with lots of cream and sugar.

"What the hell do you want?"

Crowley's upper lip creased in a bloodless smile. "Oh, I thought you and I could have a talk about your little friend Mark."

P. J. frowned, little wrinkles that had just been added to his face in the last few months growing more prominent with the gesture. "What about him, Jonathan? Just once in your life, get to the point."

His late night guest frowned down from where he stood, as P. J. wiped the sleep from his eyes. "Really, Philly, you've lost a great deal of your manners lately. You were a lot easier to get along with when you were still in college."

P. J. threw his coffee mug at Crowley. Crowley ducked to one side and watched as it shattered against the wall, bleeding tan fluids. P. J. pointed one finger in his face as he got off the bed. "You bastard! You can go ahead and threaten me all you goddamn well please, you can beat me and you can terrify me and you can harass me, but don't you ever lay a hand on a member of my family again!"

Crowley held up a warding hand as the author stormed across the room in his boxer shorts. Phil Sanderson glowered at his nemesis and his nemesis smiled kindly in return. "Phil,

I can tell you're upset with me. Would this have to do with your nephew?"

"You're damn right it does! Where the hell do you get off doing that to a sixteen year old boy?"

Crowley grinned a challenge and despite himself, P. J. Sanderson felt like running. "The little shit deserved it. Besides, he hit me first. I've still got the right to defend myself, don't I Philly?"

"You and I both know you could have taken him down without all the added punishments, Crowley. It wasn't necessary for you to hurt him that badly." The writer looked sullen now, not angry.

Crowley flopped down on the bed, his legs crossed at the ankle and sipped from his own mug of coffee. "You're absolutely right, but then I figured the little shit deserved something for what he did to Mark Howell's face." He flashed another quick smile and looked his host in the eye. "Which brings me back to my original reason for calling on you so late at night."

P. J. started picking the shards of his coffee mug off of the carpeted floor, waiting for his guest to continue. After watching him finish the cleanup job by mopping the floor and wall with a dirty shirt, Crowley did. "Mark's the one. Whatever you and your friends did when you were kids, he's the one that's paying for it now. Nice of you to help him with the book, but I don't think that's quite going to make up for what's likely to happen to him."

"What do you mean?"

"I mean, if I'm too late to stop the changes going on in his body, I'm going to have to kill him." The tone was the same he would use to discuss the weather and P. J. resented it.

"Where do you get off making those kinds of judgments, Crowley? The boy hasn't harmed anyone." P. J. hated the whine that had started in his voice, but he hated the idea of this man hurting Mark even more.

"Everyone has their calling in life, Phil. You have your writing and I have my own job. I don't always like it, but there it is." Crowley looked at him as with a dawning realization: "Oh, come on, Phillip. You don't really think I want to hurt the boy, do you?"

P. J. stared back in absolute silence.

"I didn't play with the wrong books, Philly, you did. I didn't let my nephew run around beating on the new kid in school, you did.

"Tell me, whatever happened to Alex Harris, Philly? I know you had the time and money to look for him. What did you find? Is he alive? Did he die of a drug overdose?" The pleasant tone completely left Crowley at that moment. His voice dropped two octaves and he stood up. "What did you find out, Phil? Did you find out that his little brother arranged an accident at the age of five? Did you, maybe, find out that a few years later, his brother and his mom moved to the East Coast?"

P. J. Sanderson stepped back, as Jonathan Crowley came closer. He stopped backing up only because the wall stopped him. Crowley leaned into his face, the grin on his face looking like the smile of a shark.

"How's this one? Did you know that his precious little brother Todd met a pretty little girl all of fifteen and nailed her, got her pregnant? Or that he took off like a bat out of hell as soon as he heard she was pregnant? Her name back then was Jennifer Gallagher. She had a little boy, she named him Mark. Then she got married to a nice man named Joe and they lived happily ever after.

"Until whatever you woke up in the woods started making things happen. Things that ensured Mark's arrival in Summitville. Here's one last coincidence for you: Mark Howell, son of Jennifer Gallagher and Todd Harris, managed to get his face pulverized by the local shit heads. He managed to get himself hurt on a rock somewhere out in those woods. I'd be willing to bet you money that the rock that cut him was the very same rock you made those little chicken blood sacrifices on. Maybe, just maybe, he even got himself cut on the very same stone that hurt poor little Todd so long ago. I looked at the spell you say your friend read. To work properly, it requires the blood of a lamb. It never specifies how much blood, or even if the blood has to be a particular sex. It just says the blood of a lamb."

Crowley pulled back a little, P. J. found he could breath again.

"What do you suppose the chances are that Mark was a virgin when he landed on that rock? My guess would be pretty damn good. He only started shaping up after the accident.

"You're right Philly. Mark didn't do shit. He doesn't deserve to be punished for what's happened to him. But killing you wouldn't change a single thing."

Crowley smiled again for P. J.'s benefit. Then he turned and walked away from the writer. P. J. started to collapse then, all of his worst suspicions confirmed by this terrible, frightful man. Crowley paused at the door, smile gone again. "You think about that, Philly, the next time you want to ask me what right I have to judge. I'm going to do my best for that boy, because he seems like a good kid. But, if I fail, if I end up having to kill him, it's on your head. Not mine."

Crowley left. Some time later, after the crying jag had run its course, Phillip Sanderson went down to his bookstore's main room and took all of the rare antique books he'd collected over the years to his bed room. It took the rest of the night and a good portion of the morning, but eventually he managed to burn them all in his bedroom fireplace. One by one, page by page.

7

Mark was asleep, Jenny was asleep; Joe had the house entirely to himself. Joe was having difficulty understanding the way his wife had been acting over the last few weeks and as much as he hated himself for it, he was going to find out why. In order to find out why, Joe broke the second cardinal unspoken law of the Howell Residence. He entered one of the other family member's private domains.

When they had moved out here from Atlanta, Joe had jokingly suggested that there were enough rooms in the house to let everyone have a room all to themselves as work space. Jenny and Mark had taken the joke seriously and the den as well as two of the extra rooms were suddenly declared off limits by the family almost as soon as they had settled in.

Joe had broken the first unspoken law, always knock before entering the bathroom, more than once. But he had never broken the second before now.

Feeling as if he'd committed an actual crime, Joe entered Jenny's workroom. Surrounding the walls were unfinished canvases and pencil sketches that dated all the way back to when they had first met. There were illustrations from literary magazines, children's books and even her one "real" book cover, spread in organized disarray, around all of the walls and even resting on the couch where she sometimes napped. On the far wall, where the light was most likely at its best during the day, was Jenny's drawing table. At present it too was covered with unfinished works, the difference being that these would soon be finished.

Joe didn't know what he expected to find in the room, but he started with the drawing table in the hopes that whatever it was, it would be easy to locate. Under the first layer of cute animal sketches he found more of the same. Under the second layer of Bristol board, he found something he had not expected.

Buried as if by sheer accident, Joe found odd sketches of a wooded area, but they were like no woods he had ever seen before. The trees twisted in a mockery of what nature had intended, as if they were made of unbaked clay and someone had tortured the lifelike duplicates. Figures were hinted at, but never clearly shown, dancing around the malformed aspen and oaks. They too had the wrong shape, a slander of what nature had intended. The figures were too small to be human, too large to be rodents, and they stood for the most part on their hind legs.

The second of the sketches was much like the first, but in this one there was a large stone. Sitting on the edge of the stone was a young man Joe assumed to be Mark, until he studied the face closely. There was something missing from his face, something obvious that Joe couldn't see. After a moment, it dawned on him; the boy's scar was gone. Not a large thing to notice, not a vastly important detail, but one that Jenny would certainly have placed if she had been drawing her son.

There was only one other person Joe had ever seen that looked so much like Mark and that was his father. For just a brief moment, Joe was prepared to tear the picture into shreds in a fit of jealousy. Then he recalled Jenny's off-hand comment that she was considering a children's book, one that she would write herself. It would only be natural to use her own son and equally natural to leave the scar off of his face. No child wanted to read a book that was realistically drawn with the hero being scarred for life.

The third picture revealed the strange creatures at Mark's feet to be Fairies, laughing gaily and dancing in celebration. Mark's face was filled with wonder and the woods seemed less threatening than they had in the previous two illustrations. Joe smiled at the subtlety used by Jenny in achieving surprise, not only for Mark, but for the readers as well.

Feeling foolish, he set the pictures back down and covered them over with the two layers that had covered them previously. He crept back out of the room and gently closed the door.

Inside of fifteen minutes, he was asleep next to his wife, content in the knowledge that she was only acting strangely because she was preoccupied with her work. Joe reflected briefly, before falling asleep, on just how lucky he was to have Jenny as a wife. She was everything he had ever wanted in a life long companion.

Downstairs in Jenny's workroom, the final two pictures went unnoticed. Perhaps if Joe had seen them, he would have realized that something really was wrong. In the first, Mark stood next to himself; one Mark had a scarred face, the other did not. Behind the two Mark's stood two women of different heights and physiques that were only seen as silhouettes in the twisted woods. In the last illustration, the stone in the clearing had somehow grown larger and both Marks were screwing the women, now clearly seen in the clearing's light. The Scarred Mark was joined with Cassie Monroe, the smooth featured Mark was joined with Jennifer Howell. A very careful study of the stone's shape might have revealed the profiled face of Joseph Howell screaming. An even closer study would have probably revealed the rest of Joseph Howell's body, outlined in the stone as it seemed to merge with the stone.

8

Tony, Tyler, and Lisa all spent the night in the same room at the Clinic. Lisa because she was still under observation, Tony just in case there was something more serious than a broken nose and a few bruised ribs and Tyler because he was too tired for the walk home and his parents were both asleep by now. Tony had long since fallen asleep; the tortures his body had been put through demanded rest. Lisa and Tyler sat on her bed together, holding hands and normally saying nothing at all.

It was after a particularly long silence that Lisa whispered her desperate question to Tyler. "Tyler? What happened to me?"

Tyler did his best to feign ignorance. "What do you mean? You got hit by a drunk driver."

Lisa shook her head, fear adding extra moisture to her eyes. "Don't be an asshole, Tyler. Car accidents don't make you pregnant." She studied his face while he did his best to hide what had happened. "Tyler, I want to know what happened. I can't even remember where I was going, but I think I was on my way to see you. Please, tell me?"

Tyler looked away from her, afraid of seeing her face, afraid of telling her even a part of the truth. She placed her hand on his cheek and gently forced him to look at her. "I can't tell you, Lisa. I just can't." He was only whispering, still he heard his voice break and hated himself for the sign of weakness.

Lisa did the one thing certain to break his resolve, she started to cry. The tears were silent and he knew that she wasn't forcing crocodile tears to ensure his cooperation, but the effect was still the same. They held each other tightly for several minutes and then he told her. He left out that the rapist had looked exactly like Mark, he left out all that the rapist had supposedly done to her. He held her when she cried again, and this time he joined her.

They talked long into the night, in fact they were still talking when the sun rose past the mountain tops surrounding Summitville and into the early morning sky.

Around eight thirty, Lisa fell asleep. Tyler moved carefully off of the bed so as not to disturb her slumber and sat in the one chair assigned for visitors. He thought long and hard about what they had discussed, her pregnancy. Lisa had decided to get an abortion. The A-word. Tyler agreed with her, but he knew her father would go through the roof when he heard about it. Oh, her mom would understand, but her dad was going to blow a gasket the second the dreaded A-word was mentioned.

Tyler didn't care what the bastard thought about it; it wasn't his body that would be growing a rapist's unwanted child. He wasn't the one that would have to go to school wearing maternity dresses. Lisa had developed a reputation as a tease a long time ago and even the best of behavior for her last two years of school wouldn't make a damn bit of difference in the long run. The assholes in town would still run around saying that she had only gotten what she deserved. It was one thing to keep a rape quiet when school was out and everyone thought she was just in the hospital for a car accident, but it would be quite another to keep the voices down in another couple of months. Pregnancies just weren't meant to hide on someone as hippy as Lisa: she had what his father affectionately called "birthing hips." As soon as she started showing at all, her trim figure would balloon below the waistline. There was no way in hell she'd be able to hide the fact that she was knocked up. Lisa had had more than her share of grief for one lifetime in the last few hours, let alone in the last month: Tyler would be damned before he'd let her flabby-assed bastard of a father force her to carry an unwanted child.

If he had to, he'd bite the old fart's nuts off to make his point known.

9

The confrontation came a little over two hours later, when Doctor Lewis made the call to Lisa's mom and told her about the consent forms that would need to be filled out. Lisa's mom didn't get along all that well with her husband, that was a fact known far and wide in town. But she wasn't nasty enough not to let her husband in on a decision of that size. The man turned his big ol' Cadillac around just as soon as he had hung up the cellular phone and he broke every speed limit set in the state of Colorado getting to the clinic.

Tyler was ready for him when he tried to force his way into Lisa's room for a screaming match. If the man had looked even remotely rational, Tyler would have left him alone; but the purple color of the man's face told him that the only reason he was here was to explode all over his wife and his youngest daughter about how immoral the idea of abortion was and to probably call the both of them sluts. No doubt the man was certain his daughter would be condemned to Hell as the result of an abortion. He probably thought that calling her names was a good way of expressing his beliefs and conveying the urgency of the matter as regarded her immortal Soul. Tyler was having none of it.

Tyler Wilson, a boy known for using the English weapon as a scalpel in an effort to injure as many people as possible that offended him, stopped the man with twenty-one softly spoken and mostly polite words. "If you go in there and threaten Lisa or call her any names at all, Mister Scarrabelli, I'll kill you. Sir."

Rafael Scarrabelli was a very large man, standing just at six feet tall and weighing in somewhere around two hundred and fifty pounds. He had the kind of build that spoke of sports in his youth and too much relaxation later; he was pudgy, but there was a great deal of muscle hidden under the excess flesh. In addition, Rafael Scarrabelli was a man who was used to brow-beating his employees and his family into submission with remarkably little difficulty—he often used bribes to get his way with the family, but only because it was easier. Nobody in their right mind took on Anthony Scarrabelli: one way or another, he always won.

He took one look at the skinny young man in front of him and stopped cold in his tracks. He looked at the door behind the young man and got ready to move forward. He wouldn't mind plowing through the little runt if necessary. He looked down at the boy and then at the figure behind the boy and stopped again.

Rafael knew every face in town. If anyone had lived in Summitville for more than a week, he knew them. The man with the feral smile was no one he had ever seen before. He never said a word, that man with the smile, but his eyes spoke for him just the same. His eyes said that Rafael Scarrabelli really should listen closely to what the boy had just said, because the smiling man would back the words himself, if need be. His eyes said that no amount of money would stop either the boy or the man behind him from coming at him with every means available to stop him.

The boy's stance said he meant business, his grim posture made clear that he meant every word he'd said. That was a nasty thought in and of itself. The casual way in which the man behind him leaned against the walls with his hands in his pockets, smiling that unsettling smile, said that the man would do much more than the boy had promised. He wouldn't just kill Rafael, he'd make Rafael wish to be killed.

Rafael was drawn back to Tyler's face as the boy started talking; explaining that he and Lisa had spent the night discussing all of the options and just how much humiliation Lisa would go through. In his own way, the boy made sense. Despite himself, Rafael Scarrabelli calmed down. He listened to what the boy said and in the end he found himself agreeing with him.

In the long run, it was Tyler's mouth, that weapon most often used to do harm, that helped Rafael Scarrabelli see a little reason instead of hellfire. When he finally sat down in the waiting room with Tyler, he noticed that the Man with the Feral Grin was gone. He found himself wondering if the man had ever been there at all. Tyler Wilson hadn't seemed to notice him.

He and Tyler talked for over an hour, mostly about Lisa and how Tyler felt for her. By the end of the conversation, they had all but become friends. At first Rafael didn't really like the kid much, but he came to respect him. They went in to visit Lisa together. Anthony drove off for a few minutes beforehand and came back with two bouquets of flowers. He told Tyler that he would expect to be paid back for the roses and even gave Tyler the receipt.

Tyler agreed and gave the roses to Lisa. Rafael Scarrabelli gave her the carnations. Lisa seemed to love both bouquets equally.

Later, after her folks had left and Tony had checked out, she cried long and hard, wondering if she had made the right decision. Tyler did his best to console her, hugging when she needed a hug, giving her space when she needed to be left alone.

If he seemed a little preoccupied, it was because she had waited until her family was gone and they were alone before crying. She never said the words that day, but in his eyes that proved the love he had grown to feel for Lisa was returned.

10

While Tyler was finally beginning to grasp the depth of his and Lisa's mutual affections, his older brother Patrick was having a revelation of his own. Dave Brundvandt meant to kill him.

Dave had come up to the house a little after noon and had apparently decided that the time for formalities was over. This time, he had brought a baseball bat along for reasons that Patrick just didn't want to think about. Dave didn't bother knocking, he reached for the door handle and stepped inside as if he belonged there. If Patrick had not been stepping out of the shower at the time, he would never have noticed. Most of his time in the house was spent absorbed in a movie or some other distraction, but with the bathroom window situated above the front door, he had but to look outside and see Brundvandt.

The problem, as Patrick saw it, was that he had to get the hell away from the house and somehow get to the sheriff, without encountering Dave in the process. This presented a number of problems, not the least of which was Patrick's own lack of clothing at the moment. Patrick slipped from the bathroom into his own room as carefully as he could. He had only the knowledge of which parts of the floor squeaked when stepped upon to aid him in his quest. Safely in his room, Patrick slipped on yesterday's shorts and pulled his tennis shoes in place after locking the door.

In the hallway, he heard the rickety squeal of the floorboard outside his room taking extra weight. The doorknob tried to turn at the same time that Patrick was kicking the screen off of his window.

From behind the locked door, he heard Dave's mild tones. "Patrick? You in there? Hello?"

Discretion stopped his tongue from making a snide comment and he slipped through his window, pushing the sliding
glass frame in place after him. Patrick had been slipping out
of the house for years and took full advantage of the tree that
grew in the front yard to make his get away again. This time,
however, he was not so lucky as to go unnoticed. Dave
Brundvandt came out the window just as he was reaching the
lawn below.

Patrick started for his car before remembering that his keys
were on the dresser where he always left them. He turned the
corner of the house running as fast as he could, spotting Dave's
two-point landing in the grass as he did. Dave looked remarkably calm, and that scared Patrick all the more; only lunatics
like Jason Voorhees and Michael Myers stayed calm when
wielding implements of destruction.

The way Patrick saw it, his only hope lay in the woods.
He truly wished he could think of something else; the woods
had stopped being friendly in his eyes the same night he
had his chemical nightmare about Mark munching on
Tommy Blake, instead of the usual late night snack. What
the hell else could he do? The Summitville Baseball Mas-
sacre was about to take place if he stopped now. He heard
Dave closing on him, the footsteps sounding louder and
quicker by the second. Adrenaline does wonderful things
to terrified muscles—he poured on some extra speed. The
woods were right in front of him.

Patrick didn't have time to focus on Dave any longer, he
was busy dodging trees left and right. The woods had never
seemed quite so full of the large wooden obstacles in the past.
Patrick zigzagged randomly. He'd been in these woods for
most of his life and had no fear of getting lost. He knew he
was gaining the distance he needed and risked a look back.

Dave was nowhere to be seen. That wasn't necessarily a
good thing...for all he knew Dave was right behind him even
now. Patrick looked around, trying to orient himself in the
shade of the trees. Nothing looked familiar.

Patrick refused to accept that; he knew these woods like the back of his hand, had spent almost as much time unconsciously studying them as he had the hairs on the back of that hand. The woods he was standing in were not the same woods he had grown up with. But they had to be, he hadn't run all that far.

Off to his left he heard the sound of a thick twig breaking. He turned to look and that direction and there stood Dave Brundvandt. Shit, Dave had spotted him.

"Dave, let's talk about this, okay?"

"I tried to talk about this before, you didn't want to."

"Dave, I really don't want you hitting me with that thing. C'mon, put it down okay? A joke's a joke, but this ain't even funny."

Brundvandt plodded forward, stepping over roots and branches that Patrick wished would leap up and trip him. "I'm not laughing, Patrick, I'm gonna bust you up." Patrick felt his knees start knocking. Without the running, the adrenaline was simply making his whole body jumpy. "You shouldn't have told me to fuck off, Patrick. Now you went and made me mad."

Not quite as dynamic as the guys in the comic books, but the point came across just as well from Patrick's point of view. Patrick started running again.

Before he'd gone more than a hundred yards, Patrick broke into an unexpected clearing. Cursing his luck he tried to bolt to the left. Dave Brundvandt was already there somehow and slapped the baseball bat into Patrick's right arm, which flared hot for a second and then grew numb. Patrick grunted and stumbled backwards, managing to keep his feet.

There was a huge slab of rock in the center of the clearing, almost as if the trees that surrounded the rock refused to get any closer than they had to. Patrick's mind realized that the boulder had use as a potential shield against Dave's bludgeon and ran as quickly as he could to the other side, cradling his battered arm in his free hand.

Dave was smarter than Patrick would have honestly given him credit for. Instead of going around the boulder, he scampered to the top of the rock. He looked down on Patrick from a good four feet off of the ground and lifted the bat above his head like a lumberjack preparing to chop into wood.

Golden opportunities come too seldom in life to pass them by; Patrick jumped about two feet up and planted his fist right in the center of Dave's scrotum. Dave dropped the bat, dropped to his knees and fell off of the rock, in about three seconds flat. He rolled on the ground with both hands trying to comfort his battered privates, while Patrick went for the baseball bat.

Blood colored light filtered in to take the natural colors away from the woods. Looking at Dave Brundvandt on the ground left Patrick as unaffected as if he was looking at a fly caught in a spider's web. Dave struggled feebly, trying to stand up through his pain. Patrick calmly kicked him in the side of the head for his troubles.

Dave had been terrorizing Patrick for over three weeks now and enough was enough. Patrick hefted the baseball bat in his left hand, shifting his grip so that the bat could be managed with only his good arm. He didn't say anything and in that moment he might have been surprised by how expressionless his face had become. Like Dave's, or Michael Myers', or Jason Voorhees'.

Dave tried to beg. Patrick was having none of it. The beating went on for almost fifteen minutes, the screaming had stopped after about three. The wet breathing sounds continued until the very end.

Heaving the bloodied bat into the woods, Patrick went home. There was so much to do…Dave's car had to be gone by the time his parents both got to the house. Patrick thanked God for the luck of having two working parents.

By the time Patrick managed to get the car in motion, the sun was starting a slow crawl towards the western horizon. The chase and fight had taken a lot longer than Patrick had

realized, it was after two in the afternoon by the time he managed to fire the engine in Dave Brundvandt's car. Somehow
he knew that Dave wouldn't mind. Patrick had learned how
to hotwire cars from one of P. J. Sanderson's books; he was
grateful for the man's diligence in research. The only real problem was that the book had made it all seem so much easier
than it was in real life.

It was a bumpy trip over paths that were not meant to be
traveled by car, but an hour later, he drove Dave's hot-wired
car into the waters of Lake Overtree. The odds were against
anyone seeing the tracks. The woods were normally deserted,
and few people bothered to walk in that area. Even if they
did, he was fairly certain the tracks would mean nothing to
anyone not actively looking for them. By four o'clock in the
afternoon he was making himself a late lunch of Beenie
Weenies and Cheetos. The shower's hot water faded from his
body, replaced by the almost painful cold of water that was
not given a chance to heat, before Patrick felt clean again.
Even that did not stop a ravenous hunger from building in his
body. Beenie Weenies and Cheetos, them's goood eatin'!

Dave had screamed just like a girl as the old baseball
bat cracked bones in his body. Somehow, that made it all
seem okay.

Chapter Seventeen

1

Word of the Brundvandt boy's disappearance didn't really surprise very many people; it was almost expected from the Brundvandt brood. The parents were notorious for their drunken fits of rage and more than one of Dave Brundvandt's older siblings had taken to flight as a good way to avoid the regular beatings at the Brundvandt homestead.

Word of Chuck Hanson's disappearance was different in effect; the adults in Summitville stopped being as friendly and open as they normally were. Nobody could have said that Hanson was the best sheriff ever, but he was better than nothing at all. Without his normal appearance on the streets, nobody really felt that they could trust their neighbors any longer. It was a sad turn of events in the paranoid little town. The summer was almost over and for the first time in a long while, children didn't dare moan and groan about having to go back to school. They were afraid of gathering their parents' attention.

Everyone wanted to make the most of the last week. Lisa and Tyler were no exceptions. Mostly, they wanted to spend time together, get to know each other all over again. It was a little awkward at first. Lisa was certain that the knowledge of her having been raped, even if she couldn't honestly remember the incident, would make her less attractive to Tyler. Tyler was quick to prove her wrong; he doted on her every move just as much as he had before the incident had occurred.

It was on Wednesday, that last week before school started again, that the couple got together with Mark and Cassie for a picnic on the shore of Overtree. The day would have been perfect, save for the continuing strange looks that Tyler threw at Mark when he was certain his friend wasn't looking. Mark did notice, but he did his best to ignore the look. It seemed almost like a mixture of curiosity, hatred, and fear. That was nonsense, of course, but Mark couldn't help noticing. He made a mental note to have a chat with Tyler later; no sense in ruining the fun for everyone involved, was there?

Even the looks seemed to fade after about a half an hour, but they came back with a vengeance when Mark brought up the name of Jonathan Crowley. Tyler was surprised to hear that they had met and even more surprised to hear that Mark thought he was a great guy. Crowley had been by only the night before, to tell Mark how much he had enjoyed the manuscript that Mark had given to him. Tyler was fairly convinced that he was hearing things. He resolved to meet up with Crowley as soon as possible; something here was decidedly rotten in Summitville and he suspected that the rot came from Crowley.

For Lisa and Cassie's part, they talked about everything. The guys talked with them, but for some reason there seemed to be messages going around to which the guys were not privy. In later years, they might have gained the wisdom to understand the language that the girls were speaking, but they were not nearly experienced enough at that time.

It was later in the afternoon, after they had finished eating the huge amounts of food that Tyler had prepared—all of it edible and surely nutritious, but about as tasty as chalk—when they got down to serious talk.

Cassie started it off by talking about the book she and Mark were working on together. "I think it'll work out pretty well and maybe we'll even become a regular writing team, if Dopey over here ever manages to wake up before noon." She smiled and squeezed his hand to take the sting out of her words. Her smile managed to bring a quick grin to Mark's own face and they both made goo-goo eyes until Lisa interrupted.

"Are you sure that's what you want to do with your lives? I mean, I feel like I'm behind the times here. I haven't even decided what courses to take for electives this year, let alone where I want to be when I'm thirty."

Tyler came back immediately with a patented Tyler remark. "Where else: barefoot and pregnant, cleaning the kitchen floor while I watch football on ESPN." It was a touch too soon after the abortion for that kind of comment and Tyler realized it as soon as the words were out of his mouth. Before he could think of a way to take the comment back, Mark intervened.

"Got that wrong again, Tyler. Lisa'll be watching the movies based on Cassie an' me's books. You'll be scrubbing the floor." Tyler was so grateful for the save, he barely felt the hard elbow Cassie practically drove through his chest.

Lisa managed to force a smile, accepting the apology in Tyler's eyes. After that, the conversation started to lag. Mark was having none of it and decided it was time for everyone to go swimming. He volunteered Tyler to be first, effortlessly tossing him the five feet it took to land him in the lake.

Tyler came up gasping for air and Mark and he both laughed about it. For some reason, the girls weren't laughing. Lisa was the one that hit the mystery question on the nose. "When the hell did you become Superman, Mark?"

Mark looked perplexed, but the implications hit Tyler instantly. Mark was sitting Indian style on the ground, yet he had reached over and tossed him a good five or six feet through the air. He wasn't a very heavy guy by anyone's standards, but nobody he had ever known could have tossed him that far with that much ease.

Mark looked around at everyone for a few seconds before the full impact of what he had done sank in. Lisa and Tyler both looked scared, Cassie probably would have too, but she knew him better and for some reason that seemed to take the sting out of what she had just seen. Mark seriously doubted that even Tony could have made that kind of throw.

That seemed to take all the fun out of the day, within half an hour everyone was on their way home. Except for Mark.

After seeing Cassie to the door and giving her a quick goodbye peck on the lips, he wandered off into the woods. He needed to think and he always did his best thinking in his special place.

2

Jonathan Crowley had watched the entire picnic, busying himself with a pocket knife and a good piece of whittling wood. He cut the soft pad of his thumb open when he saw Mark toss Tyler. Hissing back a curse, he closed the knife and watched the reactions of the people with the Howell boy. Tyler looked scared, Lisa looked nervous and appreciative of the raw strength such an effort took. Cassie looked excited. In Crowley's opinion things had gone on more than long enough. He slipped the wooden carving into his shirt pocket and started following Mark Howell.

Crowley watched as Mark kissed his lady love goodbye and slipped into the shadows until Mark had again entered the woods. He followed at a fair distance, enough to ensure that Mark didn't catch a glimpse from his periphery and watched until the boy hit the clearing. Crowley stopped at the spot in the woods where the trees changed; something in the woods was warping the very nature of the greenery, making the entire area seem less real, more menacing. His view was good enough to allow him to track Mark Howell with his eyes.

At first the boy sat alone on the rock, then, tentatively, the Folk made their presence known. The boy smiled broadly as the creatures came to him. They were tiny smudges of shadow from where Crowley stood; he knew the boy was seeing Them in an entirely different light. Then Howell was enchanted by Them, laughing with Them and allowing Them to crawl all over him like a seething mass of tarantulas. Crowley watched the way that the beings caressed him, stroking his skin in awe, as if he were made of expensive silks rather than human flesh.

After perhaps twenty minutes of remaining completely motionless, Crowley was rewarded for his patience. The boy closed his eyes and fell into an unnatural slumber as the tiny creatures covered his body entirely. Slowly, with incredibly light touches, he saw the creatures reach into Mark Howell's body with Their hands and actually start moving about under his skin.

They continued their manipulations for well over an hour, touching different portions of his body and seemingly wading through his flesh as if it were made of water. When They had finished, They faded into the woods around the clearing; some hid in the trees, some scurried under leaves seemingly too small to conceal them. In a matter of less than a minute They had disappeared from sight.

Still Crowley watched without moving, ignoring every painful protest of his body. In another five minutes, the boy stood up and walked away from the clearing, looking for all the world like a healthy, happy, teenager on his way to adulthood. Crowley knew better now. The boy was being changed into something that should not, could not be permitted to exist.

He followed Mark Howell all the way to his home, watching as he entered through the front door. The hatred he felt for the little creatures was increased with every step he took. He liked Mark Howell, liked his mother and his stepfather. He knew he had to end the troubles now, provided it wasn't well past the point of no return.

He'd never seen the Folk take so long just to make minor adjustments. If he was right, They knew he was here. That would make Them dangerous. If he was lucky, it would also make Them careless. One way or another, the Folk and Their Changeling would be no more by morning.

3

It was dinnertime in Summitville. Loosely translated that meant that most of the people that lived in town were at the diner or at the Chinese restaurant, or at home, eating their suppers. Most of the town ate around six-thirty at night, allowing just enough time for the commute from Denver and Boulder with a few minutes left over to relax beforehand. P. J. Sanderson was not eating like most of the town, but then he was hardly a normal resident. P. J. was instead gathering together his supplies for a last chance at redemption.

He could remember even after all of these years, the approximate location of the Stone in the woods near Overtree. It was the Stone that had caused all of the troubles in town and he, along with Alex, had been the one to cause the Stone's awakening. To P. J.'s way of thinking, that made him responsible for eliminating the accursed thing.

Everything he needed was in his suitcase: a flashlight, a thermos of coffee in case he got hopelessly lost and needed the caffeine rush, and four homemade Molotov cocktails. In this case, the homemade bombs were loaded with pebbles, nails and other debris. With any luck, they'd explode and blow his target into fragments. If not, maybe the fire would do the job. He'd have preferred dynamite, but it wasn't exactly easy to get the stuff, and these would have to do the trick. As an extra precaution, he carried a pack of three Bic lighters in their unopened package in his jacket. He stepped out of the Basilisk's front door and proceeded towards his car.

After a moment of nervous fumbling, he pulled the car keys from inside his jacket and unlocked the door. He tossed the bag towards the passenger side without thinking about the four bottles of gasoline that were nestled within. Fortunately, Jonathan Crowley was there to catch the bag.

"Hello, Phillip. I'm so glad you didn't disappoint me."

P. J. grabbed at his chest, willing his heart to start beating again as he backpedaled away from the driver's side door. "Jesus Christ! What the hell are you doing here!"

Crowley grinned. "Waiting for you, Phil. And please, there's no reason to scream. I thought you might like a little help on your hunting trip."

"What the hell do you know about it? You never make mistakes, you never do anything wrong. Leave me alone, you bastard."

Crowley made a show of looking wounded. "Phil, you cut me to the quick. I want to help and you're going to deny me?"

P. J. practically snarled his reply. "You're goddamned right I'm going to deny you! Get the hell out of my car! *Now!*"

Crowley chuckled at the rage on the author's face and slid smoothly out of the passenger door. Somehow he managed to shake his head good-naturedly at the same time that he was staring P. J. in the face. "Ah, Phillip. That's the spirit I like to see. It's misdirected, mind you, but that's the fire I always knew you had in there somewhere. Sure you won't change your mind about the company? I'll even promise not to get in the way."

"Fuck you, Crowley."

"Heh. Have it your way. See ya around." Crowley turned sharply on his heel and walked towards town. P. J. almost managed to convince himself that he was happy to see him go. He finished the climb into the car and started the engine.

He drove carefully, wanting more than at any time in his life to avoid even a fender bender. He might have written about homemade bombs that didn't explode on contact, but that didn't mean he trusted the ones he had made. No ego here, thanks just the same.

Ten minutes later he pulled into the parking lot of the Charles S. Westphalen High School and killed the motor. He double checked everything in the bag, pausing long enough to wonder if he could dodge all of the bits of metal and leftover nail heads he had added to the Molotovs, before he got out of the car.

P. J. Sanderson stared in awe at the sight of Jonathan Crowley waiting for him. The man was looking quite relaxed and casual, except for that damnable grin on his face. "Hi, Philly! What the hell took you so long?"

4

Rick Lewis sat in his office at the clinic, mind going over everything that had occurred in the last year; no matter how hard he tried, he could not get the pieces to add up properly. The dreams he had started having about Mark Howell scared him almost as much as the deaths that had haunted him since Tanya Billingsley's body had been found.

Now, as the true topper of everything else, Chuck Har son was gone. Chuck had many flaws in Rick's eyes, but cowardice wasn't one of them. There was no way in hell that Chuck would have left voluntarily. He didn't have it in him.

Rick was a different case, he was giving serious thought to packing his bags and getting out of Summitville as quickly as possible. The town held nothing for him, not even pleasant memories of past relationships. The only reason he had stayed here at all was so that he could spend extra hours on his research and all that had gotten him recently was a severe headache when he thought about the stuff he affectionately called 'goop'.

That was another problem with this town; the little scab in the mountains was haunted. Rick wasn't fond of thinking along those lines, but by God if Chuck Hanson said he'd seen a ghost then Rick believed him. Chuck didn't have the imagination for ghosts, and spooky stuff did not keep in line with the type of tall tales Rick had heard the man tell in the past.

Rick sipped at his decaf and sighed. Getting out of town sounded better every day. Every hour. There was only one thing that stopped him from leaving right this very minute: the clinic. Summitville wasn't exactly brimming over with doctors, there was Rick himself and the Posten brothers and three General Practitioners, who were effectively useless, taking care of the town. Tim and Jack were great guys, but they were only paramedics. Neither of them really had the drive to be doctors and even a town of only fifteen hundred needed at least one full-time doctor.

Obligations and considerations were the only things keeping Rick in town. He was rapidly learning to hate his morals. Other doctors got to make money on the side writing unnecessary prescriptions and charging an extra rate on people who had really good insurance. Not him, no sir that wouldn't be right. Other doctors had lives in the places where they lived; girlfriends, wives, sometimes both. The only romantic consideration Rick had experienced while in Summitville had been Jackie and she had left earlier today with her pipe smoking beau. As if he'd ever have a chance with even a homely girl in a town as anal retentive as this one. Shit, you practically had to show your pedigree to the people in this town to get them to smile.

So why the hell did he stay? Why would anyone in their right mind stay in a place that resented his or her existence? Just to please a roommate from college? Out of a sense of moral obligation? Nobody in their right mind would. Unless that somebody was as big a moron as he was. Pouring himself another cup of decaf, Rick settled back behind his desk to sort over all the writings on the last year's death toll. Hell, Chuck was gone, and half of the remaining police force in the little town was out trying to find any clues as to where he would have disappeared. As it was, there were already several volunteers out scratching around in the woods, searching for any sign of the sheriff. That left Rick, and *somebody* had to figure out what was going on in town.

5

P. J. looked over at his unwanted assistant and decided he could no longer take the silence between them. Just for the sake of conversation, he asked him what he thought they should do when they found the Stone. As soon as Crowley opened his mouth, P. J. Sanderson regretted his question; Crowley's response was as snide as the author had expected. "What makes you so sure the Stone has anything to do with what's going on,

Philly? Maybe the Stone is just a coincidence. Maybe it's not the same stone you used at all."

"You don't believe that anymore than I do."

"True," the impossibly younger man responded. "I just want to understand your reasoning."

"It's the only possible answer, Crowley. Nothing else even begins to make sense. Not unless my nephew had something to do with the book and I know him better than that. He's read too many of my stories to screw with anything that powerful. Back to my question, what should we do about it?"

Crowley looked back at him and shrugged. "Destroying the damned thing would be a good start."

"How do you propose we do that? I don't recall there being a guide to destroying magical stones anywhere in that book of yours."

Crowley stiffened slightly at that. "It's not my book." The words were very slow, deliberate. "It's your book."

"Well, it *was* my book. It's in your possession now and I personally want nothing more to do with it. Call it a gift from an admirer." The sarcasm-laced comment simply brought another smile to Crowley's plain face.

"My, my, my," Crowley crooned. "Giving up on those childhood memories so easily?"

"Kiss my ass. If I knew then what I know now, I'd have burned the book a long time ago." P. J. glared at his companion.

"Mmmm. No doubt. Pity you didn't know then, hunh? Maybe you wouldn't be trying to avenge your honor with the man you think has done so much to besmirch it."

"I don't recall asking you along for the ride."

"Somebody has to make sure you do it right."

Silence welled between them, P. J. found himself wondering why he even tried. The self-righteous bastard next to him cared nothing about anything save himself. That and maybe the continued humiliation of P. J.

Up ahead of them the trees were denser, drawn together in an almost solid wall. Crowley took the lead very abruptly and pushed off to the left. P. J. stared at the man's back, wishing that he had a gun. No, with the way things had been going he'd only wing Crowley and that would likely piss the man off.

P. J. shivered visibly at the thought. He'd never actually seen Crowley angry and hoped to avoid it as long as possible. Forever would be a good starting place. Up ahead of him, Crowley turned and smiled. He pointed towards a break between two of the malformed red oaks that blended into the formidable wall then he brought one finger to his lips in a gesture that suggested silence.

P. J. joined him and stared into the clearing. His eyes refused to accept what he saw there. The stone, almost certainly the one at which he and his friends had cast their "mock magic spell" all those years ago if his faded memories were right about the lay of the land, thrust out of the ground and pointed to the crescent moon far above. It towered a full seven feet above the fertile soil.

The look on Jonathan Crowley's face was challenging, daring him to destroy the monolithic rock. P. J. nodded grimly and opened his battered overnight bag, reaching for a Molotov cocktail.

6

Mark lay in his bed, tossing fitfully while locked in the throes of a feverish dream. One second he was with Cassie, laughing or making tender love, the next second he was atop Lisa, pounding mercilessly at her. A second later the dream would repeat with Cassie and Lisa's roles reversed and again it would rush through his brain in the original order. Throughout the dreams he could hear the whisper-voices of his special friends calling for him to decide, to make a choice between the two girls.

Then the dream warped and changed into the distant memories of Tony and the Asshole Patrol beating him into the ground; behind them, Jonathan Crowley and P. J. Sanderson looked on, laughing at Mark's pain, then joining the younger men in the fun. Joe was there too, calling him a little pansy and telling him to fight like a man.

Everything went all crazy and instead of him being beaten on, he was being held in place by Tony and his goons while Crowley and P. J. stomped on his beautiful little friends in Their special place. His special place. He could see Their delicate bodies breaking like spun glass, leaking crimson stains into the carpet of grass. Crowley and P. J. were grinding Them into the ground, laughing at the sight of their helpless victims' death throes.

Mark Howell sat up in his bed, eyes narrowed into gashes of unbridled rage. From his throat came a sound half whimper and half scream. He didn't bother with clothes, he stepped from his room and headed for the front door. His friends were in trouble. That was all that mattered.

7

From her vantage point in the hallway, Jenny watched and smiled. Only a short time longer and everything would be like it was supposed to be. Mark was going to the woods, soon the whole family would be together again. She knew the time was almost here, Todd kept telling her so in her dreams, telling her that soon, he would be coming for her.

Just like right after he left, when he told her to care for the baby, promising that he would be with her again someday, the dreams were too vivid to only be dreams. Somehow he was contacting her.

He'd watched over her for a long time, waiting until the time was right for them to be together again. He'd told her so. He knew every place where she had lived, every thought that ran through her mind. He understood about why Joe had been important to her and he forgave her her indiscretions.

There was only one thing that he urged her to take care of, only one obstacle between them being together forever. Joe.

Joe wouldn't understand the way things were. He wouldn't see why she had spent so much time quietly urging him to go for the better job from town to town. Joe had already almost ruined everything with his wanting to move to New York, where he claimed the money was better and they could have an even bigger home, an even better life together than the one they were having now.

Poor Joe, there was a lot he just didn't understand. She supposed she might miss him from time to time, but that wouldn't stop her from killing him. Anything to be with Todd.

She quietly worked her way down the stairs, towards the kitchen. Her biggest problem right then was trying to decide if a knife was the best way to kill her husband.

8

Tyler felt the sick dread of déjà vu as he watched Mark heading deliberately towards the woods. Of course, the last time he'd seen Mark doing this, he had been with Cassie and he had been wearing clothes. Tyler had a very bad feeling about what was happening. No real forethought went into his getting dressed. Jeans, T-shirt, Reeboks; that pretty much covered everything. Tyler didn't even worry about being quiet. He just took off out the back door in the kitchen.

It took him a second to find Mark, but when he did he called out immediately. None of that bullshit about not waking sleepwalkers, too much stuff could happen to Mark out in the woods at night. Mark gave no sense of having heard him.

Tyler ran as quickly as he could to his friend's side. Mark did not bother to acknowledge him. He just kept walking. "Yo, Howie, wake up guy." Nothing. "Hey Mark! Mark! Earth to Mark, come in Mark!" Still no response from the walking dead. Not good.

Desperate times called for stupid actions; Tyler tripped him. Mark landed on his face and got right back up, intent on what was ahead of him. He paid Tyler no mind whatsoever.

If there was one thing Tyler hated in the world, it was being ignored. He waited for Mark to get past him again, watched the machine-like motion of his friend's legs—doing his best to ignore the third leg swinging like a metronome—and tackled him at the knees. Physics demanded that Mark go down, it also demanded that he land unceremoniously on top of Tyler. Tyler prayed mightily to any gods that might be up there, that absolutely no one on the planet with a camera was in sight of the tangled mass the two of them made.

Whatever Mark's problem was, it apparently stopped him from being able to use common sense. He got back up again. Tyler hooked his foot around the larger boy's ankle and sent him sprawling a third time.

It took seven more tries before Mark started to come out of his daze. By that time, Mark was covered in mulch and the muddied remains of the early morning's dew.

He didn't want to, he really did not want to, but the stupid look on Mark's face, compounded by Mark's realization that he was butt naked in the woods, sent Tyler into a laughing fit. He loaned Mark his t-shirt, for all the protection it provided, and the two of them went on their way back to the Red Oaks subdivision. Mark forced a promise of silence out of Tyler. Still chuckling, Tyler agreed, but only after threatening to tell Cassie.

9

Jennifer Howell had the knife in her hand and was halfway up the stairs by the time that Todd's voice called out to her. "No, Jenny. Not just yet. It's going to take me a little longer than I thought. Kill him tomorrow night. By then it will be too late."

Jenny slipped the knife back into its holder, drank a glass of water and crawled back into bed with her husband. Joe stirred and awoke. To avoid any foolish questions, she kissed him hard on the mouth. Then she followed through with what he was obviously expecting after such a kiss, reminding herself that it would be the last time. For memory's sake, she made it count.

10

Crowley watched from the sidelines as P. J. Sanderson made his attempts with the Molotov cocktails. He watched the man carefully set the bottles out and then just as carefully unwrap the package of lighters he had purchased especially for this night. He nodded enthusiastically as the writer cautioned him to step back and then lit the fuses. He shook his head sadly as the homemade bombs shattered across the stone's surface without catching the stone afire.

Crowley managed to keep his laughter down, the Folk did not. The Folk had expected the Hunter to do something dangerous and had almost destroyed the Chosen One in the process. Against a normal man They had no reason to endanger Mark Howell, against The Hunter it would have been necessary in order to preserve Themselves. The laughter of the Folk, sounding so much like the wind through the trees, was as much out of the need for catharsis as it was out of sheer amusement at the author's folly.

Contrary to popular legend in Summitville, Albert "Stoney" Miles had not set the fire that destroyed Summit Town so long ago by accident. He had meant to destroy what he had called forth. He never dreamed that They would have Their own reasons for wanting to be summoned, or that They might not do as he requested of Them. This time They believed Themselves ready; this time They had fire-proofed the woods.

They called the Chosen out of his dream and They called the Chosen's mother from her cold murderous rage. If all went as planned, They could be ready tomorrow. Until then, the Chosen needed his rest and the Chosen's mother still had her uses. They watched and waited. "Soon," They whispered. "Tomorrow," They promised.

11

Crowley was almost gentle as he led the confused man from the clearing. Sanderson simply could not comprehend what had happened. The man kept looking at him, begging with glazed eyes for an explanation of what had just happened. Crowley decided to have mercy on him.

"They adapt," he explained. "They've already been stopped with fire once. They won't let it happen again."

P. J. Sanderson opened and closed his mouth several times before finally making his voice work. "I-I thought it was just the Stone out there, who are 'They?'"

Crowley tried to work that out in his own mind, tried to explain in terms simple enough for the dazed man to grasp. It wasn't that Sanderson was stupid by any means; it was that he had just had his world shaken to its very foundations. One expects things to work in a certain way, one expects burning gasoline to burn as certainly as one expects the sun to come up every morning. Burning gasoline in a compressed space would, one expects, explode with a decent amount of force. He could sympathize with the man's problem, he'd suffered the same disillusionment some time ago. "They're whatever Mark has made them. I believe that They are the Fair Folk; Goblins, Elves, Faeries, Bogey Men, call Them what you want. But this is a different country, one where the rules don't apply the same way they did in Ireland and the rest of the British Isles." He looked at the writer's face, waiting for him to soak those phrases in before he continued. "Don't hold me to that, I don't know what the hell They are. That's just a guess."

"I don't know much about Them at all, except for what Stoney Miles wrote in his journal. Frankly, the man babbled too much for me to even trust that very much. I looked over that entire book, Phil and you want to know a secret? Not a single spell written in that journal was accurately reproduced. Whatever he managed to call forth that first time was probably something that just needed some kind invitation to get here. Truth is, I don't even think it takes a spell to let them through. I think it just takes the desire."

Sanderson looked at him for a few moments as they walked and then he looked at the ground. Crowley watched the man's jaw muscles clench and unclench a dozen times in conjunction with his fists balling and relaxing. He could have dodged the fist that came up and hit him in the side of his jaw. He could have stopped that fist about fifty different ways. He chose not to.

Sanderson stood over him with eyes intense in their rage. Crowley looked up from the ground with a smile on his face as the writer screamed. "You bastard! You've spent half of your time in Summitville berating me for what I did to Mark Howell; accusing me of every crime in the book and threatening me every time you looked me in the face. *Now* you say that I'm not even to blame?!" He kicked at Crowley, and this time Crowley blocked it. Then he yanked the author off of his feet and gathered his legs beneath him.

P. J. Sanderson lay on the ground, on the verge of tears for a good five minutes, while Crowley studied the woods without really paying them much attention.

Finally, from his position on the ground, Sanderson asked the question that Crowley was waiting to hear. "Why? How could you do that to a person? Goddamn you, how could you do a thing like that?"

Crowley helped him to his feet, dusting off the back of his jacket. As they started to walk again, with Crowley guiding the tear-blinded writer, Crowley finally answered his question. "I did it for a lot of reasons, Phil. I did it because you have an ego almost as big as mine and I'm jealous of my ego's size. I did it because once upon a time you *did* call something forth with a written spell and that something could have caused a lot of grief. I did it because you're the type that would eventually have called something else with one of your books, or maybe even worse, written the recipe down in one of your trashy novels."

Crowley stopped speaking until they were finally out of the woods, back where Sanderson had parked his car. When the man was seated and his seat belt was in place, Crowley finished his statement. "Mostly though, I did it because I said 'I think' you didn't call Them up with your little spells. I don't *know* that you didn't call Them up. In my eyes, even if it's only the intent that calls Them forth, one three year old boy has already paid the price for your little Halloween prank and one fifteen year old boy is in the process of paying that price." He looked the writer in the face, staring deeply into his eyes the entire time that he finished his explanation.

"Maybe it was your intent that called Them up, maybe it was your friend Alex's. Hell, maybe it was even his little brother Todd. I just don't know for certain. You should be glad of that Phil. Because if I did know for certain that it was you, I wouldn't just be ragging on you like I have been. I'd have killed you by now."

Jonathan Crowley smiled angelically at the man he'd tormented and terrified, both in life and in dreams, over the last twenty years. He patted the man on his shoulder, before sauntering off towards the street, calling over his shoulder as he went: "You think about that, Philly. Think really hard about it. Someday I might even find the proof I'm looking for and if that time comes…Well, then I won't let you have a free shot at my mug."

P. J. sat behind the wheel for the better part of an hour without turning on the car's engine. He ignored the cold that covered his body as he tried to decide who had called the creatures forth. When he finally started home, the answer was still lost to him.

12

In the woods outside of Summitville, lying just under the edge of Lake Overtree, a stone sat glistening in the early morning light. Around the stone there sat a gathering of dusky shadows. The shadows thought for a long time about the Hunter and about the Chosen One and his mother and his possible mates.

When the thinking was done, the shadows approached the Stone and reached through to its very core with Their thoughts. The smooth grass at their feet started to shake, rippling like the Overtree in a hurricane force wind, and then the ground erupted. From the minds of the shadows and the bones of two dead men, the Stone was urged to make its creations. Chuck Hanson's remains were used to create a Hunter for the shadows. Dave Brundvandts' battered corpse was infused with a new life as well, as a number of the shadows possessed a real body for the second time in their existence. Dave's body was remolded and repainted by the power of the Stone. When it had been filled by the shadows, Todd Harris stood looking down at the remaining shadows and smiled. Todd had been dead for sometime now and he had to admit it felt good to be back.

Chuck Hanson strode casually out of the woods, his memories intact and his perceptions perverted. He was glad to be alive again too. He had been afraid of Jonathan Crowley, now he knew better. Crowley was just a man.

Crowley might be a tough cookie when it came to dealing with the Folk and other creatures of that type, but a good old fashioned pistol would take him down in a heartbeat. He fired a cigarette after scraping the residual slime of his rebirth off of the lighter. Damn, but that did taste fine. The rest of the slime, or ectoplasm as Rick kept calling it, faded away as he walked into the sunlight.

By the time he reached the spot where the Folk had buried His truck, They had already placed it back on solid ground; the old beat-up vehicle was a little dirty, but no worse for wear. It was time to see how Rick was doing on his research. If Rick was really lucky and hadn't made any real progress, he would be allowed to live. He hoped that Rick was still stumped; Rick was His friend after all and he didn't want to kill him.

Walking in the other direction, Todd Harris smiled and enjoyed the feel of the sun on his skin. It had been too long since he had enjoyed this. Behind him, another group of the shadows ran and scurried, as the terrain demanded. He had promised Jenny immortality, and it was a promise he meant to keep.

Why hadn't They all thought of this before? If the Chosen worked out properly and if His mate or even mates worked out as well, They could create enough bodies for each of Them. And wouldn't that be grand; a body per shadow.

Somehow, Todd didn't think that Jenny would mind making more babies, and he knew he wouldn't mind. That Jenny was a wild one. If the Shadow Hunter did its work, they would have nothing to fear. Todd Harris was certain that it would all work out in the end.

And he was really looking forward to meeting Joe. That brought a smile to his face that just wouldn't go away. Just imagining Joe's surprise was going to be reward enough. The idea that he would be able to keep Jenny afterwards only made the bargain all that much sweeter. So he'd been dead for fifteen years, so what? It had been worth the wait.

Chapter Eighteen

1

The morning broke slowly in Summitville. Those with business in Denver and Boulder wearily made their ways to cars and started on their ritual quest for another day's pay. Those with businesses in Summitville proper started their own rituals of setting up their shops and restaurants for the day ahead.

Early in the pre-dawn morning, a cold front had slipped past the natural barrier of the Rockies; the resulting fog had crept just as stealthily from Lake Overtree and into the crisp air above Summitville. From a vantage point above Summitville, all that could be seen through the blanketing white haze was the occasional rooftop of the older buildings in town. From below the sheath of mist, the sun was a pale, staring eye with hardly enough light to make it noticeable.

Most of the people in town were quite used to the phenomenon—it was just another day and not even a pretty one at that. Rick didn't think he would ever grow so adjusted to the sight. The fog was enchanting and oddly unsettling at the same time; it was like the idea of spending Christmas with the wrong family. It was Christmas and there was a certain comfort to be found in the rituals executed, but it still felt wrong. When he allowed himself to think about such things, Rick realized that the whole town seemed to give off the same feelings sometimes.

Rick had fallen asleep on his desk again, fortunate enough to have brewed a full pot of coffee before he actually reached blissful unconsciousness. The burner was still hot, and the remaining liquid had probably reduced to something just a little darker than India Ink. He shook his head in self-disgust. One of these days, he was certain, his luck would run out and he

would find himself and the building burning to the ground before he had a chance to wake up. Cheery thoughts for the
morning's first light.

The doctor stumbled into the break room and reached for
the coffee filters. Decaf was fine for late at night, but he needed
the real stuff to start his brain on the path of rational thought
again. After pouring fresh grounds in the filter, he reached for
the half-filled pot, preparing to dump the remaining India Ink
from the glass urn. Chuck Hanson's brawny hand stopped
him. "You don't want to pour that out, Rick, I just made it."

Rick decided that he would wait for full consciousness
before screaming at his friend, right now he was too goddamned
tired. "Where the hell have you been for the last week?"

Chuck smiled his All-is-right-with-the-world-as-we-know-
it grin and handed his old roomie a fresh mug of coffee. "I had
some thinking to do is all. I'm back now."

"Do you think that, maybe, if it's not too much to ask, you
could let everyone know where the fuck you're going before
you take off next time?" To anyone who didn't know them, it
would have seemed like a screaming match without the
screams. It was just the way the two of them had always communicated. Even back in college, Rick had always stood his
ground with Chuck Hanson.

Chuck slurped noisily at his too-hot coffee and eyed Rick
from over the lip of his mug. "Anything new happen while I
was gone? You and your lady friend find anything out?"

Rick scowled back at the big man and scooped half a cup
of sugar into his cup. "No, me an' my 'lady friend' didn't
figure out shit. How about you, figure out who's next on the
list? Any notions as to what the hell is going on in this damned
town? Oh, I almost forgot, that Brundvandt kid, the oldest
one that hasn't left town, apparently did. Leave town, that is.
Went missing sometime around when you took off. Deputy
Dave has all the juicy information, assuming that he hasn't
disappeared too. If the Brundvandt kid's one of ours, he hasn't
been brought to me yet."

"He'll show up. Ain't the first time the little snot's gone runnin' off to Denver or some such for a week." Chuck munched on a cinnamon donut from the box he'd brought along. When he offered the confections to Rick, the man dove eagerly into the sugar covered calorie bombs. "Probably ran himself into a spot of trouble with his dad and beat a path out of town."

"Hmm. Whatever."

"Nothin' new, hunh?"

Rick shook his head sadly. "At this point, Chuck, I'd be better off just letting it all sit for a few days, to be honest. I just keep running in the same circles again and again."

Hanson nodded his head and seemed to think about that for a while. "So go home and get some decent sleep. Take a couple of days to rest. Maybe we'll figure it out later. No offense, but you look like shit."

"None taken."

The two of them chattered for another twenty minutes and when they were finished, both went on their separate ways to separate destinations. Rick went home and collapsed on his bed. What was once Chuck Hanson went off to kill a man.

2

Mark settled down after his run and waited for the inevitable to occur. Five minutes later, it did. Tyler came up and pounded on the door. Still feeling horribly embarrassed about the previous night, Mark opened the door and escorted his friend into the den. Tyler pulled a normal Tyler stunt and got right to the point. "So, how's the moon tan coming along Howie?"

Mark held his hands before him and groaned. "Please, God, please, don't tell anyone about that. I don't know what the hell came over me, I really don't."

Tyler smiled pleasantly. "I won't tell anyone, relax." He pulled a suspicious-looking piece of paper from his shirt pocket and passed it over to Mark with a flourish. "I don't need to tell anyone, I already pasted this to all the doors in the neighborhood."

Mark looked at the writings on the paper and made threatening gestures towards Tyler. If he hadn't known that Tyler wouldn't pull that kind of crap, he would have rammed the paper down his friend's throat. Still, it felt good to just goof around with Tyler—somehow they just never seemed to have the time anymore. Tyler punched Mark in the bicep to get his attention.

"Just what were you doing out there anyway, Howie? You scared the hell out of me, I mean two moons in Summitville...one's bad enough, ya know?"

"Ha ha ha, very funny."

Tyler sobered up momentarily, still smiling, but not smirking. "Seriously, you okay? I mean, you took some pretty nasty falls out there."

Mark thought about how to answer as he ran into the kitchen to grab them each a Pepsi. "Yeah, I'm fine. Not even a scratch. I really don't remember much of anything, 'cept you laughing your ass off and me standing there butt naked. I guess I was sleepwalking."

"You think?" Tyler was throwing his Gee-I-never-would-have-thought-of-that-one/All-too-innocent look at Mark. When Mark glared instead of smiling about it, Tyler shrugged and filled him in again on all of the details. He finished up his story with a question: "Do you remember what you were dreaming about?"

Mark flashed on images of he and Cassie holding hands, interspersed with vivid flashes of Lisa struggling underneath his weight. "No," he lied, "I can't remember anything except that Cassie was there."

Mark pulled on his hair, tugging sharply at the mane that Tyler saw was growing longer every day. Then he stared at Tyler with such an intense expression of fear that Tyler was tempted to leave, equally tempted to hold him close, protect him. "Tyler, do you think I'm going crazy?"

"You mean do I think you belong behind the bars in the Lakeside Institute for the Mentally and Emotionally Impaired?" Tyler shrugged and shook his head. "No. You're weird, so am I for what it's worth, but I don't think you're ready for the rubber room. You don't belong in one of those anymore than I do." Tyler's face got that sadistic smile back in place and he winked at Mark. "You just need to get laid, Howie. Hell, you might even need to get laid more than I do."

Mark couldn't decide if Tyler was being serious or not; knowing Tyler well enough, he asked for clarification. "Shit, Mark. We've gone over this before. You're in the middle of a King Kong sized growth spurt, you've got hormones they don't even have names for going gonzo all over the inside of your body. Look, when Patrick had his last growth spurt, he was a basket case for a year and a half. Y'know why? 'Cause he didn't get laid." Tyler lit up his three dollar smirk again. "It's a scientifically proven fact, Howie."

The thought roamed around in the back of Mark's head while they talked. By the end of the conversation, Mark was more than halfway convinced that Tyler was right.

3

Tony Scarrabelli walked down the main stretch of the strip, doing nothing that had to be done and basically enjoying the last day of weekday freedom before school started again. The day was beautiful, now that the early morning caul of fog had faded under the sun's gaze. It meant nothing at all to Tony, he just had to get the hell out of the house before he went crazy.

It was a bad situation at home these days. His two older sisters were bitching about how much money they needed as allowance for college and his dear old Dad was doing everything but actually calling them leeches. Mom of course was no where near the house when his father was home and when she was there, she was bitching about how little time he spent with his children.

To add to the merriment, Dad the understanding had suspended Tony's wheels for the week before school, screaming
about how Tony needed to learn how to drive responsibly.
Tony knew how to drive, he'd received an A-Plus on his Driver's
Ed course at school. He just didn't give a shit. Tony figured
the old bastard was still pissed about the near miss with the
Gravel Shower. So was he, he'd been hoping for a bull's eye
on the fat old fart.

Tony shifted his thoughts away from the bad things going
on in his life and tried to recapture his fading good spirits as he
scratched at the bandages covering his nose. In front of B.
Dalton's, on the side of the street that everyone called "The
Mall," Tony stared at his reflection in the plate glass window.
He looked much as he always had, except for the blaring white
tape in the center of his face and the chipped incisor in his
mouth. He did his best to follow the Tyler Wilson train of
cheerful thoughts and reminded himself that at least Crowley
hadn't broken his jaw.

Tony's starting smile faded as he saw the reflection of
Jonathan Crowley behind his own image in the bookstore window. Idly he noticed that Uncle Phil's latest had just reached
the top ten charts. The reflected Crowley waved and from
behind him he heard the overly pleasant tones of the man's
voice. "How's the nose, Tony?"

Tony's bowels tried to freeze, his heart did a stuttering
double take and his voice quivered as he responded. "It'll
do." He hated the tremor he heard; even more, he hated the
way his knees were starting to shake.

Crowley's reflection locked eyes with his in the window
and Tony forced himself to resist the urge to run. "I just
wanted to apologize for that, Tony. I really shouldn't have
taken it out on you, but I was just having a bad day, y'know?
Sometimes things aren't going the way you'd like them to
and you just have this urge, the urge to beat the shit out of
whoever gets in your way, even if they haven't done anything wrong at all." Tony felt himself nodding, couldn't

recall giving his brain that order, but that was okay. As long as it pleased Crowley. He swallowed the dry lump in his throat. "No hard feelings, hunh Tony?"

Tony tried again to swallow the yellow fear in his throat; nothing doing, the damned thing was there to stay. Instead of trying to speak again, he nodded and shrugged at the same time. The smile he attempted looked pained in the window's reflection. He saw the reflected Crowley walk towards him and he flinched, almost wet his pants. Crowley's reflection smiled again, right up next to his own shaking reflection. Crowley's hand reached out and patted Tony on the top of his head, like a dog that had done well. "Good boy. I'm glad we had this little talk, aren't you?" Tony again felt his head nod of its own volition. When Crowley's voice started again, it was laced with a honey sweet threat. "Listen, I want you to do me a favor, okay?" Tony thought frantically about how many times he had used that exact same tone of voice on the kids that were smaller than him. A part of his psyche cried out that he had changed, that what Crowley was doing was unfair; the righteous voice didn't have the strength to make it up to his fear-tightened vocal cords. Tears of shame threatened to fall from his eyes, the sting of unborn tears making his shattered nose itch furiously. Again, Tony felt himself nodding. "Great," Crowley crooned. "Yes sir, that's just fine." Crowley's fingers caressed the back of Tony's neck, violence implied in every gentle stroke of the hand. "I want you to keep an eye on Mark Howell for me. Could you do that? I can't tell you how much it would mean to me."

Crowley's hand moved down to Tony's shoulder. The voice grew even sweeter, even more menacing. "You can do that for me, can't you Tony?" The soft tones were emphasized by a steadily increasing pressure on Tony's shoulder, one that just avoided being truly painful. Tony nodded hard enough to blur his vision. When he stopped nodding, he was surprised to see how pale his reflection had grown, doubly surprised by the sweat he felt beading on his forehead and under his arms. Butterflies hatched in his stomach and beat at his insides with their wings. "You're a real pal, Tony. Listen, you do this for me and there's a hundred bucks in it for you. Deal?" Even without the incentive of money, Tony would have nodded again. Both of them knew it and the slow, sarcastic wink that Crowley threw from his reflection made the situation very clear. Tony felt the paper press into his hand as he watched his reflection grasp at the offered prize. "You call me if he does anything too weird, okay Tony? Here's my number. Just let it ring four times and then hang up. I'll know who called." Crowley's reflection backed slowly away from his own. The face of his assailant grew stern for just a moment as he continued. "I'm counting on you, Tony. Don't let me down. I'd hate to see any more strains put on our relationship." The smile, the one that made Tony feel faint, flashed on Crowley's face again. "Talk at'cha later, Tony. You stay cool, okay?" Tony nodded vigorously and closed his eyes to stop the first spillage of humiliating tears.

When he opened his eyes, he was alone. His reflection was alone. Tony wanted nothing as much as he wanted the comfort of his home. But that would have been foolish. Instead he turned sharply and started towards the Red Oaks Subdivision and Mark Howell.

When he was a safe distance from the town, in a spot where no one could see him, Tony finally let the violent shaking and the tears win out. He cried for five minutes, hating himself for his cowardice, hating himself for what he let be done to him. He swore to God that he would never, not as long as he lived, ever do to another person what he had done so often in the past. He was fairly convinced that if he did, Crowley would come back for him.

Never, never again.

4

While Tony was learning what it felt like to be truly scared, Cassie was doing her last minute shopping for school. She had missed the entire exchange between Crowley and Tony as she did her shopping inside of Evvy's Boutique. Evvy's was, to Cassie's thinking, the only clothing store in Summitville worth noticing; she was trying to decide between two pair of jeans, that to the casual shopper would have appeared identical, when Chuck Hanson walked past.

Cassie waved enthusiastically after spotting the man, but he didn't seem to notice. Cassie frowned. Sheriff Hanson always noticed when someone in town noticed him, it was like a special set of eyes was in his head just for recognizing a friendly wave. Well, even sheriffs were allowed to have off days, she just hoped that he was okay. It just wasn't like the man not to wave back, or at least to tip that big old hat of his.

The jeans finally recaptured her attention and she went back to her careful study of the denim. After a few more minutes of intense observation, Cassie decided to go with both pairs. Evelyn Pratt wasn't in the store that day, she had broken her ankle just a week earlier when stepping off of the curb in front of the store, so it was up to her niece, Kathy Olsen, to take care of the pre-school rush. Kathy was the first to point out that her aunt normally managed to injure herself directly before the busiest seasons at the store reached their peaks. Cassie was equally fast on the draw and pointed out the benefits of having an aunt who sold you your clothes at wholesale, on top of paying you to do what you loved anyway. Kathy agreed to the logic in Cassie's argument, but pointed out that the job wouldn't be half as much fun if she couldn't gripe about it whenever possible. Had Cassie been carrying a tape recorder for her annual fall clothes shopping spree over the last three years, she would have been hard pressed to notice any real differences in the conversations. It was a part of the ritual, like part of a dance; it just wouldn't have been the same without the words.

Cassie paid her bill and said her good-byes to the older girl, pausing long enough to give her a hug and her best wishes for a good start at the university over in Denver. Then she was off, her hands filled with packages and her mind filled with thoughts of Mark. It was a glorious day, the temperature was perfect, the air was sweet and on this last weekend of the summer, Cassie had decided to consummate her relationship with Mark. There was no more debate, no more bouncing the idea around in her head, she just knew that it was time.

Cassie slipped her new clothes into the basket on her ten-speed bike, dreaming simultaneously about Mark and the new car her parents had promised her for her next birthday. Everything about that Friday morning brought pleasant fantasies into Cassie's mind, it was just that kind of day for her.

Cassie had one more stop to make before going home. She pedaled her Schwinn over to B. Dalton's; the latest issue of Writer's Digest was due out, along with a book she had special ordered on women in the writing industry. She intended to know everything she possibly could about the business of writing before she cemented any plans for the future; unlike Mark, she wanted all the gory details on publishing that she could locate. P. J. was a great source of information, but of late he simply hadn't been in the mood to deal with questions from either Mark or Cassie. That was okay, everyone had their off days and everyone was entitled to their times of privacy. Besides, she didn't want to bother the man too much on the small things, better to push for favors on the big stuff than on a thousand little details she could learn on her own.

Looking to her right, as she signaled to turn in that very direction, she saw Mark's friend Jonathan Crowley and waved. He started to return the gesture and then froze, eyes looking past her, to the other side of the street. As Cassie came to a stop, she turned to see what had captured the man's attention. Off to her left, slightly in front of her and on the other side of the street, she saw Chuck Hanson reaching for his gun.

Cassie stood perfectly still, as immobile as a bird paralyzed by the eyes of a snake. Hanson's gun gleamed blue-black in the bright sunlight as he aimed the barrel straight at Cassie's head. The only thought that would stay with her was that today was too nice a day to end up being murdered.

Then the ten-foot wide barrel shifted slightly and Cassie realized that death was not meant for her that day. Half a dozen blessings of thanks went in the direction of God, never having actually passed her lips. The gun had never seemed that large while resting in its holster and her eyes tracked the slow steady movement of the muzzle as it moved away from her.

The hypnotic effect of staring death in the face wore off and Cassie dropped off of her bike, hugging the asphalt for all that she was worth. To her left, almost in perfect synchronization with the sound of shattering glass on her right, the sound of thunder ripped open the early morning bliss.

5

Crowley did a very fast backward walk away from where the girl stood on her bike, his eyes never leaving Hanson. She had no part in what Hanson wanted and Crowley saw no reason for her to die. The grim look cast his way from Hanson's stern face softened for just a second, a small nod of thanks almost completing itself before he squeezed the trigger on the .38 revolver.

The idea of dodging a bullet is ludicrous. Crowley dodged away from where the gun was pointed and simply prayed that the bullet was not already in transit. It saved his life. The show window of B. Daltons spiderwebbed and collapsed on itself as a copy of Judith Krantz's latest best seller jumped towards the cash register inside the store. Crowley didn't have the time to take notice.

From forty feet away, Hanson started to take aim again. Jonathan Crowley crab-walked to the shelter of a nearby car. He had known that the Folk would retaliate for last night's interference, but he had not known that the sheriff was Theirs. That was the worst part of being in his present situation: he hated surprises.

The cement off to his right screamed in protest as a bullet missed his head. Now was not the time for complaints and Crowley chastised himself for his stupidity. The little bastards had learned a few tricks and he was not at all pleased to see what They had pulled out of Their sleeves.

The next bullet hadn't come his way yet and Crowley had already given a hundred count. Hanson was playing it smart, waiting to see what Crowley was going to do. Peeking under the car, he could just make out the Sheriff's boots. They were motionless. *Okay,* he thought. *Girl as hostage is useless here. He's perfectly willing to kill her in order to get to me.* A dozen other tentative plans came to mind: they were dismissed just as quickly. The sheriff was in no mood to play games.

He looked behind himself, assessing the stores on the row and wondering which ones would be useful. No, B. Dalton's did not have anything that he could use against the sheriff. No again, Wing Pu's Chinese Garden was closed, the potential weapons locked away from him. Buddy's Hardware was also closed, a sky blue sign with movable red arms in set into a clock face pointed to the noon hour, with the important message WE'LL BE BACK AT...above the clock and the message at the bottom: THANKS FOR YOUR PATRONAGE in bright red letters. The Healthy Housewife was open. A quick scan of the window told him all he needed to know.

The girl, Cassie, was starting to stand up and Hanson turned to scream at her, warning her to stay down. As far as Crowley could tell, it was now or never. He bolted for the Happy Housewife, hearing the gun go off just before he realized that he had been shot. Crowley bounced off the side of Buddy's, right before he reached the Housewife. The plate glass door was mentally added to the number of casualties, but he wasn't certain if it was the force of his push or another damn bullet that had caused it to break. The stupid cowbell tied to the inside handle had rattled too much for him to know one way or the other. First he got hurt, then he lost the count on bullets. Now he was just plain getting pissed off.

Inside the store proper, he grabbed the portly owner and pushed hard at her chest. With a squeal of terror, she went down and he landed on top of her. The woman looked both terrified and furious, but before she could scream rape or start beating on his face with her huge fists, he politely asked, "Excuse me, Ma'am. Could you tell me where you keep your spices?"

Alberta Kornfeld just knew the man was a serial killer. Fortunately, all the books she read, along with her true detective magazines, had informed her that cooperating with a psycho-rapist-serial killer was the best way to live through the experience, so she knew just what to do. Folding one arm over her ample bosom and clenching both thighs together as fiercely as she could, she pointed with her free hand to the wall behind the cash register. The very polite homicidal maniac nodded his thanks and winked at her before he scurried over to the counter where the register rested. She was very glad that she had deposited her receipts last night instead of waiting for today; one could never tell what all a man might want to take.

Crowley grabbed the spices that he needed and poured the contents of both bottles into his hand, regretting the excess that spilled to the ground. He crouched behind the counter and watched the front door, warning the quivering storeowner to stay down when she started coming his way and demanding payment for the bottles of spice. His arm was starting to piss him off, the small amount of blood that came from the wound told him that it was nothing serious, but it hurt like hell and he just didn't have the time to deal with it right then.

He tried to wait patiently, but the sounds of the woman breathing and the sound of his own thudding heart beat made him all too aware of the fact that Hanson hadn't shown up yet. Crowley's nerves were starting to send him false signals, which could get his head blown off. Hanson should have shown by now. The front of the store was very clear in his sights and not even a shadow had moved yet. The hairs of Crowley's neck started crawling around like a wrestling group of puppies. One minute. Two minutes. Three minutes, Four...

Behind him, he heard the not-so-happy-and-none too-healthy-storeowner gasp. He turned away from the front of the store, almost certain that he was making a horrible mistake, and saw Hanson aiming the revolver at his face. The "Employees Only" door in the rear of the store was softly closing behind him.

Crowley threw the Nature's Own All Natural Lemon Pepper and Nature's Own Sea Salt into the sheriff's face as hard as he could. Instinct made the sheriff's hands go to his face. Surprise made him fire into the ceiling of the heath food store. Citric acid, salt, and pepper flew into the man's eyes before they could completely close and Crowley smiled at the sound of Hanson's screams. It was music to his ears, a good harmony to go with the rhythmic beating of his heart.

Crowley stood, watching as the sheriff rubbed frantically at his eyes, howling out his pain and backing up. Sympathetic tears started in his own eyes as he thought of what the man's rubbing must be doing; that didn't stop him from kicking him in the head just as hard as he could. Hanson grunted and hit the floor, already struggling back to his feet.

The Healthy Housewife, forgotten momentarily in the struggle, made her presence known as she sank her teeth into the meaty part of Crowley's left calf. "Oww! Shit woman, what the hell are you doing?!" She didn't bother to answer his question, instead she started shaking her head back and forth, rather like a bulldog with a rat in its jaws.

Crowley did a staggering hop in the air, tearing a few muscles in his calf as he lost his balance and landed on the woman with his full weight. Alberta Kornfeld whooofed out the air in her lungs and was forced to try gathering more air repeatedly as Crowley climbed off of her. Her squealed protests were falling on deaf ears and for added measure,

Crowley gave a solid stomp on her buttocks as he again regained his footing.

He stood at almost exactly the same moment as Chuck Hanson. Hanson was obviously beyond seeing, his eyes were bloodied and watering madly. That did not stop him from shooting Crowley in the same arm again. Crowley let out a shriek worthy of the Healthy Housewife and aimed a side kick into the sheriff's stomach. He followed through with an elbow to the man's face and vicious punch to the man's throat.

Hanson looked barely fazed by the killing blows. He moved quickly and pointed the barrel of his revolver directly into Crowley's face. He squeezed the trigger three times.

Nothing happened.

Crowley laughed with a serious edge of hysteria and started in on the sheriff with everything he had. He threw cookbooks, Nature's Own Sunflower oil, bottles of all-natural herbal extracts and half a dozen kicks at the man. Hanson kept going down and getting right back up. All the while, the Healthy Housewife continued her screaming tirade, "You get that psycho bastard, Chuck! You take his ass to jail! I'm gonna sue you, I'm gonna press charges, you rapist!" The words were screamed again and again, a Holy litany meant to ward of the evil that was John Crowley. The only reason Crowley didn't bother with breaking the woman's fat neck was that he was occupied with Hanson. But, it was sorely tempting to take the extra risk.

Crowley dodged behind the sheriff of Summitville and Summitville County. Cursing and flailing wildly, the man tried his best to stop him. When Crowley managed to wrap one arm around the lower jaw of the man, Hanson sank his teeth into Crowley's forearm. Crowley gritted his teeth and wrapped his other arm around Hanson's forehead. With a sound half like firecrackers and half like a zipper being pulled, Crowley broke the sheriff's neck.

Yep. That did the trick. Hanson fell to the ground and stayed there. Crowley closed his eyes for a moment, trying not to think about what he had just done. He'd liked Hanson, he really had.

Behind him, the Healthy Housewife started screaming, not with anger but with fear. Crowley opened his eyes and saw why; the flesh on Hanson's body was rotting away, putrefying and wisping away like steam in a cold winter wind. The smell was reminiscent of burning hair. Crowley managed not to gag. The Healthy Housewife was not as lucky and tossed her Carob Coated cookies all over the floor.

Crowley looked down on her and smiled. "I'd like to pay for the damages, but I'm afraid the money will now be needed to stitch up my calf. Not to worry, I won't press charges."

Outside the store, he smiled politely at Cassie Monroe and told her it was all right to get off the ground; he even went so far as to help her to her feet. He righted her bike and asked her to let Mark know that he said "Hi." Then he was on his way, after making certain that she was uninjured.

Crowley was feeling good about himself as he hobbled towards his motel room. The sun was warm on his flesh and his injuries were already mending themselves, the annoying itch of healing telling him that he would be just fine in an hour or so.

He couldn't help breaking into his habitual grin as he walked. They knew he was coming for Them and They had attacked him. The thought sent chills of pleasure through his entire body. A good fight was just about the best way he could think of to start the weekend.

6

Rick Lewis took one look at the body that Dave Palance had called him about and then he threw up. It wasn't so much the state of advance decay on the body, nor even the horrid stench that wafted from the black ichor that stained the bones to an antique brown. It was the clothes on the corpse. Until he had actually seen the body and the familiar hat that lay next to the well-known scuffed boots, he could pretend that this was not who Dave claimed. He could pretend that the man he had been talking to only hours ago, his best friend in the world, Chuck Hanson, was still alive.

The voiding of his morning's breakfast felt good in comparison to the grief in his heart.

Deputy Dave, looking at least as pale as Rick felt and shaking visibly, was doing his best to get all of the information he could from Alberta Kornfeld; he was having a great deal of trouble getting the facts, because he was also doing his very best to give the woman solace. Rick personally couldn't give a heap of shit if the woman felt all right about the world or not. Like so many of the people in Summitville, she had never acknowledge Rick's existence unless it was absolutely necessary. He heard her talking of the man that had done whatever had been done to Rick's best friend without ever really listening to a word she said.

Rick picked up the battered old Stetson with the sweat stains and dents that had become so familiar to him and forced the tears that were struggling to be free away from his eyes. No one in this shit hole town had earned the right to see him cry; the only person who had was dead. *That's all she wrote,* he thought. *I've had it with this town. I don't give a good goddamn what happens to these people. Goodbye Summitville, hello wherever. Anyplace is better than here.*

Rick stood up, gently placing the hat where he had found it and walked away from the crime scene. Let the town find someone else to do their dirty work, Rick Lewis didn't care anymore. He stepped out into the overly bright daylight, leaving behind his cares for who had killed Chuck Hanson and why. None of it was worth the grief.

On the sidewalk outside the Healthy Housewife, Stacy Calhoun was talking to the little redhead that Mark Howell could almost always be seen with. Rick stared for a long time, noticing the girl's grief and Stacy Calhoun's. Rick tried to fight against it, but some things can't be resisted. He charged across the short distance between himself and Cassie Monroe—Yeah, that was her name—and yanked her violently towards himself. His rage kept the words quiet, low and menacing. They were coming out all wrong, but he had to at least *try* to warn her. "Cassie, isn't it?" She nodded her answer, looking pale, but in control; she was the one who'd had the sense to call the deputies, everyone else stood around gawking, just as soon as they deemed it safe to stick their heads out of their still locked doors. "Do yourself a favor, Cassie. Stay as far away from your boyfriend as you can. He's dangerous, you could be the next one hurt."

Cassie started to protest, still too affected by what had happened to clearly think through what he had just said. Stacy Calhoun didn't have that problem. Her mother had taught her two things a long time ago: First, you never surrender your dreams, at least not without trying your hardest to achieve them. The second important lesson was that the time for grief and displays of violent emotion was after the work was done. Stacy's hazel eyes flashed in her round face and she grabbed hold of Rick Lewis, pulling him away from the poor girl he was assaulting.

"What the hell's gotten into you, Rick?" she demanded, her voice a furious whisper. "What kind of nonsense is that to say to the poor girl at a time like this! You want to give her advice on her love life, you just wait for another day. Merciful God, where did you ever learn your manners?"

Rick tried to brush the deputy off, furious at her for having interrupted his warnings to Cassie Monroe. She held on even tighter than before, shouting in his face with her authoritative *I Am An Officer Of The Law, and I Will Punish You If You Don't Behave Yourself* voice. "You can stop that right now, mister! I don't want a scene, but I'll haul your ass down to the jail right now if you don't calm yourself down!"

Rick turned and stared at Stacy Calhoun for all of three seconds, then he went back to try and warn Cassie again. His leaving town was delayed substantially by the deputy having to carry out her threat. Rick would have never thought it possible— Stacy was a good deal shorter than he was and at least sixty pounds lighter. She took him down at the knees and had him handcuffed in less time than it would have taken him to write a prescription; her mother Dino had never bothered with a bouncer in all of her time as proprietor of the bar and grill named after herself, and she had taught Stacy well.

7

Jennifer Howell was happier than she had been since before Mark was born. Very soon now, as soon as Mark got back from wherever he had gone off to with his friends, her family would be complete again. Beside her in her bed, Todd smiled happily and caressed her hip. That had been the best sex she'd had in...well, since the last time she had been with Todd...and it looked like he would be ready to go at it again in just a few minutes.

Right after Joe had driven off towards Denver that morning, Jenny had climbed back into bed for an extra hour of sleep. In less than half that time, Todd had climbed through the second floor window into her bedroom. They had a lot to discuss after fifteen years of separation, but that was something that could wait until after the first lovemaking sessions were finished. Fifteen years without a competent lover had been fifteen years too many in Jenny's eyes.

By the time they had finished and both cleaned up with a shower, Mark had gone out. He left a note that said he'd be back by suppertime. That was fine with Jenny, it gave her more time with her first love, time she put to good use.

Smiling into his eyes, Jenny was amazed at how very little he had changed. He had a few more wrinkles and just the right touch of gray at the temples to make him look sexier than ever, but that was it. The largest difference between her first husband and her son was the scar that her Mark would carry for the rest of his life. They were identical otherwise, build, height, width, even the ways in which they moved, all were identical. Without the scar she would have been confused to see them in the same room together. Maybe Todd swaggered a little more than her son, but otherwise...

She moaned, caught off guard by the sudden pleasure of his hands probing one of her sensitive spots, moaned again as his fingers were joined by his tongue. They only had enough time left for a quickie, however—the day was moving on and she still had to prepare for when Joe got home.

Her last coherent thought, before the moment's passions carried her away, was that the garage would probably be the best place for killing her husband. Cement cleaned up easier than linoleum or carpet, and there promised to be a great deal of blood spilled by the time she got done with Joe. Whole lakes of it.

8

Tyler and Tony seemed to want nothing more than to have some fun in the sun on the last day of weekday freedom for the summer. Mark was with them one hundred per cent. They were up at the Overtree, and despite the long-standing rumors of the lake being haunted, despite even the grisly discovery of Tommy Blake's body at the beginning of the summer, they were enjoying the cool waters. Youth and bravado easily overrode any fears they had of the lake. And if Mark and Tony found Tyler's suggestion to go swimming there morbid, they never let it show. Truth be told, the Overtree held the same sort of fascination as a haunted house. It was a sign of courage to go into the waters and come out in one piece. The trio was taking turns climbing one of the massive red oaks that rested partially in the lake and diving from its branches a good fifteen feet into the water. Mark and Tony had made an unofficial competition of the fun and games and Mark watched Tony make a dive that barely left a ripple in the lake's surface. It was a beautiful dive. Mark knew he could beat it. He wondered idly how much pain driving into the water was causing the lump on Tony's broken nose, but the answer seemed to be very little indeed, if the happy expression on Tony's face was an indicator.

There seemed to be an odd sort of tension in the air, judging by the strange expressions that swam just under the surface of Tyler and Tony's faces, in the way they kept looking at each other when they thought that Mark wouldn't notice. Mark did his best to ignore the strange looks. This was the last day of freedom that he would be able to spend exclusively with these two. The weekend proper was dedicated to Cassie alone.

Mark thought about Cassie as he climbed from the waters and started towards the massive oak again. His mind seldom strayed from thoughts of Cassie for very long. The texture of the rough bark under his hands and the pads of his feet, as he started to climb towards the diving branch, even this made him think of Cassie and how lucky he was to be with her, how much he loved her.

He was amazed at how much his world had changed in the last year, amazed again to realize that a year had passed since he had come to Summitville. One year ago, to the very day, he had first laid eyes on the town. A year ago, he had been certain that nothing but pain waited for him in the future. He flashed back to the first time he had seen Cassie, waving and smiling as she jogged past the Howell family getting out of their car and setting foot on Summitville soil for the very first time. He had prayed then that he would be accepted in Summitville; now he knew that he was. Not by everyone, surely, but by the ones that counted.

Below him, the sounds of Tyler and Tony goading him to dive pulled him from his reverie. Mark decided it was time to show the two what a real swan dive looked like. He glanced above him at the next well-positioned branch on the monolithic tree. It was fully fifteen feet above the one from which they normally dived, a minimum of thirty feet above the waters. Mark grinned at the thought of one-upping Tony and started to climb.

Below him, an impossible distance away, Tyler and Tony looked on, two small islands in the flawless glittering mirror of the sky above. He could hear Tyler calling out for him to go back down to the lower branch; he could hear Tony calling for him not to be stupid. None of that mattered, this was the last day of freedom, and the last day with friends before the whole school thing fucked it up again. Just this once, he was going to fly...

To show his friends that he wasn't the least bit afraid, he actually danced a fast-footed jig on the branch, pirouetting and bowing as his feet blurred. He never lost his balance. Tony and Tyler below held their breath, waiting for the fatal fall that seemed inevitable. Mark backed up to the very base of the branch, the sun on his face warming him and showing for all his almost perfect smile, marred only by the faded scar on his cheek.

It was the best he had ever done. He ran with a grace and power that would have made the finest Olympic athlete lower his head in shame. His feet left the branch only to come crashing down at the very end and he was lifted into the air, his own velocity and the resiliency of the branch throwing him farther than he had ever gone before. For that one second, he thought he knew what it must be like to be God. He felt as if he were looking down upon all creation and he saw that it was good.

Mark's shadow blocked out the sun, for that one timeless second. And in that one second, he saw the waters of the Overtree stripped of the beautiful glare that had been present all day, he saw past the glimmer of the sky and into the depths of the waters. He saw the chrome bumper of Dave Brundvandt's car winking back at him from just below the water's surface. He was headed straight for the grinning silver light.

From Tony and Tyler's perspective, it looked like Mark had done a belly flop. Only he had done a belly flop on his face. They had watched the stunning dive from within the cool waters, amazed at their friend's audacity; no one dove from a branch that high up, no one. It was a thing of beauty, right up until he was about five feet above the waters. Then Mark's arms flailed and he hit the water.

When you see someone hit the water, from any height, you expect to hear a splash. It's one of the unspoken laws of nature. What Tony and Tyler heard was a solid *"Whoooong!"* followed immediately by the originally expected splash, as Mark, his face bleeding profusely, looking like a tomato dropped from around thirty feet, sailed away from the water for just a moment, arching backwards and spewing blood, oh dear God, so very much blood, before he slapped into the water again, some ten feet from where they were.

Tyler let out a little gasp, suddenly unable to breathe as his heart stopped for a second, then kicked into overdrive. Tony was more direct in his statement. "Fuck Me! Mark! Oh, fuck me, God damn it all to hell!" His voice broke several times as he spoke, and the color drained from his face before he started moving desperately towards where Mark hit the water.

Tony cut through the waters like the fin on a shark, plowing through the waves and heading towards where Mark had disappeared. There was nothing to see. Mark was gone.

9

They had never worked so fast in all of Their long existence. The Folk covered Mark's flesh with Their own, shifting the color of Their skins to match that of the waters. They were painfully aware that the ones They could not harm were above Them, trying to save the Chosen One. They also knew that the friends could only cause him death.

There was no time for subtlety: They reached into his flesh, mending shattered bones and placing his delicate eyes where they belonged. They mended the pulp of his brain as best They could, They altered his memories and hid from his mind the knowledge that he had just died. When They were finished, They forced air into his still lungs, made his heart beat again. They gave him back his life.

Mark came out of the waters only a few feet from where he'd hit the chrome bumper, gasping for air.

10

Tony and Tyler were searching frantically for his body. The air was sweeter even than when he had dived into the depths and it burned as he sucked it into himself greedily. He had been down there a long time, but now and then you had to test your limits.

Tyler and Tony stared at him as if he were a ghost. Tyler was the first to break from the silence that held them all for several seconds, the first to escape from the mind-numbing certainty that Mark was dead. Tyler was certain that Mark had pulled a fast one and he was furious with his friend. Through wet glass lenses, he looked at his friend. Even with corrective lenses, his eyes would never be twenty-twenty—he allowed himself to believe the lie his mind made up, surely he had simply imagined that Mark was truly injured.

While Tyler and Mark laughed about the situation, calling names and insulting each other's heritage, Tony went over what he had seen again and again. He had seen blood, he had seen teeth flying free from a shattered face, he had seen Mark flopping backwards like a fish hooked on a line and heaved towards the fisherman's boat. All Tony could think about was the conversation he had had earlier, with Jonathan Crowley. Tony was torn by the warring emotions, loyalty to a friend and fear of an enemy. Fear that Crowley would hurt him again.

Crowley...

Tony lied about when he had to be home, he told Mark and Tyler that he would see them later.

Crowley...

He dressed quickly and all but ran all the way to the Charles S. Westphalen High School parking lot. The school had a pay phone, it even had an undamaged phone book, not that Tony needed it. He already had the number he needed in his pocket. He even found a quarter covered by lint in the same pocket.

Crowley...
Tony hated himself even as he dialed the number.
He'd always hated cowards.

Chapter Nineteen

1

Crowley felt his beeper vibrate four times in his pocket and then grow lifeless again. Something had happened with the Howell boy. Despite his wishes, something had happened to scare Tony Scarrabelli enough to make him call. He didn't hesitate; he stepped away from his table in McDonald's and left the smiling face of Ronald McDonald behind. There was no outward sign of his grief; rules forbade the showing of grief before or after the show was ended.

Smile firmly in place, Crowley walked towards the edge of town in the direction of Lake Overtree. Crowley walked almost everywhere when he was busy doing what he did. Cars had a nasty tendency to explode or lose their brakes during business hours. Besides, the walk would do him good; his calf was still a little stiff right now.

They were watching him, too afraid to actually approach him outright. That wasn't the way They operated. He could feel Their hatred directed at him and it was soothing, a balm for the wounds he had suffered earlier in the day. Just for fun, he located one of the little creatures and stared it in the eyes until it ran away.

Behind him a car was slowing. He forced back the thought of Sheriff Chuck Hanson coming back for round two and made his body relax; tension would only slow down his reaction time. The car behind him honked its horn. He turned to face whatever was there.

Joe Howell waved happily through the open window across from the driver's seat. "Need a ride somewhere, Jonathan?"

Crowley smiled, a different smile than he usually wore when on the job. "I'd like that Joe. I was actually on my way to see you and yours anyway." The smile became a smirk, slightly ironic in the way it sat on his face. "Town like this, you need to see a friendly face now and then."

Joe laughed at that and pulled the lock on the passenger side door. "I know what you mean, if it wasn't for Sam Watkins giving me the okay around town, I don't think any of the family would have friends here." Joe frowned for a moment, then brightened back up immediately. "Listen, why don't you come on over and join us for dinner. I know Mark would love to see you again. You can tell him about some of the interviews you've done. If you've talked to Stephen King or Clive Barker, you ought to be set for life."

"Well, I haven't had the pleasure of those two, but I've talked to a few of the big guys in horror fiction. Maybe we'll see what others Mark likes, chances are decent that I've met 'em."

"Great. That'll just make his day. He's a good kid, y'know?" It seemed to Crowley that the man wanted to say something more, something that simply had to be taken off of his chest before the weight crushed him to a pulp. He nodded quietly and waited for Joe to start up. It took an extra ten minutes to get to the Howell residence after Joe started, but it was worth it. Joe talked a great deal about how he'd mistreated Mark in the earlier years. He hadn't abused him, he'd just not known how to show the boy he cared.

Crowley listened sympathetically, nodding and frowning in all the right places. He soaked the information into himself as if it was water and he was a dry sponge. The knowledge would come in handy when it came time to kill Mark Howell.

2

Jennifer Howell hissed between her teeth and waved her beloved Todd back out of sight. "Damn, he brought John Crowley with him. We can't do anything with him here."

Behind her, she heard the returned sentiment of Todd. "Why not? He's just another person trying to keep us apart."

She shot a quick look over her shoulder at him, puzzled by the sound of his voice. He was standing in the shadows, hidden almost entirely from her view. "Listen, he's stronger than you might think, but he's got weaknesses. Kill him first, I'll handle Joe. But you have to kill him first, okay Jenny?"

Still having to pinch herself, in order to make sure she wasn't dreaming Todd's reappearance, Jenny nodded. A short trip to the kitchen brought her a carving knife long enough to penetrate deeply, sharp as a razor and strong enough to survive impact with a few bones. Half a minute after that she was situated under the garage stairs, hiding in the darkness, and peering between the slats in the wooden steps. She crouched lower as the electric hum and rumble of the powered garage door opener started up. After the slow ascent growled to a halt, Joe pulled his car inside and killed the engine. Jenny watched from the short staircase that led to the house proper as he and John Crowley climbed out of the car. For just a second, she thought that Crowley had noticed her. His eyes seemed to stop right on her body as he looked around, but then he turned to more of Joe's inane conversation.

Joe seemed to think Crowley's opinion was of the utmost importance on something to do with Mark. Curiosity aroused, she listened. "I just need to know that he doesn't hold a grudge, does that make sense to you John?"

Crowley turned his head entirely from her, but it was too far for her to charge the man still ten feet away—she felt certain Joe would call out a warning if she came flying towards them with the knife in her hands. The wooden handle was doing a fine job of absorbing her nervous perspiration. She shifted her grip on the knife and flinched when cold light danced across the blade's surface. Neither of them appeared to notice. "Joe, if Mark held a grudge against you, I think you'd know by now. You've got a great son and a wife that obviously loves you. Relax a little. Don't always act like happiness is a bad thing. Sure, now and then you might wish for something better in this world, hell, you might even wish that you'd married someone else, but life is what you make of it and you are what life makes of you. Sometimes the best things in the world seem like they're already in someone else's hands."

Jenny watched, trying to ignore the words that Crowley was speaking. She could not; it was almost as if he was talking to her, instead of to Joe. From the look of puzzlement on Joe's face, she half suspected he *was* talking to her.

Crowley patiently continued, in the voice of a marriage counselor. Something in his voice, the timbre and inflections, seemed almost to mesmerize her. Her limbs felt heavy and her brain sluggish. "Let me give you an example; Mark's real dad took off, right? Along comes Joe Howell, maybe not a perfect guy, but certainly not a knife wielding maniac, and he falls in love with Mark's mom and he marries her. Well, nobody explained in advance that he was going to be taking on a kid as well." He stopped Joe's protest as they started on the stairs. Joe obviously wanted to explain that he had known about Mark before the wedding. "Let me finish, Joe, then you can point out the bad parts in my argument. Okay?" Joe nodded reluctantly as they started towards the doorway above. They walked right past Jenny. She didn't attack. She wanted to hear the end of Jonathan's argument.

"I realize you knew about Mark, maybe you'd even gone to a couple of movies or whatever with the kid, but knowing something with your head isn't the same as knowing something with your heart." Crowley stopped them both at the top of the stairs. Jenny stayed put, knowing that she would never get a better chance at Crowley. "Jenny might very well still be in love with Mark's dad, but she's not with him. Granted, he took off and left her alone with Mark, but she could just as easily have gotten an abortion and gone on seeing the guy. Maybe if she had, he'd have stuck around. Maybe he even promised her he'd be back someday and she held on to that promise. But she married you. Maybe a good part of the marriage idea came from wanting a father for her son, maybe she felt the influence would do him good."

Crowley leaned in close to Joe then, looking like he was about to tell him the most important secret that Joe could ever hope to hear. "I think that maybe she did marry you for those reasons. Maybe she was waiting for her lover-boy to come running back into her life so she could have him and Mark and leave you behind. But if she was, that was a long time ago. By your own admission, she makes plenty of money as an illustrator. She could have left you a long time back and still made a good enough living to keep her son happy. By your own admission, you never took enough time with Mark when he was younger. Jenny's not a stupid woman: if she was, you'd never have married her. Do you think she would have stuck with someone who was wrong for her only son if she didn't have to?"

Crowley stared into Joe's uncertain eyes and slowly shook his head. Joe seemed to find returning the shake of his head necessary. Crowley's smile grew larger, as Jenny found herself shaking her head. "That's right. She would have left a long time ago if she didn't feel you were the right one for Mark, or if she didn't love you. Hell, at Mark's present age, she could dump you like a sack of garbage without it having any real effect on the boy."

"She could maybe even find her old boyfriend and start all over, because he wouldn't have to worry about the hard part of raising a son. In his eyes all of this would be perfect. You did the hard work and she did the hard work and all he had to do was wait for the worst of it to be over. But what if she got pregnant again? Do you think that bastard would wait around for her? Hell No! He'd be gone for fifteen years in a heartbeat!"

"And if Jenny was stupid enough to divorce you over a loser like that, then she'd deserve the loneliness she'd get for her troubles. Wouldn't she?" Joe nodded, whatever doubts he'd been having apparently solved. "There. Only a woman of monumental stupidity would wait for a man all of her life after that man had abandoned her. If Jenny didn't love you, and if Jenny didn't know that you were the best thing for Mark, she'd have split a long time ago. And if Jenny is smart enough to realize that you're the best thing that ever happened to her and her son, then your fears are pointless."

Crowley opened the door and ushered Joe into his own kitchen. The shockingly wise expression on his face won Joe over to his side. Jenny reeled in confusion, wondering if maybe she was about to make a horrible mistake by killing Crowley. How could she hope to make Joe forgive her? Above her, blocking the light from finding the spot in the unfinished wall where she hid, Crowley finished his argument. "If you're worried about what Mark is thinking of you, talk to him. Ask him how he feels and tell him that you realize you made a horrible mistake. Ask him to forgive you. If he says no, then that's something you'll have to live with. But, if he says yes, you can work on making up for a lot of lost time. Personally, I think he'll say yes. Mark's a good kid. One of the best it's been my pleasure to meet." There was an element of sadness in his voice that chilled Jennifer Howell. A tone in his voice that made him seem to regret that one of the best kids he'd ever met was soon to be gone from his life for all time. Jenny bit her lip, praying that she was hearing something in his voice incorrectly.

"Listen, Joe, you go inside, I think I left my wallet in the car. I'll be right with you." She heard Joe mumble something, his voice too choked to speak properly. From where she was, Jenny could see Crowley's wallet in his right back pocket. The door above her closed and she heard Crowley's soft tread coming back down the stairs.

Jenny tried to force her body even further back into her cubbyhole. It was no good, Crowley sat to the right of where she hid, his tail bone resting lightly on a stair parallel to her trembling hands. He stared straight ahead, not looking towards Jenny at all. She knew with a certain sickening dread, that he was aware of both her and the weapon she was holding.

She watched as he lifted one hand to his face and rested his chin in the palm of that hand. Then, ever so casually, he held out his free hand to take the knife from her. Crying silent tears, she gave the weapon over. He placed it on the far side of his body, still staring into the darkened garage below.

Crowley spoke softly, words laced with cold hatred and disgust. "I don't know how long your lover over there has been back," he whispered. "I don't even care. But I want you to dry your eyes and I want you to think about what I said." Jenny started to cry in earnest, small hiccuping sounds coming from her throat and grief twisting her lovely face into a fearful mask.

In the shadows below she heard the stirring of something moving slowly. It didn't sound human by the way it scraped the floor with its feet. She could hear the bellows of its powerful lungs sucking in air. From that darkness something hissed her name, one part grief and four parts rage. Jenny found herself remembering the only fight she ever had with Todd, long years ago. He had beaten her with balled fists on that occasion. She remembered that the fight had started because of something she had said. Something about wanting him to be there forever. When she had mentioned to him the idea of getting an abortion so that they could be together. After he had slapped her senseless, he had made love to her, gently but urgently, telling her that he would be back when the time was right.

Long before that, when they had first started dating, he'd promised to be with her forever. Crowley's words were ripping through a dream she had built for herself half a lifetime ago. She had been dreaming of Todd being back since the day he had left, had used that dream as armor against everything that went wrong in her life. Now Jennifer Gallagher Howell realized that the same dream had protected her from everything that had gone right in her life as well.

Crowley gently placed a hand on her face and she held it there closely. Her tears fell freely and burned away the defensive shell she had donned so long ago. She couldn't tell how long they stayed that way, with Crowley giving her strength as Todd hissed her name coldly from the shadows. Finally, he pulled his hand away and wiped at her tear-stained cheeks.

"Now's the time, Jenny. Joe or Todd. Make up your mind. Pick one and go. Do it now."

Jenny found she really didn't have to think very hard about her decision; she turned her head away from the past and charged up the stairs. Behind her she heard the anguished scream of her lover as she slammed the door.

Joe was dozing on the couch in the living room, his soft snores undisturbed as she turned on the light to hold the night's approaching darkness at bay. Jenny slipped her own body next to his on the sofa. The area was small, but Joe's arms pulled her close, enclosing her in his warmth. She drifted to sleep with tears still in her eyes, as the battle for her soul raged on below.

3

Crowley reminded himself that he had seen worse, as the Todd-thing came out of the shadows. He forced himself to remember horrors he would rather have forgotten, as the brute came forward. One look was wasted on the knife next to him; it would never pierce the hide on the beast.

The Todd-thing spoke through lips plated in thick scales. "You little fuck! You ruined everything! Jenny was mine!" With the last words, he stepped into the light of the only bulb that was active in the garage. Crowley was right, he had seen worse. But not much worse. The Todd-thing's body was supported by thick powerful legs and by arms as wide as Crowley's torso. The arms were long, longer than a gorilla's, and the whole body was covered with thick green-gray hide, folding over on itself like the thick skin of a rhino. Bristling patches of fur ran across the body in the same areas where it could cover a man's. The fur was black in some places and gray in others. In a voice thick with hatred, the Todd-thing spoke again. "I waited so long, how could you do this to me?" To Crowley, it sounded as petulant as a three-year-old boy. Its tail lashed out behind the massive body, sweeping boxes of transmission fluid and oil across the length of the garage. Crowley didn't much like the look of the spiked ridges that sprouted from the tail.

They stared at each other for a long moment, both wondering who would make the first move. Crowley had time to study the low-slung jaw that looked quite capable of biting his head off. Thrusting tusks gleamed wetly in the yellow light from the bulb above its head. He looked past the grinning maw and past even the bat-like slits the beast called a nose, to the burning eyes hidden under its heavy brow. The eyes were as blue as the evening sky, just like the eyes of the creature's son.

Crowley started to smile and a laugh came from deep within him, lifting outward from his body in waves of malevolence. He stared the Todd-thing deep in the eyes as growing recognition bloomed in those orbs. Somehow, the foolish beast had supposed it could gain the upper hand.

The Todd-thing knew fear as the Hunter stepped forward, shedding its guise of humanity. Those of the Folk who comprised the Todd-thing shrieked in terror as Crowley stepped under the pool of light They had hastily vacated.

Too late, the Todd-thing remembered why it was that it had feared the Hunter. The sound of its breaking bones was buried beneath the shrieking maddened laughter of Jonathan Crowley. The Todd-thing's attempts at escape were futile. The Hunter batted it about as if it were the smallest of children and he a brutal adult who felt it needed severe discipline.

The Todd-thing was long dead before the laughter broke and fell into sobs of self-disgust. Crowley worked quickly to dispose of the remains.

Above him, in the house proper, Jenny and Joe found escape from the nightmares that had haunted their brief sleep. They smiled quickly and got to work on dinner at the same time that Jonathan Crowley came up the stairs smiling sheepishly and explaining that his wallet had been better hidden than he had thought. Joe made coffee while Jenny silently thanked her savior for what he had done.

Crowley smiled affably while they sipped at the warm brew, waiting for Mark to come home. In Crowley's eyes, this was turning out to be a fine day indeed.

4

Rick Lewis sat in the Summitville County Jail's single holding cell until after the sun had set. Then Stacy took pity on him and let him go. He wasn't very grateful, but he thanked her anyway. His right shoulder burned from where she had wrenched it behind his back earlier and his scraped knees had become a source of constant annoyance. None of those scrapes and injuries mattered the least in comparison to the throbbing of his head.

He was afraid, as afraid as he had ever been in his life. Rick Lewis had been visited by a ghost in his sleep, he was certain of that. Chuck Hanson had looked down on him while he was asleep and gently awakened him, stopping his cries of fear with a reproachful look. When Hanson told him to get up, he did, convinced that it was all just a dream by the lack of aches and pains in his body. Hanson smiled, as if reading his mind and pointed back to the slumbering form of his own body on the cot behind him. As much as Rick wanted to talk, no words would go past his lips.

Against his better judgment, he followed Hanson as the dead man walked away. He knew it was impossible to walk through walls and doors and trees and even the ground, but he did just that, with Hanson clearing the path. Chuck would pass through any physical object that should have blocked them, merely wade through it as if it weren't there, and Rick simply followed suit. Oddly, the one time he tried the same thing without Hanson going before him—a chair that was nearby, a target for him to experiment against—the attempt failed. Rick didn't question this ability, nor did he wonder why they were walking into the woods; he knew that patience would answer all of his questions in the long run. He also suspected that he would not like the explanations.

Eventually they came to a spot in the woods where the trees forced themselves away from what was growing in their soil, seemingly ashamed of what dwelled in their midst. It appeared to be a stone, but Rick was not fooled by the image. Stones do not have heartbeats. The thing pulsed strongly with a rhythmic beat all its own, expanding and contracting and above all else, growing. Even to Rick's naked eye, it could be seen to be growing, like a malignant cancer caught on video and fast-forwarded: the progress was still gradual, but actually visible to the naked eye. Soon it would tower over the trees; soon you would be able to see it from Summitville proper.

This isn't the first time, Rick. The voice in his head was Chuck's and Rick felt himself shiver, tried to make believe that it was only a dream, tried to remember that Chuck was dead. Chuck shook his head sadly, lit a spectral cigarette with ghostly hands. The doctor couldn't help wondering where the hell a ghost would get a cigarette. What? The phantoms of cigarettes smoked in the distant past? He shook his head, reminding himself that anything was possible in dreams. *It's more than a dream and yes, I'm still dead. Get used to it, Rick. The world is moving on again.*

Rick tried to block the sounds of Hanson's voice with his hands, but to no avail. The sounds didn't bother with his ears; they went straight into his head. *Don't turn away from me Rick, I need your help.* There was a long silence in his dream haunting and then Chuck added the one word he could not resist, the one word Chuck almost never bothered with. *Please.*

"What the hell can I do! I don't know how to help you, Chuck. Goddamn it, man, what the hell am I supposed to do!" The frustration simply could not hide itself any longer. A year's worth of bitterness spilled from his mouth, he raged at the specter before him, wanting nothing more than to be left alone by the ghosts of his own past. He screamed and ranted, throwing insults at his friend's memory, throwing fits at the friend who had dared to die on him.

Through it all, Chuck Hanson stood still, looking sadly at the man he loved as if he were a brother, the only man from other than Summitville that he had ever liked. Ever loved. *I'm sorry, Rick. I couldn't stay. Lord knows I didn't want to end up like this. Please, help me be free. I'll tell you all I can, but you've got to help me. Summitville was all I ever had, I can't stand to see it die this way.*

Rick stared long and hard at his dead friend, finally nodding his agreement, knowing that he would regret the assistance. "So, tell me what to do."

Chuck Hanson smiled. It was a smile of rare beauty for the man, making him look as he had in life, back in college, when he could pretend that the world was still his for the grabbing. *Watch closely, Rick, I only have the strength to do this once...*

5

The world shifted, changed and emptied of so much that had made it familiar. It may have only been a dream, but it was a very realistic delusion, more real than some parts of Rick's life had ever been. The land was arid, dusty in a way that even the driest sections of the Sahara shouldn't be. There was no sign of life to be found. There were no trees, there was not even a hollow spot in the ground, where the Overtree should be. Instead, there was a mountain. Still, Rick new instinctively that he stood on the same soils as he had a moment before, perhaps a thousand millennia before Man would come to walk on the earth.

From above him in the night's skies, he could see the light of a falling star. There, far away but growing closer. The oddest light he had ever seen. Whatever it was, he expected it to strike the ground at any moment. He cringed and mentally prepared himself for death. He heard Chuck Hanson's good natured booming from behind him. *Shit, Rick. I'm here to show you, not kill you. You're right in a way, this is only a dream. It's just a dream that I made you have. Now open your eyes and look.*

Rick stared at the fiery light from far above, growing closer and closer. His eyes should have been seared by the powerful sickly glow; instead they simply absorbed knowledge. Before the Fire could hit the earth, it burned itself out. From the center of what had been a raging sun, something fell to the ground. It landed gently, falling at his feet.

Rick turned away from the oddity for a second, looking at the image of Chuck Hanson and frowning. "I thought for sure that must be the cause of the Overtree, a meteor hitting the mountain top or something."

No, again with the laughter, but softer now, little more than a chuckle. *No that's another story, one not even I am privy to. Keep watching, Rick.*

Rick stared at the small lump that had fallen to the ground. What it was he couldn't have said, but where it fell was obvious. It had fallen where the Stone now grew from the ground near Overtree. The lump shimmied, forced itself into the ground and hid from his sight.

Centuries passed in the blink of an eye and the whole barren land formed life, things not seen before by mankind and long gone before the first human walked, strode across the earth and into the shades of the past as Rick Lewis watched. And then the Stone broke the ground, rising like the first shoots from some vile, malicious seed.

It was a cancerous thing, but unable to grow, it seemed, without help. It sat and waited, until a lonely, scared young boy was beaten and lay bloodied across its surface. Twice then it moved, sending strange mockeries from its veined surface to wreak havoc. Once it was thwarted by fire, once Rick could not see what stopped its attempts to grow, but it had seemingly been stopped.

Now it grew. Like a fungus rising from a bloated corpse, it seethed and grew. Bloating, reaching heights it had never achieved before. Rick had the repulsive notion that it would soon explode like a puffball, sending millions of spores into the air. He shivered at the thought.

He was back in the woods, just as he knew they really were. He never wanted to find out in person, but he knew that soon he would do just that. "Is that what really happened? The Mushroom From Outer Space?"

Hanson smiled, shook his mane of brown hair. *No, but it's close enough. It's all you or I could hope to understand. All I can say for sure is that it's alive and it wants to grow somehow. Rick, you can't let that happen. Please, stop this thing from growing anymore.*

"How? How can I stop it? Chuck, I don't even know what it is."

Chuck Hanson faded from view and the woods soon followed, as Rick awoke to the sound of Stacy Calhoun unlocking the cell door. She was pretty, but at that moment, even with tear-stains marking her face and a nose made red from crying, she looked lovelier than any woman he had ever seen.

"I 'spect you'll be wanting to leave now, Rick. Go on home." She turned away without another word, walking slowly back to where her desk sat. Aside from Rick she was the only person there. Neither of them said another word as Rick walked out of the Sheriff's offices, grumbling thanks, and towards the small house he had called his own since moving to Summitville.

Rick desperately wanted to leave town, wanted to run from the troubles as quickly as his legs would carry him. Instead, he looked into the phone book for the address of P. J. Sanderson. He remembered no words, could think of nothing said by his ghostly friend, but he knew that Chuck wanted him and Sanderson together.

The author answered on the first ring and somehow Rick knew the man had been waiting for his call.

Chapter Twenty

1

Despite her best efforts Cassie could not find a comfortable way to lie on the bed. She felt feverish, her body ached. Her entire body felt like it was sunburned inside and out. She wanted rest; she wanted even more to be with Mark.

That decision made, Cassie climbed out of her traitorous bed and started pulling on clothes. Jeans and a thin t-shirt were all she had the patience for, more than that and she would have felt constricted. Below her, she could hear the sounds of her parents arguing politely in the living room. Heavens forbid that they should argue like real people, or in any way reflect the fact that they had feelings. Thinking about her parents was starting to piss her off, so she thought of Mark instead.

Cassie had no desire to be interrogated by her parents. She slipped from the second story window. She landed roughly, hard enough to have sprained her ankles at the very least a month ago. Now the impact didn't even faze her; like the young man on her mind, Cassie Monroe had been going through changes.

It was all she could do to walk. Her muscles jumped under her skin and made most of her body feel as if someone had carefully removed all of her bones. She acknowledged the need to see Mark, the actual physical addiction that burned through her body, only on the faintest levels of consciousness. Mostly she simply stumbled on, glancing off of whatever obstacle came into her path. Around her the shadows moved, tiny entities that gently guided her fever-burned body towards the woods. Towards the pulsating Stone that rested just under the Overtree.

2

Lisa Scarrabelli writhed on her bed, mind locked in a hideous vision of the atrocities that had been done to her. She whimpered in her sleep as she remembered what Mark Howell had done to her, hands drawing into talons and clawing roughly at the sheets. Her teeth were bared in a rictus of pain and fury, her brows knitted over closed eyes that flashed everywhere, seeking for a place to escape from the nightmares she was forced to endure.

Lisa felt her body violated again, felt all of the pain that she had suffered at Mark Howell's hands repeated for the seventh time that night. Each time the dream-visions started again, fear was burned out of her, replaced with a fiery hatred that grew stronger and stronger.

Tony Scarrabelli, asleep on the chair at Lisa's vanity table, as he had been every night since she had been allowed out of the hospital, awoke to the sound of rending fabric. He swiped the sleep from his eyes with a tired hand and then gazed at his sister. What he saw made him awaken almost instantaneously and was a vision he was certain he would never forget.

Lisa stood atop her bed, holding the tattered remains of her covers in her hands. Her eyes were closed and her entire body was coiled with tension. Every muscle on her frame stood out in perfect relief as she stepped purposefully from the bed and started towards the door of her bedroom. Tony was too shocked to try stopping her. Tony watched as she opened the door and strode from the room, an angry Amazon warrior, or perhaps a Valkyrie, on her way to do battle with the enemy. Tony didn't stop her. Instead he grabbed the cellular phone in the living room and dialed Tyler's number as he followed her out the front door.

Tony had to move quickly to cover the extra distance as she opened the driver's side door of his car and started the engine. He made the passenger's side door and climbed in even as the car was starting to move. Tyler answered the phone on the first ring and somehow Tony wasn't surprised.

3

A great portion of Summitville's population went to sleep at the ridiculously early hour of nine o'clock that night. Most of the exceptions were the pieces in a game they could not hope to fully understand. P. J. Sanderson met with Rick Lewis outside of the Basilisk. Neither of them carried any weapons, save the flashlights that both clutched tightly in their hands. There was little discussion, both were far too nervous to try speaking in more than short, brusque sentences. They had compared notes earlier, talking for a long time on the phone, before P. J. finally spoke up about what neither wanted to think about. Whatever was happening was obviously coming to a head. The situation had gone on for far too long already and the only certainty was that they needed to stop the thing that rested in the woods near Lake Overtree.

Less than fifteen minutes later they headed towards the sheriff's offices, stopping only long enough to grab two of the shotguns from the weapons locker that Chuck Hanson had never bothered to keep locked. After getting halfway to the woods, they remembered to get the shells for the weapons and turned back to the sheriff's offices for just that reason. Neither of them paid the least bit of attention to the slumbering form of Stacy Calhoun. She reciprocated, staying soundly asleep through their noisy search for shotgun shells.

The nervous men stopped at the parking lot of Westphalen High, at approximately the same time that Tony and Tyler followed Lisa Scarrabelli into the woods.

Nearby, Jonathan Crowley allowed himself a small, tight smile. If all went according to Crowley's plans, they would meet up at around the same time, near the Stone that grew even larger as it started moving its own pieces into place...

4

Jonathan Crowley walked into the darkened woods as if it was noon and he was perfectly at home. To anyone that could have seen him, he would have looked perfectly at ease. Truth to tell, he was more than a little nervous. This was one of the rare times when he was almost certain that he was walking to his death. Naturally the knowledge that he could soon be deceased did nothing to stop his smile from growing larger with anticipation of the battle to come. The thought of wiping the Stone and the Folk from the face of the earth was more than enough to make up for a little fear, and as for death, well, it wouldn't be the first time.

A blur of motion off to the right caught Crowley's attention. As he looked that way, towards the center of the Overtree, he saw the column of pure white mist lift into the air above the placid waters. The mist was unnaturally thick. Ropy tendrils lifted from the depths of the quickly coalescing cloud and spread outwards, expanding the fog in a solid wall as they merged. In less than a minute, the column had bloated to three times its original thickness and it showed no sign of slowing.

Every town, no matter how pristine, has its secrets. It wasn't Crowley's place to even begin guessing all of the secrets of Summitville. But one of those secrets had just decided to force itself from the waters and it looked intent on Crowley's demise. There were forms buried in that thick mist, shades or actual corpses, and they were coming towards John Crowley with all the moans and shrieks of dead things that could find no peace. Their bodies were encompassed in a Kirlian aura the same color as the flesh that fell from their forms, a queasy gray that bordered on the color of aspen trees in the late autumn. The increasing howls of pain that came from them told Crowley that they were coming closer with more certainty than the slight expansion of their dimensions.

For the briefest of seconds, Crowley was afraid. He knew the fears that any normal person would know when approached by dead things that refused to stay dead. Then he remembered who and what he really was.

Crowley smiled as he approached the edge of the lake. His smile grew even wider as he considered that perhaps this was all that the Folk could think of to scare him. By the time he and the specters met in combat, Crowley's laughs were drowning out their screams of damnation.

5

Mark Howell lay in his special place, comforted by the sweet dreams that encased him, unaware that the final changes were taking place in his body. The Folk did not touch him. They were far too busy dealing with Crowley and his interlopers. Instead, the Stone upon which he rested made the last of the changes Itself.

The granite-like substance liquefied beneath him, and where his body met with the viscous fluid, his flesh was peeled away, making room for the raping tentacles of rock that buried themselves in his body, in his soul. All that had been Mark Howell was removed, replaced by the alien thoughts that the Stone wanted his lifeless shell to hold. The Stone finished the final changes, moving more quickly than the Folk could ever hope to. It sealed the ruptured, ravaged flesh of Mark Howell's body back together, leaving no sign that it had ever been disturbed.

When Mark Howell again opened his eyes, all thoughts of friendship, all thoughts of past pleasures and pains were gone, removed like a cancer and replaced with a mind as alien to this flesh as the creature that had created it. Sky blue eyes looked upon the world and found it wanting.

Less than a hundred yards away stood Cassie Monroe, ready at last to join with her mate.

6

Lisa stormed through the woods, ignoring all pleas from Tony and Tyler, plodding through the natural undergrowth and into the unnatural writhing mass of green that surrounded the Stone in Its resting place.

Tyler was bleeding from a dozen small cuts and grazes and beside him Tony was faring no better. Every time they came within a few feet of Lisa, obstacles appeared where there were none a second before. Tyler did his best to avoid the roots and small stones that seemed to literally grow out of the ground where he placed his feet, but to no avail. Beside him, Tony again fell to his knees, grunting in pain and immediately climbing to his feet and following his sister. Tyler watched Tony's every move carefully. His glasses had fallen off and disappeared almost a quarter of a mile ago and with the speed at which Lisa walked, oddly unobstructed by the treacherous flooring of the woods, he'd had no time to look for them. Without Tony's blurred form beside him, Tyler would have been lost long ago.

The two scrabbled desperately to keep up with Lisa, losing more ground by the minute. Finally, they saw her break between two of the fog shrouded trees into a clearing and with renewed energy charged towards the opening. An opening that was suddenly, irrevocably, gone. The trees had moved, seemed to shrug themselves towards each other and then it was all gone, nothing left of the clearing, just a wall of foliage too closely knit together for even Tyler's frame to squeeze through.

"Fuck! God damn it all!" Tony's voice was incredibly loud in the odd silence of the woods; even without the clarity that his glasses brought, Tyler could see the frustration on Tony's face. The two stood together, staring at the brooding barricade before them, wondering just how they were going to get past it, how they were ever going to find Lisa again. *If* they were ever going to see Lisa again.

7

The silence between Rick Lewis and P. J. Sanderson was uncomfortable. Both were locked into thoughts of how they could destroy the demons held within the woods and equally into thoughts of Chuck Hanson. Both mourned the man they had each called their best friend at different points in their life. Both wondered if they could have done more for him during his time in their lives.

The two were so lost in thought that they made it much easier for the Folk to read them, to find what made them afraid, and to imitate that fear. The first of the fears to manifest was the deepest rooted fear in Rick's mind, a fear that even Rick himself had forgotten about.

It started as an itch, directly after a slight scraping of his arm against one of the skeletal aspen trees that made so substantial a portion of the woods below the lake. Rick shifted the shotgun he carried under his right arm into a comfortable position and then reached over to scratch at the distraction. As his nails struck the flesh of his arm, he cried out, dropping the loaded firearm and clutching at the burning pain that launched itself through his wrist and up to his elbow.

P. J. looked over at the doctor with concern, fearing that he had been attacked by something. He was relieved to see that there were no vampires surrounding his associate, no werewolves feasting on his neck.

Then he saw the wound. P. J.'s eyes grew wide at the sight of the blood flowing from the gash on Rick's left arm, awestruck by the flaps of tattered flash that draped from the wound. "Dear god, Lewis, what have you done to yourself?" P. J. set down his own .12 gauge and walked over to where the man was clasping his arm tightly, trying to slow the considerable flow of blood with his free hand.

"Unh, damn, what the hell did I do?" Lewis was looking down at his arm with equal surprise, looking more puzzled than pained. "Shit, I don't think I even brought a Bandaid with me. Shine the light over here, would you?" P. J. Sanderson did so gladly, happy to have finally met a doctor that didn't panic at the sight of his own blood.

The light shone onto the wound and Lewis removed his hand, allowing for an undisturbed viewing of the carnage. Sanderson was appalled. The gash slid along the full length of the man's forearm and looked to be about three inches deep. "Rick, what the devil did you do? Never mind that, we've got to get you to the clinic, as quickly as we can."

The two men turned away from their target in the woods, pausing only long enough for the author to grab up both shotguns. Before they had gone ten feet, Rick Lewis dropped to his knees, squealing out his surprise at the sudden increase in pain.

Sanderson set down both of the shotguns and again grabbed the flashlight to see what was wrong, peering at the wound intently, along with Lewis.

"What the hell is going on here?" Lewis laughed slightly, hysteria edging his voice, as the two men looked at the odd patch of white that was now in the very heart of the wound. Before their eyes it started growing. For all the world, the only thought that came to Sanderson's mind was that someone had filled the bloodied hole with shaving cream, from the inside of the raw cut. The white patch grew in size and forced the flowing blood out of the channel before bringing the crimson flow to a trickle and then stopping the leakage entirely.

Lewis looked at Sanderson with an odd sort of smile. "It doesn't even hurt, it feels just fine. Heh, maybe there's someone on our side in all of this crap."

"Don't you think we should get to the clinic?"

Lewis looked at the wound, touched the rapidly stiffening lump and shrugged. "We came this far and I don't think I'll get the guts to try this a second time. Something stopped the bleeding and something stopped the pain. For all I know, the whole thing is knitting itself together while we speak. It even feels that way, the way your skin itches under a scab. I feel good enough to go on, if you do."

P. J. looked at the man skeptically. *How the hell could something like that not hurt?* he thought for only a few seconds. "Let's get out to the clearing then. I don't think I'd get the nerve to try this a second time either."

Together the two men set off, heading again towards the Stone in the heart of the woods. As they progressed, the fog around them grew thicker and thicker, burgeoning heavy enough to make them forget about conversation as they focused all of their attention on the meager light that illuminated the path they walked. Several minutes passed in relative silence, before P. J. asked Rick how he was doing.

The man's response was that he was fine except for the gnats he kept swatting away. "What gnats? I haven't run across any as yet."

"You haven't?"

"Unh unh. Not too many bugs come out to feed in a fog like this, to the best of my knowledge."

His only response for half a minute was the sound of Lewis' breathing. The breaths slowly built in speed, until at last, the man spoke in a voice that was barely a croaking whisper. "Could you shine your light over at me and t-tell me w-what you see?"

P. J. aimed his light in the direction of the doctor's voice, stepping closer to the man so that he could see what might be covering him other than the fog. "Oh, Lewis. Oh sweet Jesus."

Rick stood bathed in the yellow light of the six cell torch, eyes wide and body trembling. His face was pulled in a rictus of fear, almost comical in its proportions. From the top of his head, all the way down to the tops of his penny loafers, the man was covered in small flesh colored forms, skittering and crawling over him as if he were a log and they were termites. Rick Lewis flinched one eye shut reflexively, as one of the countless spiders actually walked across his naked eye's surface. The spider, small as it was, was crushed into his eye, pulped as its delicate, hairless body was pinched between his eye's lids.

P. J. shook his head in denial, watched the man shaking violently before him and took an automatic step backwards.

"Please don't leave me! Oh shit, P. J.; help me, please!" The man's trembling voice forced P. J. into action and he stepped forward to start slapping the creatures off of his friend. The first swing knocked more than fifty of the creatures into a gelid goo, the second did the same. P. J. fought back his bile, swallowing hard again and again and feeling the reflex at the back of his throat try to force anything that might be in his stomach back out. He continued slapping at the tiny creatures, pausing only when one was swift enough to climb onto his own body.

He was busy flicking the one off of his own wrist when he heard Rick whimper-shriek. Looking at the man again, P. J. saw that the arachnids chasing aimlessly over his body were starting to grow, swelling like blood fattened ticks and growing darker, hairier as the went. By the time he had finally knocked the spider off of his own hand, the rest of the little monstrosities of Rick Lewis had grown to the size of cherry tomatoes. P. J. stepped back again, caught off guard, and the creatures continued to grow in size.

It was more than he could take. P. J. Sanderson turned his back on Rick Lewis and ran, dodging trees and jumping over small shrubs with an agility he would have long thought gone from his body had he been capable of rational thought. Instinct guided him around the obstacles in his path and directly towards the Stone in the center of the woods. He looked over his shoulder only once and by that point, there was nothing to be seen of Rick Lewis' body under the increasing waves of tarantula-sized spiders that were crawling from their nest on his bloodied arm.

P. J. whined incoherently to himself, praying that the sounds he heard from behind him were only the sounds of the leaves from the forest's floor settling down again and not the sounds of giant spider legs charging after him.

He never heard the muffled cries that came from Rick Lewis' throat, never heard the pained whimpers that continued for the next fifteen minutes, somewhere behind him. Even if he had, it wouldn't have mattered. Perhaps nothing ever would again.

8

A little over two miles from Summitville proper, just over a mile from the Red Oaks subdivision, the Basilisk Bookstore lay quiet, as still as the grave. The Folk spent several minutes outside the main entrance to the bookstore before finally slipping through the obstructing door. There was little curiosity about the many tales wrapped in paper, and the comic books garnered no interest from the Folk either. But the large silent figure in the corner, the one entombed in a glass case, that was another story entirely.

The Folk climbed atop the case, surrounded the case from all directions and slowly melted through the dust laden glass. The figure moved not at all, seemingly unimpressed by any threat that the Folk might make. No protest came from the hulking brute as They violated its skin, pushing into the latex and foam rubber, slipping into the mannequin on which it rested.

Once inside the silent figure, They formed Themselves to accommodate the structural differences that separated the demonic form from Their normal prey. Empty sockets were filled with Their mass, becoming fully functioning eyes, with reptilian pupils. Muscles were developed to accommodate flight, latex teeth were hardened, as was the skin. Though still flexible, the epidermis grew as strong as the stone it was designed to look like.

They tested the wings and the slightest shrug of Their new limbs shattered the glass coffin. They sniffed the air with Their new nose, satisfied with Their olfactory senses. Blood flowed through the veins and arteries that They created and as one, They commanded Their new form to walk.

Sligis the Gargoyle stepped away from the fiction that he had been and through the brick wall that kept him inside of the Basilisk. The bellow of triumph that ripped past his stony lips was thunderous and with a few small steps Sligis was soon in flight, ready at last to face his creator.

9

Jonathan Crowley met the shadows in the fog eagerly. He was ready for whatever they decided to throw his way and he was prepared to cause them serious harm. What he was not ready for, was the fact that they were not there. His leap was met with no resistance whatsoever and the collision he had expected was met a few seconds later, when he landed in the waters of the Overtree.

Had it happened to someone else, anyone in Summitville perhaps, or even one of the Folk, he would have laughed. As it was the only thing that stopped him from screaming out his rage at the insult was the water that lapped around his neck. The lake was deceptively deep here. After a brief reflection, he decided it really was a rather ridiculous situation and silently scolded himself for getting too cocky, too ready to fight whatever was thrown at him by the enemy.

Chuckling to himself, he started towards the bank only a few feet from him. And that was when the creatures he had seen above the lake's waters attacked him from below. Water-softened flesh and nearly petrified bone reached for his ankle and yanked him under the water's surface.

Crowley opened his eyes, trying to see through the silt that lifted from the lake's bottom. No luck. He lashed out with his free foot at the force that held firmly to his ankle. There was no give, he was caught. Something rotten grabbed at him around the waist, pulling him further from the shore. Hellish green light glared from behind hollowed sockets and the muck-covered teeth of the mortal remains that swam in front of him latched onto his leg, just above the knee.

The pain was too much, too sudden and Crowley screamed out the remaining air in his lungs. He started to reach for the figure on his leg, the same one that surrounded his waist, but was hampered by the sudden arm that locked around his throat from behind.

The more he struggled, the more the dead creatures folded themselves around him, pinning his arms, his legs, even his neck, so that he could do nothing but try to slip free without success. The only sound he could hear any longer was the sound of his heart pounding in his ears, drowning out even the sound of the waters that pushed at his eardrums as he was forced further and further into the depths of the lake. What little light had been present grew fainter—or perhaps he was blacking out. He saw only the darkness, lit slightly by the filthy green light that rolled from the corpses around him.

Panic started to build in his arrhythmic heart, his struggles burning away the oxygen in his blood and weakening him further. *Stupid! Just plain goddamn stupid!* He chastised himself, knowing that there was no one else present to take care of the job for him. The rage grew stronger, even as his heartbeat weakened, stuttered, preparing to stop completely. Jonathan Crowley forced himself to stop struggling, knowing that it would do him no good, knowing that it was already too late.

He cleared his mind.

He opened his mouth.

He said forbidden words where none could hear them, watching the bubbles of air flow upward, away from his sinking form. The figures that held him grew panicked, broke away from him, trying to escape before it was too late.

They never had a chance.

10

From their spot in the woods, Tyler and Tony heard the sounds of what seemed to be multiple explosions and a few seconds later, looking in the direction of the unnatural sounds, saw a geyser of water lift from the Overtree far above them.

"What now?" asked Tyler, looking at Tony and trying desperately to see him clearly.

Tony continued to look only at the lake, shaking his head slightly. "Dunno." He could no longer think…it hurt to even try. Everything seemed to hurt: the healing bruises on his body, the chip from his tooth, the cracks in his rib cage and most of all his soul.

How many blows was his psyche supposed to take before he broke? He had been bested at the one thing he could ever do well, fighting. He had been terrified by a man that was no taller than him and a good deal lighter in proportion. He had betrayed a friend and now he had lost his sister to whatever was out here in the woods. Tony desperately wanted his mother's arms around him, comforting him as they had when he was so much younger and his parents had still been capable of love.

The pain was so extreme that he simply grew numb. Tony Scarrabelli had never been meant to handle pressure and the last few days had drained him of all his fight. The man that Tyler was looking towards for leadership and or advice was simply not capable of helping him. Tyler would have never thought it possible.

Tony looked at the lake for a few more minutes, listening to the complete silence of the woods, and then he started walking. Tyler watched with a slack jaw, unable to conceive of what he was seeing—or almost seeing at any rate. "Tony where the hell are you going?"

Tony looked over his shoulder with eyes on the verge of tears, shook his head and continued on his way.

Tyler started walking after him, indignant surprise and a little fear of being by himself in the woods spurring him on. "Tony. Hel-lo, earth to Tony, are you in there? We have to get Lisa, remember?" Tony started walking a little faster, Tyler matched the pace, noticing idly that he was having no trouble avoiding all of the pitfalls that had sent him stumbling earlier.

"Tony, goddamn it if you don't come back here I'm gonna hit you." There was a sight he could see vividly: his fist would probably do about as much to Tony as it would to one of the trees around them. Tony kept walking, ignoring Tyler completely. "Tony, I'm not kidding damn it, get the hell back over here." Nothing. The larger boy kept on walking and Tyler was momentarily reminded of Mark walking through the woods just the night before. "Tony, one last chance. Come back here, you pussy."

Tony kept on going, his shoulders hitching and his body shaking. Tyler lowered his head and charged like a bull, hitting Tony in the square of his back and dropping them both to the ground. Before Tony could turn over, Tyler was pounding with balled up hands—they really couldn't be called fists, had he actually been using fists, his thumbs wouldn't have been tucked inside of his fingers—actually calling Tony all of the names that Tony had for so long called him. "Come back here you fucking queer! You're not leaving her out here alone! I won't let you! Get back over there you sonuvabitch!" There were more words, but they were mostly blubbered phrases that meant nothing in the long and short of it all.

Tony stared at Tyler with wide eyes, watching the smaller boy's fists come up and down, driving like pistons, but only causing glancing blows. Tony had automatically pulled into a defensive posture, fully expecting to get hurt by the punches and instead only getting pushed around a little. For perhaps the first time in his life, he really contemplated the differences between himself and Tyler in physical size.

Earlier in the day, Tony had experienced the catharsis brought on by crying, now he experienced the cleansing catharsis of laughter. He howled his laughs out of his body, laughing so long and so hard that his eyes watered and his stomach muscles cramped and his cracked ribs burned. Tyler kept hitting him for several moments and Tony couldn't help but laugh even harder when the fists struck him, laughing so hard that he literally could not catch his breath.

Somewhere along the way, Tyler joined in on the chuckles and the two of them ended the one-sided fight with both participants on their backs, staring at the heavy fog around them and sharing a moment of almost-sanity.

Then Crowley showed up, spoiling everything. At least until they got a look at his muck covered body and the water that dripped from his hair. The sour expression on his muddied face was all that it took to start them laughing again.

11

P. J. Sanderson thought he heard laughter in the distance, shook his head to expel such thoughts and continued on his way. The guns were gone, Rick Lewis was gone *dead! Eaten by mutant spiders from outer space!* but it didn't matter. Now or never, he had a mess to clean up. He was tired of running and too worried about Mark to do anything but go on.

Next to him, one of the small streams that trickled from the Overtree whispered to itself. He stooped next to the lazily moving waters, cupped a double handful and washed it over his tired face. The freshness replaced the musty smell of his sweat, refreshing his body if not his spirit.

"Too old for this shit. Too old to run from monsters. Just plain too old, Phil. That's what you are. Too fucking old." The words were only for himself. But apparently something agreed with him, because it replied with a hellborn shriek that shook the ground under his feet.

He may have been older than he liked to think about, but for the second time that night adrenaline shot into his system like a brew from the fountain of youth. P. J. Sanderson turned his head sharply, sending a painful knot of burning heat into his neck, and gazed over his shoulder and up at the creature that could make a noise straight from his worst nightmares. The beast matched up with the sound of his dark dreams perfectly.

For the life of him, the author couldn't accept that Sligis was hovering above his head. He took in the scaly gray hide, he took in the eyes that matched his own personal vision of the gargoyle, he even noticed that the veins on the leathery wings were perfect down to the last detail. He just refused to accept what his eyes were seeing.

Sligis landed before him, sinking a good inch and a half into the ground where his carved stone feet made contact with the earth. The clear burning hatred that showed itself on the creature's face was exactly right, perfect in every detail that his mind had created. The flaring stone nostrils, so like a vampire bat's, the fangs that matched, the serpentine tongue that licked at the edge of the lipless mouth as the mouth was drawn into a victorious smile, all of it was exactly as it should be, better by far than the costume that sat in his shop. Hell, this Sligis even had a tail that lashed slowly as it approached his prey. *That would be me* P. J. mused, as Sligis stepped slowly forward.

For the second time that night, P. J. Sanderson started hurdling obstacles left and right, heading straight for the Stone in the center of the woods. Behind him he left a seven foot monster and a sizable portion of his sanity. The former at least seemed intent on joining up with him again.

12

Mark Howell, Cassie Monroe, and Lisa Scarrabelli all stared at each other. Only one of them truly saw anything and that one was hardly what he had once been. What had been Mark Howell smiled in triumph, slowly removing his clothes, feeling the body that housed Its strange mind start to respond to the ideas now forming.

Behind and above Mark Howell's body, the Stone pulsed, sending out alien thoughts and pulling the Folk home, back to Their Creator. The massive pillar heaved, growing still larger, forcing more of itself out of the ground and eagerly awaiting the return of its children.

The tortured, subdued minds of Cassie and Lisa screamed, and their bodies did likewise. One screamed with fear and pain, the other with ecstatic pleasure. The cause of both was the same.

13

The screams caught the attention of P. J. Sanderson, even as he caught the attention of Jonathan Crowley, Tyler Wilson, and his own nephew. Behind the author, they spotted the massive shape of Sligis the Gargoyle, even as that hideous figure grew closer to its target. The pursued and pursuer were coming directly towards them and John Crowley assessed the situation quickly, doing the only thing he could think of to save the author.

Jonathan Crowley stuck his foot out and sent P. J. Sanderson sliding across the ground, just as Sligis reached out and grabbed where the author had been a second before. Sligis turned his head and hissed loudly at the interloper, just before the figure stiffened and slammed into the trees that surrounded the Stone's clearing. What had just seconds before been half a ton of animated granite once again became a Hollywood costume and the mannequin it encased and flopped to the ground, tearing itself into fragments as the Folk escaped Their vessel.

The Folk stared at Crowley, Tony, and Tyler, then shifted Their gaze towards P. J. Sanderson's battered form, as he pushed himself up off the ground, trying to stand and failing. They fluctuated, shifting and reforming as Their attention focused on each individual. Silent and shadowy, They stared at the only remaining forces that would try to stop Them. Then They charged the barrier of trees, disappearing into the clearing that was blocked to the mere humans.

Tony and Tyler stared at the space where They had been, too unsettled to think coherently. Jonathan Crowley sauntered over to where P. J. Sanderson was still attempting to stand and assisted the man to his feet. Sanderson nodded his thanks, not really certain how to take the kindness from his nemesis.

Crowley flashed a million watt smile at the man who looked easily fifteen years older, patted him on the back, helping to knock loose some of the thick layer of filth on P. J.'s clothes. "Good to see you Philly. I thought maybe you'd wussed out on me."

The author stared at him with confused eyes. "You're dirty. Somehow I didn't think you could get dirty." He felt foolish as he said the words, but they came from his mouth before he could stop them.

Crowley chuckled, shook his head slightly and grinned even wider than before. "That's what I like about you, Philly. You're never at a lack for stupid things to say." He stared at P. J. Sanderson with what almost looked like affection in his eyes and then looked over at the two young men standing near by. "Well, looks like this is all of us," he mused. "So, what do you say we all go kill a monster or two."

Chapter Twenty-One

1

Tony stared at the surroundings glumly, with no real hope of breaking past the barricading trees and into the grove beyond. He glanced over at Jonathan Crowley, almost afraid to voice his question. "Uh, how are we supposed to get past all the trees?"

Crowley looked back at him as if he had lost his mind. "Easy, you just ignore the ones that aren't there."

Tyler looked over at the man in much the same way that Crowley had just looked at Tony, and asked the obvious question. "And how the hell are we supposed to know which ones 'aren't there?' They all look and feel pretty goddamn real from over here."

Crowley put on his thousand-watt grin again, shaking his head as if he were talking to a skeptical child about the reality of Santa Claus. Without preamble, he grabbed a handful of dried leaves and dirt from the ground and tossed it directly at the trees. The dirt did the natural thing and bounced off of the trunks of the trees. Well, most of them, anyway. One of the trees failed to stop the light projectiles and Tyler looked on amazed as the soil sailed through the bark of the monolithic red oak. "You just have to know how to look, it's kind of like watching where the magician's hands are, if you catch my meaning."

"Sonovabitch." Tyler walked over to the spot where the earth had failed to bounce and touched it with his hand. It felt completely solid. "How the hell did you do that?" Just to convince his senses that he had not gone completely insane, Tyler tossed some dirt of his own at the target tree. It passed right through the wood.

"Fuck me…" Tony replied to the second failure on the part of the tree. P. J. Sanderson echoed the words.

Without further preamble, Crowley walked into the tree, fading from view as he did so. "The tough part is convincing your body to agree with what your mind already knows. It's not really here, it never was."

The three remaining men stared at the tree for a few seconds and P. J. made his move. "If that bastard can do it, so can I." and with that, he too merged into the tree. Tony was next and lastly Tyler.

Stepping through the illusion was unsettling at best. None of the men, with the exception of Crowley, could accept the lack of solidity at its face value and whenever they wavered in their resolve, they could feel the start of the pressure around them, the pressure of a forty-foot tall tree completely surrounding them. Fear as much as denial is what finally allowed them through the illusion. Crowley deliberately did not specify what would have happened if they had turned back, though he was sorely tempted to, with Sanderson.

Crowley broke back into the reality of the clearing first, stepping quickly aside to allow the others through without collision. He stared around with eyes that were mere slits in his face, nose wrinkled in disgust and teeth bared. At that moment he made P. J. think of a wolf, just by the expression on his face.

The four men looked at the clearing, unsettled by what they saw, terrified by the implications. The clearing was impossibly large, larger than the area should have permitted, larger than the town of Summitville. And at the clearing's heart, thrusting from the ground like a mountain in Its own right, the Stone pulsed, brooding protectively over the three figures at Its base.

The entire area around the Stone was surrounded by a small ocean of the Folk. Fear gave Them a reality They had lacked before. Shaped by the minds of Their foes and by the mind of Mark Howell, the Folk were both beautiful and frightening.

They stood only a few inches in height, with soft pearlescent skin and flowing hair of every possible color. The Folk shifted from foot to foot, stretching wings that resemble a bat's in structure and a butterfly's in color. The shapes that They held fluctuated, changing subtly as They perceived the fears of Their enemies. Sibilant whispers came from Their mouths, mouths which were rapidly filling with tusk-like fangs.

Lisa Scarrabelli and Cassie Monroe lay at the foot of the towering Stone, apparently unconscious but seemingly unharmed. Directly in front of them stood Mark Howell. Or rather, what had been Mark Howell. The face was the same, as was the body. But the stance, the posture that he assumed, those were as different from Mark Howell as the sun was from the moon. The easy way in which he crossed his arms, the casual contempt that was sneered across his face, these were not expressions even really known to Mark Howell.

As if in slow motion, the sneer changed, grew into a smile that put John Crowley's to shame. Mark's eyes pulsed with a rhythmic light, the same color as the Stone behind him. Tatters were all that remained of his clothes and his hair was wild, blown around his head in a halo of darkness.

But the voice, the voice was as cold and alien as the surface of a distant, dead star. "Too late, Hunter, the boy is ours now." The words were not in English, but everyone understood them just the same.

The others were distantly aware of Crowley cursing under his breath as Mark Howell stepped forward. Mark's arms were spread wide, his athletic chest rippled with the motions, his arms flexed casually and his voice bellowed forth thunderously. "Come to me."

The Folk responded instantly, breaking into clouds of darkness that whirled and tore at the air on their way to Their master. In a matter of seconds, Mark Howell's body was surrounded, sheathed in a nebulous cloud of non-light that wove about his body, embracing, merging. The Darkness completely hid the body of Mark Howell; all that could be seen was a writhing black mass that shifted, and warped, dancing in the air that Mark Howell should have been breathing.

Crowley stepped forward and the darkness grew eyes. The golden irised eyes stared malevolently at the approaching figure and the entire mass of darkness contracted briefly.

Crowley took another step forward and the darkness exploded.

2

P. J. Sanderson stared around himself in shock, but there was nothing to see save an endless field of black in all directions. There was nothing to hear, feel, or smell. The taste that filled his mouth made him think of clotted blood and other, far worse things. Phillip James Sanderson was far from the bravest man on the planet, but everyone has their limits. P. J. had just reached well beyond his own limits and now was the time to stop the nonsense.

"Show yourself," he demanded, ready for whatever would come his way. His body was tensed, ready for motion. Nothing at all happened. He repeated his demands and though there was nothing yet to see, nothing yet to hear, he knew that he had been heard this time and he knew that the answer to his demands was on the way.

After long minutes, a blue light, painful on eyes that had tried to adapt to absolute darkness, split the black field before his eyes. P. J. closed his eyes partially against the sudden glare. The source of the light was uneven, wavering around the edges. Something stood in the center of the brightness. The luminescence was too much, P. J. could not decide what it was that stood waiting for him. "Who's there?"

No response.

"I don't know who you are, but I want the boy back. I want him left alone." P. J. hated the whining edge he heard in his own voice, but there was nothing to be done about it.

The figure did not move, it made no responding sounds.

P. J. stood equally still for several long minutes and then he started forward, ready to do battle for the soul of Mark Howell. Before him, something shifted in the glowing, electric blue pool.

It took an endless span of time to reach the light, to reach his opponent, but when he did, P. J. Sanderson knew that he had made a horrible mistake. Something cold and wet grabbed hold of his arm as he tried to back away. The light faded into nothingness as P. J. Sanderson screamed.

3

Tyler was closest to Jonathan Crowley. He almost heard the words that came out of the man's mouth. Even as he strained to hear them more carefully, the darkness disappeared. To his left, the very visibly shaken Tony stood looking around, eyes wide and face pale. A light blanket of sweat covered his body. To his right, Jonathan Crowley stood calmly, looking utterly unfazed by the sudden darkness that had swallowed them all. For his own part, Tyler felt a very strong urge to take a leak.

In front of them, Mark Howell still stood in the same pose, a slight smile on his otherwise expressionless face. Behind him, Lisa was starting to move, standing up with a murderous expression on her face. Cassie was still out cold, her face as calm and angelic as ever, more so when compared to the expression that twisted Lisa's beauty into something feral.

Mark Howell looked directly at Jonathan Crowley. "One down. Three to go. Who should We take next?" It was only at that moment that Tyler realized the absence of P. J. Sanderson. He felt his heart grow cold. In the last six months he had grown very close to the author and to have forgotten the man's presence there made him feel incredibly small. Mark Howell had apparently killed him. The implications left Tyler too numb to feel much of anything.

Jonathan Crowley was still smiling, shaking his head softly. "What the hell makes you think of wiping out Philly as a success? I mean, he meant a lot more to you than he ever did to me, Mark." At that moment, Tyler wished he had a gun with which to kill Crowley. "Hell, Howell, that doesn't even qualify as having won a battle, let alone the war."

Tony came out of his blank-eyed daze, shaking his head and whispering the word "No" under his breath repeatedly. Rational thought took to wing and Tony charged across the fifty feet that separated him from Mark Howell with a scream trying to boil out of his mouth. Tyler watched Tony's powerful legs tear the ground apart, mesmerized by the way his muscles shifted and contracted across the planes of his body. Crowley watched as well, shaking his head again and knowing, it seemed, that Tony didn't have a chance.

Three feet away from his target, Tony launched himself into the air, ready to collide with Mark Howell, ready to break his once-friend into pieces for causing harm to his Uncle Phil. Tony's brutal face was made ugly by combined rage and grief.

Mark Howell very calmly stepped to the side, moving in a blur and timed a perfect backhand at Tony's face. Tyler was certain he heard something break as Tony's head snapped to the side. Tyler felt a bleak darkness slide into his body and soul as he watched Tony fall to the ground, no longer able to move, no longer conscious. Tyler saw that he was breathing, wondered whether or not he would ever be conscious or able to move again.

Beside him, Jonathan Crowley called out. "No, Tony, wait. Stop. You'll never be able to hurt him." The words were dry, sarcastic and unnecessarily cruel. Tyler felt the fires of his own anger flare brighter and was not certain if he was truly angry with Crowley or with Mark. The only certainty was that he was indeed very angry.

Crowley said only one word, "Now." Lisa Scarrabelli attacked Mark Howell. It was preposterous, really, her soft little form going up against the mass and bulk of Mark Howell. More preposterous still, she was doing a much better job of it than her brother had. Crowley grinned, enjoying the show and glad he'd given Lisa a little something to help her fuel her rage and strength.

The first blow struck Mark from behind and it wasn't what Tyler thought of as a "Girl's punch." It was a double fisted full swing that hit rather like a sledgehammer. Mark's head snapped forward and his knees buckled. He dropped to all fours, with a dazed look that was much more along the lines of the old Mark, than the new "improved" Mark. Before he could recover, Lisa had hauled back her leg and shot her foot between his own legs, hitting hard in a spot that simply had to hurt like hell. Mark's eyes flew wide, his mouth dropped open and she kicked him there again. Then a third time, apparently intent on kicking his testicles hard enough to launch them from his throat. Tyler stared on in numb surprise and Crowley crossed his arms, smiling more broadly than he had all night.

Crowley placed an arm on Tyler's shoulder and Tyler could hear the mirth in his voice. "Gee, he's gonna feel that tomorrow, if he lives through it."

Lisa developed a new tactic after about seven good shots to Mark's groin and stomped hard on his lower back, in the kidney region. Mark let out a deep groan, thrashed feebly and thrashed again as she repeated the process.

Tyler stepped forward to help him, feeling like a machine with a programmed automatic pilot and was stopped by Crowley. "This is her part of the fight, Tyler. Don't you think she's earned it?"

"She'll kill him!" Couldn't the man see reason?

"I doubt it, but she'll certainly soften him up."

Tyler flashed on Lisa lying pale and battered in the hospital bed of her room in the clinic, shook his head at the thought and stopped trying to go forward. She'd progressed to kicking Mark in the side of his head while the brief conversation was carried out. Tyler could see that she was winding down, her energy fading as she vented her rage.

Tyler did something he would have never really thought himself capable of: he stood by while a defenseless individual was battered. He kept watching and waiting, waiting for when she would be done. Finally, in an obvious state of exhaustion,

Lisa fell back from Mark. She slumped down on the ground and cried tears of bitter rage and frustration. Even then, Tyler only watched.

Crowley on the other hand, went immediately for Mark. The man reached into one of his pockets, pulled out a small leather bag and began sprinkling the contents on and around Mark Howell. Again he said odd words, words that made absolutely no sense. For once, he wasn't smiling.

Mark couldn't have jumped more or harder, if someone had set an electrified hot-wire against his leg. His mouth was stretched wide—it was obvious that he was trying to scream, but no sound came out. Every muscle in his body stood sharply out, vibrating and convulsing. His chest bellowed in and out, air trying to reach his lungs and failing. His arms tried frantically to reach the source of pain in his back, but the black-green powder may as well have been attached with Krazy Glue for all the good his efforts came to. Crowley finished with whatever he was mumbling and stepped back as Mark Howell hit the ground.

Crowley looked down upon his foe with no expression on his mobile face and then he said one more word.

Mark Howell was lifted into the air, thrown really, and a bolt of painful white light lanced outward from his back, striking the Stone behind him, missing Lisa's head by mere inches. The light grew even brighter, draining all of the color from everything around it, bathing the clearing in a field of luminescence that seemed as powerful as a hundred suns at high noon. Tyler smelled burning flesh.

Crowley grinned.

Mark Howell landed on the ground like a inflatable doll filled with bones. No tension, just a rattling thud that left him laying in what was obviously a painful position.

Crowley smiled at Tyler. "Well, that's that. Now, I need you to move as quickly as you can, I need you to move everyone out of the area." There was no room for questions. Tyler grabbed Lisa under the arms and started hauling her out of the way. He was relieved to see that she was apparently unharmed. Crowley grabbed Tony, yanked him by his heels and dragged his motionless form away from the spot where it had landed earlier.

Next Tyler grabbed Mark and Crowley grabbed Cassie. Her skin was feverish, but that would have to wait, whatever was going to happen was obviously bad, judging from the distance that Crowley hauled his burdens away from the Stone.

5

P. J. Sanderson fought desperately, struggling against the wet formless mass that was doing its best to destroy him. He fought not out of desperation or fear for himself, for he knew that if he ran, the thing would let him be. Instead he fought for the shimmering image of Mark Howell that lay far across the seemingly endless, shapeless room in which he found himself.

He pulled and cursed, trying to reach to the other side of the area, gaining inches only to be pulled back yards. He felt that he was beginning to understand how this game was played. All he had to do was fight against the tide of this creature's bulk, rather like fighting a small ocean, and reach Mark.

Several people had died at the…Hands? Claws? Tentacles? of this creature. All that had crossed its path had become pieces of rotting meat. There should have been no escape from the flabby, multicolored puddle that was busily wrapping itself around his legs up to the thighs. But he was mostly unharmed. Why? Because of all the people that had died under strange circumstances, only he was close to Mark Howell. Somehow, in some way that made no true sense to him, the creature was barred from causing him irreparable harm.

P. J. was very glad to hear it. He'd already seen the strange flotsam and jetsam of this living ocean and most of it was still recognizable. He knew that his tears were likely still mingling with the—just what the hell was it anyway?— that surrounded him. He didn't really have time to acknowledge them at this point.

P. J. thrashed in the stuff that was growing thicker, more solid in an attempt to slow him further. It needn't have bothered…as it already was, he could feel his heart's frantic beatings trying to pound out of his sternum. His brain was trying to explain that he would be okay, but every instinct in his body was demanding more energy, more adrenaline, in order to let him fight on. He was beginning to wonder if a heart attack was going to hit him.

Pseudopods of oil-slicked goo reached for him, wrapping around his waist and covering his lower arms. P. J.'s emotions finally won over logic and he tried to break away with renewed energy. No dice, the thing had him as solidly as a web holds flies. Something happened then—what had seemed almost mindless became suddenly more alive than it had been before.

Energies of every color flowed into the mass, revitalizing the cancerous lump, filling it with a hideous strength that had not been there before. Awareness grew over the amorphous demon, its every motion suddenly pulled into focus. With a sickening drop in his stomach, P. J. Sanderson was heaved into the center of the creature and suddenly made to realize that he had been horribly, horribly wrong.

The creature at the heart of Mark's problems didn't need him alive at all. It simply hadn't noticed him before.

P. J. Sanderson was pulled into the flaccid depths of the monstrosity and as he was dragged down, he felt the awesome, terrifying *awareness* that he had not before sensed, aimed at a careful examination of what it had within its grasp. P. J. Sanderson's mind shut down. Sometimes, it's better not to know what is happening to you.

6

Mark Howell was at peace, floating in a paradise of pleasant dreams and even more pleasant sensations. Cassie was with him and Lisa was there too. And the only reason that either of them was there was to pleasure him in any way he saw fit. Utopia was his.

There was nothing to fear, no pain, no suffering of any type, just that annoying feeling that he was missing something important. Someone was calling his name, calling with an urgency that he did not understand. What could possibly be important enough to disturb him? Was that P. J.? He looked around, could see nothing in any direction that resembled his friend, until he looked over at Cassie.

There was something wrong with her. She was unmoving, still smiling just as she had the last time he had actually looked at her. Almost as if he was watching a film, her body flickered a few times and then she suddenly remembered how to speak. "Is everything all right, Mark?"

He nodded, looked towards Lisa and the same thing happened again. She flickered, then moved, asking the exact same question. She was smiling, despite what he had done to her earlier. He was mildly fascinated by how quickly she had recovered from all those bruises...

There it was again, P. J.'s voice, coming from somewhere behind Cassie. He started to move, but neither of his companions did. Then they both started up again, asking if everything was okay...Was there anything he needed...How could they help him?

Mark frowned, not understanding why they couldn't hear P. J.'s desperate cries. Annoyed by them, he pushed them aside, not bothering to apologize; here he was king and could do as he pleased. He demanded that P. J. show himself and for just a second, he thought he saw P. J. in the distance, screaming, drowning. Then P. J. was next to him, smiling the same old smile, dressed in a battered pair of jeans and a short sleeve dress shirt. Yet, over the "Can I help you, Mark? Is everything okay?" question, he could swear he still heard P. J. screaming.

Mark tried walking towards the faint voice, but a wall was in his way. That hadn't been there before, had it? He ordered a door put into that wall—he was after all, the king of this land—but nothing happened. He turned back to look at P. J., thinking to ask Cassie a question, and watched with mild surprise as P. J. actually blinked away, to be replaced by Cassie.

"How did you do that?" he demanded petulantly.

"Is there something wrong, Mark? Can I do anything for you?" Her smile was as bright as a sunny day. He was really starting to get pissed off about her damn smile too. The voice was suddenly clearer than it had been and Mark Howell wondered if perhaps someone was playing tricks on him.

7

Jonathan Crowley looked at the tower of stone that stood before him. It was huge, swollen with the power he had just returned to it; power that had until a few moments ago, fueled the possession of Mark Howell. As Crowley watched, the Stone heaved itself out of the ground, swelling even larger. Crowley had seen more in his long life than he often cared to remember; the Lord knew he had done more than he wanted to think about. But he had never before run across anything quite like this.

He would have been afraid, but he knew it was at least half show. Whatever concealed itself in the Stone was something that considered itself too vulnerable to be seen in its true form. That in and of itself was a good sign. The toughest part would be convincing the creature to show itself.

As if determined to let him know that It felt no fear—and truth be told It did not—the Stone heaved convulsively one more time, rearing up to an unprecedented height. Crowley stepped forward, ready at last to do battle.

8

While Jonathan Crowley was preparing to fight, Tyler Wilson was doing his best to rouse Lisa and Cassie. Tony was already conscious, though just barely and was moaning in pain over the broken jaw that Mark had delivered to him. Mark was lying perfectly still and Tyler was afraid to approach him, because from where he sat a few feet away, he did not appear to be breathing. Lisa was conscious, but she was moving sporadically at best, little jerks and shivers that made her whole body seem as if it were on the edge of a massive seizure. Next to her, Cassie was still sleeping.

Tyler was amazed by how beautiful the two girls were and more than a touch disgusted with the part of his mind that found their vulnerability arousing. He gently shook Lisa in an attempt to rouse her from her stupor. He shook her arm, calling her name softly. There was no response. The whole thing could have almost been comical, there was nothing that he could do, nothing that he could say that would help anyone and he was the only one here, except for Crowley, that was unscathed by the whole thing. His only loss so far had been his glasses and that was hardly a loss at all.

Tyler was still busy trying to do anything at all to comfort his beloved, when Mark Howell stood up and very quietly, very quickly moved to where he could best attack Jonathan Crowley.

9

P. J. had pretty much accepted his fate. He was a goner and more than anyone else he could think of, he deserved to die. Wasn't it all his fault to begin with? Hadn't he been the one that summoned the—whatever the hell this thing was—in the first place? Yes, it was best to let it all end. No more pain. No more suffering. No more tears.

Through the suffocating darkness that was forcing itself into his lungs, he felt strong fingers gripping his arm. He felt powerful muscles pulling at his slumped body. There was light and oh, sweet Jesus, it was *good!*

P. J. coughed the phlegmy substance from his mouth and throat, hacking the mucous from his lungs with painful, body-wracking coughs, until he could at last feel cool clean air flowing into his chest again. Perhaps he was wrong, perhaps he wanted to live more than he had ever suspected, because nothing had ever felt so fine as the oxygen that stirred in his system, forcing him to live despite his own attempts to surrender.

He fell to his knees on ground that was suddenly clean and relatively dry. He felt comforting hands holding him in place as he lost what little he had managed to eat earlier in the day—hadn't he already tossed his cookies? The day had been too damn long, he couldn't remember. He almost didn't recognize the voice that spoke to him, almost missed the voice that had meant the most to him in his life. "Hey, Philly. Don't you have a life or two to save?" Such a musical voice, even from well beyond the grave. "I think my nephew might need your help, guy, and I think maybe your kids might need your help too."

"How did you know about that? That's supposed to be a secret." The protest was feeble at best. P. J. Sanderson looked at Alex Harris and kept on looking. As beautiful as he had been in life, Alex was even more incredible to look on here, wherever "here" was.

There was a stunning look of serenity on Alex's face, a look of contentment and yes, even happiness that had always been lacking from his best friend's face in life. He looked so perfect, so utterly angelic, that P. J. felt the urge to cry. "No secrets here, Philly, just good feelings. We'll see each other again."

Alex was leading him towards a pool of darkness that seemed impossibly black, forbidding, and full of pain. P. J. didn't want to go. He started to resist Alex's gentle urgings. "No, I want to stay here, with you. I love you Alex, I can't go back there. Nobody loves me over there. It all hurts."

Alex smiled, half sad, half happy, all too beautiful. "You'd be surprised by who loves you over there, P.J. ...you really would. Go on. I can't go back...I'd join you if I could, but there are rules that have to be followed."

It was hardly even a push, more a gentle touch at the small of the back, and P. J. felt himself falling into the darkness again, felt himself hurled towards the world that he had grown afraid of. He wanted to scream, he wanted to cry, instead he simply let himself go, comforted by the last words his Best Friend Ever had to say as he fell. "I love you too, Philly, we'll see each other soon."

10

Mark sat in his little throne room and watched as the static images kept trying to ask him how he felt and how they could serve him. Much as he tried to ignore it, he felt his friend's pain and heard his friend's tearful cries from beyond his little paradise.

Enough was enough. It was time to be a friend again, instead of a friendly face. P. J. had helped him so often, so many times. How could he let him drown in the blackness? Still, there was a painfully selfish voice in his head that demanded he stay right where he was, that insisted that silence was golden and that he would really be much happier with his dreams, no matter how strange or perverse they became.

Mark Howell decided that he had let that voice have run of the show long enough. He had been sitting back and letting that voice handle things for most of a year now and this was where it had to end. Mark Howell struck the wall of his Special Place as hard as he could and the wall shattered like fragile glass. Really, that's all it had ever been anyway, the delicate fabric of daydreams. How could he expect the happiest of dreams to be more substantial than they could be in real life?

P. J. was going under for the last time, he could see the way that the author's struggles with the miasmic blackness were fading. Mark reached out with hands freshly bloodied and pulled his surrogate father from the depths of his own pain. God, P. J. had never seemed heavier, never before had he seemed to be a burden. *Maybe,* he thought as he shouldered the barely conscious man, *maybe that's what all of the people you love are, burdens meant to keep you anchored.* That was okay, Mark had lived without the burdens for far too long. It was a weight he would happily accept.

11

Crowley reached for the Stone at the same time that Mark Howell hit him in the back of his head. It wasn't a love tap, it wasn't meant to just get his attention, it was meant to drive his face through the pulsating Stone before him. The blow was damned near successful. Crowley felt the cartilage in his nose give way against the granite surface.

He rested there for only a second, chastising himself for turning his back on an enemy playing possum and then he turned to face his opponent. Mark's face still had that unnaturally alert expression, that same self-satisfied smirk of glee. If Jonathan Crowley'd had any friends, those friends would have pointed out that the look on his face matched exactly and precisely with the look on Mark Howell's face at that moment—and then they would have run screaming. If Crowley had had any friends, they could have told you that the shit wasn't just going to hit the fan, it was going to tear that fan apart. But Crowley didn't have any friends, nor had he ever really wanted any.

He felt more alive than he had for the last twelve decades. There was no dancing, no weaving and testing of one another's abilities, there was only combat.

The two foes met on equal grounds, squaring off and assaulting each other with fists that fairly blurred from view with each and every shot. Teeth were knocked loose from grinning mouths and bones were broken in the both of them. Crowley delivered a killing blow to Mark Howell's kidneys and received a ruptured spleen for his troubles. Muscles were ripped free from bones by hands that were strong enough to bend steel bars and blows that would have shattered oak trees were dealt out to vulnerable joints that refused to stay broken. For every strike that landed, there was a rapid healing of ruptured organic matter that would have made doctors around the world crazy for the secret.

All Tyler Wilson could do was watch, and all that the Stone could do was pull the strings on Its puppet. Tyler was mesmerized by the sheer ferocity of the attacks, stunned by the savage power that was unleashed. He could actually feel the vibrations from the battering, where he sat some fifteen feet away. And the two of them just kept smiling. It was like, well, it was like they were both just having a damn fine time killing each other again and again.

He was too busy with the fight to notice the odd bulging of the Stone behind the combatants, too busy to notice the Stone in the process of trying to give birth to what It had earlier swallowed. Or trying *not* to give birth.

Tony was not. Tony was wallowing in his own pain, but he was not too busy to hear the muffled screams of his uncle. It was hard, too goddamn hard to get up and try again. He had been beaten every single time he let himself stand up for anything at all in the last few days. It was much easier just to lay here and let these things take care of themselves, thank you just the same.

But, damn it, that was his uncle. That was the man that had been more of a father to him than his own father had ever been. That was the man he had let down at every turn, the man that kept forgiving him, kept having faith in him when he no longer had faith in himself, and he just couldn't make himself lie still. Tony got to his hands and knees and started over to the lump in the side of the Stone. The lump that would not rest.

It hurt to crawl and so he walked. It wasn't fast enough just to walk and so he ran. It was too far to run and so he fell and he started crawling again. But he eventually reached that spot in the Stone, that wart that grew at a cancerous rate on the side of the shifting granite rock in the center of the woods. He touched the Stone and the Stone burned him for his insolence. His fingers were blistered and the tips smelled like roasting pork.

He was too tired to cry and he was too angry to stop. As in all times in Tony Scarrabelli's past, it was rage that fueled him on to greater things. The same rage that let him lift twice his own weight in a max-out on his bench press, let him pull back his left hand and drive his fist into the heart of the Stone.

The Stone screamed and the surface of the Stone broke, even as Tony's hand was shattered. He wanted to hit the Stone again, he wanted to lash out at all the pain the thing in the Stone had caused him, had caused his friends and even the pain that it had caused Mark Howell. But the pain was too much. His hands screamed in silent protest and he felt the blood seep out of a dozen open wounds onto the pulpy mass of his left hand. Tony pulled himself into a fetal position and cried quietly. But the pain was only physical, it was no longer the shameful pain of cowardice. He could live with that.

12

P. J. hit the actual surface of the real world in a rush of fluids. He fell to his knees and again felt the intoxicating charge of oxygen to his lungs. He looked at the grass beneath him and saw blood and knew that it was not his own. Then he saw his nephew lying curled into a ball on the ground and he pulled the boy to him. He shielded the boy with his own body, knowing that it was all about to end.

He felt more than saw all that truly made Mark Howell who he was go running towards the thing that inhabited his body. He felt more than heard the primal scream that came from the spirit of Mark Howell as it charged towards its natural home.

He actually saw the triumphant smile fade from Mark Howell's physical face as he turned to look at the oncoming spirit that demanded its rightful place back.

In a voice that was made equally of anger and sorrow, he heard the words that erupted from Mark Howell's body. "No! It's not fair! I was winning! I was winniinngg!"

Jonathan Crowley delivered one last telling blow to Mark Howell's spine at the same time that whatever had inhabited

Mark's body was forced back to the Stone by the sum of Mark's being. P. J. heard the sound of Mark's spine cracking at the same time that the Stone exploded.

Fire lashed at the skies under the Overtree. Flames ripped at the heavens and blasted the fog into nothingness. There was no heat from the blaze; there was only an amazingly powerful cold. P. J. Sanderson felt the frost that formed across his back, felt the hair on his head grow brittle and break off, snapped by the winds that howled across the forest. He forced his eyes to close, forced his body closer to that of his nephew's. He had to watch out for Tony, who else would?

He did not see the lake covered in frost, frozen in mid-wave as the turbulence ripped through the atmosphere; he did not see the windows in Summitville blasted free from their frames to litter the interiors of damned near every home in town. He did not see the stain of whatever had been here in the woods eradicated by the force of Mark's denial. But he certainly felt them all as he lay there sheltering his nephew— *Yes. Nephew, that's all I can ever let him be, all I can ever let him know*—he felt all that and he heard the obnoxious voice of Jonathan Crowley even through the titanic explosion. "Ouch. Shit that's just *got* to hurt."

Then, almost as an afterthought to the initial blast, the ground beneath P. J. and everyone else bucked, kicking trees from the soil and splitting the earth near the stone into jagged, open wounds. The Stone shrieked in protest as it died. P. J. Sanderson's world reeled physically then, instead of only spinning out of control in his mind and heart. Who can say how deeply the source of all Mark's granted wishes had rooted itself into the soil where once Summit Town had grown and thriven? How deep were the roots of the thing? How far did they go?

Whatever the case, the Stone, the thing that hid in the shape of a gray pillar of rock, heaved itself from the ground in a rage. Like a monolithic wyrm, the rough craggy thing thrust from its resting place with a roar of protest. Fragments of its outer shell split away, revealing a darkness that numbed the mind, as it moved for the first time since it came to rest in the area. From the edge of the Overtree and all the way into Summitville proper, the earth shuddered as the Stone thrashed, trying to escape the pain of being denied its victory. Though no buildings actually toppled, the houses in the Red Oaks subdivision suffered structural damage the likes of which the architects would never have imagined possible. Walls split, floors buckled, and plaster ceilings spider-webbed from the force. The Basilisk shuddered violently, and P. J.'s proud display of his printed works collapsed as the glass shelves and cabinet doors disintegrated.

The heavy ice, just recently formed on Lake Overtree, splintered and broke into fragments, while the streets of Summitville buckled in protest to the thing's final spasms. In the area where Dave Brundvandt's parents still wondered what had happened to their son, the tremors were strong enough to rupture water pipes and knock telephone poles from the ground like broken matchsticks. No lives were lost, but several cars were among the victims of the incident. P. J. Sanderson looked on as the Stone rose high into the air, a column of blistered, broken rock that threatened to topple itself and crush them all. It tottered, swaying for a moment, and then finally fell towards the author and the youths with him, the final gesture of a frustrated god.

The impact P. J. knew was coming never occurred. Even as he covered Tony's body with his own, closing his eyes tightly in a vain effort to protect the boy, the massive bludgeoning shape fragmented, shattering into a fine dust that sifted down from above, coating everything for the length of two football fields. Before the dust had a chance to settle, it evaporated like so much dry ice on a hot skillet.

Then it was over.

Below him, P. J. felt his nephew stir, whimpering with the pain of his ruined hand. He heard the cries of his niece and the gentle shushing sounds of Tyler Wilson's voice. He heard the moans of Cassie Monroe as she started to awaken, and he heard the absolute silence of the forest.

Finally he allowed himself to look and was surprised by the light that illuminated the woods around him. The sun was rising and slowly the animals that had dared to stay finally began to claim back their territories. It didn't take much longer for others to return.

Mark Howell lay awkwardly on the ground, broken in a bad way. Of Jonathan Crowley, there was no sign.

Epilogue

(Excerpt from the unpublished autobiography of Phillip James Sanderson)

It's been a year. I guess it's time to talk about the changes that have come over Summitville. Where to start is the only real question and I guess that even that is a simple enough question to answer.

I'll start at the ending. After it was all said and done, after the thing was gone and Crowley had disappeared, I had to run for help, along with Tyler who miraculously managed to find his glasses. It took about two hours all told to get paramedics out to the spot and if Tim hadn't been one of them, it would likely have taken even longer. Tim's a strange one, almost too friendly for a person born in Summitville, but he has to be I guess; it must come with the territory, working in Denver and all. The worst of the injuries were those that fell on Mark. Crowley had apparently managed to rupture a few of his vertebrae in the fight and whatever left him apparently decided that it was done doing him favors. Mark had to be secured to a gurney and carried out of the woods over paths that would have been treacherous in the best of situations.

He's alive, and no permanent damage was done to his spinal cord, and for that he should be grateful. They expect him to be fully mobile by the end of the year. For now he needs a cane and upon occasion he still needs his wheel chair. I know that he will be happy indeed to be away from his wheel chair once and for all. He put on some weight as a result of being immobile for so long, but that's probably for the best. It probably means that whatever influence held him, is finally gone. Sometimes you could doubt that—he still has a tendency to stare into infinity when no one is looking. Maybe that's just natural, he always struck me as a dreamer.

Tony's hand may never be the same. The surgeons did their very best and he is able to flex his hand, able to make a fist and even to lift light weights, but you can see the pain on his face when the winter came, you could almost feel the swelling of his still-healing bones.

He seems a little more withdrawn for all that he has gone through and he is most certainly more cautious when it comes to physical activities, but for the most part my *nephew* is growing up very well indeed.

Lisa is another story entirely. She seems almost completely recovered from the traumas she was forced to endure, but I can't help wondering. I think that she will pull through, so long as she has Tyler by her side. He's really an amazing boy. Never have I seen anyone so dedicated to protecting the girl he loves. Now and then he is almost too protective and now and then Lisa lets him know it, but for the most part, I think she loves him almost as much as he loves her. There have been discussions between them of marriage, I think, but so far Lisa is winning the day with her practicality. I imagine that Tyler will never be fully satisfied to wait, but then a beautiful girl has always seemed to be his major weakness. I suspect that he is as in love with the idea of being in love as he is with my *niece*. That's okay, I believe that they will find their happiness together.

If only the same could be said for Cassie and Mark. Cassie lost interest in Mark almost immediately after the incident under the Overtree. I suspect that there are worse fates than losing your first girlfriend, but I also suspect that Mark can think of none. They have become friends and I imagine that they will always be friends, but the pain that Mark lets show when they are together and she is looking away from him is almost enough to break my heart. He is already going through so much, what with Joe and his mother separated. Joe seems ready to reconcile with his wife, but I don't know if she is ready yet. I wonder if Jenny is angry at herself, the town, her husband, or her son. Who can say? Such is the way that life goes—it moves on when you least expect it.

Life goes on in Summitville as well, minus a few
people who will be missed. Chuck is gone from the world
and Summitville had the good sense to put Stacy
Calhoun in his place as the sheriff. She really is the only
qualified person who was born in town and I think that
Dave Palance knows it as well. Besides, Dino very much
wanted her daughter to become sheriff some day and no
one in their right mind would think to cross her. The
woman can be an unholy terror when she wants to be.

Rick Lewis has been replaced by another out of town
doctor, at least for as long as it takes Tim to finish his
medical training. He'll make a good doctor someday
and in the meantime, Summitville is tolerating Doctor King. He at least is originally from Boulder and
that's not so far a distance; the people here can almost
pretend that he's a neighbor. Almost.

The youngsters that have died are missed in their
own ways, but not as much as the adults that died. They
had yet to make their worth known to Summitville and
that is a sad thing. They will never get the chance to—
that opportunity was stolen from them.

As for me, I thought about leaving this miserable
little town for a while, but much as it pains me to admit it, the damned place has grown on me. I have my
writing, I have my books and I have my friends. I guess
in the long and short of it, that's all that really matters.

Oh and I have two other writers in town these days.
Despite the fact that their love refused to blossom,
Mark and Cassie collaborate beautifully. Their first
combined book has received several positive reviews
and I hear a lot of comments on how well they write
together, how mature the level of their writing is considering their ages.

I hope the book does better than Mark's first attempt. I suspect it will. They work well together. One
day, if life gives them the opportunity, they may well
make a lovely couple.

These days I'm more of an optimist than I used to
be. That, or I'm getting sentimental and mushy in my
old age. I think they will get together. If an old man

can forgive himself for his many transgressions, even so late in his life, then two young people can eventually come to realize that not all they felt for each other was the work of an outside force.

I have forgiven myself.

I know now that whether or not I had performed a magic spell in the woods so long ago, things would have been pretty much the same. I think that the thing under the Overtree had enough power to make us do its bidding. There was no control to be had by me, or by Alex, or even by little Todd. We were all just pawns, just pieces to be moved in a game that is probably going on elsewhere by now.

I got a post card from Jonathan Crowley; it came from Hawaii. Short and sweet, all it said was "Hope you're keeping your nose clean, Philly. I'm still watching you." It wasn't signed. It didn't have to be. I threw it away.

That chapter of my life is closed. Life is moving on, and I intend to enjoy the ride for as long as I can.

Phillip James Sanderson

NIGHT IN THE LONESOME OCTOBER
RICHARD LAYMON

Everything changes for Ed that day in the fall semester when he gets a letter from Holly, the girl he loves. Holly is in love with someone else. That night, heartbroken and half mad with despair, Ed can't sleep, so he decides to go for a walk. But it's a dark, scary night in the lonesome October, and Ed is not alone. . . .

There are others out there in the night, roaming the streets, lurking in the darkness—waiting to show Ed just how different his world could be. Some of them are enticing, like the beautiful girl who wants to teach Ed about the wonders of the night. Some are disturbing and threatening. Some are deadly . . . and in search of prey.

SECOND CHANCE
CHET WILLIAMSON

You are invited to a party. A reunion of old college friends who haven't seen each other since the late 1960s. It should be a blast, with great music and fond memories. But be forewarned, it won't all be good. Two of the friends at the party weren't invited. In fact, they died back in college. But once they show up, the nostalgia will turn to a dark reality as all the guests find themselves hurled back to the '60s. And when they return to the present, it's a different world than the one they left. History has changed and the long-dead friends are still alive—including one intent on destroying them all.

MOON
ON THE
WATER
MORT CASTLE

It's a strange world—one filled with the unexpected, the chilling. It's our world, but with an ominous twist. This is the world revealed by Mort Castle in the brilliant stories collected here—our everyday lives seen in a new and shattering light. These stories show us the horror that may be waiting for us around the next corner or lurking in our own homes. Through these disquieting tales you will discover a world you thought you knew . . . and a darker one you'll never forget.